Praise for *An Unpresentable Glory*

"*An Unpresentable Glory* is a spiritual pilgrimage, a fairy tale, and a mystery all in one, but most of all it is a story about the unexpected miracles that come when you give of yourself for someone else. Eleanor Gustafson writes with humor and heart."

—SARA GOFF
Author of *I Always Cry at Weddings*

"Eleanor Gustafson is a sensitive and skilled writer who has not only an authentic relationship with the Lord, but a powerful relationship with language. You feel the beauty of an enchanting Westchester garden and the bitter cold of a North Dakota winter as she deftly weaves a disparate cast of powerfully presented characters and settings into this tale of love, loss, redemption, and unpresentable service. Gustafson puts 1 Corinthians 12:22-27 into action in *An Unpresentable Glory*. Yah, you betcha!"

—RALPH D. JAMES
Author of *Premium Mixed Nuts: An Anthology*

"The lives of Jay and Linda twist and turn like paths in her garden—from light to shade, from a trollish darkness of injustice and fear, anger, grief, and regret, to the light of God's love, forgiveness, and new life. Shock and uncertainty become epiphanies. Loose ends come together, the unpresentables make us pause and consider. The novel has substance, the style smooth as a current of cool water over rounded stones. A pleasure."

—SIGRID FOWLER
Author of *Don't Tell the Rabbi* Series

"Gustafson's literary treatment of a theme of redemption and restoration is set in a literal garden of delights. It is both a parable and a provocative contemporary story, crafted by a writer who is skilled, precise, and imaginative in her use of words."

—LATAYNE C. SCOTT
Award-winning author of *A Conspiracy of Breath* and
Latter-day Cipher

"In *An Unpresentable Glory*, Ellie Gustafson has spun another tale that will stay with the reader long after the last page has turned. This unlikely love story is as timely as the latest scandal out of Washington and as timeless as the long history of human tragedy.

"From the mystery of the opening pages through a myriad of twists and turns and surprises to the tantalizing questions of the epilogue, an intricate plot draws the reader ever deeper into the lives of Linda, "Jay," and a sprawling cast of lovingly-drawn supporting characters.

"*An Unpresentable Glory* is not about politics, or gardening, or immigration, or marital love and honor; and yet all of these are here in rich and intriguing detail. Like the paths of a well-designed garden, Jay and Linda's lives lead in unexpected directions, but ultimately point to the gracious hand of the God of mercy."

—SALLY WILKINS
Writer and Teacher

"In *An Unpresentable Glory*, Gustafson weaves an intricate plot of unexpected twists and turns surrounding Kileenda Jensen and a stranger she finds sprawled in her renowned garden. God's grace and providence govern every episode of this tale of searching and sacrifice that will leave the reader's soul enriched."

—BRENDA COX
Author of *Tethered: The Life of Henrietta Hall Shuck, The First American Woman Missionary to China* (Finalist for Best Books Award and Foreword INDIES Award)

CONTINUED ON PAGE 367

an Unpresentable Glory

A NOVEL

Eleanor K. Gustafson

Ambassador International

GREENVILLE, SOUTH CAROLINA & BELFAST, NORTHERN IRELAND

www.ambassador-international.com

An Unpresentable Glory

Printed in the United States of America

This is a fictional work. Names, characters, places, and incidents are either the product of the author's imagination, or the author was given permission by the store owners to mention their names and places of business.

ISBN: 978-1-62020-842-7
eISBN: 978-1-62020-853-3

Scripture taken from the Holy Bible, New International Version®, NIV® Copyright ©1973, 1978, 1984, 2011 by Biblica, Inc.® Used by permission. All rights reserved worldwide.

Cover Design & Page Layout by Hannah Nichols
Ebook Conversion by Anna Riebe Raats

AMBASSADOR INTERNATIONAL
Emerald House
411 University Ridge, Suite B14
Greenville, SC 29601, USA
www.ambassador-international.com

AMBASSADOR BOOKS
The Mount
2 Woodstock Link
Belfast, BT6 8DD, Northern Ireland, UK
www.ambassadormedia.co.uk

The colophon is a trademark of Ambassador, a Christian publishing company.

To Debby, whose long-term, dedicated mentoring began with my first novel, Appalachian Spring, *and carried through subsequent books. Also to Sue, Marilyn, Martha, Lowell, Bob and Jeanne, David and Kate, John and Betty—my faithful support system over the past three novels. My heartfelt gratitude to each of you for standing by me with love and prayer.*

Preface

THE NIGHT BEFORE MY HUSBAND'S dad died, I volunteered to take the night shift, as a bladder infection made him restless and required constant attention. I sat beside him, serving him—my *father-in-law*—as needed. But through those difficult hours, I felt I was on holy ground, the room peopled with angels.

This awkward stint of servanthood affected me profoundly, eventually moving me to write *An Unpresentable Glory*. Whatever hidden, "unpresentable" ways He asks us to serve may reflect God's glory more vividly than our more well-dressed benevolences. Places or situations that are awkward and not for public view may become God's platform for displaying His love. This love could be for all to see (presentable) or only for the eyes of the participants.

This *unpresentable* thread is woven across political, gardening, and Native American venues through various acts of kindness and caring that similarly need protection from public view. Over all of these happenings, God's glory is revealed through a developing fabric of strength, courage, spiritual growth, responsibility, and love.

The bottom line: God can cover our messes with His glory—if we submit to and trust Him wholeheartedly.

An Unpresentable Glory is a love story, but not a romance in the technical sense. I want readers to recognize love in its many guises, not all of them comfortable or socially approachable. Our hearts long for God's love, and that, too, may come in unexpected ways. Watch for His appearances in this story, and enjoy the ride.

" . . . those parts of the body that seem to be weaker are indispensable, and the parts that we think are less honorable we treat with special honor. And the parts that are unpresentable are treated with special modesty, while our presentable parts need no special treatment. But God has put the body together, giving greater honor to the parts that lacked it, so that there should be no division in the body, but that its parts should have equal concern for each other. If one part suffers, every part suffers with it; if one part is honored, every part rejoices with it. Now you are the body of Christ, and each one of you is a part of it."

—1 Corinthians 12:22-27

Chapter 1

ON HER RETURN FROM CHURCH, Kileenda Jensen discovered a problem, and it had nothing to do with her name. Hardly anyone called her Kileenda. Early on, her parents shortened her name to Leenda, which quickly morphed to Linda. Now she herself, on all but the most serious and sacred of documents, signed herself as Linda. Though her parents, deeply rooted in Westchester County, New York, had made tiresomely sure she knew her uncommon heritage and social standing, Linda herself was comfortable with a plain name because her real worth did not rest on money or position.

Her immediate problem lay face-down between her perennial border and clematis arbor—more specifically, a man who looked to be either dead or unconscious. She assumed the less bleak view and spoke to him.

"Hello. Are you all right?"

Stupid question. He was obviously not all right, but she could see neither blood nor bruise. Inordinately handsome, yes—but what was wrong?

A gray eye opened tentatively, then closed. "I'm . . . in your way."

His voice conjured up Uncle Joshua reading *The Velveteen Rabbit*. Comforting, caring . . . and a hint of a smile, perhaps?

But comforting voices from the past were irrelevant. This man, right now, needed care. She knelt beside him. "What can I do for you? Are you ill? Did you fall?"

"No," he said. "Just. Catch. My. Breath."

"I could call 911. Or take you to a doctor. It's Sunday, but—"

The fleeting smile vanished. "No! I'll be all right." He straightened his splayed limbs and turned on his side to look at her. *In his forties?* she wondered. His drawn, pinched face hurt his looks only marginally.

"Delphiniums . . . dragged me in and . . . "

Linda sat back and laughed. "Stop! You have to do better than that. You can't see my yard from the road, and with the gate closed . . . Maybe you came from the nature preserve next door? Doesn't seem—"

"Yes . . . off the trail . . . "

"A bit," she replied tartly. "Two roads and twelve 'Posted' signs. But what's to be done with you? You obviously can't finish your hike—or whatever you were doing—and you don't want me to call 911. Who can I call?"

"Please. Give me a minute. I'll be all right."

Her mouth pursed. "You're not all right." She evaluated the stranger, weighing her options. His eyes were glazing, his skin pallid. Whatever was wrong wasn't improving. He couldn't be feigning illness; she was sure of that. Nevertheless, could he be trusted indoors? She recklessly decided to test the theory.

"Can you walk to my house? A hundred feet or so?"

His face turned fractionally incredulous. "You don't mean that. Your husband . . .

"I'm not married. I live alone." *Dumb! Why tell him that?*

He shook his head and echoed her thoughts. "What are you thinking? Why—"

He broke off and draped an arm over his face in a gesture of helplessness.

She grimaced. "Never mind. I'm thinking you're going downhill fast; and if I don't get you indoors, I'll have to care for you out here, and that *would* be hard. I could go call the police. But if I move toward the house, you'll crawl away, and I don't want to be responsible for what might happen to you." She spoke in a rush, then brushed a twig from his gray sweatshirt. "Yes, this tops the list of "Stupid Things to Do," but I can tell a lot from a person's eyes, mouth, and the way he talks; and you pass. Just raising the question speaks well of you. Now, if I help you along, will you come into my house? And quickly, please. You're a bit much to carry."

He looked at her bleakly, then away. "The cost . . ." he said to the sky. "I know what's wrong . . . not life threatening. Time . . . sleep . . . couple days. But *please* don't tell anyone I'm here." He looked back, imploring. "Not a hooligan. Promise." He closed his eyes, rocking his head forlornly. "Please. Go inside. Forget. A poor time . . . delphiniums . . ."

She leaned over and grasped his arm. "You're fading. Come," she said gently. "Check my indoor flowers."

With her help, he pulled himself to his full height of six-plus feet, his face turning to chalk. He bent to force blood to his head; and when he straightened, she wondered if he'd make it to the stone patio, let alone the house.

By sheer grit, he did make it. Once inside her sprawling, dark-wooded house, he pulled for the nearest chair, but she murmured, "This way," and steered him down a cool hallway to a small bedroom. He staggered toward the bed, but she held him back long enough to yank off the bedspread and pull back the sheet and blanket.

"Now, sit, but let's get your sweatshirt off before you lie down. Much easier."

After she worked it off, he fell on the double pillows as though unconscious. She untied his sneakers and drew them off, but his jeans gave her pause. He had wet himself. Did it happen on the way in? Whenever, it required action—right away. She knew how to undress men, having cared for her father in his last days, but this was different. Was this man asleep, or maybe unconscious?

That would be best for such a procedure. She decided to wait a few minutes.

She sat down and blew a breath. What was wrong, and what could she do about it? He had said it wasn't life threatening, but shouldn't she call a doctor? *This is really stupid. A man—in my house—mysteriously ill—requesting secrecy.* Was there any identification? No wristwatch even, and nothing bulged in his pockets. *Who is this guy?*

She studied his broad head and tapered, stubbly jaw. Only his temples and chin showed signs of gray. His nose sketched an irregular line down his face, and an untidy clump of hair fell across his bloodless forehead. She reached to pick wisps of hemlock detritus from hair that itself resembled hemlock bark—scraggy, with a reddish tinge. Yes, he had come from the preserve, one of the few stands of hemlock in Westchester County.

He seemed cool to her touch—too cool, actually. No fever. No rash. Pulse rapid, but steady. No sign of a cold or congestion. A virus, perhaps? Lyme disease? She had no clue. He could die right here in her guest bedroom. How would she explain that? He had said it wasn't life threatening, but had she done the right thing? If she'd gone inside for her phone, how far could he possibly have crawled? Certainly not through her locked gate. And why wasn't she calling 911, despite what he'd asked? She shook her head and sighed. What I've done, I've done—stupid or not. *Lord, You dumped this man here. Help me care for him with dignity and honor.*

Heart accelerating and hands trembling, she unfastened his button and zipper. Pulling the sheet over him, she grabbed jeans and underwear and tugged the clothing below his hips, keeping watch on his eyes. Relieved at no response, she worked them the rest of the way off, then checked his pockets. Nothing but lint and hemlock needles—proof positive of the woods route. She sighed, took his clothing to the laundry basket, and hunted for an alternate garment to cover his nakedness. An old pair of roomy pajamas would give him a trace of dignity. More maneuvering under the sheet, and she had him tucked up and apparently un-aware—or unconcerned—about the procedure. What next? Water is always good for what ails you. Lots of water. Should she give him Aspirin? No. Allergies and all. Water, though, should be safe. She went to the kitchen and drew a pitcher of warmish water. With glass and articulated straw, she returned to the bedroom. But did he need water more than sleep? To find out, she stroked his head until his gray eyes opened.

"A drink of water? Try a sip." His eyes closed again; but to her surprise, his mouth opened, and he drew most of the glassful through the straw.

Sleep and water seemed good. And time, he had said. He slept as she ate her sandwich and nectarine, and every hour she pushed as much water as he would take.

Toward evening, after he drank, his eyes remained open with a frantic, deer-in-the-headlights expression. Uh-oh. Water in, water out. He must be desperate. What to do? She couldn't get him up; he could hardly open his mouth. Her only option was to go at it forthrightly and see what happened.

She'd need a container. Her father had used a plastic urinal, but that was long gone. A bottle, maybe? She ran to the kitchen and settled on a quart-sized plastic container that looked ideal, but as she hurried to the bedside, she realized the mouth was none too big. Major complication. Why hadn't she grabbed a yo-gurt container? No time now; his eyes were fixed on her.

"I have a jar. Can you manage it?" She smiled brightly.

His hand crept toward the bottle, but when he tried to grasp it, his eyes closed in despair.

All right. Forthrightness. She couldn't even fall back on father experience here. Her dad had been able to see to himself until the day he died.

She drew off sheet and pajamas, watching his face closely. No panic—yet. With a big breath, she positioned the container appropriately. "Okay—go to it." For a moment, she wondered if she should've grabbed a larger container, but the stream finally stopped, and she covered him again. The relief on his face was unmistakable. She patted his arm and went out to empty the catch. When she returned, his breathing was again heavy with sleep. She backed off and scrabbled in the kitchen for a yogurt tub.

At night, he slept a lot, and she slept little on the floor with her three-cushion bed and pillow. She checked him several times, terrified at the thought of finding a cold body. Though not cold, he remained far too cool to suit her. She rubbed his arms and legs and spread an extra blanket.

Linda reflected on what she'd done so far. She'd been right in bringing him indoors, taking off his clothing. She had served him in his time of need, and the very doing of it became a moment of glory, with angels present in the room, serving her as she served him. She had felt this tangible Presence the night before her father died as she watched over him alone, her mother being on the point of collapse.

At daybreak, the sound of water in the yogurt tub woke Linda. She was about to spring up but thought better of it and waited till he resettled. He had carefully set the container where it wouldn't be kicked over, and she tiptoed out to empty and rinse it.

When she returned, his eyes were open, dark and sunken, his skin pasty. She stroked his head. "You do exist behind those eyelids."

He murmured, "I blink; therefore, I am."

She laughed heartily. Nothing wrong with his wit. "Do I hear Descartes chuckling from his grave?" She put glass and straw to his lips. "How about something to eat? Never mind. I'll bring something, and we'll see what you're up for."

She returned with a tray of bland digestibles—applesauce, mashed banana, dry toast. He raised his hand. "No banana. Brought this on."

Her eyebrows went up. "Ooh! Glad to have that bit of information." She propped him with yet another pillow and fed him the rest, as much as he would take. As she brushed away crumbs, she asked, "Am I allowed to call you anything other than sir?"

His crooked smile brought warmth to the sunken contours of his face. "How about Jay? Your name?"

She considered saying *Kileenda,* but changed it to Linda. But why had her face grown warm?

"Linda." He tasted it. "Linda. Beautiful name, beautiful person." He smiled wryly. "Does illness excuse lame lines?"

Linda rolled her eyes. "Well, either you're outrageously gracious or hopelessly blind."

"Do I have to choose between outrageous and hopeless?"

She smiled impishly. "Um . . . let's not go there." She picked up the tray. "Can I get anything else for you?"

He smiled but shook his head. "You've been . . . more than kind." And she understood what he meant.

Chapter 2

LATER THAT MORNING, HE GOT himself to the bathroom and was able to shower. Though weak, he seemed much improved. He ate in bits and pieces throughout the day, sometimes lying down, sometimes in a recliner. Toward evening, he sat in the gracious sitting area off the kitchen, staring out the expansive window that measured Linda's garden from the perennial border on the left to the arched bridge and island gazebo on the right. His moroseness, though, was broken only when Linda brought him something, her warm, brown eyes doling out lavish doses of compassion and comfort. They talked little and only about the flowers she had gathered or the wren outside the window. He knew flowers and inquired about birds.

He wasn't sure where he was. "I remember crossing the Hudson but don't think I got as far as Connecticut."

"We're close—ten miles, maybe. You're in Abington, New York, in Westchester Country, where rich snobs flock before they migrate south." She laughed self-deprecatingly.

"And your garden is a way station?"

"Touché! Yes, they do land here once in a while, usually in July. Where did you cross the river?"

He shook his head. "I don't know. Drove some hilly, squirrelly roads." He shrugged.

"Bear Mountain Bridge, for sure. You picked a beautiful entrance to Westchester."

"Huh! It picked me; dumped me in your garden."

"What took you to the nature preserve? Were you looking for hemlocks?" She laughed at his confused look. "No, probably not. The county has only a few stands, and tree lovers often come just to gawk." "Huh! Don't know hemlocks, but I saw the sign and thought a walk might perk me up. Didn't realize what was coming on. This medical problem doesn't happen often, and I'm sorry you got dumped on." He grinned wryly.

Linda stood and put a hand on his arm. "Well, we'll see." She smiled and turned toward the kitchen.

That night Linda left Jay on his own but felt uneasy. As predicted, he was getting better and was shifting from self-focus to . . . what? Was a move on her the next part of his recovery? He had called her beautiful as a joke. She was not beautiful, as she had often noted in her mirror—a narrow face and assorted freckles, her father's nose, and unremarkable, brown eyes. She kept her lustrous, coppery hair cut short and out of the way of gardening tasks.

Her friend Bonnie often described her face as a window. "It shows the real you—warm, intelligent, competent, full of grace. People can tell right off that you care." Linda didn't know about that, but wealth and a well-cast body made her attractive to men— thus, vulnerable. Not with men in general. She had learned to handle pushy types. But in public, she could never be herself, had to always be on alert.

Jay seemed different, though. Had he been movie-star handsome, she wouldn't have considered taking him in. Men with smooth, perfect features were often fake, hollow, self-centered opportunists who never had to struggle to make or keep a friend. Jay's good looks had been roughened by life or by whatever inner problems he carried. Like Uncle Joshua, he was tall. His face bore the outdoor ruggedness of Walter Beamer from church, and his body was as trim and fit as Bonnie's husband before he took sick and died. Jay's eyes cared, too; she could see that. They reached out with kindness and genuine interest. And that self-deprecating smile showed no self-absorption that she could see. Against this sort of man, she could not defend herself. Did he have any idea of the power he held, ill as he was?

Jay graduated outdoors to the deck. Linda had tucked a lounge chair under the overarching trellis, and the two-tiered, sibilant water accent quickly lulled him to sleep. She worked close by, then turned to see him watching her. "You're awake. Am I bothering you?"

He pointed to the purple clusters on the vine overhead. "They attacked me—the color . . . fragrance . . . "

"Wisteria. Did you plan your arrival so you could see it in bloom?" She laughed. "Can I get you something?"

"That's a serious tool in your hand. Not digging up the vine, I hope."

"No, wisteria is tough. Actually, I'm creating a fairy garden— well, a troll garden, my father's Nordic roots and all. I have this vague plan and a few ingredients." She held up a small, rustic cabin and a curved bridge. "And my troll." She displayed an ugly, deformed depiction of the Nordic folk creature. "They're always up to mischief, hiding under bridges and other unseemly places. I need to tuck my little guy so only his face shows." She positioned him first one way, then another. "There. How does that look?"

Jay grunted. "He looks almost as bad as I feel. Any water under your bridge?"

She grimaced. "I don't know what to do there—maybe a mirror strip or cloth or . . . " She frowned, studying the miniature garden.

Jay rolled to his side to see better. "Two levels of water. Draw out of the upper, maybe? Run it under the bridge, then back into the lower—"

"Oh!" she cried. "Why didn't I see that? A little repositioning here." She dug a new spot for the bridge and troll. "Some greenery will hide the channel perfectly."

"Greenery?"

"Fake. Miniature plants, some looking like trees, others shrubs. There's a big market for them—complete with contests and all—but this is just for fun. Should be in good shape for the July garden tour."

"July. I wish . . . " Jay lay back, grimacing, with eyes closed.

Linda stood and brushed her hands together. "Time for a bit of juice. Sit tight till I come back."

In the afternoon, Jay shuffled from sun to one of Linda's shaded, garden "rooms." His five-star alcove was what Linda called her "cave"—a cool, tight space, the entrance marked by two tumbles of large stones, each with its own texture and personality. Inside the bower, a cloth-backed swing and footrest hung from a high oak limb. Cradling his body in supreme comfort, the chair needed only a gentle shove to trigger perpetual motion.

"I tried to figure how long one push would last," he later told Linda. "But when I woke up, I was hanging there, stone still."

Linda guarded him fiercely, her driveway gate barred against whoever might come by, especially Jorge and his Hispanic garden crew. Putting Bonnie off was the bigger problem. They were close enough to read each other's mind.

"For all intents and purposes, Bonnie, I'm away for a few days," she told her. "I have things that really can't be interrupted. Please understand."

Jay's moroseness worsened that first day outdoors, obviously troubled, anxious, restless. Finally, she knelt beside him. "Look at me," she ordered.

He did, reluctantly.

"You're melting down before my eyes, and I think I know why. You've been here three days and have decided that's long enough.

You should get out of my hair; and at the same time, you know perfectly well you can't. And what should you do about it? Am I right?"

His eyes dropped, giving the answer, and she hurried on before he could say anything.

"Jay, can you trust me to care for you the rest of this week? After that, we'll need to think through our options if you still can't be on your own."

He looked away and cleared his throat uncomfortably. "I'm not sure you know what you're offering. There's more to this than meets the eye. And why would you trust me?"

Yes, her own question, but she pinned her eyes on him again. "Are you a criminal or illegal?" She laughed. "Is there a difference?"

"Huh!" His crooked smile broke through again. "In some venues, I'd say yes! Loudly." He drew a breath. "But the way you're thinking of it, no. I'm not on anyone's *Wanted* list. I'm Eagle-Scout clean." He grinned, then quickly reverted to serious. "Nevertheless, trusting me is too much to ask."

"Jay, that's a dodge. You're afraid to let go and trust. You're used to being in control and don't like your position here."

He looked up sharply, but she forged ahead.

"Autonomy is the air you breathe. And I don't say that negatively," she added, watching his face. "It's my climate, too. I'd have just as hard a time if the tables were turned. The question is, can you allow me to do for you what you cannot do for yourself right now? Can you trust me to protect you and not take advantage? I am trusting that you won't take advantage of me, and that's saying a lot, as you reminded me in front of the delphiniums."

He closed his eyes and leaned back in the chair, pale and anguished. She stood and put her hand on his shoulder. "I'll give you five minutes to struggle with reality and then come back to receive your graceful surrender."

He smiled unwillingly, but when she returned, he raised his hand and said softly, "White flag."

"Super," she said. "You have till Saturday to rest and allow yourself to heal."

A sprinkle of starlings landed nearby and began scavenging the lawn. The birds seemed to divert his focus from some unfathomable struggle within, but only for a moment. He spoke, his eyes still on the flock. "You've given me an inestimable gift—one so costly, I could never pay it back. One day you may know, but for now . . . " He couldn't go on.

Linda watched compassionately, then turned and headed for her rose garden. She came back with an exquisite blossom and held it out. "Look at this, Jay. Look closely. Is there any flower that comes close to matching a rose's perfection in terms of form, color, fragrance, some indefinable magnificence? If we tried to grasp the essence of this one flower, we'd fall apart—die, perhaps, under the weight of its glory. But what do we do? We pick it, look admiringly—first at arm's length, then with a sniff—and finally put it in a vase and get on with the day. That's the only way we can deal with such things." She smiled. "So, my lost but trustworthy fellow, rejoice that you fetched up in a safe place and get on with the day.

"Now," she went on briskly, "you've been in this glum spot quite long enough. How about a different location of your choice?"

His face lifted, and he looked around. "Yah, I know where I'd *like* to go, but it's . . . pretty far, like *over the river and through the woods.*"

"Ha! The gazebo! Well, why not? I think I can get you there, but getting back . . . ? Worth a try, though. We can stop at any point, but I need a piece of equipment. Sit tight. Be right back."

She returned with folding chair in hand, and Jay laughed.

"I pictured you with your garden cart, ready to haul me there."

Linda hooted. "Smashing idea! Those carts are a marvel, I will say. I might manage a hundred pounds, but—mmm?" She surveyed him ruefully. "Two hundred? I don't think so."

They began the long trudge to the arched bridge and tiny island. "All right. Time to rest." She opened the chair and instructed him to study a blue urn set in a pink, flowery surround. "You like it? My mom's favorite focal piece, but somehow, it doesn't fit this setting. What do you say?"

Jay shook his head, smiling. "You're an operator, you know that? Directing people's minds. Are you CEO of some big corporation?"

"Huh! CEO of my garden." She smiled. "If you won't play my game, we'll move on."

They made their way haltingly across the bridge and into the screened gazebo with its elegant wicker table and matching furniture. She settled him on the lounge chair and watched as his eyes swept across lily pads to breath-catching rhododendrons behind a patch of cattails. Birds caroled overhead, and the scent of water and mud and herbage only heightened the beauty spread before them. She took pleasure in his enjoyment. Great pleasure.

The next morning brought a dramatic change in both attitude and strength. But still, when Jay was alone, he sat pensive, staring into space. When she came with a drink or some roasted vegetables, he brightened, joking about the track she was wearing across the lawn. When she left him, he again lapsed into inscrutability, like sun and clouds warring overhead. The old anxiety was gone— she could see that—but was he sad? Perplexed? She could read neither his body nor his mind. Nor could she read his verbal accent. *Yah* instead of *yeah*? What part of the country was he from?

Chapter 3

THAT EVENING, JAY SAT ON the couch in the dark-beamed living room with its stone fireplace large enough to roast a small pig. He leaned toward the coffee table and thumbed through gardening magazines while Linda cleaned up the kitchen. As she closed the door of the dishwasher, she heard a soft *hey* from the adjacent room.

"*Hey,* what?" she asked.

"That's you on this magazine, and a whole article about you and your garden!"

She moved to the door to look at the cover. "Oh, that's an old one—a year ago, maybe? Don't believe everything you read. Haven't you learned that?" She grinned at him.

He huffed. "You better believe!" But as though he had said more than he intended, he quickly flipped pages and got to the article. "I didn't realize this bit of paradise was so famous." He read aloud:

> "True gardeners are a breed apart. Many people grow things, but few are true artists. Linda Jensen of Abington, New York, is a diva among gardeners. Not only does she have an eye for beauty in the arrangement sense, but she also understands the beauty of landscape, of soil, of air, and of water."

"Understated," muttered Jay and continued reading.

"She is also modest. 'I inherited the garden,' she says. 'Both of my parents—my father, especially—did the hard work, not just of design, but of digging and planting and suffering heartbreak over wind and ice damage. And Aunt Gladys. She could sniff out the finest stock—all before computers came on the scene. Those people are the real heroes; I just receive the bouquets.'"

Linda grimaced. "'Receive bouquets.' What a cornball line! Actually—" Her face turned droll. "I'm tempted to write about 'Grotesque Gardens I Have Seen.' One had a bank of petunias with two bony cleomes poking up like scarecrows on a wedding cake."

Jay laughed. "No clue what a cleome is, but I get the picture."

Later, in the den off of the kitchen, they sat over tea and talked comfortably against a backdrop of classical music. Before this, questions had been chosen carefully—nothing personal, nothing controversial. They had circled warily until they found common ground in music, literature, and the like. Now talking was easy.

"You've traveled a lot," he said. "That's clear. What country would you go back to, if you could?"

Linda looked toward the kitchen as the refrigerator laid its ice "eggs." "I think . . . Scotland," she said. "I'm not sure why. It's beautiful, but so are other places, especially if money's no object."

Jay cocked his head. "Go on. I'm interested."

She sat silent a moment. "Besides a genetic connection—my mom was a wee bit Scottish—I think for me, circumstance played a major part. I took Bonnie there after her husband died, and we toured, saw the sights, hiked among sheep. But it was the people we loved. Solicitous, caring. The tone, the tenor of the place. Coming home was hard—for both of us."

Jay said simply, "I'm sorry."

And she knew he was.

She found him knowledgeable about history, Native American Indians in particular; and while he said nothing about his own travels, he, too, had obviously seen the world. A bit of Spanish music with vocalist and guitar took them conversationally to Spain. And when Linda got up to close the sliding door off the kitchen, she returned with fingers snapping overhead and eyes flashing, swirling and stomping in a spontaneous, improvised dance. Jay drew a sharp breath, eyes wide. Linda quickly dropped to her chair.

"I'm sorry." She smiled contritely. "Bonnie and I took flamenco lessons last winter. You just *have* to do something with that kind of music." She shifted the dialogue to safer territory. "How do you know so much about Native Americans?" she asked.

Jay cupped his face in his hands, but before Linda could adroitly try another topic, he looked up. "Native Americans." He spoke the words as though milling some inner grist. "They were here before we were, doing their thing—hunting; growing corn, beans, and squash; fighting each other. They moved from place to place as needed, with no concept of private property. They even fought differently, finding more honor in just touching an enemy and getting away with their own scalp intact. Kept score of such acts of bravery. 'Counting coup,' they called it. White man comes along and gets help from the Indians early on; but the inevitable happens, and soon they're at each other's scalps. The natives push back when their hunting and agriculture lands get taken over. They, of course, don't understand well-meant offers to pay for these lands. Who in their world could comprehend *owning* forest and fields? You *use* land; you don't *own* it."

He stopped, hands again in front of his mouth, then looked up apologetically. "I hope I'm not boring you."

"Oh, no! This is your passion; I can tell."

"Passion . . . perhaps. Guilt, maybe? Yah, I know there were bad Indians as well as bad whites, but the whites had technology, organization. And guns. Plus, they sprinkled disease and alcohol like fairy dust, and the natives were beaten inwardly, as well as outwardly. They did have their own big guns—warriors like Sitting Bull, Crazy Horse, Chief Joseph, Geronimo . . ." His voice trailed off. "In the end, a lot of horror, a lot of shame."

"Was this diplomatic failure, or was it inevitable? I mean, did it *have* to come out with the natives being shoved aside so the whites . . . Well—" She shrugged. "Just *saying* it sounds awful."

"I've asked that question, and nobody has a good answer. It's history—ours and theirs—and I—" He stopped abruptly, looked down, then gave her a crooked smile. "How did we get on such a gloomy subject, anyway?"

"My Spanish war dance did it."

They both laughed and talked late into the evening, as though neither wanted the conversation to end.

The first morning they had breakfasted together, Linda tentatively brought out her Bible and a devotional booklet. Seeing no aversion, she made it a daily practice. Sometimes she asked Jay to read the Bible part. He could find the passage easily and read expressively. Except for one morning. The topic was *God's Prodigal Son,* with a passage from Hosea, chapter eleven. Jay began reading.

"When Israel was a child, I loved him, and out of Egypt I called my son." He spoke strongly until he reached the words, *"It was I who taught Ephraim to walk, taking them by the arms; but they did not realize it was I who healed them. I led them with—"* His voice caught, and he could not go on. After a moment of uncomfortable silence, he said, "I'm sorry. It just hit me . . ."

Linda took the Bible from him. "Never mind. We'll talk of prodigals another time. Is it all right for me to pray for you?"

He nodded almost imperceptibly, a trace of fear in his eyes.

She drew a big breath and closed her eyes.

"Lord God, You touched a sore spot in Jay's heart just now. I can't ask You to take it away, but please redeem it and make it useful—perhaps for someone else who's hurting who comes along his way."

She straightened with a smile. "Now—it's beautiful out there this morning after last night's shower, and the garden is calling your name. Have you checked all my 'rooms'? Did you find the forest glade down the little path?"

"Do you work all night, making new places for me to explore?"

His eyes held both gratitude and pain.

Throughout the day, he prowled the graceful sweep of annual and perennial beds, sometimes bending to pull a weed. "I'm glad you tolerate a weed or two. There's hope for me in such a place."

"Huh!" She bent to yank an offender. "Try finding a garden without weeds! Think this way: Gardens are the exception on this planet; weeds are the norm. This is their world. We march in with order and design, and weeds just laugh. The strong guys come in and take over, doing what they want in their chosen environment. Think kudzu, bully of the south, or oriental bittersweet that's taking over the northeast. My garden is temporary, at best. Only God's garden will last forever."

Jay's eyebrows went up. "Do I hear a weed warrior speaking?"

"Oh, yes! My entire life has centered on pulling weeds. Sidebar here—have you ever considered that only the rich can afford decorative gardens? Poor folks grow food, but the rich can afford order and design. I was born rich, and my parents loved flowers. I grew up with that orderly paradigm. My mother took me from the cradle and plunked me down with clear orders: 'Pull this, but not this.'"

"Whoa! Hold on. *Rich,* as in everyone here is rich, and the rest of the world is poor? I've seen—"

"Well, yes and no. Even the poor of this country sometimes buy cheap flowers for their doorstep, but generally, the size and quality of a garden is an accurate measure of the owner's wealth.

"But aside from that," she continued, "the two great forces at war are wilderness and asphalt. Ultimately, weeds will win and can break down even concrete. But they can be useful—for eating and for beauty. You can eat violets, y'know. Plants are weeds only if they're a nuisance."

Jay was silent a moment, a soft smile on his face. "Linda's 'philosophy of weeds.' Keep going; I love this."

"I could go on for hours." She raised a comic eyebrow. "Aggressive weeds muscle in like strongmen. Some plants can stand up to them; other are fragile and thrive only with my strong-arm protection." She smiled wryly and plunged her trowel into soft soil.

"Is this what you write in your magazine articles?"

She laughed. "Well, a line or two when I can get away with it, but most gardeners want *practical* stuff—planting times, insect control, best times to water. Boring."

"Well, they're the poorer. You should plant seeds in their minds."

Jay's favorite place remained the island and its shaded haven of beauty. There they sat long over meals, talking science, philosophy, poetry. By now, Linda felt safe. This man would not cross her boundaries, and breezes of free exchange blew the curtains of her soul. She tried to avoid defining what else she felt. How does one camouflage an awkward, ill-timed blush?

On Friday evening, as twilight shifted toward darkness, Jay produced a burgundy silk scarf from his jeans pocket and arranged it deftly on the wide-mesh, tobacco-hued wicker table. "Found this on the far side of your butterfly garden. Reconstructing the scene of the crime, I'd say you were waging war on noxious weeds. The scarf got in your way; you whipped it off with your clean left hand and left it in the care of the nearest shrub. Only you forgot."

Linda tipped her head and laughed. "I wondered what had become of that."

He then produced a lilac pillar candle from behind a triad of potted greenery. "I made sure it had been lit at least once. Wouldn't want to wreck some arcane *objet d'art*." He bent again to the shrubbery. "I'm sorry. The lighter came from your fireplace and doesn't fit the color scheme. Could you do something about that next time?" His face froze, and he reached for the last item, a perfectly formed, silvery pink rose, its fragrance turning the air warm. "This I just plain purloined. Stole it. I return it now to its maker and minder with . . . with . . . " He couldn't finish. He took a quick breath and searched the woven ceiling of the gazebo as though for help. "Thank you," he said finally, but the words left unspoken brought tears to Linda's eyes.

The candle flickered against the strengthening night. Wood thrushes in the darkening wood performed evensong. Jay and Linda sat silent in the terrifying beauty of the moment, unable to think of a thing to say that would ward off heartbreak.

Finally, with a big breath, Jay spoke the dreaded words, and Linda's heart turned to ice. "Tomorrow . . . is leave time—leave this safe place, this haven of healing." She could feel, more than see, the anguish in his eyes as he studied the single flame. "I can hardly bear . . . " He stopped, then smiled brightly. "But bear we must. Could we eat early, say, seven o'clock?"

"Of course. Whenever you want. Let me drive you somewhere. You're not ready to set off on foot quite yet."

Momentary alarm rose to his eyes. "Ready or not, I'll retrace. I can do that. Thanks for the offer, but it just . . . wouldn't do."

She nodded, recognizing unsafe territory.

Breakfast was somber. Linda shuffled dishes and fought tears as Jay struggled with his French toast. She would not cry, not while he was there. Afterward, she could seek the emptiness of her garden.

"I've packed a lunch," she said. "I know it's extra weight, but eat the heavy stuff first."

"In other words, I carry it one way or another." Their smiles were fleeting. He folded his napkin carefully, deliberately. "Thank you. I'll go brush, finish . . ." He stood abruptly and turned toward the bedroom. Linda's hands shook so badly she could hardly carry the dishes.

When they came together at the patio door, both were pale, both were wretched. He stowed the lunch and bottle of water in a backpack Linda had found in the basement, then straightened. "What can I say? What can I possibly say? Thank you?" He waved his hand deprecatingly. "Offer you money? If I did that, you'd lighten my load by a head."

Linda's laugh almost uncorked her tears.

"I am forever in your debt; I cannot possibly repay. We may never meet again—" He drew a ragged breath. "But I will not forget. *I will not ever forget.*"

He drew himself up. "You have done me great honor, and I learned early that I could trust you."

He did not spell it out, but she knew what he meant.

He went on to more puzzling words. "I trusted you, and some day, you may know just how much you hold in your hands." He looked through the glass door, beyond the beds and shrubs, the bridge, the gazebo. "But—" He shrugged and grinned. "If everything goes south, I'll sneak back and hire on as your gardener. I know where you hide your weeds."

Linda laughed, but the moment had come, and neither of them could say their lines. The agony was palpable.

"I must go," he said softly, stretching the backs of his fingers toward her cheek, then deliberately closing his fist and drawing away, eyes still clinging to hers.

"Yes . . . go to your wife." Linda's voice was a bare whisper.

His eyes froze, then dropped revealingly, but he said nothing. Linda tried to smile, then bent to the backpack. He picked it up, and she helped settle it in place. She could do that. He could not touch her, but she, the caregiver, could do whatever was needed. She had done so in his time of need and had felt honored to serve him that way. Now he was in need again, and she could do the necessary thing. She gave the pack a final pat, then shifted her hands to his shoulders and propelled him through the doorway. "Godspeed, Jay. Godspeed . . . Godspeed . . . "

Chapter 4

JAY LEFT THE PROPERTY BY the same route he had come, but his emotions drove him through scruffy underbrush to the magnificent stand of mature hemlocks—which he noticed only because Linda had mentioned them. Anger sent small cones flying, and upon reaching his rented Lexus, he punched the keypad viciously. He dug under his seat for the packet containing watch, wallet, cell phone, keys, and wedding ring. Why had he left everything in the car? Pure luck? He couldn't imagine how the week would have gone if he'd had ID on him. He sighed. Did Linda's God drop him there as a test? For him or for her? And what might come of such a week?

When his plane landed, he started to phone Martin, then changed his mind. Martin could spot scars on his liver, and he wasn't ready for that. Justin, his car "hostler," would ask how his week went, and reading the weather, would stop talking and let Jay sit back with eyes closed. That he could handle.

But it was Martin, not Justin, who pulled his Hummer to the airport curb. Jay's jaw clenched, and he couldn't even force a smile. He needed Martin but couldn't bring himself to like him. Martin, his face in a permanent snarl, might once have made a respectable drill sergeant, but now his heft could turn a person's foot to mush. His spotted head and jutting jaw gave him the semblance of a mangy pit bull—or perhaps a troll. His appearance, however, veiled a well-fueled, high-powered intelligence.

This intelligence, linked with administrative skills, induced Jay to put up with him—a superb aide, ombudsman, spokesman, and marshal of irksome matters. Martin could bring order to paper in a wind tunnel. He kept the home base running smoothly and saw to Jay's daily, weekly, monthly, and yearly schedule. He knew more about Jay's finances than Jay did. In short, he was indispensable—and knew it.

"Welcome home!" he said. "Been a long week?"

"Seven days. Yes. What happened to Justin?"

"Just obeying orders. Told him to buzz me if or when you called. Wanted to get first take on what you've been up to."

"Martin, I'm too tired for the drill. Can't take it. Is everything all right here? Glynneth?"

"She's fine. Asking questions, though—like the rest of us. Let's start with *where have you been?* Then move to *what have you been doing?*"

"I've been away, and I've been thinking—a lot. There's your answer. I've even been sick. I'm okay now, just tired. Do you get that, Martin?"

"You have an important phone call to make. Do you get that?"

"I do. But I also have a wife who needs my attention. Now. With two frogs the same size, you pick the more important to swallow first, and my wife trumps everything else."

"Your wife has Charlotte; an hour longer won't make any—"

"Martin, back off. I will see Glynneth first. I need to. Go cool your—"

"Hoo! A bit testy, aren't we?"

"Martin—"

"All right. Go see Glynneth. I'm sure she'll have her latest threads to show off." His voice slabbered sarcasm.

Before getting the new dress count, Jay had to negotiate Charlotte, Glynneth's saucy personal assistant, waiting for him in the reading nook outside the upstairs suite. She uncoiled from the loveseat, her nutmeg-colored face dimpling. He picked through his collection of smiles for one he hoped would work. One had to be careful with Charlotte.

"Charlotte! Did you miss me? How's Glynneth doing? I hear she's been laying dress snares for me."

Mischief danced from her eyes. "Oh, yassuh. Wait'll you see!"

"Is she ready to see me now, or would later be—"

"Whenevuh you say, Mistuh. Yassuh, she—"

Jay closed his eyes, pulling up his best frown in an effort to abort an irrepressible grin. "Charlotte, cut that out!"

She flipped her head, dark eyes dancing. "Now, Mistuh . . . "

"*Stop talking like that!* How many times have I asked you—no, *ordered* you—"

"Oh, at least a thousand."

"Then stop playing. Talk sensibly. You do sometimes. You're smarter than the rest of us put together." He turned away, the grin having won. The very presence of Charlotte evoked laughter. "Why do I put up with you?" he asked, trying to be fierce. "Your salary comes out of my pocket—your *handsome* salary, I might add. Yes, you're funny. Yes, you know how to make Glynneth dance to your tune. You—"

Charlotte drew her graceful form into a dramatic pose that on anyone else would seem provocative, but no one dared think along those lines for fear of being instantly incinerated. "You threatening to cut my salary? You know better than that. I'm indispensable."

"Yah, you and Martin. But how else can I stop your game?"

She raised an eyebrow and let her tongue peek through her lips.

"Charlotte, don't go cute on me!" he said warningly. "It's not funny, not now. Can't you see—" He broke off. *"Please—*just *tell* me what I'm in for with Glynneth. Is she angry about my being away so long?"

Charlotte's coppery eyes went stone serious and scanned Jay up and down, much like an electronic device.

"What's the matter? Is something wrong? Glynneth—"

"Only with you. You just come off a week. You're tired, scared, and if I had to guess, I'd say every bone in your heart is broken and needs fixin', and you're afraid to talk about it. You'd like to slide in with your wife without her or anybody else noticing."

Jay closed his eyes. She was right. He needed a hole to crawl in . . . If any person could "fix" him, Charlotte would be the one, and he had no idea why.

"Yes, I'm tired, and no, I don't want to talk about it—not now, anyway. Just tell Glynneth I'm here, waiting to see her." His voice took a plaintive turn he didn't intend, especially in front of this woman he couldn't begin to comprehend.

Her eyes squinted fractionally, but she turned and, on her way to the door of the suite, muttered just loudly enough, "Yassuh, I'll tell Glynneth an' leave you here to let the good Lord speak what you need to hear."

"Charlotte, *please.*" This wasn't the *fix* he was looking for.

She stopped and turned back, again totally serious, and Jay looked at her, eyes frantically wide as though seeing her for the first time. "Something I said?" she asked with a raised eyebrow. "Or is somebody else talking?"

He thought a moment. "No . . . yes . . . no . . . "

"What don't you understand?"

He hesitated, then shook his head with a sigh. "There's not much I do understand about you, but we'll talk later—maybe. Please tell Glynneth I'm home. Ask her what she's going to do about it."

Glynneth was ready for him. As Jay softly called her name, she glided from the sitting room, tall and regal in a long, black, velvety sheath with high collar and low neckline, and he was suddenly immobilized. He might have inhaled deeply but found himself unable to breathe. Her hair—today a deep, rich mahogany the color of chestnuts—fell softly over her shoulders, setting off the topaz pendant that flashed unearthly gold over her ivory skin. She stopped, struck a pose, then with perfect timing moved toward him.

Jay, his breathing apparatus finally working, held out his arms but did not clasp her. Instead, he explored the silk-soft contours of her arms and leaned to kiss first her cheek, then her hands and both arms, and finally her neck with a passion that brought sudden color to her face.

"*Glynneth.*"

He breathed the word, then took her face in his hands. Her eyes widened, and her mouth opened; but even with her heightened desire, he knew better than to even brush her lips. "Glynneth, I'm home. Never have I seen you so beautiful. Please—come to bed with me. Right now. Just as you are. What better garment could you wear? I am *stunned*, stupefied."

Glynneth drew a shaky breath, but a smile broke the intensity of the moment. "Dearest one, I hunted so long for this. I knew just what I wanted, and when I saw it, I was sure you'd like the draped look." She ran her hand over the soft gathers along her left hip.

"You got it right, my love. I do like it. Now come with me. Let's make the most of your splendid dress," and he tried to draw her toward the bedroom. He desperately needed her. His body cried out for hers.

"Oh, silly! I can't wear this." She pulled away and drew him instead toward two overstuffed chairs. "Please, love—wait till bedtime. I'll wear your favorite nightgown. You haven't actually seen it, but I know it will be your favorite. Now, sit here and tell me about your week. How are things down south? I'm assuming that's where you were."

Jay hid a crooked smile, tempted to pull her toward the bed. He knew it wouldn't work, though, and settled in the chair, relieved that she wasn't upset about his being away so long. Her armor of beauty had once again proven impenetrable. He sighed. "No. I was out east, actually. It was a crazy week in a number of ways. I was sick for some of it and slept a lot, thought a lot."

"About what?"

"About us. About our future."

"That's what made you sick?" She tipped her head, eyes twinkling.

He smiled, too, glad that her concern went no deeper than this rare joke.

They chatted for a half hour, and Jay finally gave up trying to move her to the bedroom. He knew it was hopeless. He had dutifully worshiped at her altar, but the idol, as always, proved false. She would sleep in his bed, granting him the empty shell of her body, but only after he had fallen asleep.

He left to tackle the other big frog.

Chapter 5

LINDA JENSEN AND BONNIE MARSDEN had been best buddies since high school. They'd roomed together in college, scheduled major events around the other's convenience, wept together over tragedies and disappointments, and laughed together on the far side of tears. Now in their early thirties, they read each other as a person reads a newspaper.

Linda knew that Bonnie knew that something was afoot. Even though Bonnie had not made an issue over Linda shutting herself away, she would search for an explanation under the theory that Linda was no better at hiding secrets than she was herself.

Actually, Linda did hide her secret reasonably well. She gave herself a half day to cry and another half to practice appearing normal. Then she called Bonnie.

"Seems like forever since we've spent time just *being*. Whaddaya say to an overnight trip to the Big Apple? Shopping, dinner, and a second go on *Les Mis*. Remember to bring two hankies this time! I'll get tickets." For a price; she knew that. But a place to disguise her emotions was worth a scalper's wage. Somehow, she had to appear normal, even with her mind skateboarding.

She had so much to process, especially those last moments at the door. That Jay was married was clear. How had that escaped her? That he wore no wedding ring was not an excuse; other people, for reasons of comfort or safety, did not wear rings. She had simply overlooked—or stifled—the likelihood of his being married. That he wished he were not—at least right then—was likewise clear, and she didn't know what to do with that.

Then, his final words. *I've trusted you, and some day you may know just how much you hold in your hands.* Her ground seemed to tremble under the weight of that trust. What did it mean? She bore some terrible responsibility that she could barely grasp. She must not tell anyone he'd been there, and more particularly, she must not reveal what she had done for him. Not to Bonnie, not to anyone. And while staggering under that burden, she somehow had to appear normal.

Bonnie had eyed her those first days, but even she seemed to dismiss the strange interlude. Life in Abington, forty miles from New York City, went on—church things, charity things, boating things on the Hudson, cheering things (as when Bonnie's nephew pitched a no-hitter). Politics were a hot topic, with this being an election year. Both sides were sorting themselves out prior to the conventions in August. Closer to home and far down the political ladder, an eighteenth-district congressional hopeful spoke at the Fourth of July children's event on the Abington sports field. He was tedious, the children obnoxious. Linda mentally deleted the event from next year's calendar. Boring unpleasantness was a poor prelude to the annual garden tour the following week.

Each year, the Abington Garden Club featured Linda's magnificent display in their advertising brochures. She was, by far, their greatest draw. *Fashioning the grounds of her ancestral home after an Old English estate garden,* the tour brochure read, *Linda Jensen and her parents transformed what was once a lumpy, uninteresting bit of swamp into a horticultural fairyland behind her stone-and-wood, Tudor-styled house. Highlights include a three-season perennial border, a four-season forest path, a number of varied and lovingly designed garden rooms for private moments of meditation, and, of course, the island with its splendid arched bridge and gazebo. This is one garden you won't want to miss.*

With this bit of hyperbole, expectations were high, putting pressure on Linda. Jorge, her Mexican gardener, was *Señor Pulgar Verde*—Mr. Green Thumb. Large, assertive, overbearing at times, Jorge would not hear of taking the day off, now that the work was done. "Ha!" he said with haughty acerbity, "*Nunca hecho*—never done! They need to see who created all this!"

Bonnie would be Linda's faithful right arm, but not in the garden; she could arrange flowers, but not grow them.

The day of the garden tour dawned fine and bright. The flowers felt Jorge's touch earlier than they felt the sun; and when Linda went out, he was weeding, dead-heading, and staking.

"You're worrying sinfully," Linda scolded. "Real gardens have dead blossoms. Relax! Our guests won't notice picky stuff in their oohing and aahing."

Her crew of helpers came early, too—Bonnie, of course, Marty from church, plus Charles and Emily and a few other Garden Club friends. One parking attendant manned the curved, rhododendron-lined drive, while another waited for latecomers at the broad, grassy area just off the road. The caterers arrived alarmingly late, but not as late as Reginald Norris, the club's irrepressible president. Surprisingly, he had dressed respectably for the occasion—one of Bonnie's greatest worries. His wife, Alexandra, busy managing another tour venue, must have exercised her badgering talent to bring this about. Also, on the plus side, Linda's red coreopsis, planted late, had a decent bloom, and Charles and Emily had settled the giant pot of elephant ears in a patch of sun between the bridge and the gazebo. *Jay would have approved*, she thought.

She checked the deck arrangement and bent to her troll garden, water flowing under the bridge, past the tumbledown cabin and decaying mushrooms, and disappearing through mounds of greenery into deep, haunting woods. Satisfied, she stood and eyed the seating arrangement that included a swinging chair that everyone would fight over. A built-in table nestled invisibly under the trellis; others hid their practicality under earth-toned cloths. Two umbrella tables on the lower level provided pitchers of ice water and a semblance of shade—plenty of comfort here for non-garden gawkers and weary walkers. Satisfied, Linda went indoors.

By nine-thirty, everyone was in a perfect dither, shifting food and dishes and bouquets and flower lists to people who hadn't the faintest idea what to do with them. The doorbell rang. Linda threw up her hands. "It's too early! What are the gatekeepers thinking of? Charles, dear, be a good lad and see who it is."

"Right. I'll send them sternly back to the gate and tell them to wait there!"

He was back in a moment, box in hand, looking bemused. "Flowers. From a florist. Coals to Newcastle—if anyone knows what that means anymore." He turned it over to inspect it. "Small, at least. Won't require an impossibly huge, ugly vase."

He held it toward Linda, but she shook her head. "You and Emily open it, and do something artistic, would you? Vases are under there." She waved vaguely at a bank of cupboards. "Please don't let it be a wrist corsage that I *have* to wear!"

"Ah, *artistic* is Emily's oyster, not mine. Here." He handed it to his wife.

Emily returned minutes later, a blend of mystification and awe on her face.

"I think you should look at this." She held up an exquisitely ornate, gold-etched, double-handled bud vase containing a dusky, just-opened rose.

Linda's eyes widened, and she inhaled sharply. For a moment, she was speechless, painfully aware that the dither had ceased, and everyone had turned to stare. The pounding of her heart drove all words from her brain. "It's . . . it's beautiful!" she finally managed, wishing helplessly that the elephant ears were close enough to hide behind. She took the vase and examined it minutely. "It's—who is it from?" Her voice was only a shade steadier than her hand.

"No card anywhere. I looked through everything twice, but nothing. Just stunning. Someone put time, effort, and money into this. The vase alone . . . But I found just the place for it. The mantel. I set it there for a moment, and it plays off the gold frame of the Latour and the splash of red in the painting itself. The perfect setting." She reached out to take it, but Linda held back and shook her head.

"No. It's got to go in the gazebo."

"The gazebo! You must be joking. That's the worst possible place! It's much too formal for the gazebo."

"That's where it has to be." She ran to her bedroom and rummaged through a drawer. She picked up the burgundy scarf Jay had purloined, then discarded it for a filmy yellow one. In the dining room, she opened more drawers.

"Bonnie! Do I have any gold or yellow candles? Where is she?" Her hands shook uncontrollably as she grabbed a pair of gold candleholders from the cupboard above and continued her search.

Bonnie came from the patio and went to the proper drawer. "All the gold candles you could possibly want. What is it? What have you got?"

"Thank you. I'll be right back. Guests will be coming soon. Where's Reggie? He should be out front by now."

She ran through the garden, over the bridge, and opened the magnet-fastened screen door of the gazebo. She set the vase carefully on the floor and unceremoniously removed the huge, riotous bouquet from the table. With hands that would not stop shaking, she began work on her display. She couldn't get the scarf to drape properly and looked around frantically. Putting everything down, she went out to search the watery surround. A small, richly hued chunk of wood lay half in the water. A few shakes got it reasonably drip-free, and she hurried to try it out. After setting it this way and that, she finally got the scarf draped and the vase and candles positioned just right. She stepped back to survey the effect. Almost, but not quite.

She turned and ran to the rose garden, picked a blossom from her Double Delight Hybrid Tea, and hurried back to sprinkle the red-yellow-white petals on the ends of the scarf. Yes! Perfect! She struggled momentarily with tears, but a glance at her watch sent her back over the bridge, not bothering to refasten the screen door. Swamps incubate mosquitoes. *Get real,* she murmured.

Bonnie met her with a look of concern. "Linda, are you all right? Emily told me—"

Linda laughed and hoped that, for once, Bonnie would be fooled by its fraudulence. "I'm sorry. I get these crazy ideas, and you know how I am sometimes." She shrugged ingratiatingly. "If you get a chance, go see if you like the arrangement."

People came and went throughout the day. Bonnie took charge indoors, Linda outside. She led groups and individuals through the labyrinth of annuals and perennials, roses, shaded ferns, rock gardens, garden rooms, and, of course, her marvelous water feature with its arched bridge, island, and gazebo. On the bluestone patio, chairs, juice drinks, and an assortment of tea brought respite and comfort to weary guests.

Linda searched the crowd closely, hoping—but fearing even more—that he might come, his wife at his side. They would admire the garden and express gratitude for her kindness to him, and they'd all laugh over his misadventure. He would surely take his wife to the gazebo. What of her arrangement? What would he think? Had Linda been wrong, after all, to make it so dramatic? Now, she hoped fervently that he wouldn't come, but yet . . .

She forced herself back to her real guests. Some had come to admire and gush, some to talk serious horticulture. Many mentioned her gazebo display, and she did not know how to respond. But as always, she loved the event and drew strength from the air of enthusiasm. She hoped sincerely that other gardeners in the tour brochure were not eating the bread of loneliness because of her.

By late afternoon, the crowd had thinned, but a few settled for the night, or so it seemed. The caterers wanted to leave, but the stalwarts called for another round of food and drink so they could continue talking. They sat on the deck with its enormous bouquet, water accent, and nestled fairy garden. Conversation bounced between men and women like intersecting tennis matches.

" . . . the perennial mess in the Middle East. All terrorists have to do to bring this country down is annihilate either the Yankees or the Red Sox . . . "

"Did anyone hear that mahvelous mezzo Ava Shillingham in her Lincoln Center debut? Such a voice—so warm and sensual. But the *songs* she chose—or were they chosen for her? I can't imagine her . . . "

" . . . or both. Wouldn't have to destroy our technology—just our down-home, baseball heart. With all the 'incidents' lately— the January subway thing and all—terrorism will heat up both conventions next month."

"Linda, dear, how did you arrange such splendid weather this year? Does your church pray for weeks ahead?"

"You laugh about how little it would take to destroy us! Just a single EMP attack, now with Iran *and* North Korea having the—"

"Would you spell that out, please? Not up for alphabet soup."

"Speaking of soup, Hazel Guthrie served the most *mahvelous* . . . "

"E-M-P—electro-magnetic pulse. If even a small bomb goes off high over Missouri, the electro-magnetic pulse effect would wipe out the electronics in the entire . . . "

" . . . this chawming little boutique on Condor Island. Hardly anyone knows about it, and . . . "

"Who will the Dems put up against Nelson Graham? A governor will be hard to—"

"Roger Hanily, of course. The only person with a ghost of a chance of beating a Reaganite like Graham. And given Beltway politics, Hanily will pick Dan Coyne for sure. The big question is who will Graham pick for his VP?"

" . . . take Margaret Hanstead to that boutique. *No* taste whatsoever! Her outfit last week—shabby shoes, cheap purse . . . "

"Linda, dear, how did your Right to Life walk go? Such a controversial cause. Did *anybody* sign up to support you?"

"Actually, I brought in . . . "

" . . . assuming Graham pulls in the last remaining electoral votes."

"*Everyone* knows shoes and purse make the woman. Everyone except Margaret . . . "

"Well, he needs someone more centrist. Senator Darson, maybe, or even Shirley Gladstone. She'd bridge the—"

"Howard, dawhling, did you say Shirley Gladstone?"

"Yes, I did. She—"

"We bumped into her at the polo match last winter. Our cruise to Barbados—do you remem—"

"Shirley Gladstone—playing polo? On a cruise ship? I know they're big, but I can't believe—"

"Oh, *Howard.* Do be sensible. She wasn't on our cruise ship. I don't know how she got to Barbados. Chawming woman—folksy, down to earth, don't you think? And why ever are you talking about her in the first place, my dear?"

"If Nelson Graham becomes the Republican candidate at the convention next month, he might name her as his running mate, and just think—you'd be on bumping terms with the future vice president of the United States."

Linda retreated to the kitchen, too tired for cruises or candidates; and after shifting the remaining food to her own pans, she sent the catering crew to their well-earned rest, while grimly longing for her own bed. Bonnie, seeing her weariness, marched on the patio and gathered up dishes and food as a naked hint for the remaining guests to leave. By ten o'clock, they were gone and the kitchen and patio clean. Bonnie pushed Linda toward her bedroom and then let herself out the door.

Chapter 6

THE HOUSE WHERE GLYNNETH DWELLED was not a mansion, but it had been designed for the couple by the esteemed architect Clement Sillsbury and given as a wedding gift by Jay's parents. High on a hill west of the river, it suited her well. Glynneth loved heights; she loved the sweeping view and the shifting mood of the river below. Plus, privacy came along with property tracts the size of Connecticut or Rhode Island. The house itself had been functionally landscaped and collected perfunctory murmurs of admiration. But in Jay's eyes, it seemed packaged and sterile against Linda's gardens.

Indoors, the downstairs arranged itself into a number of large and small rooms—a kitchen that pleased even Mrs. Liles, their cook *extraordinaire* and master of multiple cuisines; a dining room large enough to seat at least twenty; a formal, well-appointed great room; and a sunken sitting room for more casual relaxation. In addition to Martin's office, two smaller rooms served flexibly as needed—a workspace, a room for private conversations, or an emergency bedroom. An intimate tearoom, hardly more than a large closet, backed off the dining room. The only touch of full-blown Victoriana in the house, this tiny room enlarged the souls of the privileged few who gained entry there.

Upstairs, the master suite contained a large and small bedroom—one lush with lace, the other with bold lines and subdued colors. A sitting room with flowered, overstuffed couches and a ruffled lounge chair adjoined the bedrooms. One of two baths held a spa tub and double-sized shower; the other was more modest in every way. A miniscule exercise room contained basic, feminized equipment.

To the north or front side of the house, Charlotte's bedroom and bath were comfortably large and well-furnished, and Jay had insisted that her tastes—not Glynneth's—be reflected. Charlotte must be kept happy, by all means.

Charlotte held the reins in this household. Though small in stature, she had emerged early as the authority figure. All the staff, including Martin, feared her. When she first came on the scene, Martin had sparred in an effort to mark his territory, but her eyes and body language proved more aggressive than his weight-throwing, and he seldom visited her fiefdom upstairs.

Charlotte had obtained her position three years earlier just by knocking on the door. Martin the Terrible had attempted to send her packing, but she bellied up to him, bullet eyes unholstered, and Martin quickly summoned his boss.

When Jay came to the sitting room, Charlotte's slender, five-foot-three frame conveyed elegance—her hair black and curved inward, just below ear level; her skin the color of lightly creamed coffee; her face expressively intelligent; her clothing a smooth, natural extension of who she was. Jay wondered then and afterward if Charlotte always dressed elegantly or if she made whatever clothing she wore look elegant.

"I am Charlotte, and I have come to care for your wife," she announced, her voice honey soft.

Jay's shoulders tightened, instantly defensive. *This woman— here in my house like some brash window washer but asking to tend to my wife.* No. He needed to say only, "I'm sorry; we don't need your services," but the words wouldn't come. Her incandescent eyes blocked them, shut them down. Who was she? What was going on? Normally, categorizing people came easy, but this woman . . .

He cleared his throat.

"My wife . . . we're, uh, not in need—"

She looked pityingly at his lined face and spoke gently.

"Your wife is in deep pain, and you're in need, as well. She would be my first priority, but helping your wife might ease your pain."

Again, Jay stiffened. What could she know of his pain? Was this a media plant? He could not permit this bizarre intrusion into his grief. He straightened in an attempt to speak firmly, but that failed, too. "I . . . don't know what to say to you. Who sent you here? Obviously, you know about our tragedy, but—"

Charlotte responded by assessing the chair arrangement in the sunroom. With feline sinuousness, she directed Jay to one of them. "Shall we sit down?"

He sat, strangely helpless. "Um . . . Miss . . . ?"

"Charlotte will do for now."

"Well. Charlotte." He coughed uncomfortably. "Can you tell me about yourself—your background, training, college deg—" Why was he asking these questions?

Charlotte leaned toward him compassionately. "College degrees can't help your wife, and my background is irrelevant. You'll need to check that, but I think you'll find everything in order. Your wife is buried under grief and shame, and she needs help. Please—ask any question you want, but God sent me here, and I came. I want to love your wife whole again and bring comfort to you, as well."

God sent her. *God?* God who had destroyed his wife and his life? To him, God could be a handy tool, but this woman, holding out . . . what? She appeared as unbending as the Washington Monument. Yet in terms of warmth, compassion, and caring, Lincoln, on the far end of the Mall, seemed a more appropriate metaphor. She was also offering him a different sort of wealth. Money he knew, but not this currency. Comfort. Help in bearing the unbearable. Jay bent under the sheer weight of such unexpected succor. One part of his brain resisted this wild and possibly dangerous proposition, erecting a barricade worthy of the French Revolution. The rest of his brain was on its knees, a ragged, beggarly supplicant reaching with trembling hands for whatever scrap of peace might be salvaged. Could this woman—who appeared capable of running the United Nations—manage Glynneth?

The beggar part won, and his mind turned to drafting an immediate rebuild of the upstairs to provide proper accommodations. Whoever this person was, wherever she had come from, seemed almost a miracle worthy of . . . God.

"All right, Charlotte, supposing I were to take you up on this—and I'm not—"

"Of course. I understand."

"What would your requirements be—salary-wise, schedule, housing—I'm assuming you'd choose to live here." Why was he suggesting that? His right brain was still at work.

"Of course. The only way I could help your wife is to live here. Salary—" She shrugged. "Room and board—I'm assuming the board part?" She smiled. "I only ask that I be free to attend church at least once a week—maybe twice, perhaps—on Sunday, or another evening if that would be better."

"So, you'd like a flexible schedule?"

She studied the Georgia O'Keefe painting over the fireplace, then directed her eyes to Jay. "Let's clarify *flexible*."

Jay tensed under an expected barrage.

"Caring for your wife is my top priority and is not flexible, no matter the day or hour. Your authority is also fixed. Everything else *is* flexible. I'll need to earn respect in this house, of course."

Jay's tortured eyes stared at her.

"Charlotte, if you could accomplish only a fraction of what you're offering, I'd be forever in your debt. Anything you need, you'd have a direct line to me, no matter where or when. We'd talk regularly to see how it's going. But right now—" He grinned crookedly. "You just might be a Godsend."

Charlotte's eyebrows lifted. "You're far too trusting here— mmm-mm. First, the background check. Second, will I get on with your wife?"

He laughed awkwardly, realizing how much faith he'd unwittingly extended. "Well, let's go meet Glynneth." He rose and ushered her toward the stairway.

When they reached Glynneth's rooms, the young woman had paused to scan the suite, signaling Jay to stay outside while she moved with cat-like smoothness toward the larger room and king-sized bed.

Glynneth lay curled on her side, eyes hidden from view. Charlotte began humming softly as she went around and lifted a knee to the bed, so she could reach the unkempt woman. She reached out her hand, holding it momentarily above Glynneth, then stroking the outer hairs of her head so lightly the woman could hardly have felt it.

"My poor, sweet dove," she sang, voice buttery and deeply caring. "I will sing your sadness, your sorrow into my heart. You, my sweet dove, will smile again—not today, not tomorrow, not the next day, but someday, someday . . ."

She settled beside Glynneth and stroked not just her hair, but her forehead, her cheeks.

"You are so pretty," she murmured. "My lovely dove. But your hair . . . " She drew out a long tress and ran it through her hands again and again. "I saw a brush on your table. Let me get it, my sweet, and we'll make this tiny piece of your beauty shine again."

Jay, watching from the entryway, leaned weakly against the doorjamb. His wife was following Charlotte's movements with a tiny spark of interest; and when Charlotte finished brushing that one strand, Glynneth put a trembling hand to her head. "So dirty," she said, her voice scarcely audible.

"Oh, yes. We'll have to doooo something about thaaat—yes!" Again, she turned words into song.

Before Charlotte left late that afternoon, she had gotten Glynneth to sit up while she fed her yogurt from the bedside table. She had prepared a soothing, scented bath, helping her in and washing her from head to toe. She had found a clean nightgown, but noted out loud that it didn't suit her well. They'd have to shop for another, she sang, maybe next week.

Charlotte's face dimpled as she reported her successes, and Jay held both her hands firmly, eyes stinging. "You're an angel straight from heaven! What you've done this day . . . You'll come tomorrow?"

"Yes, but you must check me up and down. I have character references, though not specific to this work. I've never done this before!" Her cheek dimpled. "You'll know how to dig deeper." A quirky smile played over her face, but she turned with a strange question. "Do you know American Sign Language?" Her hand made some quick movements.

Jay frowned and shook his head. "No. Is that required? I can learn. Whatever it takes to keep you here. I'll forego sleep, food—whatever."

"No!" She laughed. "A few simple signals, like, *Lay it on thick. Be warned. Thin ice here.* That sort of thing." She signed each one. "Think you could learn those?"

"I'll work hard! We'll practice whenever I'm here. And we need to talk salary."

She shook her head. "I'll be happy with room and board and a little spending money. You do what seems good. But," she added firmly, "I won't take more till we know we can all get along together."

They did get along—exceptionally well. Charlotte was with Glynneth constantly that first month—coddling, wheedling, bribing, loving her to life. Glynneth drew heavily on Charlotte, but even that flowed largely from Charlotte knowing how to insinuate herself so subtly into Glynneth's habits and moods that the woman had no idea she was being controlled.

Charlotte objected to the pay Jay gave her. "Beginner's work. I'm still learning. Wait till I get the hang of things."

"Huh! You had the 'hang of things' the moment you walked through our door, and now you're in the trenches," said Jay. "This is combat pay."

A full three weeks passed before Charlotte started calling Jay *Mistuh*—and only when they were alone.

Chapter 1

BY AUGUST, MANY OF LINDA'S perennials and roses looked frayed, but the annual beds were coming into their own—as were hibiscus and dahlia displays, plus her new planting of tall, rosy Joe-Pye, a cultivated wildflower. Several of her loyal following asked for private showings, which she happily accommodated. She did draw the line at a Vacation Bible School outing of seven-and-eight-year-olds to her backyard.

"Your garden would be perfect for our 'Fruit of the Spirit' theme," the teacher had said.

"Don't you think an orchard would be better, in terms of fruit?" Linda responded.

She might have considered a small group, but *twenty*, with all her nooks and crannies to disappear in? *Unnnh-uh*. But she promised to help Bonnie prepare a mailing for the startup of Sunday school—and immediately regretted it. The editor of *The Garden Pathe* magazine pleaded with Linda to finish her article on herbaceous borders by August fifteenth, instead of September, as originally stipulated.

"I said yes," Linda told Bonnie, "but it has to be done tonight. How about coming here to seal envelopes? Maybe I can help when brain decay sets in."

Bonnie spread out in the den, the TV volume turned low to not distract Linda in her adjoining office. The ballgame wasn't going anywhere, so she channeled through the Republican convention, golf, Chef Boninni, and finally back to the convention. Speeches, cheering, hat waving—the enduring stuff of political conventions—were an odd counterpoint to labels and stamps and curled-up seal strips. The chorus of katydids outdoors seemed a natural extension of the convention.

"Huh!" Bonnie exclaimed. "He announced, but it's no one they've been talking about."

"That's nice." Linda obviously was not following. "Bonnie, what's another word for *subjective? Arbitrary,* maybe? I'm sorry—somebody announced something."

"Graham announced his running mate."

"Who did he choose?" Linda asked. "*Capricious.* That's the word I want. *Stolid souls around you may frown on capricious plant arrangements, but rejoice in a sudden fling of whimsy.* How's that? Who did he pick?"

"Somebody Crofter. From . . . North Dakota, maybe? Nowheresville, anyway."

"Never heard of him. Senator? Governor?"

"I think he's a senator, but nobody knows much at all. This is wild! They're falling all over each other, trying to patch together something to say. This guy was totally out of sight. They don't have file photos of him, only what's happening right now at the convention. Too funny! The surprise itself is the big story; the guy himself doesn't matter."

Linda came out, curiosity aroused. "Let's see this guy. What's his name?"

"Lawrence Joseph Crofter. I never heard of him. And if nobody else has, how in the world can he help Graham win the— Linda, what's the matter?"

Linda had dropped to a chair with an inadvertent *Oh!* The color had left her face.

"What is it, Linda?"

Confusion overtook Linda. "I'm sorry. I . . . I feel strange. I think I need . . . a fast trip to the bathroom. I'll leave you to sort out Mr. What's-his-name."

"Can I help you?"

"I'll be all right."

But she was not all right. She closed the door and sank to the floor. Jay—the Republican nominee for vice president. How could that be? And what did it mean? She held her head, wanting to cry but knowing she had approximately two minutes and forty-three seconds before Bonnie would break down the door. She took deep breaths, splashed cold water on her face, and, when she heard Bonnie's step, flushed the toilet. But what could she say?

"You okay?"

"Yes. Be out in a minute." She could not fool Bonnie, but she had to try. She went out, working her hair into place and smiling brightly under her friend's scrutiny. "Sorry about that. I think *The Garden Pathe* suddenly got to me. I need a break. What do you say we get those letters finished?"

She wanted to tell Bonnie to go home, but that would never work. She would have to play her part better than any acting she'd ever done. "What have you learned about this . . . Crofter fellow?"

"Not much. I was worried about you. What happened to you?"

"I don't know. Just felt . . . weird. I'll be okay. Would you rather keep sealing or stamp? I'll do either." Never mind that her article had to go out tomorrow.

Somehow, she got through the evening with only casual reference to the frantic scramble of TV commentators to cover the sudden turn of events. Some said this was a terrible choice—a man unknown, inexperienced, nothing to bring to the ticket. Others pointed to his strengths—good voting record, impeccable morals, proven fund raiser with an outside-the-box approach. Bonnie eventually left, and Linda switched from channel to channel, watching replays of his acceptance speech, drinking in every shot, every word by and about the new running mate, trying to wrap her mind around what was happening. From North Dakota. Jay—her Jay—was possibly the next vice president of the United States, conceivably a future president. No wonder he had been quiet, preoccupied. What a solemn, unfathomable decision to have to make! Lawrence Joseph. Lawrence J. Jay . . .

The two camps reacted predictably to the announcement.

BREAKING NEWS:

In a surprise move this evening, presidential candidate Nelson Graham named Lawrence Joseph Crofter as his vice- presidential choice.

The announcement came as a total shock. Crofter, Republican senator from North Dakota, was on nobody's list of potentials. He is recognized, however, as a man of bone-deep integrity, rock-solid convictions, and a bulldog approach to the Constitution—all things that resonate with Republicans.

#FoxNews

TWEET: WHO IN THE WORLD IS LAWRENCE J. CROFTER?
Elite member of the Filthy Rich. Reactionary. Prehistoric. Racist. And horrors—LIKED Donald Trump!

CROFTER: A LISTENER, A QUESTIONER

The folks back home in North Dakota know Lawrie Crofter as a politician who talks passionately to liberals and conservatives alike about kitchen-table issues. "Look what we've done here in North Dakota," he says. "Our economy is bubbling. People have jobs and are better off than in other states. We encourage business. Your employment most likely came when someone with money invested in machinery or desks or a franchise. Not only was the investor's dream realized, but yours, as well. Greed involved? Maybe, maybe not. Some people are irresponsibly rich, but even greedy money creates jobs for those who badly need them."

#BismarckTribune

What you DON'T Know about Lawrie Crofter

Start with his background. He was born in Bismarck, North Dakota, to parents made wealthy by oil. His father was one of the pioneers of oil fracking or fracturing, a process using pressurized water to loosen shale oil and extract it through horizontal drilling. With this technology, the Bakken oil formation under the western part of North Dakota has become a highly profitable source of oil and natural gas, benefitting the entire state's economy.

Crofter earned a history degree from Brimfield College in Wisconsin and a master's degree from Harvard. He married and returned to Bismarck, where he worked with his ailing father long enough to learn about financial portfolios and to pick up an interest in his father's thwarted political dreams.

The public outpouring of tribute on the death of his parents became a turning point for him: he wanted to be like them and to develop his own personal values, whether through politics or business.

He started in city government, then ran for mayor. Just after the election, the death of the U.S. congressman representing District Thirty-Five presented a splendid opportunity for getting a conservative in Washington. Lawrence "Lawrie" Crofter would probably have won handily, but his deceased father's lectures on responsibility prodded him to keep faith with the locals who had appointed him mayor, and he declined to run. Never mind. Near the end of his term, the district again became available, and this time he ran happily and won, his earlier sacrifice paying off in constituent loyalty. After two terms of consistent, faithful-to-the-party work, he won a Senate seat. In this venue, he pleased his constituents by listening well and fighting small, personal injustices.

So—meet Lawrence J. Crofter. He speaks boldly on issues, yet with charm, grace, and substance. How come no one noticed him before this?

#BetsyWalhamYahooNews

CROFTER KNOWS ALL ABOUT GREEDY MONEY

He does know greedy money, his daddy having sucked up oil through environmentally hazardous fracking. Then there's his youthful connection to the Grainger Group with its rabble-rousing tendencies, along with early statements that cast him as hostile to gays and abortion clinics, plus his image as a morality cop. And how many moralists have gotten caught in the wrong bed?

#Warren Baldard, PotomacDemocrat

IS LAWRIE CROFTER REPUBLICAN ENOUGH?

Some Republicans out there are questioning Crofter's in-dependent thinking, especially concerning problems of poverty and immigration. Too bipartisan, maybe? Some conservatives asked if he could be trusted. "Good ques-tion," Lawrie responded. "I ask that myself. But if it's not illegal or immoral, I can go along. My job will be to make the president's job easier—or harder, if that's required."

#Newsmax

TWEET: You don't know Lawrence J. Crofter until you take his wife into account. Glynneth Burningham Crofter. HAS LAWRIE BEEN SHOPPING ELSEWHERE??

Glynneth Delia Burningham Crofter was a rich lode of muck to rake. On the surface, she was flawless—a stunning beauty from a wealthy, upstanding, Michigan family. She was intelligent, graduating from Brimfield *magna cum laude*. The two had met at college and shared an appreciation for the con-servative and academic values of the school. Full of life and fun, they breathed the same intellectual, social, and politi-cal air, and the "Wedding of the Year" filled Christ Church in downtown Grand Rapids.

Things, though, began to unravel. While Lawrie was plowing political furrows, Glynneth the Beautiful stimulated the economy with wild spending sprees—and occasionally played her physical attributes unwisely. Her indiscretions seemed paltry, but the resulting friction drew attention.

Shrewdly noting this uncomfortable attention, Glynneth had redirected her focus to another passion previously undiscovered—children worldwide—especially those swallowed up in sex-trafficking. Lawrie encouraged her interest in children suffering from cancer, starvation, or neglect. At Christmas, she packed countless shoeboxes for international distribution. Lawrie had laughed.

"With bedrooms jammed floor to ceiling with toys and toothbrushes, we have to take overnight guests to a motel! Show her an orphan, her heart goes out."

Then Glynneth got pregnant—to everyone's delight. She wore her condition stylishly and was supremely happy; and when a boy came forth, the palace burst with joy and light.

"His name is Ephraim," Glynneth had declared, pride in her eyes and voice. "It says, right in the Bible, 'Ephraim is my first-born son.'"

The light and laughter vanished, however. In less than a year, Ephraim was dead—from heat stroke when Glynneth left him sleeping in her air-conditioned car while she ran into Foster & Jones for a sale item. One bargain led to another until she forgot she had him with her, and the car ran out of gas. A period of looming legal action and threatened suicide followed; but because of the circumstances and no previous record, the charge was reduced to *gross misdemeanor* with no jail time. Had she been a shopper before, she now became obsessive: clothing, shoes, housewares, books—giving away truckloads to make room for incoming goods.

Nothing, not even her wedding dress, was too special to part with, and children became an even more obsessive charity.

HAS ANYONE ELSE NOTICED Glynneth Crofter's similarity to Abraham Lincoln's wife, Mary: wild shopping habits, death of children, odd reasoning, abrasive behavior in public? Can the country put up with another Mary Todd Lincoln? And how did Glynneth wiggle out of jail time for child neglect?

#MarshallCloverlyn

The opposition got their heads together. Lawrie Crofter had to have been driven by these problems to shop around elsewhere.

One particular opportunity came to mind—an unexplained absence late spring when he missed an important vote. "Nonsense!" said Crofter. "Would I fool around with another woman while weighing Graham's offer? I was ill. Couldn't make it back. Ask my doctor. And," he went on, "I will not tolerate attacks on my wife. Of course, she had problems after our son's death. I did, too. Who wouldn't? She's had the best of care and counseling and is recovering remarkably well. She jokingly offered to wear garbage bags through this election, so I'd say she's got it pretty much together. I am proud to be her husband."

Lawrie Crofter flew home from Washington the first weekend after Graham announced. Despite the barbs being hurled at her, Glynneth was ecstatic over this new prospect and couldn't keep her hands off of her husband. She was ready for him—new clothing, new hairdo, new eagerness.

That night—and Lawrie didn't want to count the intervening weeks—they had sex.

Glynneth jolted Linda—hard—and she didn't fully understand why. This woman who knew Jay as Lawrie suddenly emerged from obscure conjecture to hard, inescapable reality. Linda had expected that and had anticipated Glynneth's beauty. Jay was handsome. Why wouldn't his wife measure up? But it wasn't equal. Glynneth was knockdown gorgeous—one of those immoderately stunning people Linda could never trust. Her beauty made Linda appear late-winter drab. However, grief could ravage any woman, even the intelligent and gifted. What a huge challenge for Jay!

And for Linda. Now that she knew the situation, she understood—with gnawing despair—that a man as honorable as Jay would never leave his wife.

But suppose he were the sort who *would* abandon his wife? What then? She shook her head resolutely. Her only option would be to send him packing. She could never marry a man who had discarded even a difficult wife.

The hair on her neck rose when she read the suggestive report on Jay's "missing week" and his vehement denial. He would not betray her—that she knew—but they were both in peril.

Then the dead child. Linda dug deep online to research their tragedy, and her heart broke—for both of them. Ephraim. A son. No wonder Jay had had trouble reading Hosea!

Charlotte played her *Mistuh* game only with Lawrie and only when no one else was nearby. Early on, Lawrie confronted her, arms akimbo. "Charlotte, you've *got* to stop calling me that."

Charlotte, chin and eyebrows up, mirrored his arm posture. "Honey, I can call you anything I want." She wiggled her hips sideways. "But don't try that shoe on your foot. Mmm-mm. Senator Crofter could find himself in the cooler—real fast." She cocked her head impishly.

Lawrie tried exasperation. "So, this is a power play." His smile, however, proved irrepressible.

"Yassuh, plain and simple. You have the power to fire me. I have a different sort of power—power to love Glynneth, power to love you. And I think we know who will win that war." She flicked her tongue.

Lawrie stepped away, then turned back sharply. "Charlotte, you have the brain of a physicist. You could be a top attorney, a neurosurgeon, a controller for missile defense. You could have a Ph.D. in whatever field you choose. Why are you here and not doing something spectacular?"

She looked at him intently. "I have a brain, yes, and I find pleasure using it—right here. And you give me plenty to do." She cocked her head slyly. "Somebody needs to rein you in when you start riding your hobby horse *du jour*—what was it yesterday— deficit spending? You don't seem to notice people rolling their eyes whenever you get over-busy noticing the sweetness of your own voice."

"Thank you, Charlotte." Lawrie smiled dryly. "Remind me to dock your pay any time you forget to pull my plug."

Charlotte smirked, raised her hand impudently, and signed at him with rapid finger movements. *Watch your step, buddy. Don't push it.*

Chapter 8

LAWRENCE CROFTER ACTUALLY ENJOYED THIS new campaign game. Nels was close to sewing up the needed electoral votes, so it wasn't a fight for life. The long, squirrelly trips got Lawrie away from congressional food fights, and he learned the art of snatching partisan grenades and lobbing them back. Fundraising was a pain, and media smears turned ugly, pulling him from more important duties—including his marriage. His only time off would be the days surrounding presidential debates.

He had talked at length with his wife about his prolonged absences. "It's all right," Glynneth had assured him. "You're perfect for Nels. His wife came to visit last week—did you know that? Said you balance his strengths and weaknesses. She was sweet. Asked how I was feeling and if I would be all right while you're away. I told her I don't mind your being gone."

And for once, Lawrie thanked God for her vocational shopping—though this could become an expensive election. He didn't fully believe she'd like him being away and listed activities to occupy her.

"You and Charlotte could shop, then go to that play that's straight off Broadway." Never mind that Charlotte hated shopping. "Here's another idea. How about a Meet-the-Vice-President's-Wife luncheon? Upper-crust spreads are your specialty, and Charlotte is good at party logistics. Dori—my "righthand-man" from the downtown office—" He grinned. "She could make a list of—how many d'you think? Twenty-five partakers?"

"Oh, we've handled forty—remember your Senate campaign? Twenty-five is hardly more than a few friends over for tea. But Lawrie, I can't give speeches, and—"

"No, no—speeches are Dori's job. She'll find a talker or two. They'll smile and joke and tell everyone how smart you were to marry such a fine, upstanding running mate to the future president. Everybody says nice things; everybody has a good time; and the ladies will clamor to do this at least once a month. You and Charlotte are definitely up for it and could take your show on the road."

Glynneth sat silent, fingers twirling a strand of hair. "Lawrie," she said, voice tentative, almost apologetic, "I can't do much about sex trafficking, but maybe . . . I could go to Children's Hospital, visit little ones who are . . . dying, maybe, or bald from chemo . . . " Her face contorted, but she straightened determinedly. "I could do that, Lawrie. I could talk to parents about . . . " She bit her lip hard. "Would that . . . ?"

Lawrie, gripped her hand—stunned, silent. Finally, he said, "Yes, my love. It would help—enormously. *Thank you!* That act of compassion will speak louder than any words I could say. I'll handpick some people, so you won't be alone."

"Charlotte?"

"Yes, of course. Charlotte."

Lawrie could hardly believe it. Offering up her passion—on his behalf. Still, nights would remain hard; he knew that. Her demons would harry her to the point where neither shopping nor hospital visits would exorcise them. She earnestly wanted her husband to be vice president, but the price tag for both of them would be very high.

He took her hand again. "I'll call you every day," he said. "I promise."

Late August, Vice President Graham and Senator Crofter began campaigning in earnest, crisscrossing the country—New Hampshire, South Carolina, Iowa, Nevada—in a chartered jet and flashy buses, their handlers and image consultants allowing no rest on the road. What flubs—their own and the opposition's— had to be dealt with? How best could they respond to attack ads? How could they prepare for debates, both presidential and vice-presidential? Which press flacks would accompany them? Which ones would confront them at the next stop? How about personal ambush? Business or investment torpedoes? Martin had made Crofter's financial craft bombproof, and even Lawrie was moved to express gratitude to his *difficult* aide. Their political Opposition Research team had done due diligence, noting where their opponents were skating on thin ice. This alone put the two candidates well along in the art of defensive aggression.

In those early days of dig-in campaigning, the duo often appeared together to solidify the ticket. It worked well. Nelson Graham—brash, colorful, vitriolic. The more easy-going Senator Crofter—dressed casually in jeans and open neck for the "shake hands and look 'em in the eye" sort of campaigning. His tongue could be sharp and punchy, but he used that sword prudently, crowds responding positively to his unique, personal magnetism.

They polished their verbal platform with each succeeding appearance, moving from D.A.R. teas and harvest parades to hog barbecues and town hall venues. Nels appeared increasingly comfortable with his choice of a running mate.

Lawrie gloried in this transition from the down-and-dirty warfare of congressional politics. With up to six audiences per day, he could hold to his principles and, at the same time, moderate Nels's ham-handedness—another lesson from his father. He resonated with Middle America, spoke effectively to Independents, and got Hispanics laughing over his fractured Spanish. His charisma, easy-going humor, and good looks didn't hurt the ticket, though Nelson himself exuded rugged strength. An iconic, black-and-white photograph of Nels at the helm of his sailing vessel, rain pelting face and slicks, cast the desired image.

In smokestack cities, they dragged out of bed at five in the morning to talk jobs at factory entrances; in Iowa it was corn and cattle, families and freedoms. They talked terrorism, a perennial headache. The 9/11 attack had faded significantly, but January's subway disaster in Philadelphia—an acknowledged terrorist outbreak—underscored the potential for worse. "Cyber-attacks," they said, "could shut down the entire east coast."

Lawrie was not afraid to address issues of government gone bad. In a major address in New Hampshire, he began with a self-deprecating smile.

"Good evening. I'm the senator—not from Nowheresville, as this morning's newspaper said, but from *way beyond* Nowheresville. Come visit someday—if you can find us. Not a lot of people in our state, but we do have corn, cattle, and more than our share of coyotes.

"I'm guessing that many of you, if you bother to think of me at all, ask, 'Can anything good come out of North Dakota?' Sitting Bull, the great Lakota warrior did, and I'm proud to ride his considerable coattails. Others ask—legitimately—if anything good can come out of the U.S. Senate, never mind North Dakota. Good question that I often ask myself. Rot infects the entire government structure. We all know it; we've seen it. But Nelson and I, we're solid timber—pressure-treated, green-tinged. We're tackling decay that's gone unchecked for years, replacing rotting timbers with strong, durable wood. But how deep does the damage go?"

Lawrie scanned the room, gauging the attention of his audience. His eyes stopped at the short, burnished hair of a woman in the front row . . . so like Linda's. But her companion's oppositional scowl and internal arms firmly crossed against anything Lawrie might say jerked him back.

Keeping an eye on the front-row hostility, he lined out the history of the country's most vexing problems, as well as ways to promote opportunities that would benefit all levels of the economy.

With a whimsical smile, Lawrie shifted his stance and again addressed the front-row arm-crosser.

"Have you ever planted a garden? Seems easy enough. First, dig sod. A back-breaker, but once that's gone, you pull out seed packets . . . no, wait! Before planting you have to dig even deeper, adding fertilizer and maybe lime. Finally, plants start coming up. But then come *weeds*—an army of them. Strong-armed bullies that move in and take over.

"That's today's government." Lawrie, voice taut and focused, leaned to his broader audience. "Our Constitution was dug from hard soil, but it gave us a beautifully designed freedom garden with checks and balances to keep government under control. Insidiously, though, weeds have taken over. The priceless document our founding fathers crafted is now almost unrecognizable, and anyone who speaks boldly against weeds does so at great personal risk."

Lawrie stood tall. "My friends, the freedoms we cherish are being swallowed by a briar patch. We the people—you and I—*must face this stark reality.* If we don't act, vines and thorns will choke off money, jobs, and what's left of our freedoms. When that happens, we *will* crash. It's not a matter of *if* but *when.*" He reached out. "People! We must . . . act . . . *now!* Please make your vote count. Nelson Graham and Lawrie Crofter *can* and *will* make a difference!"

Loud applause. Cheers. Cameras flashing. Reporters heading out to file their stories. Lawrie fed off supporters' approbation briefly, then directed his steps toward the hostile figure in the front row.

Glued to the computer in her study, Linda hung on Jay's every word. *Jay* . . . or should she start thinking *Lawrie* in her mind? She liked the name, but, somehow, *Jay* was the name he had given himself and, perhaps, was his gift to her. And now—she smiled at this—his North Dakota *yah* pronunciation of *yeah* made perfect sense. That whole area—the Dakotas and Minnesota—was rich with its German and Scandinavian influence. Why hadn't she thought of that?

She cheered his garden illustration that had sprung from their conversation in June. They had never talked politics, but she recognized these germinal ideas and knew he felt passionate about them.

Something niggled at her, however. His eyes weren't right in this political context, but what exactly was wrong? They'd seemed okay at her house. This warrior stance had not shown up in her garden, but he'd been ill and vulnerable. A game—maybe that was it. He was playing a game, putting on a persona. Is that what politicians do? Give in on the less important to get the more important, then give up the more important to gain more power? She had told him she trusted his face, his eyes. Nothing phony back then. She shook her head and focused on the talking heads as they analyzed his speech.

In the following days, Linda avoided reports of ugly attacks but then decided she could not stand by Jay symbolically without looking his enemies in the face. *How can he take all that hate?* she wondered. *It's all lies!* Greedy, they call him. Heartless. Rapacious. Self-aggrandizing. Power hungry. But those were tags. More unsettling were assertions about his business connections, his marital problems, even his poorly explained absence in June. His responses were often harsh counterthrusts. Was this part of the political game, the balancing act?

What might the next two months hold for Jay? *And why,* she asked herself, *does it matter so much—this man I knew for only a week, a man I cannot possibly marry?* She twirled her chair away from the computer and chewed her knuckle.

Reasons paraded across her mind:

- An important and influential man had fallen into her yard.
- She had tended to his needs when he could not care for himself.
- They shared common interests.
- They had bonded in the aloneness of that short time together.

She stopped and went back to her knuckle, trying to stem the flow of tears.

- She *loved* him and, at that unbearable moment at the door, he . . . loved . . . her.

Yes, he matters.

Linda wept.

Chapter 9

LABOR DAY WEEK WAS AN odd time to celebrate anything; but for nearly a decade, Linda and Bonnie had made an annual trek to Philadelphia to mark another cancer-free year for Bonnie. She had survived not only her own bout with breast cancer, but the death of her husband, as well. The celebration was bittersweet but had become sacred to them both. They had no set agenda and did whatever came to mind. One year, they spent thousands on shopping and going to the theatre. Another, they worked among the poorest of the poor. The previous year, they signed on as chambermaids at the Ritz-Carlton Hotel and, in their course of work, got propositioned by three hotel guests, giving them weeks of laughter, as well as a few hundred dollars in pay and tips.

This year, they were touring funky art galleries and learning the art of rock climbing at a storefront gym not far from their hotel. They had just emerged from the gym, counting bruises as they walked the narrow sidewalk toward the hotel district. Bonnie stopped short.

"My purse! I knew if I put it in the bottom of the locker, I wouldn't see it, and sure enough . . . " They swung around abruptly, almost colliding with two men close behind. "Oh!" said Bonnie, recognizing the face on the right.

"Oh!" said Linda for a far different reason. The man on the left stiffened, his hand moving toward a holstered gun. Lawrence

J. Crofter stared unbelievingly at Linda, and she at him. All four stood frozen for what seemed an eternity.

Jay was the first to recover. "Nice to bump into you." He smiled. "I'm Lawrie Crofter. But I haven't had the privilege of meeting you." He looked directly at Bonnie and held out his hand. "You seem to know me, but—"

She laughed nervously. "I'm Bonnie—Bonnie Marsden. Glad to meet you."

"Bonnie!" His eyebrows lifted, and he gripped her hand tightly, compassion in his face. He then turned to Linda, hand out. "And you?"

"Kileenda," she said unaccountably and squeezed his hand hard.

Again, his eyes widened, and his hand tightened convulsively. "Beautiful name . . . " His mouth twitched, but he didn't finish the line.

If Bonnie had looked at Linda at that moment, the game would've been over.

"Where are you from? What brings you to Philadelphia?" He kept her hand, though not a nanosecond longer than was prudent. "I won't give you the pitch, but I hope you'll think of Graham and Crofter on November eighth. It's been a pleasure to run into you both." His mouth twitched impishly. "Candidate school didn't teach us how to bulldoze potential supporters with grace and elegance." His smiling eyes flicked from one to another, resting one last time on Linda, and then he stepped around and walked past the gym.

Linda's brain seized up. She could neither move nor speak; she could only feel. Her lungs convulsed; her heart contracted to walnut-size. This broadside left her grotesquely misshapen. How could she manage this emotional cataclysm? She could faint; she could cry; but she could not pretend this was simply a curious encounter. Fortunately, Bonnie had to fetch her purse. Linda had only to speak two sentences, and it would happen—first, a segue, and then something to the effect of *go do it*. But what to say? Her mind was ice, and she had seventy-six one-hundredths of a second to melt it.

Finally, she blurted, "Politicians can't even keep their shoes tied."

Bonnie looked at her. "Was his shoe untied? I didn't— Linda, *what's the matter?*"

Linda shook her head numbly and tried to grin. "Forget it. It's stupid. Just hurry in before they empty your locker." She turned her toward the gym, but Bonnie resisted.

"Linda, something's wrong. Please tell me. Is the future vice president so overwhelming that—"

"Just go!" Linda's words, like a small tsunami, picked up Bonnie and swept her into the gym. Linda leaned against a shop window, shoulders heaving. She had no time to feel, but without a plausible explanation, all would be lost. This time she'd have to lie.

When Bonnie emerged with purse in hand, Linda was ready. First, she hugged her. "I'm sorry," she said. "I shouldn't have snapped at you. I don't know what came over me. I was shaken by the sudden appearance of the candidate, I guess." She shrugged. "I lost my wits. The bodyguard, or whatever, had a gun—I saw the holster—and that jarred me. And Mr. Himself, the mystery man. Bad reaction, for sure. Will you please forgive me?"

The tears in her friend's eyes gave her permission to cry. They hugged each other long until Linda straightened. "Let's forget second-string politicians and head for some little bistro for lunch. And what gallery were we going to visit this afternoon?"

They moved on, but Linda reflected on her last glimpse of Jay before he turned a corner—his head tipped forward, hands grabbing hair—that gesture of despair she'd seen in her garden.

In September, a gardener starts thinking about stepping back and catching her breath, but, alas, not quite yet. Tall perennials need to be cut back, peonies and day lilies divided and replanted. Chrysanthemums are tucked beside frost-sensitive annuals, primed to fill the gaps. Bulbs can be planted, and if nothing else comes to mind, beds can be readied for winter.

And, of course, the ongoing Linda-Jorge tug-of-war. Yes, he was a good gardener, but so was she, and their ideas often clashed to the point of Linda pulling rank. She hated that, especially knowing he could play his trump card and walk away. She couldn't imagine a greater disaster.

Yes, September work was hard, but nights were harder. Before attempting sleep, she tried reading the Bible or even a Miss Marple mystery, but Jay rose up, demanding to be examined from every angle. She had learned much about him but longed for more. She had questions about Glynneth—the beautiful woman with an empty face. Something was wrong—beyond the death of their child. Yes, her visits to children's hospitals spoke well of her, but was the emotion real? During Jay's stay with her, Linda had studied his pain and distress, but his heartache on leaving the house raised an uncomfortable question: If he truly loved his wife, why would going home be so hard? And it wasn't just that desperate moment of parting. She'd seen his reaction in Philadelphia after their chance meeting. No matter how much she kneaded the lumpy dough, the loaf came out with Jay loving her and not his wife, Glynneth.

That left her with spiritual heartburn. She had no business loving a married man; and as a married man, he had no business loving her.

Chapter 10

BONNIE LOVED SCOTLAND. SHE'D MET her husband on a tour; and after his death and her cancer, Linda had taken her there again. They had explored castles and battlefields, hiked the wild reaches of dead-end spittals, and listened to people talk. The harder to understand the dialect, the better, from Bonnie's perspective.

Actually, any Scottish dialect would do, and when Bonnie heard a melodic burr at a local book signing organized for the hard-edged political pundit, Marshall Cloverlyn, she sucked up to the speaker like a barnacle to a tugboat.

"Are you here for Cloverlyn's political slant?" She smiled. "Or just a plant to talk Scotland with me?"

The man laughed. "I'll talk Scotland ony day. Politics'll be around a guie lot this fall. The name's Ewen."

She introduced herself and told him of her travels and what the trip she and Linda had taken had meant to her.

"Tae you pairsonally? Just whit was your pairsonal favorite, if I might ask? The Heilands, of course—awebody likes them—but whit else?"

"Now, how could I choose just one favorite? The Trossachs, maybe the Isle of Skye. Or that romantic icon, Castle Eilean Donan."

"You say you've been awe o'er Scotland, but Badcall Bay, noo—I doubt you've seen that." He smiled. "It's no on many maps, you ken, and you may no hae seen it. Nae signs, nae lay-bys with an overlook. Only villagers get the view."

"A place we *missed?* Reason enough to go back."

He took her arm. "Lait's turn from the madding crowd, shall we? Find us a sit-down. Right over thaire." He nodded toward a nearby bench.

"Di y' ken the battlefield at Culloden whare Bonny Prince Chairlie brought history doon on his head? I grew up just two miles awa."

"Did you! What a dweeb that Charlie! If I'd been Flora MacDonald, I'd have set him adrift in the Minch instead of rowing him to Skye." She sighed. "Sometimes, I wish I were a native Scotlander—all that history!"

Ewen laughed ruefully. "Aye, that's two of us." He leaned forward conspiratorially. "Prromise y' won't hold it against me, but being born in this country maikes me American."

"No!"

"Aye, sad but true. And when need be, I can talk laike one," and he rattled off a summary of Mr. Cloverlyn's talk—complete with the pundit's New England accent. "My pairrents were studying here when I happened along, and though I grew up in Scotland, they tossed me back to study on my own. But," he finished with a grin, "I've lairned that Scottish plays well here and sometimes pays big dividends. Look at the fine bit of companionship it gave me taenight!"

They laughed and continued chatting over the entire map of Scotland, paying little attention to the center of focus. A burst of hilarity signaled a shift in the discussion to the upcoming election. Ewen turned to Bonnie with a wry smile.

"Whad'ya think of Maister Nels's Bonnie Prince Lawrie? Is he pure dead brilliant as they mak him tae be, or is he as full of sinkholes as a moor?"

Bonnie shrugged, her eye on the guest author. "Haven't the foggiest idea. I don't follow politics that closely. Though," she added brightly, "my friend and I literally bumped into him in Philadelphia two weeks ago. I forgot something and turned around fast, and there he was! His bodyguard almost pulled his gun on us. He was polite and friendly, but aren't all politicians? There's gossip, I guess, but as far as I know—"

"Ay, and talk aplenty aboot a mistress, I've haird. They say his wife is rreason enough for ony man t' switch beds. A big spender, I ken, and other baggage. There's motive, ay, and opportunity. That time last spring, when he went missing. Said he wasna weel, but—"

"When exactly was that?" asked Bonnie, her eyes narrowing.

"Mid-June, I think. Gone a week."

Bonnie's mouth twisted to a wry grin. "If I didn't absolutely know better, I'd say my dearest friend could be the missing link to Lawrence Crofter."

The man's eyebrows lifted fractionally. "Tail me aboot it."

She waved self-consciously. "Oh, I get these weird thoughts. All my friends say that. But she's been behaving strangely, and that week . . . Oh, forget all that." She waved again. "The last thing I want to do is start a rumor about Linda. Just delete it, will you?" She smiled ingratiatingly.

Ewen leaned close and touched her arm. "We'll change the subject. Hoo's that?" he said conspiratorially. "Whad'ya do besides turn your back on famous authors t' talk tae a lonely Scottish American?"

"I'm a color consultant—mostly interior decorating—and I have a candle shop, as well. And you?"

"Naiver hairrd of a color and candle consultant! Interesting concept. Tell me mair aboot it. Me, I'm just a paiper poosher, but you—you whirl in color. You turn on lights for people, brighten their day."

They chatted comfortably until Ewen looked at his watch and said, "You hae tae excuse me. Time to poosh my paipers around." He grinned slyly. "Let me ken the next time you plan tae visit Scotland. I'll poot you ontae the best haggis in the whole wairld."

Bonnie shook his hand and waved him off; and as she bent to collect her bags, an acquaintance sidled up. "Pretty cozy there with Mr. MacClerhan, weren't you?"

"Who?"

"Ewen MacClerhan. Did he interview you?"

"*Interview* me? Why would I be interviewable, and who is he to even care?"

"Well, reporters do that, and as one of the top boys at Circle Television, I doubt he'd be cooling his heels at this particular book signing."

Bonnie stared at her, thunderstruck, the implications of what she had said to him slowly filtering into her brain. "What have I *done*?"

Ewen MacClerhan needed less than five hours to dig his dirt and wrap it in a news release, but he waited till morning to make an appointment with Linda to talk gardening. She fell into his trap beautifully; and after jotting down her rest-of-the-season plans, he closed his laptop and said casually, "I understand from a friend o' yours that you had a guest here the week o' June fifteenth." He knew from the look and color on her face that he had won his gamble.

Linda sank into despair. What could she do? Her attorney might advise charging slander, but it wasn't slander; it was truth. Truth misunderstood, as she had told MacClerhan while pushing him out the door.

Trying to contact Jay would only make it worse, and any attempt at denial would fail. Truth had entered her bones with her mother's milk. She *had* to tell it straight, even if it destroyed Jay. Her only option: speak truth and trust God.

What had Bonnie said? She had called last night, sounding strangely conflicted over a "nice Scottish reporter." Why hadn't Linda paid closer attention or at least remembered Bonnie's Scotland chatter? Because she'd been deleting emails during the call and had only half-listened. Bad habit. But had she paid attention, what could she have said?

She rang Bonnie but got no answer. She didn't leave a message.

The article hit the late-night television reports and online news posts.

MISTRESS ALONG THE GARDEN PATH?

Lawrence Crofter has been painted a man of virtue in broad strokes, lending moral gravitas to the Republican ticket. Now, questions have surfaced about a possible connection between him and Linda Jensen, noted gardener, author, and public speaker. Ms. Jensen has not denied the connection but refuses to comment.

When Bonnie happened on the release the following morning, she needed only seconds to realize the enormity of her carelessness. Her half-formed misgivings following her bookstore conversation thundered upon her head. She pictured herself confronting Ewen but immediately realized she would only make a bigger fool of herself.

The stew thickened quickly. After a long talk with her attorney, Linda decided that a public statement was the only way to go, and the sooner the better. She had to do this, even before dealing with Bonnie, who could only wail, "I was *used*." Linda knew that Bonnie would assume Linda's anger and would stay away. This needed to be corrected, but Linda, too, was a believer in swallowing the biggest frog first. Bonnie could wait.

The two-a.m. phone call came on Lawrie with the subtlety of a chain saw. Martin shouted into his ear. "Wake up, Lawrie. Get out of bed. Right now. Say something, Lawrie. Are you out of bed?"

"What's . . . happening?" He cleared his throat. "Something's wrong."

"Yes. Very wrong. You need to get out of bed and down to the safe room in the cellar. Now. And whatever you do, don't turn on anything—radio, TV, iPhone."

"Martin, stop. Give me a clue at least. A terrorist attack? Is Nels—?"

"I'll talk when you're in the safe room. Get there."

"Can I stop in the bathroom?"

"No. Yes, if you must. Fast, Lawrie, fast."

In little more than a minute, Lawrie picked up the phone again. "All right, I'm here. The door's locked. Can I sit down?"

"Lawrie, you've got to tell me the truth. Straight. No practice runs."

"About *what?*"

"Let me say it again: You . . . *must . . . speak . . . truth.* No hedging, dodging, dancing around. Okay?"

Lawrie took a big breath. "Okay. I'm ready."

"Tell me everything about your 'lost' week in June. Where were you? Who were you with? What *exactly* did you do—blow by blow?"

Lawrie sank into the chair and exhaled loudly.

"Answer now. I don't want you thinking up plausible answers. You must tell me the straight truth."

"Well, truth is straight, isn't it?"

"No time for games. Tell me. Now."

"All right. Obviously, somebody's talking about that—"

"No detours, Lawrie. Start now."

Fifteen seconds of silence.

"It started on Sunday. As I told you, I needed to be by myself to think through—"

"Skip that."

"I got sick. Had to have been the granola I ordered at a trendy restaurant. Must've had banana in it. Couldn't have been the egg and toast or the—"

"No time for dissecting. You got sick."

"I started feeling bad while walking a nature preserve and somehow got off the trail. I ended up on the ground near a flower bed. I thought I could keep going, but this lady came out to see if I was dead or alive. She wanted to call 911, but I begged her not to. Probably a mistake, but my brain was screwed. She got me up and into her house and to a bedroom. By then, nothing was working; and I only knew I was in bed, and she had me drinking water. I couldn't move, couldn't speak, had to wait it out." He paused a moment, but hearing Martin pull a breath, he hurried on.

"I was some better by morning but couldn't do much. I got up and mostly sat in a recliner or outdoors in her garden. I won't describe the garden; you don't want to hear that. Anyway, she cared for me but respected all boundaries. Gave me plenty of room to think, talk, just be still. I realized I was in a huge jam, but she locked her gate and cleared her calendar for the entire week just to keep me safe and away from eyes."

"And you trusted her. Why?"

"Martin, I've been in politics long enough to size up people pretty accurately. After the first day, I could read her weather. I knew she was safe." Hearing no response from Martin, Lawrie plunged on. "As I got stronger, we talked, but always on safe topics—music, history, stupid movies. She never pried or asked uncomfortable questions. Did I like her, enjoy her company? Yes, of course I did. Did I act on that? No, and she wouldn't have tolerated it.

"Saturday came, and I left. One of the last things she said was, 'You're married. Go home to your wife.' And she pushed me out the door. That was it."

Lawrie leaned back and considered what he might have said. *A love affair? Yes. But we didn't act on what we felt.* Truth, yes, but he couldn't say it out loud, especially to Martin.

Chapter 11

LAWRIE PROWLED THE HOUSE, COLD stabbing his bones. Should he wake Glynneth and prepare her for the news? Morning might be too late. But then, waking her for any reason was never a happy task, and a bombshell of this magnitude . . . He continued to prowl, then brazenly ignored Martin's television ban.

The national news had both feet in the story, with clips showing Lawrie at his benign best, Lawrie on a garden tour. They had photos of Linda but no video. They did show shots of Lawrie talking with other women in assorted close encounters, but none were even suggestive. Commentators, though, were salivating over this new sex scandal, involving a *Republican.*

He moved to his computer, and the investigative reporter, Ewen MacClerhan, came online. At the sight of his image, Lawrie's stomach lurched. He knew this man. He had once asked editorially if the death of Lawrie's son was worse than other children dying in the wake of callous Republican legislation. He was the "King of Nasty." Now Lawrie was again his target. Fury blazed within.

At five a.m., he decided to shower and dress. Martin would arrive soon, and he needed to be dressed in something more powerful than a bathrobe. Martin would not have eaten, of course, but Lawrie couldn't look at food right now. Charlotte would be getting up. What did she need to know before he talked with Glynneth?

He felt, rather than heard, Martin's arrival—akin to an earth-quake. Martin was always direct and forceful, but never before had Lawrie felt the ground quiver. Martin let himself in and, without a word, dragged Lawrie to the TV set in the kitchen, where he could make himself some coffee. Lawrie didn't tell him he'd already seen the story.

They watched for a half an hour, again without speaking, flipping channels between local, national, and cable news. Martin's phone buzzed. He looked at the ID, chewed his free thumb, punched *Talk*, and said brusquely, "I'll call back."

Lawrie looked at him, but Martin said, "Never mind." He continued switching channels repeatedly, then backed up when he heard, "Coming up, a new development. Linda Jensen will tell her side of this interesting saga."

Linda was no stranger to television interviews, but never had she spoken under such circumstances, with enemy fire frizzing her hair. Tension was thick in the Green Room; and while her attorney kept saying he believed her, she could almost see his crossed fingers. Bonnie, of course, believed her, as did her mother. Other friends assured her of their support, but money and social position were thin reeds to lean on. Her heart rate doubled when the summons came for her and her lawyer to enter the cold, cavernous studio. Shadows loomed in enormous proportions, and she cowered under them, terribly alone and afraid as they positioned her to speak. Fixing her inner vision on Jay, she drew a big breath at the technician's signal and began.

"Assuming that truth is a safer platform than lies, I will line out the facts—all of them—of my encounter with Lawrence Joseph Crofter. The telling is not easy, and I don't expect to be believed.

"On the morning of June fifteenth, I came home from church and found Senator Crofter lying on my lawn. He had evidently wandered from the adjacent nature preserve and somehow made his way onto my property. He was obviously ill but didn't want me to call for help. With no cell phone in hand, my alternatives were either to go in and call, giving him time to crawl away, or to take him into the house while he was still able to walk. I opted for the latter.

"I put him in my guest room, clothed him appropriately, and he promptly fell asleep."

Linda lifted her chin fractionally but continued on, trying to ignore the technicians, who seemed to be listening intently.

"The only name he gave me was Jay. I honored his request not to tell anyone he was there. I canceled engagements, turned off my answering machine, and secured my front gate.

"Not knowing what was wrong, I decided on sleep and water as the best treatment. This worked well until water became a problem. He was weak and needed help; but after one time, he was able to tend to himself."

Blood pounded her temples as she paused to gather breath. "Why am I opening myself up to mockery and derision? One simple reason: The names *Linda Jensen* and *Lawrence Crofter* have been added to the endless list of sex scandals; and I have received an unbelievable onslaught of ugly, salacious, vicious, and *public* attacks. I've had to change my email address and cut off phone access. I felt the truth needed to be said—*out loud*—to show that I am hiding nothing. Regrettably, the enemies of Senator Crofter have made this necessary."

A new sense of resolve strengthened her voice. "There's a deeper meaning, too, and I've thought a lot about this episode. The Bible talks about parts of the human body that we cover with more care than the parts we show. Women check their mirrors, men their zippers. The man was a stranger. I knew nothing about him: his name, his station, his government function."

She leaned toward the microphone boom.

"But *I could serve him in his illness,* and in so doing, reap what I call an *unpresentable glory*—a deep, shimmering sense of God's presence and approval of such awkward kindnesses. No one speaks comfortably about things like that, and I'm sure the moment loomed large in both of our minds. I simply felt privileged to serve him.

"As caregiver, I could touch him, but he chose not to touch me—then, or in the days of his recuperation. We talked; he helped with dishes; we enjoyed each other's company; but never did either of us step over a clearly drawn line.

"When he was well enough, he left. His last words to me were, 'I've trusted you, and someday you may know just how much you hold in your hands.' Now I know the size and shape of that trust. Lawrence Crofter knows; I know; and God knows that we have been honorable. He remained faithful to his marriage vows. I did not trespass. And that's all that matters."

She looked straight at the camera, eyes steady and resolute.

"One last word. In our current, crazy, turnaround world, movie stars, politicians, and other public figures are getting their comeuppance over sexual misbehavior, accused mostly by women. But sometimes, women accuse wrongly. I am a woman and can attest that there was no *bad* behavior in my house. May that truth uphold Senator Lawrence Crofter's good name."

When the light went off and the camera shifted, she melted and shook uncontrollably. Her lawyer helped her to a chair. How her statement would be received no longer mattered.

Predictably, Republicans cheered and made sympathetic noises, while the opposition pounced gleefully on Linda's naïve stupidity and spewed venom about religious talk providing a convenient cover for this *inconvenient* affair.

Linda, though, writhed over her dreadful *ad lib* at the end. Stupid. No sense at all. Women accuse . . . I'm a woman. And the *bad* behavior part—could that be construed as my making a *consensual* affair okay? *Yikes!* Her name—and Jay's—could be splattered across the nation.

She cowered under her lawyer's blistering tirade and longed for home. There, she could slip on a warm jacket and go to the cave room in her garden—the smallest, most confined space where she could hide from the nattering world that wanted to destroy her and the man she loved. Yes, she could say those words. She did love Jay—or at least what she knew of him from just one week. *An unpresentable love.*

Sudden lightning struck her brain: *Her way of trying to help him may have destroyed his career.* Her words—on national TV—hung heavy, like a virulent, smothering cloud. She clenched her eyes and bit her fist, face flaming in shame.

But just as suddenly, a breath of peace whispered away the cloud. She had spoken *unpresentable glory* and knew deep inside that it was good. She had felt it back in June; she had felt it today in the studio. It seemed stupid, but God had put words in her mouth. Maybe not the "bad behavior" bit, but all the rest.

She could not have Jay; he was not hers to have. But she could fight for him, protect him with every bit of integrity she could muster. But what an odd way to show love! Other women might plot ways to disengage him from his wife, who had been painted in the worst possible light. That route was not open to Linda. But the words she'd said could've been taken that way. If only she'd phrased it differently . . . *I just wanted to get across the unpresentable,* she argued with herself.

A blue jay lit on the bower roof, squawked once as though in greeting, then continued to study her. A jay. Jay. She wanted to cry but could not—not now. The bird would see, and she had to hide her grief, even from birds, and especially this blue Jay.

Lawrie's body leaped into sudden overdrive as he watched Linda speaking. His heart pounded, emotion smacking viciously. But Martin was there, watching, gauging his response. Above all, Martin must not draw conclusions. He gritted his teeth and clenched his fists, compelling his body into impassivity. Ironically, his greatest helper in this effort was the Scottish reporter. Lawrie had learned to ride the cyclones of political attack and nasty gossip, but the sheer ugliness of MacClerhan turning Ephraim's death into an attack weapon helped override his intense, unforeseen reaction upon seeing Linda.

"Martin," he growled through a clenched jaw, "I want you to get that man, one way or another. Go after MacClerhan. Search and destroy. That's what you do best. Take him out."

"Right," replied Martin. "Bring down Scotland, all guns blazing. That should play well in your campaign."

Lawrie's press encounter came that evening. Martin handed him a boilerplate statement, but he scratched most of it. There were no right words; the only effective weapon would be his own truth. He entered a pressroom full of microphones and massed antagonism. Facing the firing squad of reporters and cameras, he lifted his chin and spoke.

"Unsettling as it is to have one's toilet needs talked about publicly, what Ms. Jensen recounted is absolute truth. She did me a great service, in more ways than she told, and I owe her an enormous debt of gratitude.

"Even more unsettling is the necessity of discussing these private matters at all. Political investigation can turn acts of goodness into slime, just to gain advantage. My wife has been maligned, as have been my marriage and my reputation—to say nothing of Ms. Jensen's good name. The furor over this matter speaks more of the opposition's motives and tactics than of my supposed misdeeds. I believe the American people will judge rightly. They recognize honor when they see it, not falling for the lie that nobody lives virtuously these days. Many good, decent people honor their marriage vows, even in tough times. I am committed to my wife, and we've been faithful to each other for over twenty years. I'm not about to blow that away. Nor would I commit political suicide by romantic involvement with a stranger."

Camera flashes were getting to him. Never before had they represented more than background noise in the general ambiance of politics, but here they became blazing cannons. He tried focusing more closely on his scribbled notepad but trembled, nonetheless.

"I ask for your understanding and for your charity toward Ms. Jensen. That she refused to lie on my behalf when caught in a media trap shows her intrinsic honesty.

"I might add some facts that Ms. Jensen did not know. I went on this lonely hike, feeling uncertain about the decision I had to make. An invitation to become a candidate for vice president is no small matter. I needed to step outside myself, stripping away identity and personhood to gain objectivity. I didn't anticipate being helpless and at the mercy of a stranger."

A reporter sneezed, his handkerchief running red from a bloody nose. Lawrie waited while he worked his way toward the door, then turned back to his notes.

"The illness that overtook me is a mildly chronic one. It has a name: *Hyperkalemic Periodic Paralysis.* This was my third attack in forty years. At a quirky restaurant, the granola I ordered probably had banana in it. Afterward, I started my hike, feeling okay. When my brain turned fuzzy, I tried to get back to the car via a shortcut that wasn't. I pushed through thick brush, then found myself in a garden with a woman standing over me. I might have crawled back to the brush, as she said, but I couldn't stand without help. The illness is not life-threatening; it lasts only a few days and is generally under a doctor's supervision. With my doctor thirteen hundred miles away and my not having responded to Nelson's invitation, I felt it best to remain incognito. The decision may have been a bad one, but it was the one I made in the state I was in."

The firing squad began to fidget. Time for Martin's boilerplate.

"Mud-slinging is not a noble political tool. All political parties are guilty from time to time, but in the coming election, we intend to point up the good things that America stands for, our strengths, our potential."

Never mind, thought Lawrie vindictively, *that Nels himself is a top-tier mudslinger.*

"We have a strong, solid platform that will boost the economy, beef up security, and leave no one behind. People who stand on the rock-solid platform of truth can do that. Thank you very much."

Linda had no quarrel with his eyes after that statement.

Chapter 12

BONNIE LIVED IN A SMALL but comfortable apartment over her Abington candle shop. Her rooms—filled with color accents of wood, fabric, and wax—exuded a rare, peaceful aura of visual integrity. Sunlight streamed into the room and onto her workspace. She had a sizeable clientele, and though her candle enterprise had proven only marginally profitable, she was not hurting for money. Her shop, surrounded by upscale boutiques, featured creative arrangements and a spicy redolence that attracted browsers, especially during summer and Christmas seasons.

Her midtown location put her at a considerable distance from Linda, but the two often ate at alternating homes or at a restaurant. Their friendship spanned nearly two decades, and they cared deeply for each other. Now, though, Bonnie had inadvertently stepped into mud and tracked dirt all over Linda's life. She could argue that Linda had kept a major secret from her best friend and trusted confidante, but she couldn't argue that her personal feelings were more important than the reputation of a candidate for vice president of the United States.

Therefore, Bonnie waited in personal devastation. She kicked Ewen via the couch, beat herself for handing him an exposé, and spit at the world for deciding the fitness of political candidates from such news.

She didn't stew alone for long. Shortly after the news release, newspaper and television reporters besieged her candle shop.

Ewen wasn't among them, and that made her even more furious. Telling him off would've brought great satisfaction, but she had no words for the others. Finally, she locked the door and refused to answer the phone.

She needed to make peace with Linda, but how? Maybe make her own statement? Instead of turning the media away, why shouldn't she have her say? But which medium—newspaper, TV, online, or all three? She went to her computer and started typing.

> My friend Linda Jensen's reputation has been injured, along with that of Senator Lawrence Crofter. And I inadvertently made it happen. A reporter turned a totally innocent remark into a scurrilous bit of muck that damaged them both. I sincerely regret talking with this man and dropping the clue that led him to put together the worst possible construct.

> Might I note the irony of righteousness today being treated as something evil or nasty? Yes, today's big stories center on men's sexual misdeeds. Yet, it's the men who stick with their wife through thick and thin who get hammered. Reporters laugh. Men are liars. That's what reporters say. Sexual purity doesn't exist these days, they say. But hear me on this: a man who stays faithful to his wife will be faithful to his country.

Bonnie picked up her tea mug and swirled it absently. What would drive home her point? She set down the cup and typed rapidly.

> Scotland's political history applies here. In 1746, two unlikely characters came together—a woman named Flora MacDonald, in love with a government Redcoat, and Bonnie Prince Charlie, whose bold invasion of Scotland failed. Pushed to the Outer Hebrides with Redcoats closing in, he needed Flora to spirit him off the island and to the Isle of Skye. She dressed him as her maid and rowed fifty miles across open waters to Skye. There, friendly Jacobites helped

him escape to the continent. Much was made of this pur-
ported romance, but it was all talk. She remained true to her
young man in the same way that Lawrie Crofter remained
true to his wife.

My friend Linda Jensen is an honorable woman, a truth-teller.
I have known her for years and can attest to her character. I
believe Mr. Crofter to be a man of his word. People don't want
truth, though. Only scandal sells. But TRUTH is what measures up to reality.

Linda Jensen and Lawrie Crofter are both honorable people.
Please believe them.

Bonnie did get media attention with her statement, but her
well-meant words miscarried. The few newspapers and blogs that
printed anything at all deleted Flora and Prince Charlie, and the
only television station that picked it up edited her down to one
sentence: "I sincerely regret talking with this man and dropping
the clue that led him to the worst possible construct."

This left exactly the wrong impression.

Glynneth was in a funk. It didn't show much. She smiled and
laughed on cue, spoke when spoken to, and even went to Children's
Hospital. But Charlotte knew. Lawrie knew. Her skewed shoulders
and refusal to initiate conversations gave her away. She neglected
her makeup regimen, cried over little irritations.

"I don't feel well," she kept saying. "Can't a person not feel well
without everyone getting upset?"

Lawrie talked to Charlotte. "Is she playing games, or is it her
way of getting back at me?"

Charlotte addressed the pile of folded laundry beside her, straightening two items. "I don't know. Some days I think she really is ill, that she couldn't be faking; then she says something that makes me sure she's out to get you."

Lawrie rubbed the back of his neck. "Well, she won't say what's bothering her, but I've got to get her to talk. I'm heading out Tuesday, so I don't have much time."

He didn't need much time. That very night, Lawrie confronted her after she blew up over his flippant remark that six hundred dollars hardly seemed enough for a Scagliola bowl, considering it was imitation marble.

"Glynneth, what's wrong?" he asked. "You're not yourself. What's going on inside?" He held her as her tears subsided. "Are you thinking I really was unfaithful to you, that there's more to it than either Linda or I said in our statements?"

"No, I believe you." She looked him in the eyes. "You wouldn't do that. And you wouldn't lie. I believe you. I'm all right. Really." She straightened and smiled brightly.

"You think the news reports are right, that I'm just looking for an excuse to dump you."

"No! Of course not. You've had every reason, but you've never stepped in that direction. I'm all right, Lawrie. I'm sorry I lashed out. You were trying to be funny, and I took it wrong. Now, just try to like my new bowl, and we'll get along fine."

Lawrie was more than relieved. This was a rare exchange that wouldn't last, he knew, but for now, he was comforted.

Charlotte, too, had a moment of truth with Glynneth, who asked one morning, "Charlotte, am I going to hell?"

Charlotte considered the question as she brushed Glynneth's hair—black this month, but lusterless. She responded softly.

"God doesn't send people to hell. They choose to go. Some folks I know would prefer hell to forgiveness. They don't want to ask for forgiveness, can't even admit they need it. You know, though, don't you, honey? You know how to ask. And this, too: Jesus knew grief. He knows all about your grief."

Charlotte had things to say to Lawrie, as well, and she got in his face with her dark, steel-bullet eyes. "You been living a lie around here for a long time. You know it; I know it. You blame attack dogs outside your door; and if that don't hold water, you got your old sickness, or you're just tired. But that set of overalls has holes big enough to throw a cat through. Yes, you dress up fine, wear your best political junk. You might fool Martin, but you don't fool Charlotte. Clothes that fit you may look all right, but inside, you're an empty, Republican suit. You go to church, know the rules, keep them because not keeping them is dangerous. You don't want to be caught like others who've been tossed to croco-diles for dumb choices. Yes, you look fine and handsome outside; inside needs clothes of a different sort, clothes only God can sew."

"Charlotte—"

"Listen to me! I'm not through talking. I checked up on your Kileenda Jensen. A lot of internet space there. You landed in a safe bed. Thank God for that! Now you need to get yourself safe in the arms of Jesus."

"Charlotte, you're pouring boiling oil on me right now, you know that? You—"

"Yes, I do know. But it's not boiling oil you're feeling. It's those rags inside and the fine stuff outside that's burning. Look at Glynneth. She knows clothes can't hide pain; but she keeps trying, and new outfits are all that's holding her together right now. But she's in better shape than you think. She knows who she is and what she's done. In many ways, she's a child—plain and simple."

Lawrie grasped at that straw, his plaintive voice touched with vinegar.

"That's the one thing you haven't done, Charlotte. I've lost my wife. She's a baby, and you haven't brought her back to adulthood. You've given her childlike peace, but she can't face grown-up life."

"Not yet," said Charlotte.

"Not yet." Lawrie closed his eyes.

"I sing over her every day, sing her toward life. And let me tell you—" She shifted forward, eyes and voice turning honey soft. "I sing over you every day, too."

Lawrie looked away, though not to hide his tears. Charlotte would see them, even with his back turned.

Chapter 13

A WOMAN, CLOTHED IN ANTIQUE elegance, sat near the front of the living room in the stately McCullough Mansion in Bel Air, Maryland. She listened intently as Lawrence Crofter spoke on the importance of the long view in terms of Social Security and Medicare reform.

When the talk was over and people lined up to shake his hand, the gray-haired woman moved to a damask chair, where she could prop her chin with gloved fingers and observe the candidate as he interacted with natural grace. When she saw him check his watch, she eased out of the chair and moved behind two remaining well-wishers. He consulted his watch once more before turning to her, and her eyebrows lifted fractionally. She smiled warmly.

"I'm happy to meet you and hear you speak. Like many, I saw you as an unknown, murky shadow that no one could see into, but here you are." She smiled brightly, gauging how long she would have until he consulted his watch again. The instant his left arm moved, she stopped mid-sentence and leaned toward him familiarly.

"I believe you and I have something in common," she purred. "At least I'm assuming that one of our mutually favorite places to enjoy a cup of Earl Gray tea would be a white gazebo on a tiny island with its willow-shaded, arched bridge." She stood back to watch the effect.

The watch was forgotten. He drew a sharp breath and stared hard. Then he smiled.

"Perhaps we should talk. I believe there is a small room off to the right. May I?" He grasped her insubstantial arm, ushered her into the anteroom, and shut the door.

"Bonnie, how about coming for supper tonight, and would you bring a salad?" Linda wanted to transmit a positive signal, even while anticipating Bonnie's pro forma wail.

"Do you really want me to come?"

"Of course, I do. Would I have asked if I didn't?"

The evening would not be easy, but it had to be done.

Linda set an elegant table with a blend of fresh and dried flowers, candles, and pastoral figurines that wove in and out of the flower arrangement. She dug out the paisley napkins Bonnie had given her five years ago, the dinner place settings that had cost her mother five hundred dollars for just two sets, plus her grandmother's ornate sterling flatware. The entire spread could have been a tapestry straight out of Afghanistan. As the gate signal sounded, she ran her eyes over the table one last time, then buzzed Bonnie in.

She met her at the door, took the salad, and hugged her tightly. Bonnie burst into tears. Linda held her and rocked her gently. Then as the storm subsided, she pulled her toward the kitchen. "Come. A pot of tea is waiting. A cup will do us good. How did things go at the store today?"

"Linda—"

"Not now. We'll talk after supper. Right now, we're friends getting together after a too-long absence. I like your skirt. I don't think I've seen that one before. Is it new?"

Bonnie sank gratefully into the rocker, mug in hand. "I love your kitchen. How many times have I said that? Maybe it's this chair."

"My favorite chair in all the house?"

Bonnie laughed. "And I'm hogging it."

"You're my guest."

"It's so welcoming here, so . . . healing." Her eyes welled again.

Linda touched her in passing and said, "Did you ever get that lady straightened out who wanted two impossible color layouts?"

They chatted comfortably while Linda arranged marinated pork chops on the stove grill and turned on the hood. "I made your dietary downfall—french-fried sweet potatoes."

"And your trifle to multiply my guilt?"

"Of course! To balance off the salad."

Against a background of Bach and Vivaldi, they ate their sumptuous meal and leaned back, replete. Bonnie looked at Linda. "Thank you. I can't say it fervently enough. What you gave me tonight almost makes talking unnecessary, but not quite. Is now the time?"

Linda shook her head. "Since the bus boy's off tonight, we have cleanup and dishes." She momentarily considered sending Bonnie into the living room while she put away the leftovers but thought better of it. "You do food remains, while I bus the dishes. Five minutes and we'll be done."

When they finally sat in the den, Bonnie exclaimed and said, "Look! Outdoors." The western sky glowed with roseate tones, falling off to a deep mauve. "If I tried to duplicate those colors in my workroom, they'd look cheap and contrived. But here . . . " They sat in silence, drinking the wine of the moment and not wanting to let it go.

As the color faded, Linda reached to the table beside her and turned on the light, a jarring intrusion on the gauzy ambiance. She straightened with a look of uncomfortable resolve.

"Bonnie, I don't have to tell you how special you are to me. We've been friends for decades, and our friendship is not going to be shipwrecked over an inadvertent word spoken at the wrong time to the wrong person. I could cut to the chase and say just forget it; I forgive you; get on with life; but I think you need to talk about it. And cry," she added, reaching beneath the table for a box of tissues as Bonnie's eyes welled.

A half hour later, Bonnie had talked herself out. She apologized fifteen different ways for telling the reporter about Linda's strange behavior and for her own botched public statement. "But I was *used!*" She pounded her chair arm and went into a violent spasm of crying. When finally she could talk, the real pain and anger surfaced. "Linda, we've been friends . . . nearly all our lives, but you . . . shut me out, kept this huge secret . . . If I'd *known* . . . " Her sobs intensified.

Linda sat silent for a long moment.

"Oh, I know, I know," Bonnie moaned. "I'm not trustworthy. I know that. But knowing it doesn't make it hurt less."

Linda remained still. Then she reached over and touched Bonnie's arm. "Perhaps I'm to blame. Perhaps if I had told you what was going on, you'd have been more on your guard with Mr. MacClerhan and might not have fed him the goodies. Keep in mind: you only provided the bait; I was the one who fell into his trap. My face told it all, and that was not your fault.

"But," she went on, "it happened as it did, and given a second chance, I'd probably do the same thing—hiding it from you. The promise I made to Jay was a sacred trust; and even though I hadn't a clue who he really was, I knew I had a special obligation to protect him. Now, would I have felt the same with some thick-headed tradesman in trouble with his girlfriend? Or maybe if I saw scars and tattoos? Yes, it made a difference that Jay was the man he was. I sized him up, believed him, and trusted him immediately—for better or for worse. When we walked into the house, I wondered if he'd suddenly recover and turn on me. I won my gamble but only by God's grace."

In the silence, the honeyed tones of the living room mantel clock sounded the hour.

"We're both vulnerable, Bonnie. Naïve, transparent, easy prey for anyone who wants to trip us up. I don't think either of us owes the other an apology; but because I am genuinely sorry for having hurt you, I offer mine to you."

Again, Bonnie burst into tears and clung to Linda's hand. "I'm sorry; I'm sorry," she whispered.

Linda finally pulled away and, with a smile that was patently false, said, "Well. That's over. Now we can get on with life." She stood up and asked brightly, "What CD would you like me to put on? Are you up for Chopin or Mozart?"

Bonnie stayed another half hour, looking over material swatches that Linda's mom had dropped off for help in choosing new curtains in her living and dining rooms.

"She really wants my advice?" asked Bonnie. "Her apartment is so regal. She doesn't need my help."

"She'll make up her own mind, but it makes her feel better to ask. Lunch tomorrow at Paretti's?"

Chapter 14

THE LEFT WORKED THEIR OPPOSITION Research people hard to find corroborating witnesses to affirm their theory of sexual misbehavior on Senator Crofter's part. MSNBC reported a number of women with claims of unwanted advances—giving times, places, names of waitresses and other people who were present. This sent Lawrie reeling.

"Bunkum!" he spat. "Martin, if I've done nothing else right in politics, I've walked the line here. I know it; you know it. I've fought sex trafficking as hard as any—"

Martin humphed. "We both know that your run-of-the-mill sex pot often hides behind a noble trafficking effort. That argument won't wash. Sit down and listen." He leaned into Lawrie's face. "The only mistake you made was not letting me know right away what was going on. I would have gotten you out of there, and—"

"*Would have* doesn't cut it, Martin. I did what I did, and I can't go back and do it differently."

"Okay. Can't go back. Can go forward, though. You're neither the first nor the last to get banged around this way. Think of the snow job on Peter Parkerville. He survived and moved forward. You got people working night and day to dig you out of this. None of these accusations are going to hold up. They'll fall apart because there's no substantiation. You can't knit a sweater out of cobwebs. Now, relax, Lawrie. Let me handle the mess. You and Nels get out there with your dog-and-pony show."

For once, Lawrie was deeply grateful for Martin.

Seemingly, Glynneth had adjusted quite well to her new position in life. She didn't fuss about Lawrie's campaigning absences. She didn't shop ten hours straight as she once did. Instead, she invited friends for tea and political talk and took her mother to a movie she herself had no interest in. But still, something was wrong—the droop, lackluster grooming . . .

She did gather herself for a major trip with her mother, this one to La Rivière on the Connecticut River in Hartford—a favorite haven, where she frequently sought solace.

In her early years, Delia Burningham had been every bit as beautiful as her daughter. Now in her seventies, she remained strikingly handsome and shared Glynneth's love for shopping, though not as compulsively. She welcomed this Hartford outing and chatted happily in the back seat of the chauffeured Lincoln rental on their way to La Rivière from the airport.

"You'll love this boutique," said Glynneth. "On the edge of town, away from the interstate, but Mrs. Candell says Boston folk come regularly. Hard to believe. She's tight with Paris and Milan and knows the latest fashion trends before anyone else in the country gets them."

"Anything in particular you're looking for?" Delia reached for her silver-gray cashmere to settle around her shoulders and spoke to the driver. "Hans, dear, could you turn the air conditioner down—or up, if that's the way to get it warmer? Thank you. Is this an event with Lawrie that needs a special dress?"

Glynneth's eyes burned like dying embers. "Oh, yes. The end of the month—or is it early October? I can't remember. Anyway, I want to surprise him with just the right gown. Actually—" Her face went somber, and she reached a trembling hand to brush away imagined dirt from the back of the driver's seat. "If what I think is true, it has to be a surprise. For him *especially*."

Her mother turned with a puzzled frown, but suddenly, Hans slammed his brakes to avoid a car that had jerked rudely into his lane. The unasked question was forgotten.

When they reached the boutique in Hartford, Glynneth flowed out of the Lincoln with new energy and swished through the door of The Golden Candelabra with an effusive greeting for Mrs. Candell—immediately sealed with a hug and kiss.

Mrs. C. touched Glynneth's arm and gave her standard opening line: "I've been hoping you'd come, my dear. I have dresses set aside just for you. Please sit down while I get them from the back room."

Glynneth, born to try on dresses, stood before the three-panel mirror for the next two hours, parading and posing and fretting over her profile, finally whittling the selections to two.

When Delia's patience started to fray, Glynneth turned to the keeper of elegance. "I need to think about this overnight and come back tomorrow." She gave Mrs. Candell another hug, then pushed her to arm's length. "You won't sell either of them, will you? Thanks *so* much." With a dazzling smile, she swept out of the door, her elegantly frazzled mother following more slowly.

Chapter 15

THE FOLLOWING WEEK, THE TWO candidates, Nelson Graham and Lawrence Crofter, arrived at the first of five wine-and-cheese affairs in the Northeast and were met by an enthusiastic party of faithfuls, with the usual sprinkling of media types prowling the margins. These events were civilized, on the whole, with the principals planting seeds they hoped would produce a profitable fall harvest.

Strategy, however, demanded a major event with Lawrie and his wife appearing together. Ads had shown them going to church, walking across the lawn, and holding hands, but that wasn't enough. Though the initial buzz over Lawrie and Linda had diminished, predatory media would dig up whatever bone they could and gnaw on Lawrie's integrity, exposing him as a power-hungry, sex-driven, two-faced fraud.

The chosen event was a North Dakota fundraiser, featuring both Nelson Graham and Lawrence Crofter—along with Judson Crawford, the outrageously colorful radio talk show host. The affair would be a counterpoint of damask and crystal, against Jocelyn Shantiss, the hot new singer, and Peter Elson, the stand-up comic, who now aimed his rapier wit at the Left after an astonishing political conversion. Some advisers thought him too unseasoned for this major appearance, but Nels had talked with him at length and felt he could be trusted. And he was funny.

Glynneth asked Lawrie several times exactly where the event was to be held. "At Riversmeet Country Club, forty miles north of Bismarck," he explained patiently. "I believe we were there—at somebody's wedding reception? Can't remember exactly, but I think you were with me."

This time, Glynneth's eyes widened and stared outdoors at the darkening landscape. Lawrie, assuming she was displeased or still battling whatever illness, moved toward her. "Dearest," he began, but she turned, face alight.

"I remember it—a long lawn out back. Am I right? Is that the place?"

Lawrie smiled in relief. "Yes! You got it. Beautiful spot, the two rivers joining in a sharp point below the lawn." He swung her away from the window and planted a kiss on her forehead.

Still, though, she continued to ask anxiously about Riversmeet. An obsession somehow connected to her recent malaise? She refused, almost belligerently, to see a doctor, and her unease now seemed centered on what to wear against such a backdrop. She had come back from Hartford, eager to parade her surprise before Lawrie—a Turkish evening dress with a slotted overlay of rich mahogany atop a lustrous rose underskirt. He was suitably wowed and assured her that the gown was perfect. Her eyes had been bright and childishly excited at the prospect of the event.

She put her arms around his neck with a wistful, almost melancholy smile. "Do you love me, Lawrie?"

For an answer, he had kissed her long and deep—which she allowed, for a change—and maneuvered her toward the bedroom door, pushing it shut with his foot, and from there to the bed, all without removing his lips from hers.

Afterward, lying quietly with his arm around his grandly clad wife, Lawrie noted wryly to himself, *The most expensive sex I've ever had and worth every penny. If it takes a new dress or two to get her into bed, let the buying begin.* Never mind that she'd likely give it away the day following the event.

Lawrie and Glynneth arrived early at Riversmeet. The sprawling white clubhouse with its broad petticoat of mums and purple asters rested a comfortable distance from the two rivers. The golf fairway and its requisite buildings ranged to the right and boasted stunning views and a challenging layout. The well-manicured lawn flowed gently behind the clubhouse and toward the river. Gracious groupings of chairs and tables gave tired golfers a grand perspective of river traffic along the gleaming Missouri. A chain-link fence interrupted the lawn but did not impede the view of the slender point. The two riverbanks wore a modest fringe of brush.

The couple strolled the fence to view the rivers. "I want to be down there," Glynneth said wistfully.

"Down where? On the river?"

"No—on top. Looking down."

"Well, the fence tells us they don't want people that close to the river. Too dangerous. Think insurance claims."

Glynneth stopped and studied the landscape.

"You like high places, don't you." Lawrie looked at her. "I remember that time at Lookout Point. Couldn't—"

"I do like them," Glynneth said, a bleak smile softening her face. "They make me feel tall and strong."

Lawrie put his arm around her. "You are strong, and you'll be a strong vice president's wife. But come. We need to go in before Nels starts looking for us."

Glynneth and her Turkish gown seized the eye of all who entered the massive portico with its stately pillars and handsome, carved doors. She rose well to the occasion and greeted new arrivals with grace and warmth. Lawrie wore her proudly at his right hand.

The surrounding glitterati were equally well-coordinated, women's purses and shoes confidently displayed. But a discerning eye might note a pecking order. Nelson formed the locus for the most distinguished coterie, with Lawrie holding the next rank. The fringe consisted of retiring types or those more interested in food than politics.

The crowd expanded, and the Lawrie-Glynneth cell divided and drifted apart. When the call came for the dining room, Lawrie looked for his wife. Not spotting her, he assumed a last-minute ladies' room call and took his place at table, watching for a flash of pink and mahogany. As he was about to return to the entrance hall, a Secret Service man moved toward him. "Sir," he said, "Your wife—"

Lawrie's face paled. "Where is she?"

"Sir, somehow she got around the chain-link and is walking toward the point. She won't respond to—"

Lawrie slammed his way between the tables and headed for the front door.

"This way, sir; it's faster."

Several men were on both sides of the fence, some talking furiously on cell phones. Lawrie ran up the fence and over, snagging his tux but paying no heed.

"Stop!" he ordered the men who were moving toward the point. "Don't push her. Let me talk to her and get her back. I think she'll be all right. How did you lose track of her?" Crackling rancor masked his fear.

He jogged toward her. "Glynneth! Wait for me!"

"No, Lawrie. Don't come. I need to be alone."

"Glynneth, the photographer wants to take our picture. He likes your dress."

"He can wait. I have to be here now."

"Well, let me come with you so I can learn the power of cliffs to make me strong." He wasn't making sense. *Where was Charlotte when he needed her?* "Glynneth, wait."

"No, Lawrie. Don't come. You'll upset me, and I could fall." Her voice quavered.

"Please, Glynneth. Come this way. You're frightening me."

"Stay there. I'll be all right."

"Glynneth, you're at the point. Stop and look at the river. The ground ahead is sand. It's not safe."

"Lawrie, stay *away!* I have to do this. I have to go all the way."

He kept moving but more slowly. She continued to back away, and Lawrie panicked. "Glynneth! Watch where you're going! Wait. I'll keep you from falling."

As she turned, he hurried his pace, but she looked back, tripped on her skirt, and lurched. Lawrie sprinted. Glynneth screamed, throwing herself the last few feet toward the point. The fragile ground crumbled and slowly gave way. Lawrie grabbed mahogany, trying to get some purchase. Gravity, however, dropped them twelve feet onto a rock—Lawrie landing hard on top of Glynneth.

Charlotte insisted on being the one to tell Lawrie that Glynneth was dead. "I have a deep well of tears, but I know how to turn the spigot on and off. I know him. He knows me. I can do this."

Being intubated, Lawrie could not speak when she came in. He signed to her instead. *G-l-y.* She closed his fingers and signed back, *Gone.* She gripped his hand tightly, saying nothing, but communicating volumes of past and present pain.

Chapter 16

LINDA HAD A TASK TO accomplish somehow. She had to go to Jay in the hospital. She knew this for a certainty, even before Emily of the Garden Club spoke of the dream she'd had.

"So vivid, my dear. You were speaking at a Wisconsin Garden Club Federation pumpkin festival. Would they even have such an event? Anyway, your plane overshot the Milwaukee runway and ended up in Bismarck, North Dakota, of all places."

Bismarck. To see Jay. Linda knew the idea to be foolish, presumptuous, emotionally manipulative, and just plain stupid. Under other circumstances, she would have jumped at a chance to reconnect with Jay. But not this. Not intruding on his grief, on his pain, the loss of his *wife*. The very thought made her ill.

But going was not optional. She *had* to go to Jay—a compulsion she recognized immediately. In her younger years, her mother's look could propel an ox to gallop. No words were needed—just that look.

She felt this same compulsion now, but it made no sense. She didn't want to go—wouldn't get past the front desk or a guard outside his room. Even worse, she would be barging in on little more than an acquaintance, really, whose wife had just died tragically and who himself was badly injured. She'd be as welcome as a bed bug.

It was foolish, presumptuous, emotionally manipulative, and stupid. She wouldn't go. She couldn't do it.

But she had to. She argued with God inside the house, up and down the garden, in and out of the gazebo, but could not escape the compulsion that her ox *had* to gallop all the way out there.

She tentatively consulted her nurse friend Susan at the local Friendly's, hoping for scathing laughter.

But Susan stared in surprise across her chicken salad. "I know somebody at that hospital!"

"You're kidding!"

"No. Really. We were in nursing school together. I'll see if she's open to the idea and could get a uniform, maybe come up with somebody's ID. If anybody looks close, you're dead, but mostly they don't. I'll get back to you."

Linda sagged in defeat. "Can she be trusted not to blab?" she asked bleakly. "I'm trusting you, you know."

Susan's eyes widened, but she nodded with conviction. "I'll make sure."

Unhappily for Linda, everything fell into place. She flew to Bismarck, met Susan's friend Caitlin, who finalized arrangements while Linda checked the fit of her borrowed scrubs in a mirror.

"This will do, I think," she said. "You're skinnier than I am, but it seems comfortable. Do I look all right?"

"Close enough. I'm on night shift this week," said Caitlin. "Can we make that work?"

"Are you on his floor?"

"No, but I know the night guard, James Morrison. We come on about the same time and joke around a lot. I can get you in easier if we arrive together, but you'd have to wait till I'm free—maybe an hour or more. You could hole up in a toilet."

"Great! Splendid way to spend the night. Are there multiple stalls, or do I have to tie up a single bathroom half the night?"

"I'll find one that will do."

They made the arrangements, and Linda, clothed in costume and trepidation, met Caitlin the following night.

Linda's watch said eleven when Caitlin released her from the toilet stall and equipped her with a tray and cup of juice. Linda's hands shook, making ripples on the liquid. She could get arrested, put in jail, and do Jay irreparable harm. Her heart banged against her chest as they approached the guard.

"James James Morrison Morrison, Wetherby George Dupree," sang Caitlin. "My grandmother charmed my little brother James with that poem, and it fits you even better!" She nodded at Linda and carried on. *"Don't ever go down to the end of the town, if you don't go down with me."*

Linda hesitated, then pushed through the doorway into the dimly lit room. She slid the tray onto the table, eyes adjusting slowly. Was this sleeping man Jay, for sure? Yes, she could tell, even around bandages.

She took his hand and spoke softly. "Jay, it's Kileenda. Can you hear me? You don't need to say anything, but can you squeeze my hand?"

His eyes opened—wide—and he squeezed hard and stopped breathing. His eyes burned into hers, and he opened his mouth.

"No," she said. "Don't say anything. I have only a short time. Just listen. I'm so sorry about your wife . . . a terrible tragedy. I can't tell you how sorry . . . " Why hadn't she practiced this part? How can one truthfully say that you feel someone's pain? She drew a shaky breath.

"I have a word for you that I believe came from God. I didn't want to intrude, but I had to do it. This is what He gave me." Hands trembling, she unfolded a piece of paper, thankful in the dim light that she'd used a large font.

> . . . The Lord has anointed me . . . to comfort all who mourn, and provide for those who grieve in Zion—to

bestow on them a crown of beauty instead of ashes, the oil of joy instead of mourning, and a garment of praise instead of a spirit of despair. They will be called oaks of righteousness, a planting of the LORD for the display of his splendor (Isa. 61:1-3).

"This is God's word for you. He made that clear to me. He loves you and knows your sorrow. He is your hiding place, your refuge. I'll leave this on your tray table so you can look at it in the morning."

When she paused, he started to speak, but she hushed him.

"I have to go. If I'm caught here, we'll both be in trouble. I can't see you again, but I pray for you almost every minute. Peace be with you." She reached out and touched his head in blessing, then turned away.

She left the room, shame and regret dragging at her. He'd known she was there, but how had he felt about it? Had she simply compounded his grief in this ill-advised effort to cheer him? Her ultimate disgrace would be getting arrested on the way out. She stopped at the door, remembering the tray, but decided to leave it. Less of an encumbrance on her way to jail.

Caitlin's face showed relief at her reappearance, while James Morrison settled back to resume his long, lonely vigil.

Arrest nearly came at the nurses' station where the head nurse challenged Linda's pedigree. Caitlin drew breath to talk their way through, but the phone rang, drawing the drill sergeant's attention to more immediate problems.

Caitlin escorted Linda to the door, stretching her already-overdrawn break time to the point of almost sure reprimand. Linda drew off the faux ID.

"Be sure to thank—" She peered at the round-faced, white-haired image on the card. "—thank Edith for me. If she'd seen how little I resemble her, she might not have consented." She looked at Caitlin, then clutched her in a hug. "Thank you for putting your

job on the line for me and for the man in that room. Please protect him." Her eyes pleaded anxiously. "I think I've done what I
was supposed to, but what will come of it?" She turned Caitlin
around. "Now, hurry back before you get into more trouble."

Linda sat for a long time in the car before starting up. She had
obeyed orders; she had read and left the verses. But what had it
accomplished? More sorrow for Jay? Should she write him a letter,
or would that simply compound the trespass? She felt dirty, somehow, and dressing up in a costume seemed a part of it.

Was this another *unpresentable glory*, an act of service that
again had to be hidden? She hadn't felt any angelic presence this
time, but certain things needed to be done, and she seemed to be
the person God was picking to do them. She didn't ask to have
Jay deposited on her lawn. She didn't volunteer for this word-of-
comfort job, but one thing gripped her with absolute certainty:
God wanted her to deliver that message. She had done it, and that
would have to calm her for the moment.

When Linda's plane landed, Bonnie was there. After a quick,
stiff hug, Linda wrapped herself in silent hostility for the long
drive to the house. Bonnie insisted on going in with her and then
would not leave, despite Linda's strong signals in that direction.
Linda spun away, huffing angrily, and could no longer contain
her tears.

Bonnie gestured wildly. "I know what it's like to be lonely and
afraid, and I will not leave you."

"This is not your husband dying. This is different! I'm not
lonely. I just want to be alone!"

"You shouldn't be alone, not right now. I'll stay with you. I
want to help you."

Linda, eyes blazing, turned on her. "I don't *want* your help! Please *leave—now!*" She spun Bonnie around and shoved her toward the door and slammed it behind her.

The sound only intensified the reverberation of Bonnie's wailing sobs.

Linda dropped to the floor, clutching desperately at the silence, but it pounded on her, failing to bring even a shred of comfort. The reality of utter loneliness drove home the enormity of the words she had hurled at Bonnie. *What have I done?* Her groans turned to convulsive sobs.

While Lawrie was still in the hospital, Nels came, bearing presidential cheer and comfort. "We're all sorry as can be about your wife, m'boy, and we'll do everything we can for you and your family."

Lawrie looked at him balefully. "What family? Who's left?"

Nels staged a grimace but then went on. "Hey, man—*we're* family! We're here for you. And," he added, "this may be all to the good in the long run, even if you can't actively campaign. Sympathy's running strong. You're the hero who threw himself over the cliff in an attempt to save his wife. That plays well—very well—in politics."

Lawrie rolled to his side and curled as though being beaten.

Nels piled on more incentives. "We'll get you on every top TV spot, roll you on in your wheelchair."

Lawrie's groans intensified. "Nelson, as plain as I can say, I will not stay on the ticket. I do not want to be your vice president. Can you understand that?"

Nels looked at him in pity. "Come, now, boy. You feel bad now. Ribs hurt like crazy. I broke a couple when I was a kid. Well, I know it's more 'n just ribs, but—"

"Yes, I hurt, but my pain goes deeper than ribs. *I will not run as your vice president.* Period. End of sentence."

Nels shook his head and strode around the confines of the room, a frown working his considerable eyebrows. "Now, think a minute, boy. Do you realize what you're saying? Look what I've done for you. Picked you from a long list of men who were more than willing. Who are you? Senator from North Dakota—Nowheresville."

Lawrie eased himself over and fixed Nels's eye. "My wife is dead, less than a week. And you're telling me there are more important things to think about right now?"

"Of course not, my boy. I mourn with you. You know that. You don't get over tragedy overnight. Take as long as you like to recover. The last thing I want is to drag you out of bed and prop you in front of a TV cam." He stopped, a smile lifting his face. "But like the pope getting shot, like Reagan—"

"You're saying I'm more valuable to you here in the hospital— waving weakly, trying vainly to smile—than I would be on the campaign trail. What I'm saying is, yes, I am the senator from North Dakota—Nowheresville, if that's what you want to call it— and I will remain senator as long as North Dakotans vote for me. That's my calling; that's what I'm sticking with."

Nels stopped pacing and glared at the closed door, tornado alerts darkening his face. When he turned, his eyes were ugly slits. "I hand you the opportunity of a lifetime, and you turn around and smack my face with it. Keep the price tag in mind, Senator Crofter: If you ever go back to that floozy you stayed with, *I will destroy you and her and anyone associated with you.*"

Lawrie looked long at him, then with slow deliberation pushed the call button, his eyes never wavering. Nels turned on his heel; and as a nurse opened the door, he pasted on his best campaign smile and called cheerily over his shoulder, "I'll drop by again, my friend!"

Lawrie stared at the empty doorway and saw weeds—the gross, insinuating sort he'd learned about in Linda's garden. Clearly, Nels' threat was a cannon—fully charged and strategically aimed.

Nelson Graham lost no time in tapping Vermont Senator Charles Darson for the vice-presidential slot; and while he didn't trash Lawrie publicly, he said almost nothing about the man he had formerly admired for his honest political stance, his moral bearing, his heroic effort to save his wife.

Chapter 11

LAWRIE GOT HIMSELF OUT OF the hospital as soon as he could. The barrage of attention was getting to him—top-to-bottom medical personnel; city, state, and federal officials; the odd news vulture who managed to wriggle through the barricades. A top-brass campaign advisor was the final straw. He came, begging Lawrie to reconsider.

"The team needs you, Lawrie. Desperately. You're awesome—you know that—articulating our case more powerfully than Nels. Though don't tell him I said so." The attempted lightness didn't work, and the advisor got in only one more word before the call button flashed. "Lawrie, the *country* needs you."

No, the country didn't need him as much as he needed to go home. Home—where Charlotte would see to his needs but not hover. Home. But not to the home he knew. Martin had moved in, for one thing. He had peopled the dank, frost-blighted house with a regiment of wraiths who moved silently, demanding that he eat, drink, sleep, attend to prescribed bathroom regularity, walk a prescribed number of steps, watch a prescribed selection of vapid television programs. Life had no color, no purpose, no reason for him to be there. Even the sun, pasted on a concrete sky, warmed nothing, illumined nothing. The only figure of substance was Martin the Moldy.

In Lawrie's absence, an efficient but colorless housekeeper named Nadine had been added to the staff. One of the small rooms downstairs had been rehabbed into a drab bedroom for Lawrie, staffed by a private nurse to oversee his medical needs. He was home, but only as a specimen to be poked, prodded, and pushed.

After the first few hours of this specimen existence, Lawrie hissed with annoyance, "I was better off in the hospital. Why did I leave? Where's Charlotte when I need her? Martin, find Charlotte and—"

"Charlotte's gone. Packed up four days ago. Nobody saw her go, and she left no contact info." His face showed no regret over her absence.

"*What?*" Lawrie was stunned. "Not here? She's *got* to be here. Martin, why isn't she here? She came to the hospital and said she had to leave, but she'd be back. I expected her the next day, but she didn't come, and I got focused on . . . other things."

Martin couldn't or wouldn't tell him anything, even though Lawrie kept repeating himself with variations.

He stared in consternation. "She *left?*"

Fingertips kneading his forehead, he breathed heavily. Charlotte. The bane of his life, his captivating torment. He desperately needed her now, and she was gone. The only glimmer of light left to him had quit the household.

Lawrie deflated visibly over the next few days. Martin saw and pushed him to push himself, to get out, sit outside, go for a ride, do *something,* for goodness' sake.

Finally, Lawrie could stand it no longer. "Martin, you've prowled the room. You've made your mark here. Get out. Go find someone else's territory to pee around."

Martin's eyes narrowed. "Huh! You firing me?"

Lawrie's eyebrows flicked upward. "Hadn't thought of that, but you won't hear me complain." His eyes became slits. "I just want you out of this room—now."

Martin took a third turn around the room before answering. He stopped and glared at Lawrie. "Here's another bone for you to chew on. You turned down Nels. Not your brightest move ever, but neither was his performance. Your melodramatic exit may have ugly consequences, y'know. Just heard the latest buzz about Darson's girlie activities, and varmints are busy digging. Darson shouldn't even be in the picture. Your streak of independence could lose us the election. Have you thought of that? Lawrie, get a grip. Stand up. Be a man."

Lawrie, tongue pushing his cheek, studied Martin. With difficulty, he pulled the recliner to upright position and dragged himself to his feet, an effort as painful in the watching as in the doing.

"Now, wait—I didn't mean . . . "

Eyes steel-hard and ice-cold, Lawrie shuffled toward Martin, got in his face, and pointed with deliberation to the door.

Martin went.

Linda spent hours at her computer, googling *Senator Lawrence Crofter, Glynneth Crofter, Crofter death,* mining every scrap of information that turned up. She learned little of immediate substance beyond Jay being home, with Martin Walsh serving as spokesman. A dark thread on some sites suggested that the senator might have contributed to his wife's death, noting a number of possible motives.

She came across nasty, even filthy, posts that cobbled together bits of gossip and artful stories that twisted Glynneth's love of clothing and lust for attention into lust of a different sort. And, of course, Linda's name appeared in the tar pot. She quickly learned to discern the tone and clicked past most of them, but not before they had sown seeds of malice in her mind toward

Jay's wife and what he'd had to put up with. Earlier, she had felt compassion for this bereft woman, but even that faded beneath an even starker thought:

Now that Glynneth is dead . . .

She punched that weed back into the ground but knew it would reappear.

Linda had her own garbage to deal with, as well, and the day after her post-hospital meltdown, she went to apologize to Bonnie. It wasn't easy, and her voice shook.

"You were right about loneliness and fear, dearest Bonnie, and I realized that almost as soon as I tossed you out the door. I'm not sure you could have helped by staying, but at least I wouldn't have to be here, groveling and saying I'm sorry in twelve different languages."

"One is more than enough." Bonnie squeezed Linda. "When Andy died, you did so much for me—in multiple languages, like when I thought I was going to die along with him and then was afraid I wouldn't die, that I'd be left wrestling forever with that huge lump of loneliness." Her eyes again welled.

Linda, turning to practicality, filled Bonnie's kettle and turned it on. "We're here for each other, you and I, and a cup of tea will do us good."

Martin's warning turned prophetic. Two weeks before the election, Ewen MacClerhan rolled out his research on Nelson's new running mate, Senator Charles Darson. The reporter's bloodhound genes had again sniffed dirt. Though Darson slithered around the allegations convincingly, it left a bad smell, and the once-sure election was sure no longer.

Lawrie wallowed in wretchedness. That Nels might actually lose had seemed inconceivable. His Republican base was strong;

he'd been playing well with Independents, and even Blacks and Hispanics—though strongly Democrat—had been listening. But now, crashing poll numbers sounded a red alert in Lawrie's heart. Like the captain of the *Titanic*, he had ignored iceberg warnings and now felt the deck tilt alarmingly beneath him.

His name surfaced frequently during the remainder of the campaign, some noting that Darson's conservative bona fides might be even better for the ticket, while others heaped guilt on Lawrie for bailing out.

The political bowstring tightened.

Election night was unbearable, too close to call until very late. The returns crept in—precinct by precinct, county by county, state by state. Lawrie forced himself to stay up until Nels conceded, though keeping watch was more an act of self-flagellation than party loyalty. A squeaker, yes, but close was still loss. Roger Hanily was now president-elect of the United States, with Dan Coyne standing in triumph where Lawrie should have been. The Senate had shifted to Republican hands, but that was cold comfort on this long night.

Lawrie imploded. What had become of Nels' Opposition Research team? If McClerhan could find dirt, careful vetting could have found it, too. He mourned, though not for Nels' sake. That "friendly visit" in the hospital room had cleared his vision. Charles Nelson Graham was a hollow huckster who knew how to play the issues, the people, the voting game. He knew how to disguise his shallowness, and Lawrie had felt right about breaking with him. Now, the opposition victory validated both his decision and Nelson's political expiration date.

But the issues close to Lawrie's heart had gone down with Nels. What had that campaign advisor said? *The country needs you.* Bitter recrimination sucked Lawrie down, down, far beneath the surface of icy waters. If only he could actually drown right now . . .

Chapter 18

EVEN BEFORE THE ELECTION, LAWRIE had been trapped in a long tunnel of agony, wrestling with multiple, feverish pains—only two of which he spoke out loud. Mostly, though, he didn't speak at all. The implacable torment battering him got Martin thinking outside the box.

"Someone," he announced to the house staff, "needs to be with him at all times. Yes, I know—" He waved impatiently at several hands. "We're all close by, but we have work to do. I'm talking suicide watch." He looked at each face grimly, belligerently, as his words sank in. "Right now, he's on the cliff and wouldn't hesitate to jump. I'm posting the position, but if you know some man who could be with him without driving him to the edge, let me know. We need somebody—like yesterday."

The search began for the perfect companion, and candidates lined up. While most were crossed off quickly, Martin introduced a couple of promising applicants to Lawrie but was not heartened by his cold, hostile response. The task would be daunting.

Three days after Martin's initial announcement, one of the kitchen women came hesitantly to his office. "Yes, Carol. What is it? The dishwasher again?"

"No, sir. That's working fine. Thank you, sir, for getting it fixed."

"Good. Then what is it?" He glanced at his watch.

"Sir, there's a man in our church who'd be perfect—leastwise, I think so . . . I mean . . . " She put flustered hands to her face.

126

"You're talking about someone to be with Mr. Crofter, right?"

"Yes, sir. He's nice—quiet-like—but he don't put up with things. I mean—"

"What's his name? From your church, you say? So, he's local?"

"Yes, sir. His name's Nathan Grover. I don't know how old—maybe thirty, thirty-five."

"Where's he work now? What does he do?"

"He's got a job but hates it, so that wouldn't be a problem."

"But what kind of—"

"He's in an office he says isn't fun. People are nasty. His boss is out to get him because he's a Christian."

"Who—Nathan or the boss?"

"Nathan. He works hard, gets along, and people come to him for help—y'know, advice—sort of."

Martin sat back in his chair, arms folded, and studied what Carol was saying and not saying.

"Oh!" She sat up straight. "Maybe most important of all, his wife died two years ago, so he knows what that's like."

Martin's eyebrows went up at this, and he leaned forward again. "Do you have a phone number? And would he be interested in this position?"

"Oh, yes! I told him, and he said he'd need to pray about it and get back to me. He did last night and thinks he could help."

Martin nodded slowly, processing the *pray about it* part, then stood in dismissal after receiving Carol's paper with phone, email, and mailing information. "Carol, thanks for trying to help here." He ushered her out the door. "This person may not have the right qualifications, you know." He patted her on the shoulder. "We'll check him out, though."

He dutifully added the name to the bottom of the list; but when Lawrie became increasingly testy with even the choicest of applicants, Nathan rose to the top and was summoned for an

interview. To Martin's surprise, he measured up to Carol's glow-
ing description. Quiet but personable, with a presence and inner
substance that spoke confidence and authority. No one would call
him handsome, but his face, his beach-sand hair, and his sketchy
beard somehow made him attractive. Scandinavian, maybe?

Now Martin had to sell him to Lawrie, who at this point was
jaded and hostile. He tried to prepare Nathan for rejection. "We've
had some excellent applicants, but they've all been shot down. He
slams the door halfway through the introduction."

Nathan tipped his head and raised an eyebrow. "How about if
I just go in and you stay out here? Let me see if I can pry the gate
open a little."

Martin snorted and rolled his eyes. "Good luck to *you*!" And he
led Nathan to the sitting room.

Nathan paused at the two steps down to the warm, creamy
room. On the left, a curtained window splashed light across a
glass-topped table and six upholstered chairs. A large television
seemed uncomfortably out of place in the room's elegance and
had probably been dragged in for Lawrie's entertainment. The
wall to the right held a well-appointed fireplace with bookshelves
on either side. Other easy chairs were scattered around, though
at a respectful distance from Lawrie's opulent recliner. This chair
sat just beyond the line of sunlight streaming through a curtained
bay window that framed the wintry landscape outside. Lawrie's
face was pale, his frame shrunken, his demeanor cold and hopeless. A fast-barred gate, if ever there was one. Nathan closed his
eyes for a few seconds, then walked softly down the steps.

Instead of going directly to Lawrie, he took one of the wood-
backed chairs surrounding the table and placed it at an angle to

the recliner. He sat on it and leaned forward, elbows on his thighs. He said nothing for several moments. Finally, he straightened.

"May I call you 'Hey'—at least temporarily? 'Senator Crofter' seems a bit stiff and formal, and we're not on 'Lawrie' terms yet, so 'Hey' is the best I can come up with right now. How does that sound?" His eyes, more than his mouth, crinkled to a smile.

Lawrie's eyes widened, and his mouth moved only fractionally, as though bound by a fierce will against smiling. "You one of Martin's 'Lawrie Companion' tryouts?"

He shrugged and grinned. "Afraid so. A companion is the last thing you want right now, but Mr. Walsh will put somebody in this chair—I'm sure of that—and I, at least, won't make a lot of noise about it. Other than the few words necessary to life, I don't talk much. I have lots to read and can do computer—behind your back, if you don't like watching other people work. I assume you have wireless here?"

Lawrie nodded curtly and opened his mouth to speak, but Nathan hurried on. "In fact, I brought along a book today in case I had to wait around." He pulled a small volume from his jacket pocket. "A neat survey of Icelandic history by some unknown author, but he knows his subject and writes well. Have you seen it?" He handed it to Lawrie, who took it and looked at the title page and publishing information, then at the back cover, and read the first couple of paragraphs.

"Iceland," he said, pulling the word from some unwilling core in his being. "Eric the Red—the only thing I know about Iceland. Are you Icelandic?" he asked, looking at Nathan's light hair, then back at the book. "I'd like to read this when you're done." He handed it back. "And tell Martin he's found his man." He put out his hand. "After you get tired of 'Hey,' call me Lawrie."

Chapter 19

THEY SETTLED IN REASONABLY WELL together. Martin had drawn up a contract that included guest-room accommodations for Nathan, full board, and a sizeable stipend. In return, Nathan would be on duty twenty-four hours a day, with specified breaks and days off. His primary duty was to keep Lawrie from harming himself and, secondarily, to get him moving and out of his depression. During sleeping hours, security guard Warren would sit outside Lawrie's bedroom, but Nathan would remain within call-button distance.

For the first week, Nathan kept to Lawrie's usual schedule—breakfast for three at the glass-topped table with alternating china settings, linen napkins, and fresh flowers. Following breakfast, Lawrie showered and dressed and took to his chair. Martin would turn on the TV. Lawrie would watch for five minutes, check hockey scores, then turn it off. After a time of immobility, if not rest, Lawrie would be pulled from his chair to walk for at least twenty minutes. Lunch was at noon, followed by a nap in bed, more "exercise," and dinner at six—sometimes with guests with whom Lawrie talked or didn't. More time in the recliner followed dinner, then more force-fed television, with hockey most easily digested, and finally bed between nine and ten o'clock. Nathan, always in the same room as Lawrie, did his computer and books, occasionally reading a page to Lawrie—with no negative response.

The second week, Nathan began to modify the routine, requesting that he and Lawrie eat breakfast alone. That went over well, and Nathan pushed Martin to allow other private meals. Lawrie's relief was obvious—even to Martin—but Martin pushed back, insisting that at least four meals a week be eaten with others at the table.

"Good," said Nathan with a smile. "I was going to suggest five, but four will do." He waved his way out of Martin's office, leaving his boss off-balance.

Nathan's first war with Lawrie involved exercise. "Carol tells me you have a treadmill."

Lawrie growled. "I *detest* treadmills."

"Huh! I'm with you there. I don't want to condemn you to life on a treadmill. Just want to—"

"Treadmills are for Capitol Building squirrels."

Nathan grunted derisively. "For all I know, the Capitol Building could have donkey and elephant treadmills, but whatever's here, we'll use—briefly."

"I walk around the house for exercise."

"Right. Tortoisize. Two miles an hour, top speed. I promise you, when I find what you can comfortably do, we won't visit the treadmill except maybe for blizzards. And while you're walking, I'll read to you."

They sparred back and forth, but Lawrie finally gave in. Ignoring his faked attempts at collapse, Nathan kept him moving until he reached three miles an hour for ten minutes.

The next day, Nathan insisted that Lawrie shave, shower, and dress before breakfast. When they arrived at the table—late—they found Carol standing uncomfortably before a third place setting.

"Good morning, Carol," said Nathan. He turned to Lawrie. "I've asked Carol to join us this morning. She works hard in the kitchen, helps all these meals happen, and I thought you'd like to get to know her. She doesn't often escape pots and pans."

Getting to know Carol was obviously light-years from Lawrie's mind, but he nodded and pulled out her chair. Her hands, restless and shaking, could scarcely manage to pass dishes. Nathan lined out a monologue for a few minutes until she settled down, then asked questions about her family, what she did at church, and how she spent her spare time.

After she answered haltingly, Lawrie turned unexpectedly with his own question. "Where do you live, Carol?"

Her eyes shot wide, her breathing turned frantic as she tried to explain where her family lived.

"Yah, sure," said Lawrie. "I know the area. Used to play field hockey on Schneider's pasture. The Haldersen boys . . . Any Haldersens still around?"

"Yes." She sat up and looked straight at him. "Old Mrs. Haldersen comes to our Senior Souls group, and she talks a lot about her boys."

Lawrie grunted. "She's a talker; I remember that." He smiled. "Tell me what you do in the kitchen. Does the staff treat you well? Martin? You get on with Mrs. Liles, the cook?"

Nathan sat back, his heart smiling broadly. Now they were getting somewhere.

The next morning after the normal breakfast for two, Nathan came in with an armful of parkas, boots, hats, and mittens. "Time for outdoor exercise."

Lawrie's back went up. "There's a foot of snow out there!"

"Well, yah. The storm of the century, you might say. Doesn't often get that deep. Surely, you've walked in snow before. I can't believe some lackey goes before you with a shovel or broom to—Nooo! Delete that. Not nice. We're going out. We'll make a path. This much snow is God's gift. Let's enjoy it." He pulled on a boot and stomped down.

Lawrie reached for a boot, his face bearing a look of helpless, hopeless sadness.

"It's a beautiful day and above zero. You might even be moved to make a snow angel!"

The cold sucked breath from Lawrie's lungs, but once they got moving, he did quite well. For fifteen minutes, he actually seemed to enjoy himself, but as strength and spirits flagged, he looked hopefully toward the house.

When he got back to his chair, Nadine, the housekeeper, brought him a cup of hot chocolate. He sipped it eagerly, color and eyes brighter than they'd been in weeks.

During one of their long silences—and there were many— Nathan studied his charge. Lawrie was not only accepting him, he seemed to feel better in his company than with anyone else— more, even, than being alone. The previous day, when Nathan had come back from time off, Lawrie's face had reflected relief, if not welcome. A good sign.

But bad signs still lurked in dark corners.

Nathan talked about things he thought Lawrie should know— his church and what he did during his time off. He told Lawrie of his own wife's death and how difficult that had been, being careful to make no comparisons or hint that Lawrie was somehow not coping well. Nathan simply handed off information.

During another silence, Nathan plucked a thought from his head and held it out. "Somebody told me Charlotte used to work here."

Lawrie flinched as though Nathan had hit him, but then looked off, a mix of love and pain twisting his face. "How do you know Charlotte?"

"From church. That's where she went."

Lawrie's eyes dropped to the carpet.

Nathan went on. "Did you ever hear her sing?"

Lawrie grimaced. "All the time. She was always humming or singing to Glynneth." Again, the love-pain mix.

"No, I mean belted-out black Gospel with that thick, caramel voice of hers. She didn't sing often in church; but when she did, it shook every speck of North Dakota dust from rafters and souls. One time, she sang the 'Dakota Hymn'—I think at the baptism of one of our Native American teenagers. The Indian folk loved it. You know it? It goes, 'Many and great, O God, are Your works, Maker of earth and sky.'"

Lawrie shook his head.

"Well, it's *the* hymn for the Dakotas or Sioux and dates back to the 1800s. But when Charlotte sang, it seemed like she was taking out her heart—publicly—and holding it up to God. Like I say, she didn't sing that way often. You can't do that every day and stay alive."

Lawrie looked desolate. "She did that every day, and I didn't know . . . I didn't *know*," he said forlornly. "I wish I had heard her sing like that. So much I didn't know. Charlotte, Charlotte, *why* did you leave and not come back?" He rubbed his neck as though against some racking anguish.

Nathan was shaken by the effect of his off-hand question and the glimpse into this hidden layer of pain. He mentally filed the conversation. Charlotte, even in her absence, might prove useful somewhere down the line.

As Lawrie's inner trauma became increasingly corrosive, Nathan decided to call in his goodwill cards. "You've been sitting here way too long, marinating in . . . stuff," he announced one Monday morning. "You're able to walk and ride in a car, so I've decided you're well enough to go to church with me." He hurried on, his eye on the squall gathering in Lawrie's face. "Which do you prefer—a service on Sunday morning? Charlotte's not there to sing, I know, but it's still a good service. Or a Bible study Thursday evenings? Those are your choices. You *will* go to one of them. Which do you prefer?"

Lawrie sucked in a breath and glared, then batted the air and turned away.

"Lawrie, quit acting like a teenager. Think a moment, then make up your mind, and give me an answer. Right now, I'm in charge, and you will go to one of those places. The Bible study, by the way, is in a home, if that makes a difference. Eight guys who are willing to have you join us. Not a given, you know."

Lawrie leaned back in his chair and closed his eyes. Then he looked at the sleet-pounded window. "Nathan . . . " he began, anger morphing to plaintiveness. "Nathan, I—"

"I don't need a weather report." Nathan spoke gently. "The storm inside is worse than the blow outdoors; I can see that. I just need your preference. If you decide not to choose, then I'll take you where I think you should go."

Martin also took note of Lawrie's implacable anguish and began consulting psychiatrists. Having learned from Nathan's approach, he picked the gentlest, kindest of the bunch to sit and talk with Lawrie. Within minutes, however, Lawrie had his number. He stood and reached out his hand.

"Thank you for coming, but I'm not up for a shrink. When I am, I'll be in touch. But for now, I have other plans."

He walked with him to the door of Martin's office and leaned in. "Where's Nathan?" he asked gruffly.

When Nathan stepped into the sitting room, Lawrie looked at him, eyes narrowed. "Were you in on that little stratagem?"

Nathan smiled wryly. "No. Didn't think you'd like it, and apparently I was right." His tongue bumped out his cheek momentarily, but his face turned serious. "Martin tells me you said you had other plans. What might they be?" He raised an eyebrow. "Church or Bible study—which?"

Lawrie stared at the grayness outdoors, then turned to Nathan as though to plead one last time. His companion's implacable look, though, turned him away and brought out one final, grumpy sigh. "All right. The home thing. Now will you leave me alone?"

Nathan stood and, with a smile, put a hand on Lawrie's shoulder and took the two stairs in one step.

The "home thing," early in December, went reasonably well from Nathan's point of view. The car pulled up the snow-swirled drive to a tree-banked house and weathered barn. Lawrie, tense and hostile, remained silent through the "How y' doin's" inside the door. The group consisted of Kevin the rancher host, Mike the firefighter, Laddie the truck driver, Bruce and Jake the prison guards, Len in collision repair, and Billy, "our token American Indian," Nathan finished with a smile.

Lawrie's eyebrows went up. "Lakota?" he asked.

"Yah. Hunkpapa. One of the seven council fires of Lakota Sioux." Billy's eyes crinkled as he put out his hand. "Sitting Bull welcomes you."

Lawrie took his hand and nodded a brief but unmistakable greeting, with a soft "Hau."

Billy tightened his grip on Lawrie's hand. "Háu kȟolá—hello, friend."

They moved to the cramped kitchen for coffee and snack, trying not to step on Kevin's tabby cat that viewed this forest of legs as feline heaven. Back in the living room, the men opened their Bibles. Though Nathan had one for Lawrie, he made no attempt at finding the passages given. The men had been primed. They talked and joked throughout the discussion, their attention including Lawrie but not demanding a response. After prayer that included him, they filed past Lawrie with outstretched hands—rough and callused, nails dirt-packed. He received each shake dispassionately but put his other hand over Billy's and squeezed tighter.

As the men left, Kevin leaned toward Billy. "You the man," he whispered. "White man likes you."

"Uh-huh," said Billy. "Or was that the politician doing his thing?"

"Something clicked. We'll see."

Chapter 20

BIBLE STUDY NIGHTS WERE AWKWARD, especially at first, but Billy White Water, the Lakota Hunkpapa, held the high ground. In almost any circle, Billy manifested a latent power no one could safely ignore. Tall—roughly Lawrie's height—with a presence that spoke strength, he bore a classic, though not particularly handsome, Indian profile—his long, black hair sometimes tied back, sometimes braided. When Billy walked into a room, whether of friends or non-friends, respect was palpable. One neither presumed on nor opposed Billy lightly.

The Lakota had done his homework on the senator's interest in Indian affairs and got him talking on the subject. Lawrie, in turn, picked up on Billy's heavy-equipment contracting business as one of the native entrepreneurial successes he loved to spotlight, as well as his involvement in private relief efforts for the hard-hit Native American population. It didn't hurt, either, that Billy was a professional tracker.

"What exactly do you track?" asked Lawrie.

Billy shrugged. "Anything. Everything. Wildlife, search and rescue, missing people."

"So, you're a pro."

"I belong to the International Society of Professional Trackers, so yah."

"You teach tracking? Like maybe to wrung-out senators?"

Billy batted his arm. "We'll go out someday, see what you're made of."

Initially, the other men had felt uncomfortable with this new-comer. But Lawrie surprised them—not only by his acceptance, but also by his interest in farming, firefighting, and how the two prison guards viewed their work.

The actual Bible study on God's love, however, turned him off, and he wouldn't open his Bible. Nathan made the mistake of trying to help him find the Gospel of John. Lawrie glared back. "Genesis, Exodus, Leviticus, Numbers, Deuteronomy, Joshua, Judges, Ruth, First and Second—"

The men laughed, and Nathan looked chagrined. "Okay, okay—you know the Table of Contents better than we do. Where'd you learn it?"

"Sunday school. Where'd you learn it? I've gone to church all my life. Do I know the Bible well? No. Can I find the book of John? Yes. Do I care right now? No. I'm here because I have to be, and I don't really want to find the book of John. Get the picture?"

Nathan gripped Lawrie's knee in response but sat silent for several moments. Then he looked up and said, "We're just glad you're here. You can follow along or not. God's love doesn't de-pend on you wanting it. Now—" He straightened and turned pages. "The clearest and most basic statement about God's love is the old, familiar John 3:16. 'For God so loved the world that he gave his one and only Son, that whoever believes in him shall not perish but have eternal life."

Lawrie grimaced but said nothing.

Nathan searched him silently, then turned his head. "Billy," he said, "tell Lawrie how you became a Christian."

Lawrie slumped in his chair and rolled his eyes. "*Undoubtedly* after reading John 3:16." His mouth stiffened.

Billy stifled a smile, and he, too, sat back. "Nope. Even worse—a hymn."

"Well, yah—much worse. Which one—'This is My Father's World?'"

This time Billy did laugh. "Not far off, at least subject-wise. It's called the 'Dakota Hymn,' written by a half-breed in the 1840s. The words go—"

Lawrie frowned. "'Dakota Hymn' . . . " He looked at Nathan, who nodded and grinned.

Billy spoke out the words.

> *Many and great, O God, are your works,*
> *Maker of earth and sky.*
> *Your hands have set the heavens with stars;*
> *your fingers spread the mountains and plains.*
> *You merely spoke and waters were formed;*
> *deep seas obey your voice.*
> *Grant us communion with you, our God,*
> *though you transcend the stars.*
> *Come close to us and stay by our side:*
> *with you are found the true gifts that last.*
> *Bless us with life that never shall end,*
> *eternal life with you.*[1]

Billy bent his head, leaving Lawrie to stare uncertainly, negatives and positives dueling in his face. But then the Indian looked up. "Wasn't the hymn that got me. The story that came out of the hymn tracked me down." He leaned forward, elbows on his knees.

"The Dakota War of 1862. Broken treaties, natives getting cranky about being cheated, and land stolen. Indians went on the warpath, killing settlers. The army rode in, trapped the Indians in a ravine. Three hundred and three braves were convicted of

---

1   Joseph Renville. *Many and Great, O God,* https://hymnary.org/text/many_and_great_o_god_are_your_works.

murder and rape—some trials lasting all of five minutes. No defense attorneys. You know how it was back then." Billy watched Lawrie's face gather pain.

"The Minnesota bishop went to Washington, got in the president's face, and Lincoln had guts enough to whittle the condemned list to thirty-eight, despite political 'consequences.'" Again, he glanced at Lawrie.

"With the men on death row, the missionaries went to work. Many Indians turned Christian and were baptized." Billy looked down, his face tightening. "On December twenty-sixth, the prisoners were led to the gallows, and their women began to wail. Proudly, one man cried out, '*Mitakuyapi, nanmahon po!* Hear me, my people! Today isn't a day of defeat, but of victory. We've made peace with our Creator and will be with Him forever. Remember this day! Tell our children to tell their children: we are honorable men, and we die for a noble cause.' Then he led the group in singing the "Dakota Hymn."

> *Come close to us and stay by our side:*
> *with you are found the true gifts that last.*
> *Bless us with life that never shall end,*
> *eternal life with you.*

"Those Dakotas went to their Creator that day. Another day, when *this* Indian heard the story, he joined their band."

On the way home, Lawrie said nothing, and Nathan did nothing to staunch the aching silence.

The following morning, Nathan came into the sitting room with jackets, skates, and hockey sticks. Lawrie looked up sharply.

"Martin tells me you're a serious skater. I can move a puck around, so we'll see who wins this first matchup."

"No."

"Yes. It's either that or the treadmill. Would you rather go to the rink—closer—or to Petersen's pond—more private?"

"I choose to sit here and go nowhere."

Nathan shrugged. "There are three other men here—Warren, Justin, and Martin—ready to change your mind, and I would advise against a dustup with Martin. Now, you decide where—"

Lawrie swore, and his eyes turned vicious.

"Don't waste energy. It's nippy out there. Put your jacket on, and get in the car."

They drove in frigid silence to the bleak, isolated pond, and Lawrie shoved open the car door and yanked his skates from the back. By the time Nathan joined him at the pond's edge, he had already laced up and was hurling himself across the pond, the venom of each stride melting ice. Nathan watched in amazement, then skated more slowly around the edge with practiced ease. When Lawrie showed signs of tiring, Nathan tossed him a stick and pulled the puck from his pocket. Lawrie shuffled it down ice, then whacked it as hard as he could—directly at Nathan. The latter ducked and turned away, but the puck hit hard. Nathan bent over for several seconds, grimacing, then grabbed his stick vengefully and went after the puck. He drove it hard toward his opponent, and the two went back and forth until Lawrie tripped and fell. He lay gasping on the ice.

"You all right?" Nathan slid to a stop beside him.

"Yes," mumbled Lawrie. "You?"

"Let's see if Nadine has more hot chocolate."

They said nothing on the way home, but as they pulled their gear from the car, Lawrie put his hand on Nathan's shoulder and said softly, "Sorry."

Winter came early in New York, a freak snowstorm taking out the most ironclad chrysanthemums. Linda's soul felt equally bleak. Writing chores put her up against proposals and deadlines and run-ins with editors. End-of-the-season greenhouse inventorying wouldn't add up, and both she and Jorge threw up their hands.

"Forget the tallies," said Linda. "Try to keep better records from now on."

With Christmas looming, she should have sketched plans for tree decorating, but even that didn't heat her blood this year. One thought stalked her daily: *Now that Glynneth is dead . . .* An illicit notion, but she could not take it out of the envelope to stare it down once and for all.

This would be a long winter.

In subsequent Bible-study sessions, the men looked at assorted passages.

> "And I pray that you, being rooted and established in love, may have power . . . to grasp how wide and long and high and deep is the love of Christ."[2]

> "Who shall separate us from the love of Christ? Shall trouble or hardship or persecution or famine or nakedness or danger or sword? As it is written: 'For your sake we face death all day long.'"[3]

"Now, there's something I can identify with," said Lawrie, eyes flinty. "'Face death all day long.' Nice to hear that somebody gets a kick out of that."

---

2   Ephesians 3:17b-18
3   Romans 8:35-36a

The following week, the last meeting before Christmas, Lawrie seemed more relaxed and even joked some. They took heart. But with the lesson on Hosea eleven, everything came unglued. Nathan read,

"When Israel was a child, I loved him, and out of Egypt I called my son . . . . It was I who taught Ephraim to walk, taking them by the arms; but they did not—"[4]

Nathan stopped abruptly as Lawrie dropped his unopened Bible and slid to the floor, hands gripping the back of his head. The men were on him immediately, but Lawrie rocked back and forth.

"Something set this off, something in this chapter," said Kevin.

"Track it back," said Billy. "Lawrie as a child? Egypt? What is it, man?"

"Didn't his boy die?" asked Jake. "What was his name?"

Lawrie scrunched tighter and moved his hands to his ears.

Nathan hissed slowly and gripped Lawrie's shoulder. "Listen, my friend. You lost your Ephraim, but that's not what this passage is about. God is talking about faithless Israel, not a real child. He loved Israel like a dad who bends to feed his child. He wants them to come back before—"

Lawrie shook his head more violently. *"Please . . . "*

"You need to hear this. It's about God's *love* for His child. As you loved your child, so God loves you. 'How can I give you up, Ephraim?' He says. 'How can I treat you like junk?'"

At that moment, Kevin's cat slipped into the living room and deposited a live mouse on the floor as a plaything. The men stared at this almost-welcome alternative to the tortured pain in their midst. But Kevin got up and yanked open the front door, then came back to grab neck fur with one hand and battered mouse

---

4   Hosea 11:1

with the other, tossing them both into outer darkness. "Sorry," he muttered as he sat down.

Lawrie stared at the floor and began to laugh—hollow, joyless, on the edge of shattering. "Perfect!" he croaked. "That's it! You guys are the cat; I'm the mouse you dragged in. Not quite dead, but toss me out, too. Ten below ought to make quick work of—"

"Stop, Lawrie," said Nathan. "We're sorry about this. The whole evening went badly. I'll take you home, but first we want to pray for you."

Billy put his hand on Nathan's arm and shook his head.

Nathan sighed, then helped Lawrie to his feet. "All right, we'll go home, get you to bed. We had no idea this would touch such a deep wound. We'll talk later, but only if you want. Come. Jake's got your coat. Let's go home."

Chapter 21

LAWRIE'S DREAMS OFTEN WOKE HIM and held him sleepless for hours. The staging for the latest was Theodore Roosevelt National Park—not surprising, in that he had talked with Billy about favorite places there. In his dream, Linda appeared as a prairie dog, sometimes spitting hatred and disgust, other times laying a hand on his head, longing to give comfort. Comfort, though, as in Super Glue. Her hand stuck to his head, and he couldn't get away. He was being scalped, and her despairing look only intensified the pain.

Drenched with sweat, Lawrie got up and went to the bathroom. He then opened his dresser drawer and pulled out the paper Linda had given him in the hospital.

> " . . . to comfort all who mourn, and provide for those who grieve in Zion—to bestow on them a crown of beauty instead of ashes, the oil of joy instead of mourning, and a garment of praise instead of a spirit of despair."[5]

His hallway "keeper" got up from his chair and looked in the bedroom. "You all right, sir?" he asked.

Lawrie sighed and put the paper back in place. "Yes, Warren. Just can't sleep." He closed the drawer and curled inwardly on his bed.

---

5   Isaiah 62:2-3

Bed, though, provided no escape from Christmas preparations. The smell of baked goods polluted the entire house. Multiple trees were on every level, along with garlands, window lights, candles, wreaths, and packages under the king of trees—a fifteen-footer in the great room. *Why?* thought Lawrie. *Why so much work when the owner of this grandeur doesn't want any of it?* He had no control. None–over his own house.

He could have helped decorate but chose defiance instead. Finally, out of desperation, he pressured Nathan into multiple walks. Silent walks. Lawrie wanted to walk alone, but Nathan replied with a sardonic, "Right." Lawrie stalked rigidly, dragging a cumbersome clump of wretchedness and gall.

"I'm worried," Nathan said to Kevin over the phone. "I thought by this time he'd talk about the other night, or at least simmer down, but he's angrier than I've ever seen him, barely tolerating me. I don't know if it's Hosea or the way I handled it."

"Something punched his button, for sure," said Kevin. *"We'll get on him after Christmas."*

"If we live! The house is awash in glitter, and he can't stand it. I talked with Martin, but he thinks it's the right thing, that Lawrie will be distracted by Christmas Day activities. He may be right. Friends will be here, plus Glynneth's mom and relatives. You wouldn't believe the pile of presents from all over the state and D.C. A musical group is coming, he says. Lawrie likes music, and this is one of the top ensembles around here. That alone might save the day."

"Well, seems you got plenty goin' on. I was thinkin' of stoppin' by, but maybe not." Kevin chuckled. *"Wouldn't fly too good."*

"For sure. Some other time. I haven't actually decided, but I'd like to spend Christmas with my wife's family in Stanton. They miss her as much as I do. Would mean a lot to them—and to me."

"Do it! Leave the Christmas mess to Martin. Lawrie won't get away with nothing with all those people. . . . Maybe he'll appreciate you more. And keep warm. Looks like she's gonna turn cold tomorrow, for sure."

Nathan left for Stanton the afternoon of Christmas Eve after getting Lawrie's almost enthusiastic approval. "I'll be back early Thursday, probably before you're through sleeping off lebkuchen and presents."

Lawrie looked grim at the prospect but pushed him toward the door. "Go get ready. And . . . thank you, Nathan. Merry Christmas."

Nathan turned in surprise and risked a hug. It was received, to his even greater surprise.

As she feared, Christmas had become a downer for Linda. Normally, she found almost childish joy in tree decorating. This year, she had taken on five charity raffles but found herself short on ideas, materials, and logistical connections. She could have backed out of at least three commitments; but with Bonnie's help, they managed them all.

She and her friend spent Christmas together—a good day, all things considered. After exchanging their "under-ten" gifts in Bonnie's apartment, they went to an urban shelter to help serve a modest turkey dinner. For weeks, they'd been collecting an array of items, making up small, color-coded packets. As people left the center, the two stood at the doorway and distributed packets with a word or hug for each person. They closed the day at Linda's mother's more lavish table and basked in the satisfying light of a Christmas well spent.

That night, with nothing more than early seed catalogs to point her past Christmas, Linda visited websites that sometimes gave bits of information on Senator Lawrence J. Crofter. What she found, though, kept her up the rest of the night.

Nathan had planned to sleep late at his in-law's, badly in need of rest. But at seven o'clock, his mother-in-law's timid tap on the door woke him.

"I'm sorry, dear, but a man phoned and said to call Martin. That's the only name he gave. He said you'd have his number."

Nathan rolled over, rubbed his head, and breathed life into his body. "Okay," he finally said. "I'll get it. Thanks." He sat up and reached for his cell phone. "Martin—what's up?"

"He's gone, Nathan. He drugged Warren and got away. I called the police, and they've put out an APB. He took Glynneth's car, but we have no idea which direction he went. Come as soon as you can, and keep your phone on!"

Nathan sat a moment, phone in hand, then punched another number and waited through several rings. Then, "Joey, where's your dad?"

"He's opening presents. We all are. I didn't want to—"

"I need to talk to him, Joey. Now. Please."

Joey sighed. *"All right . . . "*

After a short silence, Billy spoke. *"Hey! Merry Christmas! What's up?"*

"Billy, Lawrie's gone. Got away in his wife's car. The police have an all-points on him, but do you have any idea which way he might have gone?"

"Yah . . . sure's if he'd said it outright. National Park. South Unit. We can find him if he didn't have too much head start."

"Martin didn't say when he left. He evidently drugged Warren, but Billy, the park will—"

"Don't waste time. You're not at the house; where are you?"

"In Stanton. We can meet along the highway. Just say where. But it's Christmas, Billy. The park'll be closed. And with fencing all around . . . "

"Yah, but Elkhorn Ranch is a through road. Has to stay open. God's in this, Nathan. Get here."

"I'll leave within ten minutes and call the guys. Some might be able to come."

"Just Kev and Mike. It's a tough climb. The others could drag. Grab food, blankets, thermos, whatever. I'll bring Joey. That'll get him over his pout. He's pretty good into tracking."

After arranging a rendezvous point, Nathan called the designated two. The four men and twelve-year-old arrived at the agreed-on spot within minutes of each other—all in long, hooded parkas. They shifted into Billy's pickup and Kevin's SUV, better suited for off-road driving. Nathan piled food and equipment into the SUV but asked to ride with Billy and Joey. They drove west to the Visitor Center exit and onto the park road north. Five miles further brought them to a wide spot where Billy worked his truck through a narrow slash and down a stretch of steep, alluvial scrabble, rough enough to whiten Nathan's knuckles.

"He'll park at the creek, then head uphill," said Billy. "See the tracks?"

Nathan didn't see the tracks and bemoaned the lack of snow. But within five minutes, they spotted the blue car under a grove of cottonwoods, hidden from a helicopter combing the area. Billy parked next to it, then took off with Joey, sweeping wide for obvious signs, then dropping to hands and knees for closer inspection. With the temperature below zero under a clear sky, Nathan was shivering, even in his parka. "At least no wind," he muttered.

The Badlands—a hostile, alien wasteland of river-eroded buttes and coulees. Deep-cut layers of sediment displayed a broad palette of colors—white, brown, red, blue, black—with sparse vegetation softening north slopes and creek and river beds. It was a beautiful place to gawk—in spring, summer, or fall—or to suffer in minus-four temperatures, as now.

Billy started praying out loud. "Gotta find him, Lord. Give us something."

Hardly had the words left his mouth when Joey hollered, "Over here!" The men hurried over. "He peed—right there," and Joey pointed proudly.

Billy squatted to examine the yellow ice. "Pee, all right, but Lawrie's or a coyote's?" He scooped up some of the icy sand and smelled it. Joey didn't wait for a verdict but crept along, searching out more signs.

"Lawrie's," Billy decided. "Coyotes don't leave that long a mark." He stood to see where Joey was. "Go left four, five yards," he hollered. "He should be heading up the slope toward that butte." He pointed and strode that way, searching the ground. Joey got in front, scanning the butte his dad had pointed out. Billy pushed past him. "Gotta find him quick, son. Before he gets up there and starts getting ideas."

Kevin and Nathan looked at each other, then at the butte with its sharp drop-offs.

Joey pounced on a marker that was invisible to the other men. Billy nodded and said, "Good. From the length of his stride, he's not hustling. This is a climb for him."

They moved haltingly, looking nervously at the sky and the amount of daylight left. "I got a couple of flashlights," said Mike, "but out here . . . I dunno."

"We'll find him. He's not that far ahead. Probably—"

Joey stopped and pointed. "Look!" he cried. "There he is!"

The other men whooped, but Billy shushed them. "Don't want him to know we're here."

But it was too late. Lawrie turned to look in their direction, then swung upward at a jog.

Chapter 22

ON THE CHRISTMAS NIGHT NEWS reports, Linda heard only that Jay had gone missing that morning, that the police were still searching, but that no one seemed to have a clue about the circumstances surrounding his disappearance. She checked weather reports in the Plains area and emailed news outlets, hoping for updated information. She even called hospitals and police stations, frightened by what she might learn but needing to at least try.

Finally, she got up, walked from room to room, turned off the tree and window lights, then built a small fire in the living room and sat on the hearth, weeping and praying. She knew nothing except that Jay was in trouble, and only God could find and help him.

That gave her a small measure of comfort.

Billy bit his lip in exasperation. "Let's go. We've got maybe three minutes to get him." He and his son took off on a dead run, clawing their way up the steep, rugged slope. The others did their best, unzipping parkas, but they dropped far behind, gasping for breath. Lawrie, too, was slowing but still scrabbled upward. "You got him in too good shape," Kevin hollered at Nathan, bringing up the rear.

"Billy knows something . . . we don't," said Nathan, breathing hard. "Something . . . not good. Gotta get him . . . before . . . the top."

Up ahead, Billy stopped, chest heaving. "Fifteen seconds. Run, Joey. Take him down!"

The boy took off, shedding his parka, and the distance closed. Lawrie fell to his knees but looked back and got to his feet at a clumsy run. Within seconds, though, Joey was on him and tackled Lawrie's leg until he flipped and fell hard on his back. The boy threw himself across Lawrie's body, his own harsh gasps blending with his father's hoarse rasping directly behind.

Billy was the first to speak. "Blanket." He called to Kevin. "Conserve . . . heat."

Kevin collapsed and clawed at his backpack. "Thermos?"

"Not yet."

Billy shook out the blanket and threw it over Lawrie, who was bellowing, "No! Leave me here!"

Billy grabbed one of his flailing hands and looked close at his fingers. "White, but no frostbite." He put his own warm glove on that hand and inspected the other before transferring his other glove. He checked Lawrie's nose, chin, and ears, then pulled a wool cap from inside his jacket and jammed it on Lawrie's head.

Lawrie's groans turned to wrenching sobs; and when he began gagging, the men rolled him over and got him to his hands and knees.

"Get it out, Lawrie." Nathan gripped his shoulder. "Poison's in there. Get it out. What's deep inside? Glynneth. Your boy. Down in your gut. Get it out. Think Charlotte, Lawrie. She'd be here with you, singing you back."

That brought more dry heaves. He dropped to his elbows, gasping for breath. "Charlotte . . . knows . . . I killed her! She'll never forgive me. I grabbed Glynneth's dress. If I hadn't, she'd 've missed the rock; I wouldn't have landed on her. *I killed her!* Charlotte could never forgive that!"

Billy stood and went to Joey. "Go back for your parka, son, and then—"

"I got it," said Nathan. "Here."

Billy took it and handed it to Joey. "Go uphill. Look at the view. I'll whistle. Stay off the sandstone ledge," he shouted after him. "Not safe." After seeing him out of earshot, he knelt again by Lawrie. "Yah, okay. Keep going."

Lawrie was shivering uncontrollably. Mike started to take off his parka, but Billy shook his head. "Nerves. He's okay—warm from running. I'm watching. Keep going, man. Get it out."

For a moment, everything stood still. Even the coyote howl across the valley hung frozen in the frigid air.

Slowly, it came. "I loved her. I hated her. She *killed* my son. But I loved her. So beautiful. I loved her. I *hated* her. She *killed Ephraim;* and when she saw him dead, she died, too—right there, right then. Never, ever the same. A child . . . addicted to . . . I hated her. I hated God for what she'd become!"

He broke down, head on his arms, weeping uncontrollably. Billy pulled a heavy scarf from his voluminous coat and wrapped Lawrie's neck. "Keep going. Tell it all."

Lawrie continued to sob, his head shaking slowly back and forth. "The whole country died . . . I sank it. The country's . . . going to hell . . . I'm to blame." He stopped.

Nathan gripped him tight. "No. You couldn't bring the country down just by getting hurt and dropping out."

Lawrie lifted his head and bellowed angrily, "No! I didn't die; *that's* the problem!"

The men exchanged puzzled looks. Kevin leaned toward him, but Lawrie went on in a cataract of pain.

"Nels wanted to use me. In a wheelchair, looking pathetic, could get more votes. I wouldn't do it. He lost the election, got mad, and threatened to wreck my life and Linda's if we ever got together." His breath became ragged. "Oh, God, I love her, and You took her away. You took Glynneth; You took the country. Nothing's left! You hate me like I hate Nelson Graham and—"

Billy and Nathan looked at each other and went into action. "Okay, got the picture," said Billy. "Time to get to work." He rolled Lawrie onto his back, tucking the blanket both under and over and repositioning the scarf. "We're going to pray you up and down, but first, a hot drink." He motioned to Kevin, who unscrewed the thermos lid and poured hot apple cider into the cup. "This'll warm you, give you energy. Careful—may be hot."

Lawrie sipped and shivered; and when the cup was empty, he lay back, teeth chattering.

The men knelt on either side of him, all but the Indian shivering. Nathan and Billy laid hands on his head, and Billy started the prayer.

"God, we got our hands on Lawrie, but Your hands have to do the work. His head, Lord, needs cleaning out. Garbage is in there, stinking so bad, he can't stand it. Lord, ream it out."

Nathan took over. "We'd stay longer on his head, Lord. That's where he hurts most, but it's cold out here."

Kevin and Mike put their hands on his chest. "God," said Kevin, "Lawrie needs fire right here. He's messed up, needs to *know,* to *feel* love and forgiveness. Move in on him, Lord. His heart is stone. Warm it. Melt it. Bring it alive."

They moved fervently down his body, praying for his arms and hands, his belly, the daddy seed that was longing for a nurturing place, and his legs and feet and where they should go—politically and otherwise. Lawrie was breathing hard, his body heaving convulsively.

Nathan finished up. "Yahweh, Lord Almighty, You set a bush on fire for Moses. It's cold in this wilderness, and Lawrie needs to feel the heat of Your love, know Your forgiveness. Do as You will. We ask this in—"

Billy cut in. "God, help us get him down before dark. No hypothermia. You can do that, Lord. Thank You. Amen." He stood abruptly and whistled toward the top of the hill.

Joey leaped over the rocks, his own teeth chattering. Billy looked him over closely. "You okay?" He dug keys from his pocket. "Take these, and Kev, give him yours. Run to the cars. Get 'em warmed. Drive 'em if you have to; we'll all need heat. *Ee-yah-yah!* Go. And check gas levels!" he hollered after the boy.

The others had gotten Lawrie to his feet, made him drink more hot cider, and had drunk a little themselves. Lawrie was pale and shivering but had calmed and was looking at the others with what appeared to be a thin ray of gratitude. When he started to walk, though, they saw he would need a man on each side to get him over the rough spots.

The sun set just as they reached the cars. "Lawrie goes in the SUV, back seat," said Billy. "Lay him flat. Get that blanket over him. He'll want to sleep." He looked at Nathan's haggard face, then turned to Joey. *"Chee-kshee,* I want you on the floor by Lawrie. Keep him covered and drinking if he's awake. Anything seems wrong, tell Kev and Mike. Nathan's coming with me."

When they got Lawrie settled and Joey at least semi-comfortable on assorted gear, Kevin and Mike turned to Billy. "What now, you think?"

Billy looked away a moment. "We'll pick up the cars and head for Dickinson, then decide about a motel for the night. Once we get in cell range, we'll contact the police."

"What about Lawrie's car?"

"Nobody'll steal it here. We'll get it later."

Nathan rubbed his face. "Um . . . I'll call Martin but not the police. The police might—"

"Yah—good thinking." Billy nodded. "The cops are way ahead of Martin in tracking cell phones. In you go, man." He shoved Nathan into the truck.

Billy pulled himself behind the wheel and examined Nathan while putting the truck in gear. "You're not much better off than Lawrie, I'd say."

Nathan leaned back, put his hands to his head, and grimaced fiercely against an emotional onslaught.

"You're safe here, buddy. This old truck has seen a lotta weepy Lakota. Y'know, I was almost more worried about you than about Lawrie up there. Didn't know if you'd crash on the hill, and I'd have to haul the two of you down. But if you're gonna crash, here's the place."

Nathan choked out a laugh and batted Billy's arm. "You're an operator, y'know that? I'm . . . grateful." And he slumped into his seat belt and wept.

Chapter 23

ON THE HIGHWAY HEADING TOWARD Dickinson, Billy slammed his brakes and swung onto a road that went south. "I think there's a motel down this way, and who's gonna search for us out here?"

They drove slowly into the small town, and Nathan pointed. "There! That's our place."

The two vehicles pulled up at a low-end motel, located comfortably off the road. The four men got out to discuss the next step. "Another hour-and-a-half and we'd have him home," said Mike. "Wouldn't he be better off in his own bed?"

The men looked at Nathan.

He rubbed his cheek thoughtfully. "The real problem is *getting* him to his own bed. There's Martin, the police, the house staff, family—it's still Christmas, y'know, and they'll all be there. Martin was livid when I told him we might not bring him home tonight. I don't want to put Lawrie through that—not tonight."

"We need to eat, too," said Kevin. "Would make it even later."

"And he needs to talk more," said Billy. "Pretty sure of that."

"You guys have done so much. I hate—" Nathan stopped and studied the gravel driveway. "Why don't you fellows go on home? I'll stay here, get him rested and talked out, and somebody could pick us up tomorrow."

Billy shook his head. "We're not leaving—at least I won't. You guys do what you want. Me and Joey are staying." His face broke into a wide grin. "How about that kid of mine? He left home a cranky boy and is going back a man."

"For sure, he saved Lawrie," said Mike. "None of us could've gotten him in time."

Billy nodded softly. "A God thing . . . and Joey!"

Kevin put a hand on Nathan's shoulder. "My car's stone dead right now. I can feel it."

"I'm in, too," said Mike. "Just need to make a phone call. I doubt the police'll track my phone!" He smiled.

Nathan rubbed his face hard. "Okay," he said finally. "I'll get us a couple of rooms, maybe connected. We'll order in some food, and—"

"It's Christmas, y'know. What's gonna be open?" asked Mike.

Billy blew through his teeth. "God got us this far; He'll dig up some manna."

Linda listened to reports, switching from channel to channel and surfing her laptop for additional information. She sagged with relief when word came of his safety but kept squeezing her hands, sensing more to the story than the reports indicated.

Bonnie called shortly after ten. *"Did I wake you?"*

"No, I'm on the computer." Linda's voice was tight.

"Are you watching? Of course, you are. I thought I'd catch headlines before I went to bed, and there it was. You know he's been found and is probably okay?"

Linda studied the grouping of snowflakes over her desk as they twirled slowly on threads. "Yeah. I saw a short clip saying they didn't know where he was, but that he was reportedly all right." She shivered, the nighttime thermostat having taken over.

"I could come over—maybe take turns watching and sleeping?"

"Thanks, Bon, but sleep is out the window for me. I'll call first thing in the morning—okay?"

"*What actually happened?*" Bonnie's voice spiraled anxiously. "*Nobody is saying anything about that. Was he kidnapped, you think?*"

Linda shrugged, her knuckles white. "Bonnie, we don't know. Maybe tomorrow . . . You go to bed. If I hear anything new, I'll call, no matter what time. Is that okay?"

They got Lawrie under the covers and cranked up the heat. That was the easy part. Food was not to be found anywhere, cooked or uncooked. Mike stepped toward the door. "I'll see if the motel clerk knows any place."

He came back, a woman in tow.

"I was just wonderin' what to do with that full kettle," she said. "We had some friends who couldn't make it last minute, and here I got a gallon of fresh-made chicken soup. How many you got here?" She started counting bodies.

Nathan stepped in front of Lawrie's face to ward off recognition. "One here," he said, motioning behind him, "and five other men." He emphasized the last word and reached over to mess Joey's black hair.

"I'll heat it and bring it in, along with dishes and spoons. Won't take but a minute."

She returned with the stockpot and ladle and set it carefully on the table. "Couldn't carry everything, but one more trip'll do it."

"Can we help?" asked Kevin.

She waved him off and bustled out, returning with spoons, napkins, and a loaf of homemade bread, including a knife and slab of butter.

The men leaned forward, all but drooling.

"Wish I had pie for you all, but what's left of ours wouldn't give you more'n a taste."

"Ma'am," said Mike fervently, "you're God's angel this Christmas day. You couldn'ta come up with a better gift, and there's plenty here! Thank you from the bottom of our empty stomachs!"

She rubbed her hands and looked exceedingly pleased, then backed out and closed the door.

Nathan went to the table and filled a dish. "Okay, Lawrie—you first. Sit up, lad!"

They all dug in; and when their bowls were empty, a soft knock sounded at the door. Kevin moved to open it, with Nathan again hiding Lawrie.

The woman held a fruit in her hand. "I hunted around, but this pomegranate is all's I could find. Maybe if you cut it in six pieces, it'll be kind of a treat. Maybe you don't—"

"Ma'am," said Mike. "What's your name, by the way? We need to mention you to God, tell Him how grateful we are."

She dimpled and shrugged self-consciously. "I'm Sophie, an' my husband's Herb. We been runnin' this motel near twenty-five years an' are mighty glad for you stoppin' by. Not much business on Christmas day."

"Sophie, you keep a good motel here," said Nathan. "Clean as a whistle. And the soup was just what we needed—hot and good. We'll settle up with you tomorrow for that."

"Oh, no!" She waved her hand. "My Christmas present! Don't want no 'settlin' up.' Just want you to . . . " She inspected the table and smiled. "Well, seems you kinda liked the bread, too."

After she left, Mike examined the round globe in his hand. "Okay, what do we do with it?

"It's got red crunchies in it," said Kevin. "I ate some once but don't know how to get at 'em."

Nathan took it from him. "Well, slice it in sixths like she said and go from there. The bread knife ought to work."

They operated on the fruit, getting red juice all over the table. "All right, every man for himself," said Nathan. "Eat the red seeds, not the white stuff."

Lawrie took a slice, but Joey backed off and shook his head. His dad cocked his head. "Give it a try, son. If you don't like it, one of us will finish it."

"Hey! You squirted me!" Mike moved away from Kevin and laughed. "We're a red mess. Look at your face!" He moved toward Kevin and took aim with his next bite. Soon, they were hooting with laughter, and Joey reached for the remaining slice. After a tentative taste, he, too, joined the "Battle of the Pomegranate."

They mopped up as best they could, and Billy said, "We all need a shower. Lawrie, you first," and he pulled off the blanket.

"Why?" Lawrie replied petulantly.

"Well, you're red, too."

"Why am I first? Am I redder or better than the rest of you?" His mouth registered several degrees below a smile.

Billy looked at him. "No games, pal. You know why we're here. No rank allowed. We're all redskins tonight. Plus, I need to see how much blood spurted after Joey's tackle. You landed hard. Ribs hurt again?"

Lawrie slumped. "Nothing broken. Joey did what he needed to." His breath caught as he looked at the boy. "And I'm sorry I made it happen." He stood uncertainly, then shrugged his shoulders. "Okay, shower. Inspect at will." This time he managed a half smile in Billy's direction.

Chapter 24

AFTER CLEANUP, BILLY SENT JOEY off to bed in the adjoining room, and the men settled around Lawrie—Nathan next to him on the room's only chair, Billy at the foot of the mattress, and Mike and Kevin perched on the adjacent bed.

"I got questions, Lawrie, if you're feelin' up to it," said Kevin. "Don't have to answer, but what you say stays here. Not even the guys back home will hear about it." He frowned and leaned to examine Lawrie more closely. "You don't look so good, bro. Want us to buzz off, let you sleep? It's been a day."

Lawrie grunted. "I'm okay. I've got questions, too, but you first."

Kevin searched the flowery bedspread between his knees for his first question. "Linda. I wanna know about her. The two of you were on TV—September, was it? Didn't know you then. And didn't know about your wife and kid, neither. But what came out on the butte put a whole new light on it. Seems Linda messed you up some. You come outta that week loving her—that what you said?"

Lawrie leaned back and studied the rough, water-stained ceiling. "I did," he said finally. "She was everything Glynneth once was—intelligent, fun, interesting—and I realize now she talked to God the same as you do. Didn't seem important then." He paused. "What I didn't tell you was one morning, when she did her Bible thing, she asked me to read the same part that put me on the floor last week."

163

"Hosea. God teaching his son to walk? Whoo! Double jolt."

"I couldn't finish. She covered for me, and that tiny act of compassion—on top of everything else—showed the stark difference between her and my bleak reality at home." He looked away. "I don't know when I first realized we cared for each other; but by week's end, it was pretty obvious, though neither of us said anything. The night before I left, we were both wretched; and walking out her door was one of the hardest things I've ever done."

"Stupid question," said Mike, "but here goes. Glynneth's dead. Nothin' anyone can do about that, so why wouldn't you pick up again with Linda?"

"Huh! Our names would be slime, even if I quit politics, and she quit gardening. Any hint of a continuing relationship would clang the sex-scandal bell again." His voice took an edge. "Believe me, I've asked countless times: why not drop out of the Senate and get on with life? If it were just me, I'd take the garbage and live with it happily, but I *will not allow that to happen to her.* Too many people out there waiting for one of us to make a move."

His eyes sought refuge in the cheap painting on the opposite wall—a tree-sheltered farmhouse and barn on the right, round hay bales stacked nearby. To the left, cattle were grazing at the base of a windmill water pump. In the foreground, feathery slough grass whitened a saucer of bottomland. Pastoral, calming—but behind the scene, a large wind turbine spread its arms like some foreboding angel. Lawrie shivered. "Political dragons can be ruthless."

Kevin shifted his leg and the subject. "We heard a lotta other hate/love stuff on the butte—love/hate Glynneth, hate Graham, hate God. You thinkin' God hates you?"

Lawrie sagged on the pillows, confusion seizing his eyes. "I don't know what to think. What you did up there . . . Not just pulling me down. That was big, and I hated you for it. But then you laid me out. I don't know what happened. Somehow, as you moved down my body . . . " He laughed awkwardly. "Y'know, if Linda had been watching, she'd 've pointed her finger and said, 'See what those guys are doing? That's an *unpresentable glory*'—like she said on TV about holding a jar for me." He rubbed his frown, his voice sounding perplexed. "What she said about *unpresentable glory* was itself unpresentable. Caused a rumpus, y'know, and only Martin was able to work it out. Not sure why she said it, but just watching her . . . " He chewed his thumb, then laughed humorlessly. "*Unpresentable . . .* "

Kevin leaned back reflectively. "I like that. *Unpresentable glory.* A Bible verse. Corinthians, is it?"

"No clue, but what you guys did up and down my body was way too unpresentable." He grinned. "Do that in my church, they'd toss you out."

Nathan chuckled. "Ever notice that God staged His really odd things outdoors? Jacob wrestling an angel, God knocking Moses flat in front of a burning bush—that sort of unpresentable stuff."

"Burning! That's it!" Lawrie sat up straight. "Cold as I was, I could feel heat or buzzing, like an electrical current. Got my attention, for sure. It was strong . . . scary. *What was it?*" He looked at each man, his body pleading for an answer.

The men leaned forward, eyes wide and questioning. Nathan started to speak, but Billy raised his hand. "Did it feel good, Lawrie, or did you want to get away from it? Saying it different, would *love* or *hate* best describe it?"

Lawrie sank back and laughed. "You guys! You shot love at me from the start, but it missed, or I was too good at ducking. Today, I couldn't duck. Yes, it was love—right inside my body." He struggled, but his voice wouldn't remain steady. "For the first time in my life, God was . . . real."

He stopped, eyes wide. "No. One other time. In the hospital." He licked moisture onto his lips. "Linda came. I don't know how, but she was there."

"To *Bismarck*?"

"Yes. She read from a piece of paper. 'Comfort those who mourn, provide for those who grieve. Beauty instead of ashes, oil of gladness, garment of praise'—something like that. And this: 'They'll be called oaks of righteousness, plants of the Lord for the display of his splendor.'"

"Isaiah," murmured Kevin.

Lawrie gritted his teeth. "She left that paper, and I kept it but deliberately didn't take it today."

"You walked away, but God wouldn't let go."

Again, Lawrie's face distorted, but he started laughing. "Yah, sent the tribe after me! He was real because you're real. Even Joey bringing me down. God said, 'Stop, stupid!'"

Mike got up and went to the temperature control on the far side of Lawrie's bed. "Anybody mind if I turn this down?"

Billy leaned toward Lawrie. "You'd've gone off the bluff, wouldn't you?"

"Yah, but maybe not right then. When I saw you, it pushed me like I pushed Glynneth until—"

Billy cut through. "It came down to seconds—that close. Thank you, Lord—*pee-lah-mah-yea*—for *perfect* timing!"

Nathan gripped Lawrie's arm. "You thanked me . . . just before I left yesterday. You knew then, didn't you? You even let me hug you. I didn't expect that."

With a soft, desolate cry, Lawrie leaned toward Nathan and punched his chest hard. He grabbed him fiercely, and the two wept unashamedly.

Billy put a hand on each head. "Merry Christmas," he said softly.

They all slept as though dead, and once they had "settled up" with Sophie and Herb, pleading the juice-wrecked room, the men parted with long, earnest hugs. Joey backed off, but Lawrie went to him, outstretched hand morphing into a quick hug.

"Hey, Hunkpapa kid, I owe you! And with some serious aches to remind me, I won't soon forget. Are we pals?"

Joey smiled shyly and leaned into the hug.

Lawrie was quiet on the drive home, but as they entered Mandan, he stared straight ahead and said, "A week from today I'll be heading back to D.C., and I want you with me for at least two weeks."

"Whoa!" said Nathan. "That's pretty abrupt." He laughed. "How long has that idea been percolating?"

"Longer than you think." His jaw shifted into a smile of sorts. "Linda got trapped by Ewen. She could've just said, 'Talk to Senator Crofter about it,' but she stood up, did the hard thing, laid the groundwork for me. I should've told Martin right off when I got home but didn't, and she's the one who got smacked in the face. I can't even apologize to her, but I can honor her name in private and live my life in the hidden shadow of that—one more *unpresentable* thing." He grinned at Nathan. "I can go to Washington, be the best senator I know how to be, and carry her name and piece of paper with me forever. And, by the way," he went on, "it's safe to call off the suicide watch. Martin won't need backup anymore." His smile morphed to residual pain.

"Yup. You're over that hump. But speaking of Martin, be warned: When we get to the house, I expect pandemonium. I'll run interference and get you to your bedroom, pleading aches and pains from an unanticipated fall." He grinned sideways. "Once you're out of the way, I'll tackle the horde and deal with the police and the media's friendly attentions."

"Nathan, it's taken me awhile to see it, but let me say it now: you're worth ten times your weight in camels!"

Chapter 25

THE STORY CAME OUT IN bits and pieces. On Christmas Day, the news had been scanty. All that was covered was that he was gone and that an all-points bulletin had been in force.

Evening reports revealed that Lawrie had been located in Theodore Roosevelt National Park and was safe.

The morning broadcasts added that a friend had followed him Christmas Day, locating him with difficulty, and because of frigid temps and a fall that had injured the senator somewhat, the two had opted for a stay in Dickinson. The authorities had spoken with him when he arrived home and were assured of his safety. Then came Martin's short squib, noting that Lawrie seemed all right, though tired and sore from his mishap.

"The good news is," Martin said with a lift in his voice, "Senator Crofter will be returning to Washington right after New Year's to resume his duties in the Senate. This little adventure seems to have given him the space he needed to make his decision."

Lawrie listened with Nathan, away from the group clustered in the TV room. After they had mined all versions of the report, from *MSNBC* to *Fox News*, Lawrie pushed the remote and swiveled around with an amused grin.

"Nathan, you're a wonder! You protected the guys; you protected Sophie and Herb; you protected me. Well done! I know Martin hammered you, but you stood up and had him mouthing platitudes about my little adventure." Then his face darkened. "I can't go to Bible study this week. I can't put the men at risk."

"You've been going regularly. It's not like something unusual."

"There's Ewen. Don't ever forget Ewen. He's out there, and I'd bet the lead crystal that this story will have him snuffling for truffles and that he knows where to dig. I will not give him any leads. Maybe someday I'll think differently about him, but not now . . . not now."

Linda was relieved by the morning news. When Martin Walsh spoke, she leaned forward, grasping the importance of his position. She was heartened by Jay's surprising decision to return to D.C. but couldn't help but feel that layers of the story remained beneath the surface.

Martin worked hard to persuade Lawrie that Nathan was no longer needed and should not accompany them to Washington. Nathan said nothing and sat back to watch the two lock horns. He had privately released Lawrie to go without him if that was best but had said nothing to Martin.

Lawrie, surprisingly, refused to battle. Ignoring the perfect storm of dust and thunder that followed him around, he made phone calls, sent emails, got out suitcases, touched base at his offices in Bismarck, Fargo, Minot, and Grand Forks. Yes, he'd have a huge backload of work but saw it as a welcome change from his black hole. Martin was an annoying fly, but swatting flies was one of Lawrie's skills.

On Saturday, he pulled Nathan out the door, away from the chaos, and headed for a faded eatery and its blue-collar clientele. The jovial grill comptroller bellowed a greeting.

"You boys both want American chop?"

"He doesn't know it yet," said Lawrie, "but he'll like it."

Nathan scanned the diner. "You come here often?" he asked incredulously.

Lawrie chuckled wryly. "Often enough to escape the mad, mad world."

But while they waited, Nathan watched Lawrie's face turn morose. "What's going on, bro?"

A hard-faced waitress plunked down heaped platters of the beef-pasta-tomato combo. "Anything else?"

"No. Looks good. Thank you."

Lawrie took a bite before replying to Nathan. "I don't know what's going on. After the motel, I felt almost whole."

"But now?" Nathan prompted.

"Now . . . I've got questions—shapeless, dark, threatening."

"You changing your mind about D.C.?"

"No. That's one thing I feel sure about. And, yes—" He grinned. "I still want you with me. I'm ready to pick up the pieces and do what I'm good at. The horror show's behind me. You guys pulled its teeth, and I'm grateful, but . . . " He studied the counter population for help in articulating the stubbornly inexpressible.

Nathan wiped his mouth with the cheap napkin. "Maybe Washington will answer some questions."

Martin continued to natter, but in the end, Lawrie made his decree. Two SUVs would go ahead with assorted helpers, books, files, equipment, and personal effects, and the three men would fly to D.C. On hearing the edict, Martin stopped harping and started bringing order to the maelstrom.

Their actual leave-taking was more traumatic than Lawrie had expected. Unwanted memory shards sliced his resolve, especially of Charlotte, who had been his life support in that household for three years. Where was she? Why had she abandoned him? He'd give anything to hear her soft *Mistuh*.

Lawrie's unresolved feelings put him in a foul mood, Martin and Nathan being the unfortunate targets. Martin flailed back, but Nathan remained calm under the familiar feel of Lawrie's anger.

On reaching Washington, they went to the Russell Senate Building and were greeted warmly by staff and well-wishers, including a number of Democrat senators and representatives, some of whom had opposed Lawrie fiercely.

"Winners can afford to be charitable," Lawrie noted sardonically to Nathan.

Martin, after his pro-forma faceoff with Connie, Lawrie's Chief of Staff, busied himself tidying the senator's office and integrating staff, some of whom were new. Lawrie managed sufficient politeness to introduce Nathan to key players, who earnestly welcomed this alternative to his *aide de camp*.

But the peace treaty didn't last, and the two battled over Lawrie's decision to forego his apartment and sleep in his "hideaway" office in the Senate wing of the Capitol.

"Mine's not grand like some of them but has a couch and lavatory. That's all I need. And a window. Some are just closet-sized boxes."

"You're kidding!" Nathan stared at him, astounded. "*Secret* offices? Is this for real?"

Lawrie shrugged. "Long history here. The rooms are basically odd spaces tucked behind statuary or tourist corridors, convenient to the chambers and hush-hush. A great place to hole up."

Nathan's back went up. "I don't care how convenient it is. You *will not* sleep in an office, no matter how grand." His eyes became dual exclamation points. "Let's go put your apartment to rights."

Lawrie huffed. "Didn't expect you to like the idea, but this is my turf, and I get to call the shots." He stalked out of the office, then halted in the marble hallway at the first door of his nine-room suite, the only entrance that stood open. He chewed his cheek indecisively, then turned in. "Might as well meet the welcomers," he said, arranging pleasantries on his face and voice.

Nathan stopped, astonished—a full-sized bison head on the left wall, bighorn sheep and pheasant to the right, and a cougar behind him. "This is your *welcoming* staff?"

"Yah. Those are the friendly ones." He turned and pointed to a trio of computer stations. "Now, these guys," he said, "they look you up and down, check your genealogy, and require you to state your business in ten words or fewer. Janis here—" He reached out a hand and drew her into a hug. "She's my first line of defense. Davis over there is Deputy Scheduler, and on the left is probably an intern who snuck in while I wasn't looking."

"Richard Cassidy, sir," and he shook Lawrie's hand.

"Richard the Lion-Hearted, undaunted by bison breath." Lawrie nodded at the head towering above. "Glad to meet you."

The two left the Russell Building and headed for Lawrie's apartment, which Nathan approved and set about organizing. "Better, for sure," he said after stowing the last empty suitcase.

Lawrie's jaw jutted, but he opened kitchen cupboards to inventory staples.

During the next few days, Nathan compiled a list of churches that sounded promising and talked with Congress members who acknowledged being Christian. These, in turn, led him to a number of Bible studies, one of which he recommended to Lawrie as they ate sandwiches in the apartment.

"I don't need a group down here," said Lawrie. "I have you guys at home, and—"

"Come on, Lawrie. How often will you see us? These fellows are into unanswerable questions."

"But I—"

"Just listen, okay? I talked with two of the men—Chase and Lucas—and they convinced me. I told them a little about you but only bare bones. It's no-nonsense, and they far outweigh us in brainpower. You need accountability right now. At least give them a try."

"Nathan, I don't *want* accountability right now. I need to catch up where I left off in August. And stop trying to 'organize' my life, as well as my apartment."

"Look. You invited me along; now put up with me."

Lawrie looked at Nathan, anger shifting to panic. With elbows on the table, he tipped his head and pulled at his hair.

"Lawrie, you're scared. God touched you on the butte, and you're afraid He'll do it again. And here I am, expecting you to walk on water, and you'd rather not right now, thank you. Am I right?"

Lawrie rose from the table and poured two cups of coffee. After putting down Nathan's cup, Lawrie continued holding his, then placed it carefully, as though sound of any sort might destroy the moment. He sank onto his chair.

"Nathan, I'm blind and groping, with nightmares as my only entertainment. Last night, it was Linda, not Glynneth, on the rocks, snow covering her body. Pallbearers carried her off." He slurped his coffee cautiously. "My only peace is my senate office. I'm at home there. I can handle that part of life. But this part . . . You want me to 'walk on water'—your words. It's madness, and I can't do it!" Again, panic burned his eyes.

"You can. You just don't know it yet. The God of the butte is the God of Chase and Lucas. They'll hold you up."

Nathan, in turn, fought against staying for the inauguration, but Lawrie insisted.

"This is a once-in-a-lifetime opportunity. Anybody can come and stand a mile away in the bitter cold, but you'll be seated and blanketed as necessary. Besides, I need you here."

His pleading eyes won the battle, but the only seat Lawrie could find for Nathan was one that Martin had ordered for a friend. When the friend became ill, Martin offered it to Nathan with a semblance of grace.

Chapter 26

AFTER THE INAUGURATION, LAWRIE SETTLED into a routine of committee meetings, conferences, strategy sessions, and of course, regular appearances in the senate chamber. He never missed a session, his long lapse needing to be seen in past tense. He camped on the phone with staff in the four home offices—Bismarck, Fargo, Minot, and Grand Forks. On television, his recovery from the tragedy drew interest—and again raised the speculation on his presidential potential. Adrenalin buoyed him through these venues, and other than marked weight loss, he appeared normal.

The mentoring group Nathan had selected was something else. No-nonsense men—three Republican congressmen and two Democrats, a judge, three businessmen, plus two local pastors. Serious Christians, they immediately zeroed in on the new guy in the box.

After his third session with them, Lawrie called Nathan. "After my first inning with the 'Big Boys,' I was sure you'd bobbled the ball."

"And your more seasoned assessment?"

"I'm lucky to be alive! They picked up on my obsession over the failed election bringing the whole country down. Well! The two Dems climbed all over me, 'audacious' being their kindest word. 'So, in your mind,' they said, 'President Hanily and his minions—including us Democrats—will not only bring the country down, but the whole world, as well. And do I hear you thinking, *Christian Democrat* is an oxymoron?'"

"Whoo! What did I get you into?"

"That's not all. Chase says I'm government. I write laws, pull strings that serve my party and career, he says, but I'll never be an effective senator unless I'm under God's governance. How's that for pruning political feathers?"

"They're fearless. We got you at low tide when you weren't exactly intimidating."

"Well, they were sort of pulling my leg, but it helped put things in perspective. And today, Judge Albert hammered home number six of his Ten Governmental Commandments: 'Thou shalt not paint thy political opponent in lurid colors, neither shalt thou whitewash thine own position.' These fellows don't mess around! Have to admit, Nathan, it's the right bunch. Six men *volunteered* as my accountability group, and in twenty minutes, they had everything they needed to know about me in plain view on the table. Couldn't hide a crumb." Lawrie laughed.

"They talk heavy stuff," he went on. "Cultural views of morality, the frog in boiling water concept . . . This is *Bible study* conversation! Nathan, I've always related well to 'religious' people—a point of pride. You guys knocked that apart. These fellows brought me down fast, but they're teaching me how to plug Scripture into real-life issues."

Lawrie was silent a moment. Then, "Nathan, they're showing me how to hang out with God. You started it, but this is a whole new world. They put me on a money diet. Live on my senatorial salary alone—subtracting a ten-percent tithe that increases a point each year."

"Well . . . "

"Well, pretty Spartan, but they live it. We met one night at Albert's house. Swankier than you guys up there, but incredibly modest here. He and his wife sold their big house to free up money. 'Live poor, give rich,' he says. But they take care of me without reserve—my congressional nannies. And they want me in a ministry to soon-to-be-released prisoners and/or teach hockey to at-risk kids."

"That'll get you down to street level."

"Street level I manage pretty well, but this is subterranean stuff—a whole new language."

"My friend, I think that group of yours is worth its weight in camels!"

Lawrie badly wanted to teach hockey, but afternoon sessions wouldn't work for him, so he entered prison—apprehensively—and felt upside down in this unknown world. A couple prisoners recognized him, but most couldn't care less that he was a U.S. senator. That he listened, asked questions, and seemed friendly satisfied them.

One scraggy, knobby-faced Hispanic caught his interest when Lawrie learned he'd been a gardener. *"Sí,* I grow up working San Juan Botanical Garden, also Montoso Gardens with *mi papi."*

"Ah! Puerto Rico," commented Lawrie.

"Sí. I come the States, find job at Chicago Botanic, first just cleanup guy but they find out I know plants. They make me planting supervisor and soon come ask *me* questions!" His back straightened, and a grin raised new facial lumps.

Lawrie asked more questions and learned he would be released within a week. "Any job prospects yet?"

The Hispanic curled into a disheartened slump, and Lawrie put a hand on his shoulder and prayed that God would open the right door at the exact time he needed it.

With catch-up work heavy on him, Lawrie remained in D.C., not returning home on weekends. His assigned committees—Indian

Affairs; Agriculture, Nutrition, and Forestry; Budget; and Energy and Natural Resources—required far more input than he'd anticipated. With the party shift in the Senate election, he found himself once again both Ranking Majority Member and Chairman of Indian Affairs, despite his long absence.

He even stayed for the February State Work Week and holed up to call constituents who had phoned or emailed. The two weeks of spring recess served as a golden lantern at the far end of his tunnel.

Anticipating this break helped him handle his three teams—administrative, legislative, and communication—going over pending bills with his legislative assistants. That, plus endless wrangling over a Natural Resources bill that had passed the House but not the Senate and was now in Conference. And somehow, on top of all that, he managed to fit in pesky television appearances. He confronted top-cat Connie and Ben, his scheduler.

"Are you guys beating the bushes for *opportunities*?" he asked. "This isn't an election year. I don't have to be the jolly face everyone goes to sleep on."

"Oh, no," said Connie with a mock frown, "we wake people up with you. And while you don't need a swelled head—" Putting a forefinger on his chest, she gave him the *stare* over her glasses. "We are, in fact, turning down all manner of interviews, press conferences, early breakfasts, and late-night talk shows. Get used to it. And the upside is you have no time for idle mischief."

Inwardly, Lawrie bowed daily to Connie and Ben, both of whom helped him prioritize and focus. Though Connie seemed always in his face, he knew without a doubt that she was the caring and unyielding bedrock beneath his political feet. Her "sex-scandal eye" never closed. If a woman—any woman—was alone with Lawrie in his office, she would make unprogrammed entrances for whatever contrived purpose, and word got around.

Martin was harder to appreciate, but he served as Lawrie's chief aide and utility man—his fullback in the political floor game.

Lawrie found the congressional "saddle" still comfortable. He breathed the air comfortably and felt the old exhilaration in the war of political wills. Before the election debacle, he had gloried in felt power; now, his focus had shifted to a different sort of Power.

"Get out there," Nathan told him over the phone, *"and raise a little dust!"*

Chapter 27

IN LATE WINTER, AFTER A warm spell had taken down most of the heavy snow pack, Linda walked outside to the hard, flat, comatose lawn that lay breathless, waiting for new growth to pump life into its cells and arteries. Winter remained sullen and frowning atop the bleak landscape, but Linda knew that spring would come. If only she could transplant that kind of certainty into her own bleakness. *Plow the soil of my soul, Lord; make me a fruitful vine.*

She jumped between the internet and television channels to watch Jay speak, sometimes against the iconic backdrop of the Capitol building, but especially on talk shows. He always appeared relaxed and ready with answers, but she saw—or imagined—things beneath the surface. He had lost weight. She noted his body language with hostile pundits. While he remained calm and ready to smile or joke, he shifted to patterns she came to recognize.

His eyes had changed for the better. No phony, on-call expressions for whatever platform; they now seemed alive and genuine. She wondered at that. Pain still skittered through eye and body talk, but what had been going on since his terrible tragedy?

Friendly venues were fun to watch. Sometimes, the conversation would shift to the aftershocks of Graham's unexpected defeat, the host lobbing softball questions. Follow-up remarks often explored possible presidential aspirations. Jay would laugh self-deprecatingly over his dusty prophet capabilities. Then he'd shift back to pain, which Linda found emotionally hard to watch.

"Yes, I've walked a dark valley, but many others are stuck in seemingly impossible situations, not able to crawl out as I have. I'm here for them, to get them safely past dragons and snares. I'm here to serve—not myself, not even the party, but the people of North Dakota and the United States of America—so help me God."

He's made for this, thought Linda. *A strong, but engaging politician with no trace of phoniness. God help him!*

As she pushed the remote and watched the television screen darken, sadness brought its own pall. Lawrie seemed to be doing well. Did he ever think of her in odd moments? That unauthorized visit in the hospital could well have soured him or even blocked all memory of her. But now that Glynneth was dead . . .

Now that Glynneth was dead . . . Lawrie sat on this thorn every day, sometimes hourly. Not as a gleam of hope, but as a driving curse on any chance he might have at happiness. His immediate line of defense against his inner longing for Linda was his iron-clad determination to protect her, whatever the cost to himself. The media had threatened him. Nelson Graham had threatened him, but the presidential candidate was little more than a blow-hard, especially when viewed against Ewen MacClerhan—a viper, a black mamba, whose crafty schemes could unleash far-reaching damage. He personified evil, but Lawrie had steel in his backbone against the combined threats.

The bigger threat to eventual happiness was his own part in his wife's death. His body had killed Glynneth, but had his heart participated in her death? At first, this inner indictment was an inchoate concept—one he could not articulate, let alone express, even to Nathan. Yes, dragons were there, ready to swallow both him and Linda, but the fiery breath of his own complicity formed an impenetrable wall against any hope of their ever reconnecting. Glynneth was dead, but had he wished it so?

Adrenalin was both fuel and refuge for Lawrie. It got him where he needed to go, past multiple dragons and snares to the brink of exhaustion. His Bible study men got on him for wearing his senator suit even to bed.

"You're killing yourself, Lawrie," said Chase. "Your armor is six inches thick. Not even David and his sling could bring you down."

"Ha!" said Lawrie. "David wasn't up against President Hanily and a hostile Congress. Next to them, Goliath was a piece of cake."

Chase took a big breath. "All right, if you can't let up everyday stuff, then knock off prison ministry, at least for a few weeks. Yes, I know—" He grinned and waved his hand at the hardening on Lawrie's face. "You'd swap us any day for the prison guys!"

"You betcha! You fellows chew me up and spit me out. They just love on me and don't care what I say."

Those men did love him, and he knew it. They managed to wrap every bit of Scripture around his heart and liver and made him say—out loud, slowly and painfully—how it applied to him in the Senate, on television, with his constituents, and with his money. When Lawrie grumbled about the endless mountain range on his immediate landscape, Albert cocked his head with a wry smile.

"We teach mountain climbing here. We're your practice wall, hand and footholds in easy reach. We hold safety ropes so you don't get hurt when you fall. Not if you fall, but *when*. You'll come to cliffs that only you can climb, but right now, we coach hand-holds and pitons for cracks. God, though, holds ropes that are truly safe."

When Lawrie called Nathan that night, he reported the conversation and said, "I needed to hear that."

"Safety ropes. I like it! Write it on your forehead."

"Nathan . . . " Long silence.

"Yah?"

"I owe you an apology, and I don't know how to make it adequate."

"For what?"

"What d'you mean 'for what?' I dragged you through hell and back—before Christmas, after Christmas. And I didn't even recognize it till tonight as the guys were talking. You accompanied a *somewhat* improved version of Lawrie to D.C., but I stayed stinkingly obnoxious. You patiently dusted me off and handed me over to these spiritual Goliaths. Nathan, I'm sorry I gave you so much grief, and if you were here, I'd bow down, head to the floor, and say it five times."

"Apology accepted, but those guys of yours got work to do in the matter of bowing down to anyone. God alone, bro; God alone."

After he hung up, Lawrie sat for a long time. He had confessed to Nathan—and almost felt guilty about how easy that apology had been. Could he even speak his other guilt? He had spoken his responsibility for the lost election, but the other offense . . .

Dear Jay,

We have finally reached High Spring here in Abington after a difficult winter, and you can interpret that any way you choose.

When I set out in my car early this morning, God, the Artist, lured my mind away from winter, and I gloried in the pastel wash of yellows and greens across the hillsides. I'm now on a college campus not noted for architectural excellence, but its landscaping shows promise, and that, of course, is why I'm here, waiting to give a lecture. At this time of year, almost any landscape looks good—bulbs, early azaleas, the multihued yellows of daffodils, forsythia and weeping willows. But most of all, I'm drinking in the fair green of new, unmown grass. And maples. Oh, those glorious maples! The reds are, of course, first to bloom but last to turn green. Right now, they are nearly as brilliant as in the fall. But I'm on a bench under a Norway maple. Later, I'll have to point out its status as a despicable invasive, but now, I'm being attacked by its heavy scent—almost fatally so. Down the path in front of me is a row of mature sugar maples—stately and magnificent in lace-fringed bridal finery. My heart aches.

I call this High Spring because winter's death has been conquered—if only for a brief moment. Death's sword will soon leave its mark, first with daffodils, then forsythia, and of course, tree blossoms that quickly carpet the ground. But for now, I can drink in the sights and smells of God's High-Spring artistry. But even with the onset of death, spring itself will carry on. Trees will leaf out; lilacs will attack me; and toads will trill just a few feet from the gazebo, again binding my heart unbearably tight.

I know Washington, D.C., is beautiful in the spring, and North Dakota must have its spring beauty, as well, though perhaps not so glorious as ours. I'm quite sure, however, that North Dakotans welcome any sort of spring more earnestly than the rest of us do. My spring lacks just one thing, one person . . . But now I must go indoors and give a dry, dusty lecture on the importance and diversity of soil bacteria. Did you know that an acre of soil can host one ton of bacteria?

I wish you a Happy Spring.

Kileenda

In the kitchen that evening, Linda gathered a handful of paper scraps she normally would have recycled and took them to the fireplace. After touching them off, she opened her notebook, read the letter one last time, then ripped it out and laid it carefully on top of the sputtering fire.

Chapter 28

EWEN MACCLERHAN INVADED LINDA'S WORLD yet again, and again she was furious. *Why* was he picking on her? This time, it couldn't be lust for headlines. What nationally known reporter would waste even five minutes on an obscure gardener such as Jorge Degas? The only reason Linda could conceive was his desire to destroy her—personally.

Jorge had been Linda's head gardener for five years. They had worked reasonably well together, and he and his crew put in countless hours getting her garden into top form for the annual garden tour. It wasn't just planting and weeding. He thought beyond routine to new plants and how they'd work in the overall design.

Jorge, though, was an autocrat and had challenged her authority on several occasions. Most of his demands were reasonable, and his crew worked tirelessly under his supervision. Linda had thanked God often for such a professional. Her gardening friends envied her, one even trying to coax him away. Jorge simply sniffed at the offer.

This time, Ewen worked from afar, and Linda learned about it only after Jorge barged into the house and blasted her, mostly in Spanish, but with enough English for her to understand that someone had accused her of hiring illegals. He left in a huff, calling down cumulative curses on her head for what she had done to him and to his reputation.

Ewen's connection did not surface right away, but she soon learned he had filed a report in a free, local newspaper—an act that could only be construed as malicious. She stomped off the deck, kicked a pile of dirt by one of the double-digs and bellowed, *"AAARGHHH!"*

But was the report true, or had Ewen manufactured it just to heap on more dirt? She went to the Immigration and Customs Enforcement website and made a few phone calls after clicking *Report Suspicious Activity*. What she learned demolished her people-reading confidence. Ewen had, indeed, done his homework in fingering Jorge's helpers as undocumented residents. They had worked as hard as or harder than Jorge; they were polite and cheerful; and as far as Linda knew, they kept their noses clean elsewhere. Definitely Dreamers. But Jorge had assured her he would not stoop to illegal hiring. That hurt, as she had trusted him with free access to the house, even when she was not at home.

Without Jorge, Linda could not possibly participate in the annual garden tour. Not only were major beds being re-dug, but Jorge's system also went with him—as had, she was finding, some valuable plants and tools. This made her even angrier. Items had disappeared off and on, but Jorge's explanations of breakage or theft out of his truck had seemed reasonable, considering his business sources and best-price venues.

After a half day of strewing anger over her lawn like fertilizer, Linda punched her cell phone. "Bonnie, can you come over? I'm in trouble and need you to help me think straight."

"Are you all right—as in not hurt?"

"I'm all right—just steaming. You're working, I know, and this could wait till—"

"Either Judy can come for a couple of hours, or I'll hang my *Closed* sign and come right away."

Bonnie arrived a half-hour later and immediately made two cups of Linda's least favorite tea—Bitter Peace. "Yes, it's yucky, but the herbs are calming, and you need that—obviously. Now, drink it, and tell me what's going on. Is this about Jorge? Last night, you weren't sure what was happening."

Linda dumped her load. Why would Jorge betray her like that? When his helpers had come, he had sworn to their legality.

"But that's not all," she went on. "I can't prove it, but a lot of small stuff—plants, tools—have been disappearing. In an operation this big, you lose things, and I don't keep track of every last seed flat."

"What happens if you're convicted of hiring illegals? What's the penalty?"

"I don't know. Do it deliberately—maybe prison. Unintentional? Probably a misdemeanor and maybe a hefty fine." Linda fished out her Bitter Peace bag and tossed it. "But that's the least of my worries. *Ewen!*" She spat out the word. "*Why* would he do this to me? Certainly not for headlines. This is a deliberate, malicious act against me and against hard-working Hispanics, who may have taken advantage but weren't doing any harm."

"Sounds like Jorge took more than advantage. What's the value of the goods he may have lifted?"

Linda sighed. "I don't have proof of theft, and if I throw that in the pot, it'll only make matters worse. I *liked* Jorge. Well . . . we managed and together made a pretty good garden."

"There are other gardeners out there."

"Right. I should go steal one?"

"No! That's not what I meant. Go online. Search for gardeners looking for work."

"What good will it do? There's no way I can get my garden any-where near tour standards. You have to communicate your vision, train and hover over each helper—to say nothing of checking and rechecking their legal status. Bonnie, I can't do all that. Just the thought . . . " She sighed and rubbed her temples. "We were double-digging some beds. Holes are everywhere. The greenhouse is a total mess. It's impossible! Did Ewen simply want to hang me on a clothesline for public view? Is this Round Two in his "Unfinished Business" folder? Whatever possessed him?"

Bonnie pulled food from Linda's refrigerator and insisted she eat a little. Then she got paper and pen and drew columns and started making lists of what needed to be done. On seeing the stark reality, Linda began melting down, but Bonnie just said, "We have to deal with this," and kept writing. At the end of the exercise, she agreed with Linda that a tour this summer was out of the question but insisted that finding a permanent gardener—not a temp—was top priority. "There are people out there. Does it have to be a man? Could a woman do the heavy work?"

"I've always worked with men and know how they operate, but if the right woman came along, we could hire some backs for heavy lifting. Bonnie, what would I do without you?" She leaned over and gave her friend a quick hug. "You've forced me to look at the big picture and think methodically. A lot of work—"

"A lot of prayer, I'm saying!"

"Yes. Thank you. I needed to hear that, especially tonight."

Chapter 29

SPRING RECESS FINALLY ARRIVED, AND Lawrie was ready for it. His Beltway study group had been after him. "Work is your escape," they said. "It keeps your mind busy till you collapse in bed. What happens then?"

He could not answer, not out loud. Yes, he was exhausted, but even that wasn't enough to beat back the dragons lying in wait. Linda . . . Charlotte . . . Ewen the Sinister. And Glynneth—double underlined in his mind. Had he been avoiding going to Bismarck for fear of that black hole?

Then, too, he didn't want to risk connecting with his guys back there. He could meet Nathan safely, and he phoned the others frequently, but it wasn't the same. His Washington group had served him well, but the men back home were bone of his bone, flesh of his flesh. They had loved him and saved his life in twenty different ways. But he could not, would not subject them to dangerous publicity.

Nathan picked him up at the airport. "No Martin?" he asked.

"No. He chose to stay—thank goodness."

Nathan slammed the rear hatch and got in the car. As the engine started, he looked at Lawrie. "This may be a dumb question, but why do you put up with Martin? Yah, he's good at what he does, but couldn't you find someone more . . . *likeable?*"

Lawrie laughed ruefully. "I inherited him from my father. In the years before he packed on tonnage, he was bright, a quick study, and invaluable. When I started sniffing political air, Dad pushed him in my direction, and I've been stuck ever since. He doesn't like me anymore than I like him, but he does like important coattails."

"Changing the subject," Nathan said, "what's your schedule these two weeks? I assume you have some constituent work across the state. But you do need to rest. You look awful, you know."

Lawrie made a face. "Thanks, friend. Yah, gotta stop pushing, for sure, but just saying it adds another layer of stress." He stared at the line of red taillights exiting the airport. He turned to Nathan with a crooked smile. "Any ideas?"

"As a matter of fact, yes. And if you got constituents who need visiting where I'm thinking, it could be a double dipper. There's this neat, guy restaurant in the boonies, northwest. Serves bison, elk, rattlesnake, and anything else they can get away with."

"Which direction? Mountrail County, maybe?"

"Yah, maybe. Not sure where it's at."

"Mountrail is reeling under assorted pressures—cultural change with the influx of oil outsiders, failing schools, even sex trafficking."

"Never mind the table of contents. Give me a date, and I'll give you the time we need to be at the restaurant. If you want, we can get a couple of rooms in a motel and just play up there a day or two. Half a day of work, a day and a half just banging around. I'll be Martin for you and make all the arrangements."

"Oh, *please* . . ."

Mountrail County wasn't much. It had some oil, a lot of farming, and a fair amount of poverty, even with the oil boom. It also had a high Native American population. The only tourist attraction was Mountrail County Courthouse. They drove . . . and drove

. . . off the U.S. highway, off the county road heading north, off the county road heading west, off a bypass road, and through a small hamlet that served as the focal point of surrounding farmland. From there, a dirt road led to Lost Elk Grotto, a dark, scruffy hangout that had an air of *men only* about it. Although no sensible elk would wander close to that area, enormous elk racks decorated the exterior. As remote as the place was, a number of trucks and jeeps sat comfortably in the sizeable parking lot.

"How'd you find this?" asked Lawrie with awe-filled voice.

"Wasn't easy." Nathan laughed. "But word gets around the guy network. Let's go in."

The indoor décor was equally inspiring, with crossbows and additional racks competing for every empty space. Full-spread turkey tails provided artistic accent. The magnum opus, a deer-antler chandelier, hung noticeably off-center. Lawrie shook his head. "The only improvement would be guns hanging off every light fixture," said Lawrie.

Nathan laughed. "If that were legal," he said, "I'm sure they'd do it. They do hold archery contests almost every week, though." He smiled, then turned as a man in a plaid shirt and greasy jeans came from what they took to be the kitchen area.

"Hey there! You must be Chuck." Nathan stuck out his hand. "I called last week about your private room?"

Chuck's eyes crinkled, and he glanced at a door on the far side of the dining room. "Been expectin' you. Come right along." He swept chairs aside to make a wider passage through the area.

Lawrie's eyes took in two unshaven men in the far corner, dressed in dirty denim and dirtier scarves, fortified with beer and cigarettes for their game of checkers. "With all the cars outside," he murmured, "I thought the place'd be full."

"The rest must be at the archery range." Nathan's laughter seemed almost uncontainable.

"Right in here, gentlemen. You got the room to yourselves, as long as you want." He held the door for them.

Nathan entered first, then stepped to the side with a grin that matched that of the maître d'.

Lawrie stopped, thunderstruck. Six men whooped and rose to greet him. "Kevin!" Lawrie cried, giving him a huge bear hug. "Jake! Mike! Laddie! Lennie!" He hugged them each in turn. "And Billy!" That hug lasted long, and Lawrie's laughter hung on the sharp edge of emotion. "You guys!" he finally said. "Wait! Where's Bruce?"

"Well, he's sorta in the hospital. Now, don't go gittin in a twist." Jake's words beat down Lawrie's alarm. "He's not bad hurt. Just a scrap with a con, an' he got thumped some. I saw him last night, an' he told me t' pound the daylights out of you," which Jake proceeded to do. "Wanted to be here bad, but we wouldn't let him."

"Anything broken?"

"Naw. He'll be okay. This happens."

"Why didn't you tell me? I could've—"

"He didn't want you to know. Felt stupid. That's his job, my job, an' sometimes y'come up on the short end. Whaddaya call it? Occo-something . . . "

"Occupational hazard." Lawrie shook his head ruefully. "You tell Bruce to watch his backside. But look at the rest of you!" He took in the other men. "Nathan, you cooked this up, didn't you?"

He answered with a big grin. "This was the best safe place I could think of. I know, for sure, Mr. Snake Slinger's on our side. I didn't tell him any more than he needed to know, but this is right down his alley. We need this time together."

Lawrie frowned accusingly. "Billy, you didn't bring Joey."

Billy shrugged, winked at the men, then whistled softly. Movement under a cloth-covered table in the corner presaged a figure that bounded out and latched onto Lawrie with a force that almost knocked him over. Billy, though, was there.

"Got your back, khólá. Figured the boy might be enthusiastic."

Lawrie swung Joey around, and they both shouted in sheer joy.

After they finally settled around the table and Nathan and Lawrie had made their choices from the day's offering of elk, bison, rattlesnake, pheasant, and rabbit, Nathan signaled the "culinary artist." With only himself on duty, the food would be slow in coming, but the men had plenty to talk about.

"Tell us about your D.C. group," said Mike. "Our eyes bugged when Nathan described the guys down there. Or maybe their language doesn't include *guy*."

Kevin hooted. "We never got a chance to work with Lawrie the senator."

"No, you didn't," replied Lawrie. "The senator hid. Wouldn't come out. You had only this big, angry puppy chewing ankles and moaning in your laps. But this being farm country, you know how to deal with hurting animals, and you did good by me."

"How's the group down there different from us?" asked Laddie.

"Well, let's see." Lawrie leaned back. "They chew ankles more eruditely—and that's a word they'd probably use. They talk about everyday power struggles—between nations, political parties, between local gangs—and now I can add between convicts and guards. That's what goes on in the real world, they say. They want me to get out of my office and relate—not to influence votes, but to touch people's lives."

"Huh!" said Laddie. "I like that. But do politicians ever stop scratching for votes?"

"That's their point. We're a class both privileged and distanced, they say. They want me to go into the backcountry, talk to people about real stuff. I should come often to Mountrail County, talk oil and gas on fracking sites, find out who got hurt recently, talk to natives here about their culture shock. You know the sex trafficking here. I'm up to my armpits in that mire, but yah—from a distance."

"We know," said Jake. "That slime's showin' up in prison now."

"But you guys—" Lawrie swished his finger around the table. "You *are* the real world—planted right here in North Dakota, a long way from D.C. and its highbrow talk. You are real people—doing agriculture, working transportation, overseeing heavy-equipment, fighting fires, patching car wrecks, and minding prison punks.

"But here's another difference between you and D.C." Lawrie leaned back with a wry smile. "If I had to describe what two birds the groups resemble, I'd say buzzards and eagles, and the only difference is that eagles have slightly better table manners. Other than that—"

The men howled. Chuck butted through the door with a tray of bread, pretzels, and assorted chips. "How's it goin'? You boys havin' too much fun in here. Gotta ask you to keep it down. My regulars out there—" He nodded vaguely toward the dining area. "They don't talk much, but they're havin' trouble hearin' thoughts go back 'n forth." He winked and clapped Lawrie on the back as he went out.

As they began to eat, Lawrie described the makeup of his other group. "Two Republicans, one Democrat, a judge, and two local pastors—that's the accountability group. The Bible study is bigger. Both pastors come for a shot of fortitude. D.C. isn't a happy place for ministry. We've got problems here in North Dakota, but there . . . Probably the same junk we deal with, but far more than any pastor can keep up with."

Lawrie stopped and studied his plate for several moments.

"At first, I had this starry-eyed idea that God provided the 'eagle' group down there just to take care of me." Shame touched his face. "You fellows didn't help, y'know—focusing totally on me. When I think back, we hardly ever talked about your problems. You set all that aside just to love on me, and I was too thick-headed to see it." He looked up pleadingly. "Getting slapped with other folks' reality down there has been good medicine."

Nathan gripped Lawrie's arm. "Hey, our job was to stuff your gut back in—first aid. Down there, you're the suit, and it's the job of the other suits to make sure your spiritual tie is straight. Two groups, two different purposes, but buzzards and eagles both are good at teaching a guy to soar on high winds."

The arrival of the main dishes got them laughing again. "Okey dokey, Joey," Jake said. "Bite into that rattlesnake!" The boy sat there, contemplating what he had ordered, then picked up his fork and manfully took a bite. His eyebrows went up. "Not bad! But—" He leaned toward his dad. "I don't think Kellsie would like it."

Billy leaned over with a grin, "That's why you're here, *Cheekshee*, and not your sister."

As they ate, Lawrie told them about his prison ministry. "That got me out of myself—fast! It's one thing to debate legislation on prison reform; it's another to see the end product of broken lives and families. What, Billy?" He looked past Nathan to his friend, whose face had suddenly gone hard. "What'd I say wrong?"

Billy's eyes shifted from his plate to the deer antlers above the door. "Not wrong. Truth."

Lawrie studied him several moments. "Y'know, for all my experience on the Indian Affairs Committee, sometimes I think I'm just play acting, making believe I'm doing something important. I can talk a pretty good game with Lakota natives, but what do I really know of their lives? For sure, they get drunk; kids waste their lives; women get banged up; schools are bad; but I know *nothing* of life in the trenches—not like you do."

The Lakota's face remained impassive.

"If or when I need to know, *please* give me a call. I'm on that committee and want to help if I can. Billy, you should be

Chairman of Indian Affairs, not me. You know far more and are better positioned to know what to do." His voice wavered, and he looked off to the side.

Billy reached around Nathan and squeezed Lawrie's shoulder. "Kȟolá. Friend. Good friend."

Leave-taking was hard. "Guys," said Lawrie, "This is my heart home. Right here, in this parking lot with you—my family, my blood kin." He rubbed his neck hard. "We gotta do this again. Maybe August? You'll be ready for more rattlesnake by then, won't you, Joey?"

The boy responded with a long hug.

Chapter 30

BONNIE SAT WITH LINDA IN the latter's small office. Winter's snowflakes over the desk had been replaced with multifaceted orbs that bounced shards of color off the walls. The two women hovered over the computer, designing a carefully worded advertisement for the position of head gardener. When satisfied, they printed a hundred full-color flyers and posted a notice in newspapers, gardening magazines, and online venues. Responses started coming, but Linda was not heartened. Most were turned down immediately; a few she interviewed, but all fell short of Jorge and his abilities.

As Linda withered under the discouraging task, Bonnie remained strong and optimistic and insisted that she and two friends meet with Linda twice a week just to pray for the right person to appear. Linda objected in scathing tones. "The *irony* of praying for this rich lady whose only real need amounts to wanting an expensive gardener! Better that we pray for orphans in Africa or the bottomless pit of Haiti disasters."

Bonnie's response was practical. "All right, we'll pray for them, too, but we will pray for a gardener. Who knows? He might turn out to be a poor Haitian."

A week later, Felipe Hierro came to her gate, announcing his desire for an interview. At first, Linda got on him for not having gone through the proper contact protocol, but then she sighed and let him in.

Clearly nervous, he lined out his gardening background and, perspiring even more, told her his prison history.

Linda's back went up. Her eyes little more than slits, she questioned his legal status. With trembling hands, he showed his documentation and stated his aim of becoming a U.S. citizen. Again, he tried to bring the conversation back to gardening and his capabilities but made a mess of it. She finally said she was sorry, but he wasn't the right person for her needs.

With a doleful, hesitant lift of his finger, Felipe stood and, with hands shaking almost beyond function, pulled a folded piece of paper from his wallet. "The lady . . . she give me this and say to show to you if you say no. So, I show to you."

Linda took it and turned it over and over, seeing nothing but a blank sheet. "What is this?"

He lifted a trembling, dirt-framed finger to the center. "There," he said.

She looked closely, then stared at him, eyes wide and frantic. "Where did you get this?"

"The lady, she give it to me to show you if—"

"What lady?"

"The lady who tell me about you need a good gardener. She say I good, and I need to show you this piece of paper with just one letter. It mean something? It don't mean nothin' to me."

Linda drew a shaky breath and sat down. "Felipe, we need to start over again. Sit down, and tell me again everything about yourself and especially the people you've talked with. You came from Washington, D.C. Do you know Senator Crofter—either while you were in prison or afterward?"

Felipe shrugged. "I talk to many, many peoples."

"Yes, but did someone talk to you particularly about gardening?"

"*Sí*. Many, many peoples help me to look for job. And this lady—" He pointed to the paper. "She want to help me."

"No—I'm talking about men, a man who might have . . . Never mind," she went on, shaking her head. "Let's go out to the garden, and you can show me what you know about flowers."

Felipe's eyes widened as he stepped through the sliding door onto the deck. He stood for a moment, taking in the scope of Linda's garden, pointing without comment at certain features and especially the gazebo. The doleful, basset-hound look dropped away and was replaced by delight and hope—obviously foreign to him on most occasions.

Linda began her usual tour commentary, apologizing for the holes and general disrepair; but Felipe took over with his own *sotto voce* inventory, nodding approval over budded delphiniums and identifying plants by their common names and, sometimes, the Latin name. Awestruck, Linda just followed and listened. Occasionally, a plant was too embryonic to be easily identified, and he would ask, then nod. He stopped at beds that were being double dug.

"What you have here?"

Her hand drew broad circles as she explained, "This area is for some of the more particular and showy perennials. Over here, I'm not sure what . . . Well, nothing definite yet for that space. One of the things we'll need to talk—"

"*Sí!*" said Felipe. "Something . . . passion, maybe." His eyes shone with excitement. "I see lily tree here, red penstemon, tall dahlias group here, there," and he pointed. "And over here." He strode to an established bed. "This good. This point to something. Show it off." He moved to the end of the planting. "But this no good here. This get lost. And this. And over here."

Linda caught her breath, struggling to keep up with his rapid-fire assessment.

"And the gazebo island. *Perfecto!* Drama *y* passion, but all around is quiet, peaceful. Good balance. You make this?" He turned to look at her as though she were hardly capable of such artistic mastery.

"Felipe," she said, voice shaking, "we need to sit in the gazebo and talk!"

Two hours later, he left, promising to return the next day with a list of references; and by the end of the week, he was happily employed. "We go at this garden *de la mano,* hand in hand," he said, face totally transformed and suddenly confident.

"Bonnie," Linda said that evening, "I'm still shaking. I can't believe this. I don't know how Jay found him or who actually gave Felipe that paper with the tiny *J,* but I do know that God heard your dogged prayers. And I'm equally sure he wasn't impressed with mine! I even invited Felipe to our church, and he almost hugged me on the spot!"

Linda listened with a smile to Bonnie's effusive response, but her mind visualized that rose *objet d'art* that Jay had sent on the occasion of her garden tour. It had to have been him. Who else? Her face gathered pain. The orbs over her desk twirled but had no light, no life. They had become blank blobs, good only for dispensing misery. When she spoke again, her voice was tight. "Bonnie, Jay landed on my lawn nearly a year ago. Is Felipe's coming another sort of . . . advent?"

The next day, Bonnie called, her voice strained. "Linda, I think you should turn on your TV. Something's happening in North Dakota, and I heard Jay's name a couple of times."

Chapter 31

WHEN LAWRIE GOT THE NEWS from an aide on his way out of the Senate chambers, he called Chief of Staff Connie immediately. "Pull whatever strings. I need a fast flight to Bismarck. I'll pack and be at the airport within an hour. Call the office up there to have someone pick me up."

Three hours later, Dori, his Bismarck office manager, met and briefed him as he tossed his carry-on in the back. "Nobody knows exactly what's happening," she said, "but we do know this. Around noon, Governor Allen stopped at the casino near Fort Yates, whether for political purposes or gaming or both. Doesn't matter. His men were with him and watching, but a ruckus at one end of the big room brought his guys close around."

With only a quick glance at the side-view mirror, Dori pulled directly in front of a taxi and ignored its swearing horn. "Then two shots came from the opposite direction. The first one hit and killed an aide, and the other clipped the governor; but from what I understand, he'll be all right."

"The aide—what was his name?"

"Pete Mulligan, age thirty; been with Allen three years. Wife, two kids."

Lawrie blew a sharp breath. "The shooter. What about him? Assuming a him."

"He got away. A lot of rumors, but nothing solid."

"Let me guess. A Lakota native." His face darkened.

"Nobody knows for sure, but it seems so. The ruckus may have been a distraction. Those involved were all Lakotas."

Lawrie covered his face, then looked up. "Where are we going?"

"I thought to the office to make you accessible, but I'll take you anywhere you want. We've been in touch with the reservation police, state police, and the mayor. And, of course, casino people. You could contact any of these, but my guess is, nobody will say anything till it gets sorted out."

Again, Lawrie let out his breath. "Okay, the office, but no news conference till I actually have something worth saying."

Dori started to speak but was interrupted by her cell phone. "Dori here . . . . You sure of that? Do you have a name? Who should we contact down there? All right, call with anything, any time." She clicked off her phone and made a sharp U-Turn to head south. "They're on somebody near Porcupine. No name yet. When he saw helicopters, he ditched his car and took to the brush. They've brought in a tracker and are circling the area."

Lawrie's face went white. "The tracker's name?"

"Don't know." She looked at him. "You all right?"

He nodded and stared straight ahead. "Get there. Keep your speed just under an accident."

They turned west toward Porcupine and then onto a dust-kicking dirt road where the state police stopped them. "I'm sorry," said an officer, "there's a problem ahead, and we'll have to ask you to come back later if you—"

"Senator Crofter." Lawrie held out his identification. "And I need to get there. I am directly involved."

The officer studied the ID and then Lawrie's face as though to connect some mysterial dots. Lawrie drew a breath to speak, but the officer said, "Yes, sir. You may go, sir, but please proceed with extreme caution."

Lawrie nodded, and Dori spun dirt getting the car in motion.

They had more trouble at the next roadblock, this one manned by a mix of well-armed tribal and non-uniformed functionaries who seemed to neither know nor care about senators, especially one who was out of place and in the way. Lawrie got out of the car and in their face. Grudgingly, they let him—but not Dori—through. Lawrie pumped his two-man escort for information. Yes, they were after a young Lakota by the name of Crawn Wolf Runner. Yes, he'd been a troublemaker on both sides of the legal fence—white and tribal. Yes, Billy White Water was the tracker. No, his son wasn't with him. They didn't know if the ruckus at the casino was part of the plan, but yes, it could have been. They'd deal with that later.

"Sir, we know this man is armed, and if he's the shooter, he has good aim. It's dangerous up ahead, and—"

"There's a staging area up ahead," Lawrie said tartly, "where other people are not getting shot. I'm going there. You can come, too, unless you're—" He stopped abruptly. "No. Sorry. You're good men, taking a risk with me. I appreciate it."

When they reached the main search-support group, Lawrie recognized a man from Minot and moved toward him. After clapping backs, Lawrie got the latest on what was happening. They had the area circled and were reasonably certain that Wolf Runner was still in there. Billy's relatively rapid advance seemed to indicate an easy-to-follow trail.

"But is that good?" asked Lawrie. "I know enough about the business to understand that an easy track could be a trap in itself or a lure that would—"

A shout to the right cut him off. "Crawn! Listen up!"

The hair on Lawrie's neck went up. Billy's voice—he was sure of it. His heart pounded. *Lord*...

"Crawn! Lay it down. You're totally surrounded. No way out. We don't want you getting hurt. Put the gun down, and come out with your hands up. You know I'll stand by you, do what I can. But know this: if you don't come out on your own, you're toast."

Lawrie strained to see Billy through the dusty underbrush and scanned the woods for a glimpse of movement. He tried to shift to a better position, but two men immediately put hands on him.

Then he saw Billy rise from the brush and cup hands around his mouth. Before the tracker had a chance to say anything, Lawrie saw his body rise and lurch, followed by the sound of gunshot that coincided with his fall to the ground. Within seconds, gunfire sounded in the focal area and was answered by a sharp cry and a shout from the woods.

"He's down!"

The men had pulled Lawrie to the ground, but he shook them loose and stumbled through the brush, shouting, "NO! Billy! When he reached him, he fell weeping to his knees, cradling Billy's head in his hands. "Billy, Billy my friend . . . Please, God, please . . . Billy, can you hear me?"

Billy's breath came in shallow gasps. A medical team searched for the wound entry and exit. "In through his chest and out near his spine, so it seems."

Kneeling on angular brush stems, Lawrie felt hands on his back, but no one tried to remove him. He continued to plead with God for Billy's life.

Working around Lawrie, the medical team checked Billy's vitals; but before they lifted him onto a stretcher, Lawrie squeezed his hand and said, *"Kȟolá* friend. God's love, my love, the other guys—we will hold you."

Billy squeezed back, flickered his eyes, and whispered, *"Kȟolá . . ."*

Billy was medevacked to Bismarck. Lawrie stood desolate on the flattened brush, watching the helicopter lift off, tears streaming down his face.

Linda and Bonnie stared at the TV, following the unfolding story as reported from Bismarck. The shooting in the casino with background footage was followed by a statement on Governor Allen's condition and the news that Aide Peter Mulligan was dead. Then came the shootout three miles northwest of Porcupine—presumed assailant Crawn Wolf Runner dead, tracker Billy White Water critically wounded. Senator Crofter had been onsite near Porcupine but was now returning to Bismarck. Reservation Chief of Police Harry Martin gave his view of the casino event and spelled out preventative measures that would be put in place. The hospital spokesman had no news on White Water, aside from his being readied for surgery. A video clip showed mourners laying flowers on the floor where Peter Mulligan had died. And, of course, talking heads speculated on recent Lakota gang activities that might have precipitated the tragedy.

Linda rubbed her temples. At least Jay was safe. Were Mulligan and White Water strangers or acquaintances? Whichever, Jay would have to say something about them, as well as about the governor. She longed, yet feared, to see him on the screen. What would or could he say, other than as chairman of the Indian Affairs Committee, he would do what he could to help prevent this sort of catastrophe, blah, blah?

"Wait!" she said. "I've got to record this."

"There he is!" exclaimed Bonnie.

"Where? I don't see him!" She looked up from hitting the Record button.

"On the right. He's coming toward—"

"Yes! I see him! Lord, help him . . . "

The mayor of Bismarck stepped to the bank of microphones at an outdoor podium outside the stolid, soaring capitol building. He held a sheaf of papers and looked appropriately solemn. "I'm standing here on a very sad occasion," he said. "We are grateful that Governor Allen's life was spared, but we grieve for the Mulligan family in this terrible loss of a brave man who—" His voice cracked, and he cleared his throat. "—who literally placed his body in front of the governor." He paused a moment to shuffle his notes. "We grieve, too, for the family of Crawn Wolf Runner and the pain they feel today. Our prayers go up for Billy White Water, as well."

As the mayor spoke, Linda and Bonnie watched a light-haired man hand Jay a cell phone. Jay listened, nodded, and attempted a smile, then handed the phone back.

The mayor turned to Jay. "We are grateful for Senator Crofter flying from Washington to be with us today. He's just back from the Porcupine encounter and perhaps can tell us more about what happened there."

He shook Jay's hand and drew him to the podium. Jay's companion reached a hand to the senator's shoulder, then stood by.

"Oh!" said Bonnie, looking at Jay's face.

Linda's lips gripped tight against tears. "Something terrible happened! Well . . . I mean . . . of course, it's terrible . . . " She bit her curled finger—hard.

Jay gripped the podium and looked down, as though to draw courage. When he looked up, his face spoke loudly. Then words came. "Senator Crofter doesn't have much to say that will be helpful on such a day. The only person here is Lawrie on one of the worst days of his life—and he's had a few. Lawrie is hurting, the politician totally stripped away. I'm standing here with naked grief like the rest of you, only I happen to be the one who was pushed in front of these microphones.

"Pete Mulligan is dead. I knew Pete—not as well as I would have liked, but had talked with him on a couple of occasions. I'm glad for what the mayor said about him, about his bravery in the course of duty. He was a good man, and I only wish . . ."

He looked down, then began again. "We failed Crawn Wolf Runner, and he is dead as a result of our failure. Now, please don't misunderstand me." Jay put up his hand. "I am not blame-shifting, making Crawn the victim. He chose to pull the trigger three times and did incalculable damage. He ran with the wrong bunch, went down the wrong trail. He needed help, guidance, structure, discipline in his life, and he didn't get any of those. We, as a community, failed him.

"Billy White Water tracked him down. And as the police were closing in, Billy shouted, 'Crawn, come out. We don't want you to get hurt. I'll stand by you. You know I'll do what I can. Just come out with your hands up.'"

His face twisted, a vagrant breeze riffling his ill-groomed hair. "Crawn's answer . . . was to shoot Billy. A double tragedy out of one gunshot, the police having to bring him down."

This time, Jay looked to the treetops for strength. "A few minutes ago, I got a call from a friend in Washington who taught me rock climbing. Not real rocks. I'm talking cliffs of a different sort—hard places in life that have no visible footholds, no pitons. My friend said on the phone, 'We're watching you, buddy, holding the rope for you. Just speak truth—your best toehold.'"

Linda and Bonnie watched a hand again go to Jay's shoulder, and Jay straightened and leaned into the microphones. "I'm here tonight, speaking truth as best I can. No platitudes. They won't work. The long, tragic war between whites and Native Americans is behind us. There was sin on both sides, but whites have a lot to answer for, and Indians have a huge lump of anger to climb over. We've *got* to get beyond this, work our way up the cliff. All of us need to reach out to the Crawns of our community, walk with them, with Billy as our example. I didn't know Pete all that well, but I do know Billy. I know he himself would have brought Crawn down, had it come to that; but if Crawn had come out with his hands up, Billy would've been the first to put an arm around him.

"I want to form a Rope Committee here." Jay paused and looked directly at the faces curved in front of him. "It's tough work. I know it; Billy knows it. Volunteer. Be a Big Brother. Make friends with a struggling mom. Be a good example, and I think you know what I'm talking about here. Gambling, drugs, alcohol, gangs—chronic problems in our community. *Don't let this tragedy be a total waste.* Teach rock climbing, hold ropes—" Another big breath to cover desperate pain. "And it's okay to cry."

Jay turned and gave his friend a quick hug as a reporter moved in. "Senator Crofter, can you tell us if there's any pending legislation that would help our situation here?"

Jay turned, his face drained of color. "I'm sorry. Senator Crofter can't come up with anything helpful; and right now, Lawrie the man needs to go see Billy in the hospital."

Bonnie sobbed openly, and Linda bit skin at the base of her thumb to keep from joining her.

Chapter 32

AFTER LOCATING THE WAITING ROOM outside the surgical unit, Lawrie and Nathan surveyed the slumped family. Nathan headed for Billy's wife, Rosa, and daughter, Kellsie, and Lawrie went to Joey. The boy turned away, raising defensive quills of grief and anger. Lawrie backed off and moved to Nathan's side. He had met Rosa and joked with Kellsie but didn't know either of them well. He simply listened as Rosa stoically told what she knew. Billy was alive, but barely. The doctors were not hopeful. Besides serious lung injury, the bullet had nicked his spine, but they couldn't assess the neurological damage. They had warned her the surgery—and the night—could be long.

As they talked, Mike, Laddie, Jake, and Len came in, and after a briefing, they all grabbed hands and prayed at length. Except for Joey, who distanced himself away as far as possible. Lawrie went over and sat three chairs from him but said nothing and didn't look at him. After a bit, he got up and took a magazine from the rack, then settled two chairs away and was pleased to see Joey—after a sideways glance—stay put. Lawrie returned the magazine, then came back and said, "Let's go for a walk."

Joey dropped his head to his hands but got up and exited the doorway without looking at Lawrie. They walked silently through assorted hallways until Lawrie took advantage of a change of direction to physically steer the boy. Seeing the lad's struggle against tears, he put an arm around him.

"Joey, it's okay to cry. I've done a lot of that today and will probably do more." When they came to a row of chairs along a windowed walkway, he pulled the boy over and sat him down. Joey melted into his arms, and they wept together.

The men took turns walking and praying. Pastor Dan joined them, as did Kevin. Lawrie had tried praying facedown but fell asleep. The others didn't disturb him. Joey and Kellsie curled in their chairs to sleep. Rosa sat straight and staring, and Nathan occasionally put his arm around her.

At three a.m., the swinging doors burst open, and they all jumped—except Lawrie. Nathan nudged him, and he leaped to his feet, frantically reorienting.

The surgeon, face lined with fatigue, nodded and said, "He's still alive, and I don't know why."

Kevin gripped his arm. "We do. You've been prayed over— brain, eyes, fingers, back, heart. And Billy the same. We give thanks to God and to you."

The doctor's face contorted, and he squeezed Kevin's hand. "No promises. We did what we could. He's in God's hands now. I know that. I *know* that."

Rosa stepped toward him. "Can we see him?"

The doctor's eyes shifted to the flickering television on the wall, then back to the woman. "It would be best, I'm thinking, if you don't see him right away. He's not awake, and the post-op folks are working hard to keep him on this side of things. Maybe tomorrow. Go home; get some sleep; and call maybe mid-morning. We'll know a little better by then." He looked around the group, then cocked a puzzled frown at Lawrie. "Aren't you—"

"Lawrie Crofter." He gripped the surgeon's hand hard. *"Thank you.* You give us hope. We need Billy." He reached around to Joey and Kellsie. "And these guys here—they need their dad."

Three days later, Lawrie returned to Washington, an important EPA bill coming to the floor. He went one last time to talk to Billy and hold his hand, but the only response was a nearly imperceptible squeeze. Lawrie had done what he could for Rosa and was pleased by early gifts that had come in response to an online fund. He would return every weekend until his state workweek at the end of May.

While in D.C., he thought long and hard about Crawn Wolf Runner's family, from all reports a bad hatch. His father was seriously alcoholic and a chronic gambler; his mother was abused and abusive; and assorted in-laws, cousins, and nephews were on a first-name basis with prison officials. But Lawrie had listened to his own words at the press conference and wanted to do something.

On his second weekend at home, he was gratified to find Billy in a rehab hospital, finally off the respirator and able to respond in limited fashion.

"Thank you, *Kȟolá*," he said hoarsely, "for helping Rosa . . . the kids."

A long silence ensued. Lawrie cleared his throat. "Billy, how are you handling what's happened? Crawn is dead, but his family . . . How do you feel about the man who altered your lives— maybe forever?"

Billy closed his eyes and said simply, "I forgive him."

Lawrie left the hospital, determined to put substance to that forgiveness. He checked his phone app for Crawn's mother's address and drove to a riverside shack on a junk-strewn lot. Sucking a big breath, he walked toward the house with more confidence than he actually felt.

His knock was answered by a lumpy, unkempt woman, whose eyes revealed a legion of demons within—anger, pain, hatred, vengeance, brutality, lostness. Lawrie stepped back from her sheer, negative force.

"Mrs. Wolf Runner?" he asked.

Her mouth curled obscenely. "Who wants t' know?"

"I'm Lawrie Crofter, here to say that I grieve with you over your son's death. This was a terrible tragedy all around, but a mother's pain is perhaps—"

She cut him off. "Whadda *you* know about a mother's pain? How can you walk in here with your white clothes and fancy car and talk to *me* about *my dead son?*"

"I'm sorry if—"

"Don't give me no sorry. Get outta here. Leave me and my dead son *alone!*" Her voice rose to a screech.

This drew another figure out of the dim recesses of the shack.

"Who's worth yer hollerin', Ma?"

This man of indiscernible age was thin and more angular than his mother, but his rutted face and eyes, in a frame of grimy black hair, were painted the same malevolent hue.

"What you want?" He addressed Lawrie.

Lawrie stuck out his hand. "You must be Crawn's brother. I'm Lawrie Crofter, and I was onsite when he was—"

The man slapped the proffered hand and stepped from the doorway to get in Lawrie's face. *"You?* The *senator?* At *our* door? *Git outta here,"* he snarled. "Git, an' don't never come back!" He dragged Lawrie away from the house and hurled him bodily at the car.

Lawrie hit hard and slid into an ignominious heap of humiliation, his Dockers and suede Henley garnished with dust and shame.

Word got around the network, and Lawrie received a summons to Billy's bedside. He entered the room, abashed, hand over the left part of his forehead. Billy said nothing at first, then, "Put your hand down. I want to see the damage." His eyes carved holes in the remnants of Lawrie's self-esteem.

Billy was clearly angry, and Lawrie stood like an offending schoolboy until the signal came to sit. They remained silent for a long time before Billy spoke. "I'm guessing your grasp of Indian Affairs got a good dose of reality today. I'm also guessing you won't prosecute Wayne Wolf Runner—though you could, you know. Assaulting a senator pretty much translates to a direct bus ride to prison; and in his case, nobody would complain, tribal or otherwise. But—"

"You kidding? If I turned him in, I'd be Chief Mud Face. Billy, I'm sorry. It was stupid; I see that now." He stopped, noting that Billy's carved-rock face had turned even harder. He closed his eyes, forehead on his hand, waiting for absolution.

It came, but with conditions. "From now on, you will not go alone onto tribal land or the Indian enclave here in town. You will always have with you someone strong to run interference, if necessary. You can be sure the Wolf pack will smear you every way they can. You're no longer safe among my people, not for a long time.

"And," he went on, "you will leave reconciliation to me. I'm the one who got shot, not you. You meant well but did it wrong. And I speak peace to you, my brother." He reached out his hand, and Lawrie shed tears.

Chapter 33

A MODEST COLLECTION OF NORTH Dakota ranchers, bankers, small-business owners, and assorted women sat in the Fountain Room at Stonycrest Inn, tugging at political issues in the presence of Senator Crofter. The sibilance of the indoor water accent against blistering heat outdoors soothed tempers and prompted the spirit of sleepiness.

As Lawrie consulted his watch toward the end of the hour, an elderly woman clothed in gauzy elegance and a rakish hat slipped inside and stood quietly near a potted plant. Lawrie's eyebrows rose fractionally; but without missing a beat, he continued his well-crafted closing statement and then went around the room with a word, a handshake, and even an occasional hug. After he had spoken to everyone, he moved toward the woman.

Before he could speak, she took his hand and said softly, "Would you prefer that I see you in your office or at your home?"

Lawrie laughed. He couldn't begin to guess who this woman was, aside from her earlier, oblique tie-in with Linda. But her eyes, the gracious curve of her words, the starch in her spine—He stopped his survey abruptly. Did that straight look remind him of Charlotte? She was not Charlotte, but the chance comparison suggested an implacable integrity on which he was willing—no, eager—to rest his emotional weight.

"I would be honored to have you in my home. Would you prefer lunch or dinner?"

Her mouth pursed coyly. "How about tea? After all, people might talk."

He laughed and gripped her hand tightly. They set a date and time; and having kept him from his constituency less than two minutes, the woman slipped out the door as unobtrusively as she had come.

Two days later, housekeeper Nadine announced his guest's arrival. Lawrie rose from his desk, brushed a thread off his dark shirt, and glanced at his hair in the mirror. His face warm with welcome, he greeted the woman, again coolly dressed, though minus the hat.

"Lawrie, dear!" She kissed his cheek and offered hers in return. He held her soft, wrinkled hands and fought the stinging in his eyes. "My dear," she said, "while you may be fooling people who see you frequently, I see the effects of bone-deep pain. In short, you look dreadful. Now, how's that for political bluntness?" She gave him a dazzling smile.

He laughed uproariously and silently gave thanks for her adroit rescue. He led her to the tearoom that had been Glynneth's favorite place for intimate entertaining. It seemed just right for this occasion.

She looked around admiringly. "Beautiful! Your wife saw to the decorating?"

"Yes, and with her in it, the house was never too big. Now, though, I'd be content with a small cape hidden in some forest."

"Yes, far too much empty space in this house for one man. A cape would fit you, but not a forest. You need people around you."

Lawrie studied this elegant, patrician lady who would not give her name. "You may call me Lady Cool Water," she said disarmingly. "That sounds quite Indian, doesn't it?" As she spoke, Lady

Cool Water ran penetrating eyes over him, as though to assess his liver and kidneys.

He smiled wryly. "You amaze me. I know nothing about you, but you see every wart on my face and wrinkle on my soul." When her eyebrows raised, he went on quickly. "Not that you're impolite or lacking grace, but somehow, you *know* me, far better than many."

"Oh, yes! I'm scanning, you know. And learning quite a bit. I mentioned pain a moment ago. Layers of it. You usually hide it well, my dear, but your press interaction after that dreadful shooting . . . " She steepled her hands over her mouth and tsked sympathetically. "You were masterful but terribly transparent. I wept for you that day."

"Thank you," he replied fervently. "That was a hard one."

They sat silent, thoughtful. Then Lawrie said, "You have a word for me?"

She straightened with a smile. "Probably far too many words. At some point you may want to look at your watch and declare a meeting you had forgotten. But I'm here to cheer you and to be of whatever help. Now, may I make tea, or do you have a paid tea-maker whose services you must use?"

After three cups of tea and an hour's conversation, the pair flowed from the tearoom, her arm in his, her face wearing a pleased expression, his face picking through assorted expressions, not sure which he should wear. As he opened the front door, she turned with a firm grip on his hand.

"Lawrie, dear, I know you'll think deeply. My apologies for a disgustingly hackneyed phrase, but it seems appropriate right now." She leaned toward him and whispered, *"Get a life!"* With a quick smile and a wave, she was gone.

Lawrie went about his affairs in whimsical distraction, settling to the point when necessary, but quick to stare at potted plants in his office or pigeons in front of the Capitol building. August arrived, bringing summer recess—most welcome this year.

But before he left for North Dakota, he felt obliged to attend a social event—one at which politicians sniff the wind to gauge political position and power. The affair, the wedding reception of Senator Lundquist's daughter, was disastrous for Lawrie, placed at a table of women who were not of his political persuasion and whose conversation leaned toward rant and incivility. The only other man at the table turned his back on Lawrie and flirted outrageously with the woman to his left. Lawrie finally asked one of the quieter of the group to dance, largely to escape the combat zone.

As they finished dancing, a woman of sparkling fire, circling the men of the room, swept closer to Lawrie. Her dusky dress exuded a diffuse, red corona, and she was color in motion.

Lawrie sensed immediately that she was after him and debated a quick dash to the men's room. Though not as drop-dead beautiful as Glynneth, this woman—tall, finely sculpted, curved in all the right places—affected him powerfully. He suddenly wanted to be with her, to take her onto the balcony and sip her nectar. He looked frantically toward his dance companion, seated once again at the table, but the woman in red was on him, settling on his shoulder and whispering provocatively, "I will see you again." She backed away to play off other males, then tapped Lawrie on her way out. "Anon," was all she said.

Lawrie, mouth and eyes resembling a cod, asked, "Who is *that?*"

"Bonnie, I know that woman! Not well, but she's *not* a woman for Jay!" Linda's furious scrolling of the internet post all but created smoke.

Bonnie frowned. "How do you know? What's her name? I didn't catch it."

"Jerusha Mitabelle Haverstone."

"You *gotta* be *joking*!"

"I'm not. She goes by Rooshie, or did way back. She's a paper relative through convoluted marriages, and I can't remember which side of the family it was. We didn't spend much time together back then. Her family had more lift to their noses than ours." Linda shook her head. "What is he *thinking* of?"

Bonnie scratched the name on a Post-It note. "It's what gossipmongers are thinking and not so much Jay."

Linda pounded her forehead. "A hundred times a day I lay him down, let him go. I know he's staying away to protect me. And I know he'll choose to marry again. I've been bracing myself for this, but . . . not *her!*"

"They're not engaged, Linda. It's simply the first hint that he's beginning to look around and thinking in that direction."

Linda continued to shake her head. "Rooshie Haverstone . . . I can't believe it."

Nathan, too, was concerned. "Lawrie, what *are* you doing? You and this woman are being watched. You're hot gossip right now, and Rooshie Haverstone's rep is not exactly glittering."

"I know that, but she plays straight with me. Yes, she's been divorced. Yes, she's a party animal and risk-taker, and I doubt she'd waste any pity on the weak. But with me, she's almost fanatically public—theatre dates, weddings, golf. She's better at golf than I, but that's not saying much," he added ruefully. "Bring on the spies. They'll get bored, for sure."

Nathan sighed. "But, *why*, Lawrie? Why this woman? I'd have a really hard time if you were to tell me you were going to marry her. And what about Linda? Is this some sort of signal you're sending her?"

"Nathan, marriage to anyone, Linda included, is totally off my charts. And let me say this loud and clear: Linda's safety is my top priority. I will not jeopardize her in any way. I'll stay away from her, not even talk about her—just to shield her from any wrong imputations. I can love her that much and in that way." He turned away momentarily, but then swung back.

"Rooshie's different, and we're on totally different footing. I think I know what I'm doing with her. I continually ask God for blinders when I need them and for eyes to see beyond fun and verve. She's a hot ticket, I admit, but it's me I have to jerk back in line, not her. She's almost ridiculously careful not to step over my lines and is the woman I need right now."

"Why? She's not a Christian. Why is she playing this game?"

"No idea, but she's the woman I need *now*. And I wouldn't think of marrying anyone who wasn't a Christian. Please—trust me on this."

After the recess, Lawrie made frequent trips home, primarily to see Billy. The Lakota was still in rehab, progressing to wheelchair use. His lung had healed reasonably, but he continued in pain. His spinal injury left his legs partially paralyzed and improving only slowly. He could not stand, though therapy was helping his muscles.

Lawrie spent hours with him and with Rosa and the children. He made sure the donated money and Billy's business were being managed effectively and that the family had no financial need. Their emotional need, though, was difficult to assess. The Indian part of their nature found refuge in stoicism and silence, and Lawrie had to morph into Lakota-speak to make them comfortable. Rosa and Kellsie were coping the best. Joey, she admitted, had been acting out and didn't like visiting his dad. The men of the church had taken him to rodeos and tribal events and were keeping him more or less stable and civil to his mother.

Billy was different. He always greeted Lawrie warmly, but they sat silent for long periods, with information flowing slowly. He unfailingly expressed gratitude for the watch care over his family but obviously ached to be doing it himself.

The long-range outlook was bleak, though not hopeless. His arm strength had returned to normal and was occasionally tested on Joey to get his attention. Slowly, he was adjusting to reality and engaging more normally with the men, but the process was painful to watch.

Lawrie remained the faithful watcher. Taking Rooshie to meet Billy, however, was out of the question. Billy's dark, Indian eyes would strip him—not her—naked.

Chapter 34

FELIPE HAD BECOME A BULLDOZER in Linda's garden. First off, he dismantled almost everything, repositioning the arbor and eliminating another focal point—the blue urn that never seemed right. At least the gazebo seemed safe. Linda panicked: Could she trust him? Could she control this Godzilla she'd turned loose? Having rid herself of one autocrat, had she ingested another? She decided to test her authority and dragged the gardener into the house for a cup of coffee.

"Felipe, you're going way too fast for me to keep up with what you're doing or even thinking. I'm your boss and pay you each week. You work hard, but I need to see us pulling in the same direction. Can you explain—slowly—what you have in mind?"

Felipe sighed, sipped some coffee, and said, "Some paper? *Dos*—no, maybe *tr*—three pieces? I will draw."

And he did draw. His coffee went cold before he finished. Arranging the papers in order, he turned to Linda and began explaining patiently, as to a child. "You see, this is big border. We have changed much, yes? But not delphiniums. They stay. I work around. More also down here to balance," and he pointed toward the far end of the border. "New home for blue urn," and he pointed two-thirds down the border. "More happy here. Pick up delphinium blue. Surround with *elegancia*." He looked up to see her wide-eyed approval. "And down here, new way to greenhouse. Shrubs to hide path. Still thinking what shrubs."

He sat up straight with what might pass as a twinkle in his eye. "And Stella d'Oros—here." He pointed to one of the papers.

Linda rolled her eyes. "Oh, pul-*ease!* Stella d'Oro daylilies are dazzling, but everyone's yard is full of them. I'm sick to death of—"

Felipe's eyes crinkled. "But nobodies has Stella d'Oro mountain." He sat back with a direct grin, which seldom happened. "And maybe Gloriosas for later bloom."

"A Stella d'Oro-Gloriosa mountain. Okay. Could you . . . "

"That rock mountain out there." He gestured beyond the sliding door. "You see it now and wonder what it is. Felipe see Stella d'Oros climb rocky mountain. *Then* peoples notice and say, 'Oh, how beautiful!' Other things, too, climb mountain, but they will see and like Stella d'Oros and Gloriosa again. Focal point *número tres*."

Linda sat back and shook her head. They went at it for another hour, Linda slowly grasping—and gasping—at the full magnitude of his vision. When he finished, she asked hesitantly, "I know next July is a long way off, but will we be ready for the garden tour? Once winter sets in, we can't dig much."

He sat silent, fingering his cup. "I think . . . we can do it. Another helper . . . ?" He looked up, fear resurrecting the hangdog look. "I no like to ask—"

Linda put her hand on his arm. "Felipe, hire who you need, *dos*, even." She grinned. "Just remember—" She leaned forward and gripped tighter. "They must be legal; they must be honest; they must work hard and do just what you say—no more, no less. I trust you, and I must be able to trust your helpers. Are we clear on that?"

Relief closed Felipe's eyes momentarily, and his mouth worked toward a shaky smile. "*Sí, sí, señorita—muy* clear! A man in church—you know Julio? He need work. Gardening? Uhhh . . . but I teach. He do okay."

Lawrie returned to D.C. in the fall, and his interaction with Rooshie took shape. She operated comfortably, drawing him to pricy restaurants whose clientele plotted to be seen there—which served Lawrie's purposes nicely. They toured museums and galleries, went to an opera, and even attended church together. Lawrie's D.C. guys had a lot to say after that appearance, but he asked for their trust, as he had Nathan.

Despite all that, he could not figure her out. Why was her behavior with him so markedly different from her reputation? It didn't make any sense. But then, she seemed to be filling Lady Cool Water's dictum for him to "get a life." That, at least, he could live with.

Christmas came, sending seismic memories through Lawrie from the previous year. Two days before the holiday, he stared out the window, reflecting on that grinding, residual pain that had driven him to the butte. He felt the icy cold, the desperate clawing up the rocky slope to escape rescue.

His cell phone rang, dragging him back to reality.

"Lawrie, love." The familiar voice rocked him. "Do you suppose you could pick me up at the airport in about fifteen minutes?"

Rooshie!

"I thought I'd surprise you."

Suddenly, last year no longer mattered.

The night before Christmas Eve, the two attended a glitzy ball at the Bismarck Radisson. They danced and dined, Lawrie's heart swelling almost to bursting point. Afterward, Rooshie drew him through the exiting crowd to an isolated cluster of white-lighted Christmas trees. They chatted about the ball and the people they had talked with, but then Rooshie's words dwindled. She moved closer to Lawrie, close enough for his pulse to increase markedly, close enough for him to catch her scent from within her fur-trimmed hood. Her mouth whispered, "Merry Christmas," but her eyes, suddenly charged, spoke a different message.

Heat took over Lawrie's face and traveled southward, his breath thickening. Provokingly, his own words, "Trust me on this, Nathan; trust me," rattled his head like the chains on Marley's ghost. Closing his eyes somehow blocked the sound, and he bent his head toward her face.

Rooshie, though, drew two fingers across his lips. Then, with the air of a conqueror, she turned and walked away, leaving him—again—kin to a cod.

That was it—one insignificant move of his head in the wrong direction, and she was gone. No one watching. Even Ewen MacClerhan could not have picked up on that move. But his thoughts beat him mercilessly. The last sex he'd had, that full-bore romp with Glynneth, grandly clad in what turned out to be her death dress . . .

The night was cold, and Lawrie, dressed in light evening wrap, began to shiver. He walked aimlessly, sometimes inside the hotel, sometimes along the midnight streets. *"Trust me on this, Nathan; trust me."* The chains fabricated from those relentless words clanged for an hour, two hours. *He could not be trusted.*

But what had he actually done? Nothing, really. He was prud-ish, overreacting. Recasting the proverbial molehill. But no, that line of thought wouldn't fly. The chains rattled alarmingly, and he knew God was staring him down. *Small things do matter.* How could he face Nathan or Billy—let alone God—after tonight? *He was unpresentable. No glory in this scene.*

He would not see Rooshie ever again. Her Christmas greet-ing, or whatever she'd said, was her farewell. He knew that. But knowing it didn't change things. He had wanted to kiss her, and his body was thinking even beyond.

But—she had stopped all that. The soft touch of her finger across his lips slammed the door. Unpredictable, unpresentable Rooshie. Had she systematically and intentionally protected him from scandal? Was she God's agent, after all?

Somehow, he got through Christmas Eve and Christmas Day. Why had she left like that? Why, indeed? And what was the meaning of it all? He had no answers.

In that time of shadow when no one knew or cared, Lawrie returned to the Hill, feeling quite like Linda's troll, hunting desperately for a place to hide. He first sought refuge in his secret chamber office, a cold, cheerless cell with little more than a table, chair, and cot—like a troll bridge, like his inner prison.

In that cramped space, he pulled out a notepad and started listing his interactions with Rooshie.

- She, the party animal, came onto me at the D.C. wedding reception.
- She planned activities—always public, always acceptable.

Protecting him from scandal? But why would Rooshie, given her provocative history . . . ? He shrugged and went back to his list.

- I became comfortable with her but knew from the start that she was not marriage material.
- She flew to N.D. to surprise me.
- We had a great time at the Radisson ball.
- Afterward, she took me outdoors to a private spot.
- She came onto me—fifteen seconds at most.
- I lost it—a total of fourteen seconds.
- She cut the cord before I could act.
- She left.

- It wasn't love, just pure sex reaction.
- Neither of them did anything.

He bit the end of his pen and studied the list. Suppose Linda had shown up that night, right while he was dragging his chains? She whom he truly loved? What could he possibly have said to her? *No, I didn't really mean that.* But he did mean those fourteen seconds. At least, his body did. And hadn't his D.C. guys worked hard at getting him to think deeply about his inner feelings and attitudes on all sorts of matters?

No one in the real world would be struggling over this. Martin would snort lewdness. His N.D. guys would say, "C'mon, pal. Think you're the only dude who ever got his pants in a twist?" His D.C. group would say, "Go easy on yourself, Lawrie. You didn't act on it, so let it go."

Yes, guys are programmed a certain way, and he'd experienced hundreds of such moments. But this was different. Way different. Not only had he enjoyed being with Rooshie, his body had been sending out slender tentacles, reaching, groping for an attachment.

He sat back and tore the page from his notepad, read it one last time, then folded it carefully, and pocketed it inside his jacket. With deliberation, he slipped off the chair and onto his knees. Thank God for stopping him before his body got the upper hand!

Rescued by grace.

He returned to his office in the Russell Building. Happily, his suite was furiously busy and heavily trafficked—chaos itself providing refuge. He welcomed stacks of legislative material, committee agendas, and news briefs, feeling safe under a pile of work. He could solidify his amendment dealing with EPA overreach.

Next morning, however, Chief-of-Staff Connie ambushed him. Passing her office, his head jerked up as he heard her on the phone.

"I'm sorry," she said. "He's buckling swash in his office right now. May I take a message?"

"*Connie!*" Lawrie roared. "Who are you talking to?"

"Nobody, actually." She set the phone down. "Just wanted to catch your attention."

Lawrie sighed, exasperation stark on his mouth. "All right—what is it?"

"Two things, actually. The first 'It' happens to be legislative assistant number four."

"We don't have four L.A.s."

"Well, then, I guess we need to drop somebody, and I have one in mind."

"All right, who's number four?"

"Right now, Conrad tanks my list."

"Conrad! He's been around for, what—two years?"

"I can excuse one or two late arrivals due to holiday excess, but c'mon—almost every day? And with L.A.-wannabes crammed outside our doors?"

"Connie," said Lawrie, brightening at this opportune good cause to help balance his books. "When he gets here, send him to me. I'll sort him out. Ah! There's your miscreant." He watched the slender figure slide deftly behind a convenient conversation. "Sic 'im." He grinned impishly and returned to his office.

Connie's nostrils flared. Fiercely silent, she stalked her culprit to his cubicle and steered him through Lawrie's door, shutting it firmly on the two of them.

When they came out, Connie met them, ready to engage, but Lawrie's face allowed no interference. The young man, wide-eyed and solemn, returned to his cubicle, breathing a soft, fervent, "Thank you, sir!"

Lawrie smiled smugly at Connie. "There. Number One. What's Number Two?"

Connie's face went dark. "Sex trafficking" was all she said.

Lawrie's face roiled into thundercloud mode.

"Body found three days ago south of Williston," said Connie. "Took two days to identify. Neela Hermandez—age thirteen. You won't want to know the details, but I want to know what you're going to do about it."

He did want details. This would legitimately shift his inner conflict to this scurrilous evil that had sneaked under cover of the oil boom, dumping broad swaths of filth over western North Dakota. Before Christmas recess, he had talked with Ross Murphy at the FBI about mounting another sting operation. The agent agreed to line up operatives and contact state and local authorities to work out details. Lawrie was to keep Governor Morgan abreast of the action. Time to go pound desks.

"I'm on it," he said as he stalked fiercely to his office.

Shaming the governor into action brought satisfaction, but this gave only temporary asylum from the implications of his close call. He still needed to talk out loud about Rooshie, the *weed* in his garden. Just before Christmas, Linda's blog had given him that new word.

> Go for a walk along a country road and search for plants we commonly call weeds. Note which ones like to hang out in your garden. Study them closely. They self-select their location, putting down roots in the most hospitable soil, light, and moisture conditions. Your garden suits them well, and there they grow into sturdy little fellows that are neither fussy nor fragile—just happy to settle into your space. Dandelions, clover, assorted grasses—these guys are quick to flourish and tough to dislodge from our manicured beds.

What can we learn from these lowborn beauties? Maybe nothing. Maybe we just breathe in their simple charm and then go home and dutifully hold the hands of the elegant darlings we have chosen to showcase in our gardens. We pay a high price for our sort of beauty; weeds simply are.

Weeds simply are. Never had Lawrie felt more weed-like. The soil of his soul welcomed even gross weeds—thistles, nettles, poison ivy. What would Linda say about those? *Kileenda* . . .

He was soon forced to conversation when Chase, Lucas, and Rick summoned him to Albert's judicial. "The word's out," said Chase. "Rooshie's gone, and you're avoiding us. What's going on?"

He took a big breath. "Yes, she's gone." He looked toward the ceiling, then at each of the men. "To put it simply, she cozied up to me in a tight, private place and then . . . just walked away. For good. She didn't actually *do* anything, and neither did I." He glared defensively at each face.

The judge eyed him as he would an incompetent lawyer. "If *she* had, *you* would have. Your good behavior depended on hers. Am I right?"

His closed-eyed, non-answer spoke clearly.

After probing and listening, the men served him steaming cups of grace—which, in the end, proved too hot to drink. Lawrie put his hands on the table, studying first his fingers and then the heavy drapes behind Albert that kept out cold air and blocked escape. Finally, he looked at his mentors, anguish in his eyes.

"Three days ago," he said, "I extended grace to one of my L.A.s, whose bad choice left him deep in debt. He knew his mistake, wanted to make it right, and took on another job—as though his job with me wasn't intense enough. Connie was ready to toss him, but I, feeling kindly . . . " He laughed sardonically. "The Bible says it's more blessed to give than receive, and that applies to grace, too.

It's far easier to *give* grace than receive it. I'm having a hard time, guys." He went back to studying the drapes.

They let him ponder a moment, then Lucas put a black hand over his. "Pride, Lawrie, pride. You felt up to handling Rooshie. It would all work out. Somehow she'd change or you would—"

"No—I knew she wasn't for me. I knew it had to end, but not like that. Why did she do that to me?"

Chase chuckled. "The question, dear fellow, is why God allowed—or told her—to do it. These days, a kiss is cheap currency. Her lesson on pleasure economics smashed your self-assurance, and maybe that's what you needed. Powerlessness, you know, is a powerful fulcrum in lifting a sinner to God. Basic physics. You have confessed, Lawrie; you are forgiven. Now, pick up that heavy ball of grace and carry it into future 'situations.'"

Chapter 35

WITH CHRISTMAS AND NEW YEAR'S long gone and everyone seeing Valentine red, Linda felt only the drippy, dreary remains of winter. She badly needed God to show up in her emotional morass, but He had stepped back, content, so it seemed, to watch her squirm.

For starters, the garden could not possibly be ready for the tour. The garden crew had toiled as best they could with weather and frozen earth, but even Felipe, as hopeful as he had been, had bowed to reality and was ready to go to the wall over his failure to produce what he had promised.

Picking up again on Lady Cool Water's cheery injunction to "get a life," Lawrie grew bold enough to invite other women to receptions or political events. But with mid-term elections approaching, on top of Senate sessions and committee meetings, he faced an intense schedule of breakfasts and as many as three evening events that often lasted till midnight. He was seen as a strong and effective voice on behalf of chosen candidates, especially gifted in bolstering their heartfelt, but sometimes poorly packaged, positions. Invitations for television interviews came frequently, hosts—friendly and otherwise—often raising the specter of the next presidential election. He was the Man, by now an eminent figure and either esteemed by the Right or ridiculed by the Left. He didn't want to even think about it, but were he to run, the experience would be akin to rafting class-five rapids on the Amazon.

A blue moon came upon the land. Lawrie claimed that evening for himself and headed to the skating arena to play hockey. He went to bed sorely bruised but felt really good for the first time in weeks.

Linda scrolled through gossip sites, taking small comfort in Jay's improved taste in women friends. Rooshie seemed gone, but others would come. Linda agonized in dark corners, beating herself for being unable to let Jay go, to marry again, to have the life she could only dream of. She knew her computer addiction was wrong, but withdrawal seemed impossible. Even Felipe's single-minded drive to reinvent her garden only shot home the painful truth that Jay would never come back to enjoy it. And why would he even want to?

"Lawrie, I need to talk to you." Martin muscled into a conversation between the senator and his new summer intern.

Lawrie's eyes went hard, but he sensed urgency. He turned to the college student. "Tyler, let's do lunch this week. You'll work with Jeremy, but I like to get to know my interns before they leave. Tell Scheduler Ben to work out a time and place—will you do that?"

The young man gripped the senator's hand, eyebrows high. Martin's brows went down. As they walked away, Martin said, "So much time on your hands you need interns to fill your schedule?"

"What's on your mind, Martin?"

"That energy bill clawing your back. I happen to know that Arnie Rasmussen is in the favors market, and an encouraging word in his ear would be a cheap deal for you."

Lawrie looked at him. "Who you been talking to?"

"Never mind who told me. I'm working with you here. Act on it, and I think you'll have one more vote in your pocket."

Lawrie rubbed his forehead, but as they passed the Senate chaplain in the hallway, his frown abruptly became a smile and a wave.

"Nathan, I'm going home this weekend. and I'm sick of eating out. How about coming to my house, and we'll put the crew to work. Anything special you'd like?"

"Yah, I've been drooling for Mrs. Liles' crab quiche and Hoppin' John. Maybe not your favorites, but you did ask. Think she could come up with those? And whatever southern greens. If you ever find yourself headed for the poorhouse, Lawrie, auction her off. You'll be financially set for life."

"What planet are you from, Nathan? Not North Dakota, for sure. Southern greens? Hoppin' John?"

Three days later, they sat at the small table in the creamy sitting room where they'd eaten so many meals. "Good choice, Nathan—fine quiche! I like it," said Lawrie. "And Mrs. Liles never batted an eye over my list."

"Huh! She probably called Alaska for crabmeat and 'Nawleans' for turnip greens. Remind me to give her a hug. But how are you doing? We haven't talked for ages. Tell me about your other guys. How's Chase? You still on their page?"

"My accountability group is down to four. Mark moved. Sam had heart bypass a month ago. But Chase, Lucas, Rick, and Albert are still on me. One of them calls nearly every week, whether here or there."

"Whoo! We're not *that* tight!"

Lawrie pointed his fork at Nathan. "You guys are grafted on my heart, and you get at me, even without saying a word. Can't get tighter than that."

"By the way, how's your money diet going?"

Lawrie laughed and bent to retrieve his napkin from the floor. "That's hard gristle to chew. This house, for instance. Should be a slam dunk for me to sell and move to a shack, but . . . " His voice trailed off.

"But you're not ready."

Laurie studied the flower arrangement. "So many memories. Glynneth's gone." His voice caught, but he went on. "Charlotte . . . I keep hoping she'll come back. Would she find me if I moved?"

Nathan set his biscuit down and leaned back. "Here's a tough question, Lawrie. Are you in love with Charlotte?"

"Huh!" Lawrie jerked back in surprise, then sat silent. "In love with Charlotte . . . Maybe I am," he said reflectively. "But not the way you're thinking." He grinned impishly. "In love with *Charlotte?* Who'd ever want to marry Charlotte? But I did love her because she loved me and was the only face of God I had back then. When she came that first time, I watched her infuse Glynneth with a tiny spark of life. I was scared to death of her, especially when she came at me with that *look.*"

He drew designs in the tablecloth with his forefinger, first a circle, then crisscross lines over it. "Charlotte was . . . *unpresentable.* I see now what that means. Her way of addressing me, of digging into my soul. We had secrets—she and I." His voice became an intense whisper. "But she *wore glory.* I see that, too. Nathan, in knowing Charlotte, *I knew love.*" He straightened and smiled at his friend. "Yes, I am in love with Charlotte."

Nathan nodded with a satisfied air. "That's good. I like it."

He picked up his biscuit, then changed the subject. "What else do your guys push you on?"

Lawrie shrugged. "Oh, stuff like balancing work and spiritual input, social issues—abortion, gender stuff—political games like double standards, hypocrisy, lying. Everyone lies, and political battles are won by those who lie most convincingly." He shifted uncomfortably. "Then race issues—especially with two blacks in the mix. Being with them keeps me from knee-jerk responses." He paused a moment. "Of course, they're cheering my fight against sex trafficking in the oil fields. The sting netted six pimps and rescued thirteen underaged kids. One thing I'm doing right." He grinned.

Nathan nodded. "That's big. Something you can feel good about.

"Here's an unrelated question," he went on. "How do you feel about Linda? Do your guys ask how much time you spend on websites that mention her, all the way down to page ten?"

"C'mon! What senator has that kind of time? And by now, she probably doesn't even remember my name."

"Right." Nathan's smile widened. "A woman who sneaks into a hospital, past a guard, in the middle of the night to see a headline-type guy probably isn't likely to forget his name. Are you back to playing stupid mental games just to kill pain—" He stopped and looked at Lawrie. "This isn't a game, is it? You really are afraid she'll forget. Your biggest nightmare."

Lawrie sagged and toyed with the single bean stranded on his plate.

"What?" said Nathan. "Something I said hit a nerve."

Without answering, Lawrie got up and leaned into the kitchen, then returned and sat down. "I cannot *ever* reconnect with Linda," he said. "It's not Nels' threats. It's not Linda forgetting me. It's not Rooshie, though she uncovered truth about me. Nathan, it's me. Yes, I will protect her till my dying breath. That's a given. But there's a reason beyond that—one I never speak of."

He bent his head on his propped hands until the air turned thick with unease. He lifted his eyes.

"*I . . . killed . . . Glynneth!*" His face contorted. "Willed her death. How many times did I wish she had died instead of Ephraim?

Would I have left her for Linda? No. But is that more noble than my wishing her dead?" His voice rose to a frenzied pitch.

Nathan sat straight and frowned. "Stop. Don't go there. You've spoken the evil. Let God come in and clean it out."

"It's not that easy. I need to see my deep, inner sin for what it is—ugly, loathsome, monstrous."

"Oh. This deep, inner sin is way beyond the grace of God, I see. Do I spot a touch of pride here? Lawrie, Satan is messing with your head. You're painting a self-portrait that just isn't true. If you had stayed behind the fence and *willed* her off the cliff, that *would* be a type of murder. But you didn't do that. Everyone witnessed your self-sacrificing effort to save her. That's not hate, Lawrie. That's authentic love that can't be faked. In that instance, love overruled whatever hate was in your heart."

Lawrie's face again went into his hands.

"You know I'm right," Nathan said softly. "Give love a chance— God's love, not Linda's, not yours. My guess is, Satan wants to drag you down. But why? What's ahead? A presidential race? We don't know, but whatever it is, you need to be free from the past."

He reached across the table and tapped Lawrie's plate. "When you go to bed tonight, chew on this: Some define God's glory as glittering splendor, too bright to look at. I say God's glory isn't some big light show. It's simply the revelation of His *grace*—that full, undeserved offer of forgiveness that only God can provide. Let Him, Lawrie. Let Him wash your heart clean."

They sat silent, neither speaking, then Lawrie looked at his watch. "I told the crew to go, but Mrs. Liles said she'd leave two slabs of sweet potato pie, and she was whipping cream when I went in." His voice was husky, but he smiled. "Come, brother. Let's eat pie together."

Chapter 36

IN EARLY JULY, LAWRIE DROVE home over the mountains of Virginia after an awkward political luncheon in Harrisonburg. The political topic had been switched at the last minute—intentionally, he felt—leaving Lawrie's team staring at each other. Personal attacks were tucked smoothly into the oppositional presentation, but he could handle that as an everyday occurrence. He couldn't handle the unpreparedness of his aides and his own clumsy performance, though. Inexcusable. Martin would never have allowed any of it to happen, but he had a doctor's appointment he said he couldn't miss. Embarrassed and sorely conflicted, Lawrie left early and drove viciously, his thoughts as dark and twisted as the winding road.

And then . . .

Later, he wondered if his life would have gone on as normal if he had stayed until the event officially ended, or if he had returned to Washington via the highway instead of back roads. But he had done neither. Instead, he drove hard on the heels of the car in front of him, forcing his mind to the sharp-curve challenge of staying on the road.

Suddenly, time stopped. Lawrie slammed his breaks and skidded to the narrow shoulder, transfixed by a drama unfolding in a series of slow-motion film clips. *Clip One:* The naked, exposed undercarriage of the car in front as it flipped over the guardrail. *Clip Two:* Hollow, obscene clunks as it rolled down the embankment.

Clip Three: The car teetering on two wheels before slamming against a tree with four-footed finality.

Lawrie fought shock, punched 911, and heaved himself from his car to scramble down the embankment. The woman driver seemed conscious, but her door and window were inoperable. Lawrie ran to the other side, horror growing over *Film Clip Number Four*: Serious smoke from under the hood and the strong smell of gasoline.

The far door against the tree had sprung open but allowed only enough room to shut off the engine and unfasten the woman's seat belt. Panic gripped him as smoke filtered into the car. How could he get her out without them both dying? He had embraced the die part for himself on the butte, but not now. Please, Lord, not now. He *had* to save this woman.

Clearly, she was injured, and pulling her through the narrow slot could hurt her more. But smoke . . . gasoline . . . He had no choice. He gripped her arm and pulled. She screamed, but the awful alternative steeled his nerve.

He could never say where he got the strength—perhaps from the power of her screams—but he dragged her to a safe distance, sheltering her body against the expected explosion.

It never came. The only sounds were her moans and his lungs, rusty and useless, desperately dragging every agonized breath.

At the hospital, they assessed her damage: concussion, broken ribs, smashed pelvis, and spinal contusion. Indeed, what might have been relatively minor injuries had become far more serious from his extraction efforts. Lawrie had scrapes and bruises and a torn muscle but was released from the hospital after one night.

Before he left, he asked to see the woman—Annalee Adams. Head bandaged and face swollen, she could only grip his hand. Surgery had repaired the major part of her injuries, but in all likelihood, she would be permanently disabled and confined to a wheelchair.

Chapter 37

WHEN LINDA SAW REPORTS OF Jay's accident, her hand shook so badly she could scarcely control the computer mouse. How seriously had he been injured? *Thank goodness there hadn't been a fire!* The hospital releasing him the next day relieved her, but as she followed various threads of the story in succeeding days, she experienced a different sort of fear. This woman seemed different from the others. The online follow-up of the accident covered a lot of ground, with photos of Ms. Adams, information about the vibrant church she attended, details about her real-estate career, and, more particularly, animated discussion of the senator's growing attachment. Annalee Adams. Rooshie had been a horror, but this woman . . .

"Linda, you've got to stop thinking like that. Breaking dishes is a bad sign." Bonnie bent to a casualty from Linda's violent load of the dishwasher. "You're in a swamp and not even trying to get out. Jay's been going out with women. Why is this one more a threat than the others?"

Linda shoved in the last tray and slammed the dishwasher door. "Because she's attractive and personable, and from all I can tell, a committed Christian. That's what makes her dangerous."

Bonnie dumped glass shards into the wastebasket and turned to Linda. "Out!" She pointed toward the deck. "Sit there and think while I make tea."

The conversation that followed included recriminations, tears, apologies, and prayer. And a big breath from Linda. "Yes. I need a new direction." She sat silent a moment. "I've had this niggling idea. Tell me what you think.

"I'm bothered that most serious gardening is done by moneyed people," she went on. "Yes, middle classers love to garden." She leaned forward. "But I'm interested in people who like gardening but who have trouble putting food on the table. Have you looked at prices in seed catalogs lately? Outta sight—to say nothing of fertilizer and mulch. I'd like to work up ways to garden on the cheap, maybe get a club going. Fall is a good time to start. Gives us time to plan."

"That's super!" Bonnie's face lit as much with relief as with the idea itself. "Let me know if I can help. You need a catchy title. How about 'Pinchpenny Planters'?"

A week after the accident, Nathan flew from Bismarck to be with Lawrie, alarmed more by his emotional shock than physical damage. Lawrie had told him that sleep especially had been hard. The movie, deeply embedded, played over and over in that same, excruciating, slow motion, with Annalee's horrendous screams becoming his own.

Yes, he had saved the woman's life. No, there was nothing he could've done to spare her further injury. Yes, she was deeply grateful just to be alive, and yes, she was trusting God to work out her situation.

"The first thing she said after she could talk was how much she appreciated my being there, holding her hand, and praying." Lawrie strode through his apartment, abstractly rubbing arm scabs. "I wreck her life, and she thanks me!"

"What do you know about this woman? What's her background?" Nathan stood and motioned to a chair. "Come, sit down. I'll get coffee."

Lawrie continued his urgent strides but finally settled. "She said she grew up in Maryland, had a good life." His face twisted derisively. "Good life. And I wrecked it."

"Lawrie, she's the one who hit the curve badly. Had she been drinking?"

"No! She misjudged the curve. That road is ter—"

"She caused the accident. You were there and saved her life."

"No, I ruined it. There was no explosion, and if I'd waited till help came—"

"There *should* have been an explosion. You did what any reasonable—"

"But even if I did save her life, was it a good thing? Would she have—"

"Oh, stop! Now you're playing God, deciding who should live and die. Lawrie, you did what you could, what you should, have done. The rest and what will come of it is in God's hands. She's not blaming you, so lay it down. Let God handle it. And don't forget the miracle part. You're both still alive."

Nathan knew, though, that this would not end the guilt trip.

Senator Crofter found himself extremely busy. Two separate caucuses were pushing him toward an official presidential run. He was now well-known and attractive to a broad spectrum of voters. Each of the caucuses saw him as far stronger than any of the other wannabees who had stepped forward.

"Man, everything's going for you here!" The mainstream captain leaned forward admiringly. "You look strong, talk strong; you stand strong on fixing the economy, the racial mess, the international quagmire. You'd be a great money-raiser with us behind you. And being single gives you latitude to go with the flow. Get on board, Lawrie. The country needs you!"

The conservative coalition noted Lawrie's rightward swing with pro-life, pro-family, and gender issues. And both saw his sex-trafficking crusade as a unifying, bipartisan bonus.

Lawrie, though, had more immediate matters on his mind. His deficit-reduction energy bill had to get on the floor before summer recess. He and his most knowledgeable legislative assistant drummed for support, talking oil, gas, coal, wind, solar, and the high cost and inefficiency of ethanol. Opponents got in his face: spending advocates, corn growers who produced ethanol, the Environmental Protection Agency, even animal rights people. Martin's tip on Rasmussen had paid off, but he still needed at least two, and possibly three, more votes. He had his scheduled speeches pretty much in hand, but no matter what he did, where he looked, he could see only this huge, ugly nut that wouldn't crack. He instructed Connie and Ben to cancel all appointments and turn away calls that were not life or death. This bill had to get to the floor, and he had only six days to make it happen.

On the fourth day, he got back to his office well after closing time and glanced through the long note Connie had left, listing people who had called and what they wanted, as well as noting some sort of kerfuffle outside a Lakota Sundance ceremony that was being held this year on the North Dakota section of Standing Rock Reservation.

Lawrie frowned. *Sundance!* There hadn't been a Sundance in the state for years, though South Dakota sometimes had one. Billy hadn't said anything about it, but their conversations were mostly about his recovery process. Lawrie didn't like being in the dark. On reflection, though, he knew that this high, holy observance representing life and rebirth was always hidden away, due to repeated outsider intrusion and lack of respect. Participants would have spent the entire year in personal preparation for the month-long event that started and ended with a full moon.

He looked back at Connie's note. *Probably should be followed up,* she had written. Lawrie shifted to the phone list again and saw *Michael Spotted Deer,* the tribal Chair. He frowned. Was this part of the "kerfuffle"? Well, too late to call tonight. Tomorrow . . .

But tomorrow, a different sort of adversary ambushed him. As Lawrie was about to enter the office of the only Dem he could possibly sway, Martin intercepted him in the hallway.

"Martin," said Lawrie, "whatever it is, I don't have time. And I don't know where I'll be at lunchtime."

He turned toward the doorway, but Martin grabbed his arm, his face grim and chalky.

"I just got a call from my doctor. He says I have Stage Three prostate cancer."

"Oh, great! What a time to tell me."

"Crofter, is that you?" A door opened down the hall, and a head shouted annoyance in his direction. "We've been waiting fifteen minutes."

Lawrie started for the door, then turned back to Martin. "I've got to go. I'll talk to you later." Then, seeing Martin's face harden, he added, "Go out and lose a hundred pounds, and it'll probably go away."

As he strode toward the open door, he stopped suddenly. *What did I just say?* He turned back abruptly. "Martin—" But Martin was gone. He grabbed his cell phone and punched a button but got no answer—then or any half-hour afterward.

Mid-afternoon, Connie muscled into another tense, heated confrontation, this time with Senator Carlson, the chief bill obstructer. She handed Lawrie a printout of the Sundance brouhaha, complete with headline and lurid photos.

As Lawrie read, his face went white, and his shoulders sagged. Hauling himself from his chair, he said nothing and simply flapped a hand toward Senator Carlson on his way out the door— grimly noting the exultant gleam on the senator's face. At times like this, the muck of the trenches sucked him down.

In his office, Lawrie sank in front of Connie's computer and looked at the news sites she had ready for him. Somehow, a group of Christians had learned of the Sundance location and had planted teenagers near the road leading to the ceremony space. This was Tree Day, the opening of the sacred observance. The Christians had remained respectfully silent, but their hand-drawn placards howled disapproval.

AND YE HAVE SEEN THEIR
ABOMINATIONS, AND THEIR IDOLS,
WOOD AND STONE, SILVER AND
GOLD, WHICH WERE AMONG THEM.
DEUT. 29:17

THEY LEFT THE HOUSE OF THE LORD
GOD OF THEIR FATHERS, AND SERVED
GROVES AND IDOLS AND **WRATH**
CAME UPON JUDAH AND JERUSALEM
FOR THIS THEIR TRESPASS.
2 CHRON. 24:18

GOD'S **WRATH** FALLS ON THOSE WHO
SERVE **NATURE** INSTEAD OF HIM.

THEN SHALL YE KNOW
THAT I AM THE **LORD**

WHEN THEIR SLAIN MEN SHALL BE
AMONG THEIR IDOLS ROUND ABOUT
THEIR ALTARS, UPON EVERY HIGH HILL,
IN ALL THE TOPS OF THE MOUNTAINS,
AND UNDER EVERY GREEN TREE,
AND UNDER EVERY THICK OAK, THE
PLACE WHERE THEY DID OFFER
SWEET SAVOUR TO ALL THEIR IDOLS.
EZEK. 6:13

WORSHIP GOD
NOT THE SUN, MOON, STARS,
TREES, FIRE, WATER...
AND HOW MANY OTHER
IDOLS DO YOU SERVE?

Lawrie's blood went cold. He scrunched his eyes and rubbed his head, muttering, "Stupid, *stupid!* And how did they know where to find the event?" He hurried over the report, noting that the only injury was a young boy who had gotten knocked down in the ensuing push and shove. "Could have been worse," said Lawrie. "Was he white or Indian?"

"He was with the Christians and presumably white," replied Connie, "but something in a later report . . ." She scrolled to a new page. "Somewhere, it says the Christians were *escorted* out and the boy taken to the hospital, but I'm not sure about . . . Here it is. Oh, my!" She gasped. "The boy, so it seems, was a Mohawk of the Iroquois Confederation! That mucks things up, doesn't it?"

"Great!" groaned Lawrie. "An Indian import from Iroquois country. New York State? Or maybe Ontario, if we're lucky. Let the Canadians sort it out. No doubt they prepped the kid for the warpath with a Mohawk haircut—the crowning touch. What were they *thinking?*"

"Well, the question is, what are you going to do about it? U.S. or Canadian, the mischief happened here, and it's yours to deal with."

He clicked through the reports. The Lakotas herded the Christians away. The boy, not even twelve, had tumbled in the fracas, hitting his head when he fell. The Christians claimed the rough treatment had put the boy's life in jeopardy. Now the Lakotas, incensed by the audacity of the whole affair, were planning some sort of counter invasion, a Christian praise concert later in the month being mentioned.

"I called Michael a while ago and told him you were on your way," said Connie. "A bit of a lie, as you were trying your best to not be on your way."

"Well, call him again, and tell him I want to meet him. And get me a plane, will you?"

"They'll be ready for you; you can be sure of that. They know you're a Christian. *Ergo,* you didn't bother responding right away."

Lawrie looked at his watch with exasperation. "Look, are you going to—"

"I'm on it. Just get yourself—"

"Good. I'm going to squeeze in a quick meeting with Castner and Howell. Let me know when you have things in hand." He pushed out the door, punching his cell phone, but still Martin would not answer. *Worse than trying to push toothpaste back in the tube.*

Fifteen minutes later, Connie appeared in Senator Castner's office, flamethrower eyes at the ready. The receptionist ducked from the heat and ushered her to the inner sanctuary.

"The boy died, and he was a Mohawk from Upstate New York. Nothing said about his hair." Connie made her stiff announcement, then turned and left the office. Lawrie leaned his head on the back of his chair, eyes closed and face taut.

"I've got to go," he told the men and knew as he left that he'd be at least one vote short.

"I've got to go," he said to Connie when he got back to his office.

"Yes, you do." Connie's eyes were cocked at him, but Lawrie worked up courage to face the flames. Martin jabbing his conscience was quite enough without adding Connie to the mix. And to make matters worse, he was afraid of Connie, but not of Martin. Trolls, though, have to start somewhere.

"Connie . . ."

"No time," she said stiffly. "We'll talk later. You've got little more than an hour to get yourself to the airport. *Don't dawdle!*"

Chapter 38

IN THE LIMO TAKING HIM to the airport, he called Billy and got blasted from that angle, too. *"It's a mess, Lawrie. If you'd gotten here yesterday, we might've pulled off a reasonable defense, but that won't happen now, apart from a miracle. The Lakotas are furious; the Mohawks have bear claws sharpened for some sort of legal action against them."*

"That doesn't make sense!" exclaimed Lawrie. "Unless I'm missing something, the boy's death was accidental, and the whites provoked the incident. Get on Attorney Jakes ASAP for advice."

Billy grunted.

"Suppose we gather the Lakota brothers to go with me to talk with Michael. Set up a private *pau wau*. What do you say?"

Billy was doubtful. *"Let me think on that. My gut tells me Michael would veto, but we'll do our thing till you get here, then talk. Bruce will pick you up. It's his day off, and Nathan can't get away."*

At first, Lawrie felt disappointed, but then a plan came to mind as he walked from Arrivals to Bruce's pickup at the curb.

"Hi, friend," he said as soon as his seatbelt clicked. "Could I borrow your phone? I need to call Martin. He might answer a call from a strange phone."

He did answer, and Lawrie had his line ready. "Please don't hang up on me, Martin. My first and most important words are, 'I'm sorry.' And that's not pro forma. Immediately after, I couldn't believe what I had said. Yes, we've chucked nasty things at each other, but this was inexcusable."

He took heart that Martin hadn't cut him off, but he didn't risk giving him space for a response. "As soon as we can manage, I want to find out what Stage Three entails, what the options are, and how I can help you through this process. Can we talk, Martin? Maybe the first of the week. I have this huge mess to deal with here in Bismarck, but as soon as I'm able, I'll give you a call. Will you answer me, Martin?"

He held his breath but was rewarded by a soft *Yes,* though he couldn't interpret the possible meanings behind it. The fact that Martin had hung up on a positive note was enough for now.

Bruce looked at him. "Don't even ask," said Lawrie, staring straight ahead. But then, he turned. "Guilt plus guilt plus guilt. What does that add up to, Bruce?"

The driver leaned back, hands tipping upward on the steering wheel and eyes crinkling. "Well," he said, "me 'n math don't work too good, but even my prison gang could answer that. They got guilt with twenty plusses."

Lawrie slumped back and put a hand on his forehead. "Yah, I know—" and they both said, "Grace," at the same time.

Bruce drove him straight to Billy's house. The Indian waved off the usual social gestures and got immediately to business. The Lakotas, he said, were planning an offensive designed to start a fight, and the Christians reportedly were calling for a region-wide spiritual mobilization and an army of strong men to surround the building with clasped hands and prayer.

"Going to Michael with any show of force won't play—with him, with the rest of the tribe. I'm sure of that. Better you face the chief alone than ask for a back full of arrows when you and the guys turn to leave."

Lawrie put his head in his hands, and no one spoke. Finally, he looked up. "You're right. I need to go alone—alone, with peace in my mouth."

Rosa insisted that Lawrie eat something. "The men fast; you eat. You need strength."

He did eat, though as little as she allowed him to get away with. Afterward, a dozen men came to read Scripture and pray with him; and when Lawrie fell asleep in the middle of a sentence, they put a pillow under his head and continued to pray.

With fear and trembling, Lawrie drove south to the reservation the next morning and entered the Standing Rock Administrative Building and the office of Tribal Chair Michael Spotted Deer. Though they had long been on first-name terms, Michael greeted him gravely as "Senator Crofter." Lawrie did not push it. Instead, he sat in the proffered chair and remained silent for a long minute before this stern, sovereign presence with classic Indian profile and long, loose, black hair. So like Billy in many ways, without the Jesus-softening that made a difference.

Finally, Lawrie looked up. "Michael, I can say nothing; I can do nothing that could possibly make up for my negligence. I can only say I'm sorry for not getting here sooner. I was busy, but that's not an excuse. My duty was to be here. My heart was speaking, too, and I didn't listen to that voice, either."

Michael sat stone-faced.

"I'm not here as your senator or to ride the good relationship we've had in the past. None of that matters. I'm here because I messed up and want to make it right, if that's possible.

"The crux of the matter is a group of Christians who insulted your people and your spiritual ceremonies. They came, ignorant of who you are and what you stand for. I haven't had time to go tell them how badly they behaved, but I will. You, though, are first."

The only movement on Michael's face was an intensified frown.

"I'm not trying to appease you. You know me better than that, Michael. What that group did was wrong. A life was lost, and that needs to be addressed, but you and your people were the ones who were . . . *invaded*. They can wait."

Lawrie was rewarded with an almost imperceptible nod. He took heart and went on.

"You also know I'm a Christian, and you're probably thinking I would side with them and hang you out to dry. This part is trickier to explain, and I ask that you bear with me. Try to hear what I say."

Pray, guys, pray! Lawrie's gut tightened.

"I'm a Christian; the group who came here are Christians. We believe basically the same thing—that God, the Great One Who is holy and can't tolerate our badness, came to walk with us in love and then chose to die, so we could live with Him forever. I believe I have that in common with the New York Christians. Now, please hear me, Michael," he added quickly, seeing the frown turn into war trenches. "We—those Christians and I—*believe* in common, but we don't *act* in common. The God Who is Love sends us out to act in love as a way of drawing people to Him. Holding up placards with Bible verses that might as well be written in Dutch is the wrong act. Those verses meant nothing to you and were rightly interpreted as messages of hate. It was not love, and I disassociate myself from that sort of thing."

Lawrie studied the disarray in the Indian's dreary, dark-hued office. No faithful staff here with *Neatness* at the top of their job descriptions. He looked at the compelling figure of the Tribal Chair across from him. "I've asked myself what I would have done differently had I led that group. Their actions gave the wrong message. I'd want mine to do better."

He settled back in his chair and crossed his legs, a whimsical smile on his face. "I could see myself handing out fried bread or offering to service latrines. White man in Indian ceremonial territory doing that? 'Sure,' they'd say. 'Right.'" He laughed. "I'd certainly come out with a better appreciation for those who do those jobs! Jesus washed feet thick with sheep muck. I could at least clean privies."

He was encouraged by a slight twitch on Michael's mouth.

Lawrie bent forward. "Michael, your people have a long history of counting coup, a warrior getting more honor for just touching an enemy instead of killing him. We might look on the New York boys as coup counters, going into enemy territory and trying to touch Indians with the power of the Gospel. But it turned out to be a bad coup and did the opposite of what they intended. They even lost one of *their* warriors."

He shifted again and looked Michael in the eye. "From what I understand, your people are planning an act of revenge, hoping to restore honor, but that would be a bad coup, as well. And the Christian community here is just as bad, looking to line up their strongmen around the building, purporting to pray as well as protect, but in reality, it will be a hostile act. No honor on either side.

"Michael, I'm suggesting that both camps try a spiritual coup, and I've had some experience along that line." He looked down, elbows on his knees, steepled hands in front of his mouth. "As you know, my wife went off a cliff behind the country club. They had fenced off the sharp drop above the river; but the chain-link had a void off to the side, and Glynneth found it." He drew a breath before going on. "I tried; the Secret Service guys tried; but for whatever reason, she was determined." He dropped his head a moment. "I could have sued the country club for poor fence maintenance, and they would have had to pay. But I didn't. No amount of money would bring Glynneth back, and what was the use? As I look back, I believe I did the right thing.

"Then there's the Wolf Runner family. I could have pushed Billy to sue them, but—" He laughed sardonically. "Just speaking the idea would have put me in real trouble! I've learned that getting on Billy's wrong side can be hazardous to your health!"

He leaned forward, smiling. "Let me tell you a story—my wrong-headed attempt at a spiritual coup. After Billy was shot and Crawn killed, I decided to go to the boy's mother and offer my help. Dumb move. In less than five minutes, I found myself bleeding in the dirt after being slammed against my car by Crawn's drunk brother. You can imagine what I heard from Billy that day!"

Even Michael laughed.

"Since then, though, Billy has done it right. He waited till Crawn's mother got beat up by her husband and ended up in the hospital. He got his boys to go to her, just to be her friend and advocate. She hasn't turned the corner, but at least she has a bit of hope for her desperate situation. What I couldn't do with my flashy attempt at a coup, the Indian Christians are doing by showing love she can understand. Coup is a noble tool, Michael, and I think your people, even more than ours, grasp what I'm talking about."

When Lawrie left the building, he stopped short. Five men, their hands on his car, were praying out loud.

Chapter 39

THE SITUATION IN BISMARCK WAS dire, even though Michael had agreed to use his influence in the tribe. Lawrie, however, felt compelled to fly to Syracuse, New York. He had to do this. His bonding with the Indian community went far deeper than the Indian Affairs Committee that he chaired, and he needed to repair the breach with Michael. He didn't know what to do about the Mohawk boy, Ronnie. Yes, technically, he'd died from an accident, but bad blood flowed on both sides. He wished he could take along his prayer band. As serious as things were at home, the New York men could be more difficult than Michael. The Senate wrangle three days ago seemed almost a picnic compared to this. And Annalee would wonder where he was. He'd try to call her. He rubbed the ache in his neck that wouldn't go away.

Lawrie had learned from reporters that the group sent to evangelize Native Americans were part of a small, rule-oriented denomination. He had considered requesting an airport pickup to give him time to get the feel of the church folk. He thought better of it, though, and decided to talk first with the boys who had been involved. He picked up a rental car and drove fifty miles north to the farm community of Welton.

As he feared, talking with just the boys was hard to arrange. The parents who met him—all men, dour and defensive—wanted to leave the boys entirely out of the discussion, but Lawrie put on his friendly, political bulldog persona and would talk only about the heat, the heavy thundershower he'd driven through, and how the corn crop was coming along this year. Finally, and largely because he made clear that he wouldn't leave until he had talked with the young men, they gave way.

Lawrie greeted each of the five boys with a warm, easy smile and a bit of hilarity as he tried to attach his memorized names to the proper face. "Let's go for a walk, shall we?"

The dour faces began to object, but Lawrie simply raised his eyebrows and said, "Dairy's big here, isn't it? I'm guessing cows are tied into your larger families somehow. Am I right?"

One man spun away in disgust, and the others followed. Lawrie turned to the boys. "Okay, guys, where you gonna take me? A brook close by or patch of shade to cool us off?"

While walking toward a pond and clump of willows, Lawrie learned that the boys ranged from fourteen—Jerry—to twenty-two—Caleb. Mitch, Peter, and James fell in between. They all had jobs of some kind, but only Caleb had any sort of plan for his life. While settling underneath the trees, the boys tightened with apprehension.

"Tell me about your faith," said Lawrie. "You obviously care about wanting people to become Christians. What does the Bible say to you?"

The boys looked at each other, then Jerry ventured softly, "'All have sinned and fallen short of the glory of God.'"[6] Peter added, "'The wages of sin is death, but the gift of God is everlasting life.'[7] And God so loved—"

"Wait, wait." Lawrie held up his hand. "For sure you know Scripture, and that's good, but I want to hear what you believe in your own words. Start from the top. You believe in God. Then what?"

They looked at each other again. "Well," said Mitch, "God created the world and put Adam and Eve in the garden, but they sinned and—"

---

6   Romans 3:23
7   Romans 6:23

Lawrie nodded. "You betcha. Mucked us all up."

"Then Jesus came and—"

"Who's Jesus?"

They looked at him with alarm.

"Tell me. Pretend I don't know."

"Um—Jesus is God's Son," said Caleb.

"God's Son? What does that mean?"

"Well . . . He's the Son of God," he finished with a lame shrug.

"Oh—two gods, maybe?"

"No!" Caleb laughed. "One God, three persons—Father, Son, and Holy Ghost."

Lawrie passed over the Ghost part. "Okay, this one God—what's he like? Is He mean? What does the Bible say? God is . . . what?"

"God is love!" chorused three.

"Bingo! God *is* love—that's what He does, and we like that."

He paused a moment as a pair of ducks glided onto the pond with a splash and satisfied flourish of wings.

"But there's another side to God that we don't like so much. Like you said, God can't tolerate sin of any kind. But the God Who loves found a way to pay our huge sin debt. How'd He do that?"

Caleb's face lit. "He died on the cross!"

"You got it! God Himself, through Jesus, came to our world and died to erase our sins and show how much He loves us. How cool is that?"

He let them work through that idea, then leaned forward. "Now the hard part."

They turned instantly solemn.

"We've had a great talk here this afternoon, haven't we? We've laughed and joked and shared our faith with each other. Are we friends?"

They nodded vigorously.

"Now, supposing I had come, face all stern, holding up plac-ards that showed how mad I was about what you did back there in Bismarck. Would we be friends then, or would you look at me as some cranky old senator who's here to rub it in?"

They looked down and were very quiet, and Jerry, the young-est, trembled visibly.

He reached out to touch the boys on either side of him. "But I didn't. I'm not here to rub anything in. But what you did in Bismarck was not appropriate—you know that. Didn't win any souls or make friends out there. And your actions had serious consequences, one of which was a boy getting killed. Yesterday, I met with Michael Spotted Deer, one of the tribal leaders—a big guy in every way—and I was really scared. We'd been friends be-fore, but when he addressed me as Senator Crofter, I knew I was in for it. The first thing I did was apologize—not for what you did, but for my not coming back from Washington when I first heard about the incident. Trying to get a bill passed made me very busy, but that didn't excuse me. I should have dropped everything and gone—it was that serious. In the conversation, I told him my beliefs were basically like yours, but that I shared my faith differ-ently—making friends one person at a time until they can hear the Good News that could change their lives. By the time we fin-ished talking, he was back to calling me Lawrie instead of Senator Crofter and shook my hand. Meant a lot. You betcha!"

He watched the ducks a moment, then looked at the boys. "Are you guys ready to apologize to Michael?"

All eyes widened with alarm.

"I'd be with you, of course. And I'd pay most of your plane fare, charging each of you only a hundred dollars. Fair enough?"

They nodded.

"We haven't talked about how you feel about your Indian friend's death."

They looked at each other, and Mitch shrugged. "Yeah, we feel bad, but we hardly knew him, so it wasn't as though—"

"You didn't *know* him?" Lawrie looked incredulous. "How did he get on your team?"

Mitch shifted uncomfortably. "Well, Ronnie was Indian, and since we were going—"

Lawrie hissed exasperation. "Ronnie *died* as a result of this foolish trip. Does anybody care? Yes, it was an accident, but the trip itself . . . Why would your folks allow this crazy stunt?"

The boys, thoroughly alarmed, all started talking in an effort to douse this unexpected blaze of anger, but Lawrie put up his hands. "This isn't your fault. I'll have plenty to say to your dads, but please—all of you—stand up. I think you need a hug right now." He put an arm around Jerry and looked from face to face. "My guess is you fellows don't see a lot of love in your home or church."

Jerry's face crumpled, and he began to sob. Lawrie held him long and hard. "God loves you. I love you, too, but not as good as He does."

He moved to Caleb and then to Mitch. "We—you guys and I—we're called to be men of love in a world that doesn't know the meaning of the word. If I've done nothing else today, I hope I've given you a tiny picture of what love is supposed to look like."

He completed the circle with James and Peter. With an arm still around the latter, he looked at them all. "May I pray for you?" he asked gently.

The boys nodded, with tears on their cheeks.

Lawrie went home wretched. His meeting with the dads had not gone well. The men denied any responsibility for endangering the boys or for Ronnie's death and refused to talk about motives.

Finally, he fell back on senatorial weight-throwing to persuade them to allow the boys to make things right in Bismarck.

"Nathan, did I do any good out there at all?" The two men were walking the Missouri River trail. "Sure, I used a cheap trick, but I desperately wanted to drag those boys toward light and away from their parents' cult, if that's what it is!"

Nathan kicked a fallen branch from the trail. "Seems you connected with the boys. That's a positive."

"Yah . . . maybe. Like tossing a Cheerio to a starving child."

"Billy met with Michael at least three times this past week, so I think we're making progress. From what he says, there's still anger, but if the Christian community can come together in good faith, we just might avoid all-out war."

Nathan stopped and stared toward the river.

"This is sort of off-subject, but I'm thinking about two Christian cultures, here and in New York. Here, it's the white-Indian cultures that don't get each other. We whites choke over accepting Indian culture as a valid way to worship. We don't see it."

"Yup. If Billy had his way, half the service would be just drums." Lawrie grinned.

Nathan grunted. "Yah, Lakotas, he says, think drums express the presence of God and heartbeat of the earth. How would *that* fly in Welton?"

Lawrie's face went abruptly sad. "Yah." He shoved his hands into his pockets. "What *is* worship, anyway? We sit in church, sing with our minds poking through yesterday's trash, say pro forma things about the sermon, then leave, our spiritual duty done."

"That straight from your D.C. guys?" Nathan grinned sideways.

Lawrie didn't laugh. Instead, he picked up a stone on the edge of the trail and heaved it viciously toward the river. It fell short by three feet. He stared bleakly.

"Go figure. Nathan, right now I feel really, really small." He again pocketed his hands with a hollow laugh. "Maybe that's my answer about running for president."

After a week of tense negotiating, the Bismarck praise concert went off reasonably well, with only two armed drunks looking for a quick arrest. A few Lakotas wandered in just to see what it was like and were met—not by Christian strongmen but by friendly welcomers handing out fried bread. During the concert itself, a poignant song of forgiveness and grace led to a moment of silence for the dead Mohawk boy, the "Dakota Hymn" immediately following. In contrast to earlier in-and-out shuffle, no one moved.

The first thing Lawrie did when he got back to Washington, before seeing Annalee—even before lunch—was to head for Martin's apartment. He knew the chances of finding him were remote, but he needed to try. Martin wasn't there. Lawrie didn't want to risk calling from his own phone. What to do? Lunch seemed the obvious alternative, and the closest eatery happened to be a Subway—and Martin happened to be there. Alone at a table. Lawrie was stunned. *Thank you, Lord!* He took the time to grab a coffee, so he wouldn't be totally empty-handed.

He started talking even before pulling back the chair. "How's it going? I just got in. A horrendous week, both with Michael Spotted Deer and the New York boys. The boys were okay. Mostly the fathers." *Uh-uh—"Poor Lawrie" talk is no way to start this conversation.* "But while traveling, I was thinking of you and how you were handling your cancer. What are they telling you?"

Martin's face was undergoing cinematic flow, from surprise to anger to pain, mixed with an appreciable dose of fear. Lawrie considered reaching out to grasp his aide's thick hand but thought better of it. You couldn't call Martin touchy-feely. Would he even talk? Lawrie sipped his coffee.

Martin chewed his lip and stared out the window, his half-eaten sub forgotten. Finally, and keeping his eyes averted, he spoke. "I don't need your sympathy."

Lawrie was ready for that one. "Of course not. You're strong in ways I'm not. I'm here as a sounding board to bounce your options off of."

"And I don't need religious talk." Still staring out the window.

"You'll have to specifically invite that one. Any time, any place, I'm available, but you have to initiate."

The window still held Martin's eyes. "The doctor already gave the overweight lecture, so I don't need that."

Lawrie grimaced. "Well, I blundered on that one. I apologize. Bad timing."

Martin stared for what seemed an eternity, then finally picked up his sub, took a bite, and again looked toward the window for the chewing part.

Lawrie worked on his coffee.

Finally, Martin looked directly at Lawrie. "Two options: surgery or radiation—or both. If it were Stage Four, we'd talk religion."

Lawrie started a smile, but Martin was not laughing.

"What can I do for you now? Are you angry? I can handle that. Afraid? You can dump it all, and I can listen and talk only when wanted. We've never been friends, Martin. We've needed and put up with each other, but we know and can trust each other pretty well. I want to be here for you through this, but you have to let me. I won't push. Deal?"

Martin looked at him for a long time, then nodded and went back to his sub.

Chapter 40

DURING THE MESS IN BISMARCK, Annalee had been transferred from the hospital to a rehabilitation facility less than thirty minutes from Lawrie. He was surprised and pleased by its closeness, and being able to visit helped sooth his inner jaggedness. He found her lying flat, a trapeze bar over her head. Her face still bore signs of severe lacerations, and even smiling was hard.

Her first interaction, though, was a joke. "How do you like my short-long haircut? Mod, don't you think? A tattoo might balance it off. Maybe some face jewelry."

Lawrie laughed. "You look fine for the shape you're in."

Fine, indeed. Her eyes shone past the swelling—beautifully rich and alive with laughter, with pain, with something just out of reach. And as her face began to reshape, he saw a lovely lily emerge from an ugly, clumped bulb. He noticed her cheek dimple; dark, wavy hair; the cut of her nose and chin; the fullness beneath her nightgown. Prettier than Linda but not Glynneth. He had to work at keeping his eyes in their proper place.

Laughter came easy for her. "I know you're a senator, but you haven't revealed your color. Red or blue?" Her eyes turned merry. "Or maybe purple."

Lawrie laughed. "Why do you say that?"

"From what I hear, only hockey produces more bruises than congressional infighting."

Lawrie shook his head wryly. "Got that right! And I'm a hockey player!"

Initially, they talked of her progress. She was healing well from her surgery and had some movement and sensation in her legs, but the long-range outlook had her permanently in a wheelchair. This stabbed Lawrie yet again, but Annalee deftly moved the conversation to areas of commonality—their faith, favorite Bible passages, books they had enjoyed. Lawrie read Scripture from his iPhone and prayed with her. She, too, prayed, giving thanks again and again for their miracle, especially since the engine had been aflame, and the car should have exploded but didn't.

This sort of interaction spoke joy to Lawrie's heart. Of the women he had dated, a couple had become good friends, but they didn't know the language of deep, spiritual communion.

Her background came out bit by bit. Parents gone. Sister in Arizona. She was a top real estate agent, wondering if she'd ever work again.

One evening, he found her troubled. "What's wrong? Bad news from your doctor? Therapy?"

"No, they say I'm doing as well as can be expected."

"But you're not satisfied with that."

"Oh, I am! The pain is awful, and I'm exhausted by noon, but I have much to be thankful for. No, a different sort of pain." She stopped a moment and looked away. Lawrie didn't push her.

"I heard about your wife." She spoke gently. "Such a tragic death! I'm sorry, Lawrie. I didn't know or maybe didn't pay attention when it happened." She took his hand and pressed it. "I feel so bad for you."

Lawrie closed his eyes, the electricity of her handgrip sending multiple messages.

In that moment, he fell in love.

"Thank you," he whispered. "That means more than you know." Pain from the past and hope for the future fused in his face. "A lot has happened since then. For one thing, I became a Christian, and God did a lot of reshaping through my support system."

"That gives me hope! My emotional crash was similar, though nobody died."

"Can you tell me about it?"

She lay silent, staring at the dark, rain-splashed window. Then she turned back with a lift to her chin. "I was . . . engaged but had to back out two weeks before the wedding. Invitations, gifts coming, dresses bought, flowers ordered . . . " She stopped and looked away again.

Lawrie stroked her hand. "Tell me only if you want."

She smiled gratefully. "I became a Christian shortly after getting engaged. Jeremy seemed fine about it and even went to church now and again. But I soon realized we weren't on the same page, and it wasn't going to work. He kept saying it could, but anger began, and I knew what I had to do." She shrugged. "It was awful, probably the worst time of my life—even worse than the accident. But—" She straightened with a smile. "That's my past, and I'm absolutely sure I did the right thing." Her chin went up. "Turned out to be a great way to lose weight!" she quipped.

Other conversations followed, and her welcoming warmth and effusive gratitude for everything he did forged silvery chains about his heart. Glynneth had been far more skilled in despair than in gratitude, and Lawrie needed this new sort of bondage. But still, the damage his rescue efforts had caused clawed at his heart.

Nathan sized him up immediately en route from the airport on a rare weekend home. As they entered the house, he said,

"Lawrie, your motives are good, but you're lugging this huge boulder of moral obligation. You've got to lay it down. Yes, you injured her, but you got her out of a car that should have blown up. A horrible way to go. If she's thought of that, she's certainly grateful for only a moderate disability. You did what you had to, and you're being supportive, but don't get her hopes up that you'll take care of her the rest of her life." He set down a suitcase.

Lawrie's back went up. "But I do have an obligation, and—" He looked Nathan straight in the eye. "I can see myself living with her for the rest of my life, and you need to know that, right up front. Now, please let me make my own decisions."

Nathan's back went up, also. "Okay—have you done a background check on her? And how does she measure up to Linda?"

Lawrie's face went black, his jaw clenched, his eyes glittering. He turned away viciously, then back. "Nathan, I've never been this close to smacking you. Go away and let me simmer down."

"Oh, but you have been close. The hockey puck. Remember?"

"Nathan—"

Nathan waved his hand and turned away. "Never mind. Not a smart thing to say. I'm sorry, and I'm leaving."

Chapter 41

LAWRIE FOUND A WARMER RECEPTION in D.C. "I care deeply for her," he told his group, "beyond just sympathy. She's attractive. She's funny. We're on the same page with God, have common interests, and—" He shrugged with a wry smile. "And yah, her body," he added to ward off the inevitable question. "She'll always need a certain level of care, but Glynneth prepped me for that. And—" he grinned, "unlike Glynneth—she's frugal! I told her about you guys pushing me to live more simply, so she joked about the frippery of my iPhone over a cheap, basic cell."

Judge Albert studied him.

"Lawrie, I get your sense of responsibility and why you want to care for her. But there are alternatives to marriage. You could set up a limited trust, something along that line. The big question: is your real motive genuine love, or is it guilt? Don't answer that now. Just think, pray, and we'll talk about it down the line."

Lawrie did think. He thought about his brawl with Nathan and knew he'd have to work through that. The D.C. guys, though, were giving him room. And Nathan would come around, he felt sure. Yes, he'd think about his motives, but he needed Annalee. He needed her sweet spirit, her companionship, and yes, her body. He wanted to hold her, kiss her, but first—first, he had to get his mind straight. Background check? Yah, maybe. But not now. Right now, he had to stand up to Nathan . . . on principle. He would not let even his best friend run his life.

The fall congressional start-up had delayed bringing the New York boys to Bismarck for their scheduled apology to Michael. When Lawrie could no longer put it off, he made arrangements to fly them out. Though the boys were terrified, their meeting with Michael Spotted Deer went well. They walked from his office, faces fused with awe and relief. Lawrie took them to church on Sunday and introduced them to his friends and to Billy, who awed them even more than had Michael.

When the service was over and Lawrie began herding them toward the van for the airport run, Caleb halted, cleared his throat, and looked to his friends for support. "People out here say 'you betcha' a lot. I know I'm not saying it right, but Lawrie, you betcha we can't hardly count the ways you helped us." His voice went shaky. "We see better now—ourselves, God. We—" But he couldn't go on.

"Guys," Lawrie said, emotion heavy on his face. "Forget hugs till we get to the airport, or I won't see to drive. You know where we live. Come visit any time, or call when you need a friendly voice. We're here for you. *Yah, you betcha!*"

One Saturday morning, Annalee greeted him with eyes twinkling. "I've been learning interesting things about you!"

Lawrie removed his jacket and settled himself by her wheelchair. "Well, I'll take *interesting* over *nasty*. What's your little bird been telling you?"

She tossed him a pert smile. "Oh, that you went out last night. With whom—Ellen or Sheila?"

Lawrie frowned and cocked his head. "What do you know about Ellen and Sheila?"

"I know their names." She laughed provocatively. "Do you know any of my male friends?" She put out her hand. "I'm joking. Please tell me about your friends."

Lawrie shifted uncomfortably. *Background check* . . . "You're right—they're friends." He named other women. "You know them, too?" He deliberately did not include Rooshie—or Linda—but still his voice held more of an edge than he intended.

Annalee turned immediately apologetic. "Oh, Lawrie! This is coming out all wrong. My funny bombed, big time. I just want to get the feel of your life. You come in; we talk about my latest therapy or the horrible dinner—not what happens in the Senate or your life after hours. I'm missing big chunks of your world! And it's your fault!" Her eyes laughed.

Lawrie squeezed her hand, but then sat back. "These women are friends; that's all. Yes, I do go out occasionally. Last night— Ellen had moved but came back for a conference. It was good to see her. Sheila—"

"Forget Sheila." She waved disarmingly. "Instead of my health report, we'll talk only about what you're up against. I want to know your struggles, so I can pray for you."

They did talk. Annalee listened well, far better than Glynneth had. Lawrie left feeling reassured and nurtured.

Nathan had accepted Lawrie's apology but was reasonably sure he didn't mean it. They did get together every time Lawrie went home, both on their best behavior but both knowing their relationship was on different footing. Nathan would not back down, though. He sensed an emotional and physical drain in Lawrie that he couldn't pinpoint. Reasoning with his friend wasn't working; the wall had grown too thick. He couldn't even talk with the other men about it for fear of making things worse. Billy appeared to grasp the bigger picture, but the Lakota would say nothing.

"Hey, you're in bed. Therapy wear you out?" Lawrie set a pot of bronze-colored chrysanthemums on the window ledge and moved to Annalee's bedside.

"Well, getting kneaded and stretched like pizza dough every day isn't a party." She screwed her face. "*Brutus*, I call him, hollers when I screech, but I'm making strides. Figurative ones, at least." She laughed. "My leg, hip, and spine will never be functionally right, but I keep at it. They won't let me leave till I can get in and out of the wheelchair and tend to myself. That's a long way off, but I'm working at it."

Lawrie shook his head. "You're something else! I can't imagine what you go through, but you stay upbeat. I heard you singing when I came in."

"My defense mechanism." She flashed a smile. "Whatever comes—why not sing? I ask God to walk me through therapy. That old hymn, 'I Come to the Garden Alone,' takes me to a place of peace." She hummed a bit, then said, "Sing with me, Lawrie."

> *And He walks with me, and He talks with me,*
> *and He tells me I am His own,*
> *And the joy we share as we tarry there . . .*

Lawrie stopped singing, suddenly conscious of his shift of focus. No longer was he walking with Jesus, or even Linda, in the garden. As he watched the rise and fall of her every breath, his mind had begun to slide into the weeds.

Charlotte came to mind—Charlotte the singer. What might she say if she were here right now? But he quickly shoved the thought under his mental bed—though he knew Charlotte could not be set aside so easily.

Chapter 42

LINDA SAT IN THE GAZEBO, feeling at peace for a change. The work of putting the garden to bed for the winter was mostly done. Felipe, his summer helpers now gone, had worked long hours, but he stubbornly refused to cash checks for any amount, other than his salary. *A Godsend,* she reflected, *in so many ways. I don't understand how Jay got him to me, but I am forever grateful.*

The rich, fall colors that had surrounded the tiny island were now muted, the only greenery in sight being rhododendrons and sword ferns. Bony tree skeletons stood dark and stark, portending the dead of winter. For now, the season was holding its breath, waiting . . . waiting.

Waiting. Linda's life seemed perpetually pre-winter, but today she felt almost comfortable with that. Felipe, her poor friends, a few weeks rest from gardening chores—the fertilizer of gratitude was doing its work, nourishing her soul—at least in this moment of darkening splendor.

The week before Thanksgiving, Lawrie dropped in to see Annalee after a luncheon at which he had spoken. "Oo!" she exclaimed. "Aren't *you* grand!" She examined the fine weave of his sleeve. "That suit must've cost more than I spend on clothes in a whole year!" She laughed. "Come to think of it, I'll need a whole new wardrobe." She cocked her head. "What do you see me wearing in a wheelchair, especially to such an event?" She lifted her arms and looked at her wheels. "Can't be black—too morbid. Bright pink—or is that standoutish? Well, wheelchairs do stand out, don't they?" She laughed cheerfully.

Then, unexpectedly, she looked directly at him. "Speaking of wheelchairs," she said, "how is Billy doing?"

Lawrie looked up sharply. "What brought that on, and how do you know about Billy?" His voice tightened a tone or two.

She smiled. "I have my ways." She leaned to break off faded blossoms from the pot on the window ledge.

"How much do you know?"

She turned the pot, checking every side, then asked, "Will he recover fully or be in a wheelchair, like me?"

Lawrie got up, put his hands in his pocket, and walked the room. Finally, he turned and said with an even tone, "I don't know where you're getting stuff about Billy or anyone else, but please understand—his name should not be linked with mine in any casual conversation. Billy's my friend. I made that plain the day he was shot. But I make every effort to protect him from undue attention."

Annalee's eyes widened.

"Lawrie, I haven't been gossiping! I had no idea he needed protecting."

"I know you didn't. I'm sorry. He's been through a lot, and any link with me could bring more grief." He sat down again. "I don't know what his future will be. He has some sensation in his legs, so getting full use is not out of the question, but there's no real movement yet. The bullet wound healed well, his lungs and all. He's strong physically, but walking? Can't say. He'll try—that I know."

"You see him when you go home?"

"Yes."

"Are those visits difficult for you?"

He moved to the bedside tray and shifted each item as though order mattered.

"Before I answer that, let me line out an unpleasant bit of Indian history. Around the turn of last century, the Bureau of Indian Affairs—a government agency, mind you—decided to 'civilize' Native Americans. One of their mottos was, 'Kill the Indian; Save the Man.' They set up boarding schools—many run by Christians, of all things—and thousands of children were dragged from their families, their culture, and their language. They were given haircuts, new names, and daily abuse—as in brutal. This attempt to assimilate Indians into our culture produced an entire generation of broken people who themselves became abusers, resorting to suicide, alcohol, and crime to deaden their pain. Billy's grandfather was one of those government-contrived disasters, and his son—Billy's dad—suffered terrible abuse. He might have walked the same trail, but God planted a neighbor who became a friend and mentor. Got him away from his toxic home and literally turned his life around. When the boy married, he determined to stop the cycle, and Billy escaped his history." Lawrie stared out the window, reaching for even more difficult words.

"I've had a few people in my life whom I've loved profoundly, and Billy is one of them. I respect him as a man of courage and absolute commitment to God, to his family, to his friends, to his enemies. He is proud of his Indian heritage. '*I am Lakota!*' he says. Doesn't say much else verbally, but his entire life is a testimony to his God commitment, and I have benefitted directly." He turned away, struggling to keep his face in order.

Annalee reached for his hand. "I want to be like Billy."

He frowned, not knowing what to make of her earnest but strange remark. He decided not to pursue it.

Nathan picked up Lawrie at the airport in early December and found him almost totally non-communicative. That wasn't like him, and his silence put Nathan on high alert. They hauled luggage inside and dropped it at the foot of the stairs. Nathan waited for the usual, pro forma *thanks and come sit down a minute,* but Lawrie stood in the hallway and fidgeted. He looked down, rubbed his left arm, bit his lip. Nathan finally said, "What?"

Lawrie took two big breaths, then looked straight at Nathan. "I'm going to ask Annalee to marry me. She still has a ways to go. She can care for herself some but can't get in and out of the wheelchair, and nobody quite knows why." His words came in a rush. "She's trying as hard as she can. Marrying her would simplify my life, not having to drive up and back. It wears thin." He tried a laugh, but it didn't work. "I'll need a bigger apartment in D.C. and adjustments here at home. A lift or elevator. Or—" He shrugged. "I could sell the house and buy a single story." He aimed a bleak smile toward the wall sconce. "Both groups should approve of downsizing. You, at least." He looked back accusingly.

"Yah," said Nathan. "That'd fix things. New house, no more Charlotte memories." He had carefully altered his phrasing from *exterminate Charlotte memories,* but even with editing, he knew he had stepped over the line. "I shouldn't have said that, Lawrie. I didn't mean to be hurtful. Well, maybe I did. Charlotte was such a positive force in your life, and I'd like her to be one now, even in absentia."

Lawrie didn't explode as he expected, but Nathan could see the pain his words had inflicted, almost a physical flinching. He put his hand on his friend's arm. "Any time you want to talk, I'll be here." He gave a squeeze and turned toward the door.

Before Annalee's accident, Republican Big Wheels had nattered about a presidential run for Lawrie. After the accident, they backed off some but were now back to full volume. This couldn't have come at a worse time. His relationship with his best, most valued friend was in shambles, and he was about to make a marriage proposal—both good reasons to think hard concerning a presidential run.

How would that decision impact his relationship with Annalee? They had joked about the presidential thing but had never talked seriously. Was now the time? He doubted she would object, especially to the First Lady part, but she had no idea of the cost—constant travel, physical and emotional drain, unrelenting hostility for both, and background searches. Would she have the backbone for a run? He didn't know and was almost afraid to ask. Dangerous waters . . .

In Washington the following week, Lawrie arrived at the Maryland rehab facility at lunchtime while trays were being distributed. He heard loud voices from Annalee's room, and an aide flounced from the room and brushed past. Lawrie's eyes followed her with question marks, but he entered the room. "What was that all about?"

Annalee made a face. "Oh, just coleslaw. Again!" She laughed. "Somebody must've dumped a truckload of cabbage out back. Lawrie, no matter how nicely I ask, they keep bringing it."

He grinned. "Easy enough to fix. I'll eat it," and he picked up the dish and her knife and shoved the slaw, bit by bit, into his mouth. "Anything else you don't like?"

"Well! Raid more of my lunch, and I'll slap your hand!" Her earlier awkwardness evaporated. "I'm so glad to see you!" Her eyes smiled rich and warm. "You're early. I didn't think you'd come at all, with your big event last night. How did it go?"

"Reasonably well, though I got in hot water on a couple of issues. Just mention marriage and family and First Amendment rights, and temperatures head for the ceiling."

"Well—" Annalee picked up her fork. "Political hot water is a poor way to get warm. I prefer hot showers myself." She flashed a playful smile.

On his way out, he spotted "Brutus," Annalee's physical therapist, and decided to ask about a possible release date. His real name was Thorsten, a god-like name that fit his physique and way of doing life. Annalee was right about that.

"Hi, Thor. Wanted to get your take on Annalee Adams. She's been here a long time now. Do you see an end in sight?"

Thor shrugged and stared at the nurse's station, and Lawrie began to wonder if he was into talking at all. Finally, the therapist spoke. "That's sort of up to her."

Lawrie frowned. "What do you mean—*up to her?*"

The therapist again shrugged. "Talk to the staff." He looked at his watch and turned away. "Gotta run."

Lawrie stared after him, perplexed. No wonder Annalee didn't enjoy her sessions. He moved to the desk to enquire of "the staff" and was referred to her doctor, who was not in that day.

"Anyone else I can talk to?"

"The charge nurse might have a minute, but we're all busy, as you can see." The woman smiled brightly. "Come. I'll take you."

The charge nurse proved equally non-informative under an umbrella of unintelligible jargon. She answered Lawrie's questions but defended Thor unequivocally.

"He's one of our best therapists. Physical therapy is painful, for obvious reasons, and patients who cooperate do benefit greatly. That's what we're here for. Ms. Adams still cannot do a transfer and needs max assist with ADLs. Now, if you'll excuse me . . . " And Lawrie was ushered out of her office—again with that same sort of bright smile.

Chapter 43

CHRISTMAS WAS NOT AT HOME as usual, and Lawrie left orders that the house be decorated only minimally. This was to be a special day—right there in Washington.

He rented a wheelchair van and took Annalee to a small restaurant, one of very few open on Christmas day. As they were led to their table, he thought back to the motel two Christmases ago and the feast provided through two angels. What were their names? He couldn't remember. He'd have to ask Nathan or Billy. Those people were gold coins he dared not lose.

This restaurant was tastefully decorated. Annalee, having somehow risen to appropriate wheelchair attire, wore a rose, low-necked affair that draped provocatively over her shoulders. Her hair, beautifully coiffed, set off ruby dangle earrings. Her color was high, and Lawrie breathed the beauty and passion of the moment. He loved this woman. Her vibrant eyes pulled him in. Her voice—warm and throaty—stroked his soul. He desperately wanted to hug her. He had held her the day of the accident. It hadn't registered back then, but the feel of her flesh left an imprint that would not go away. He needed her.

He reflected on past Christmases—the one that almost killed him, then last year with Rooshie, and now this. His heart was full, and he drank in the fervor of the occasion.

He had worked out his proposal—not there in the restaurant, but after dinner, at Brookside Gardens in Maryland, where they would view the dramatic Christmas light display. It would be an evening to remember, erasing the pain of Christmases past.

The previous two years had taught him much—about himself and about the God who had provided two tribes of men for his instruction. He had to negotiate carefully the stepping stones of this strange, new love territory. Nathan—and Billy—were watching . . . watching. To say nothing about scandal-watchers. He had to do this right.

Ordering dinner was difficult, choosing between marinated duck breast and grilled, free-range bison ribeye. They ordered both, with the agreement to share at will. Dinner couldn't have been better—the food, the conversation, the ambiance, the unspoken exchange of passion.

When they left the restaurant, Lawrie opened the passenger door of the van. "How about riding up front with me?" He grinned.

"Oh, yes—please!"

"Put your arm around my neck." With an impish grin, he lifted and placed her carefully in the front seat. He saw her wince as he settled her. "I'm sorry. I hurt you."

"No, I'm fine. You did well—better, actually, than the rehab clowns. You're good for me!" She squeezed his arm affectionately. "I wish I had you all the time."

Lawrie drew a shaky breath, but the parking lot of a restaurant was not the place for a proposal.

The ride to the gardens passed pleasantly, but as they waited in line to pay the entrance fee, a nearby deaf couple distracted Lawrie with their rapid finger movements—much too fast for him to follow their conversation. He was pleased, though, to catch a few words or phrases. They appeared to be bantering back and forth, laughing, and very much in love. But then Lawrie's blood froze, and he white-knuckled the steering wheel. A word configuration he knew far too well: *Watch your step, buddy!* Charlotte!

How often had she signed that to him? Blood pounded his head, and Annalee had to repeat a question before he heard her.

"What's wrong, Lawrie?" She looked at him closely. "Are you all right?"

"Yes. I'm sorry." He tried to laugh but couldn't. "What were you saying?"

"Well, even before we're in, I see 'money' written all over this place. The lights alone—I can't imagine the size of their electric bill! And the garden—how many missionaries could be supported with all that money? I don't know what it'll cost to get in here, but only rich people can afford—"

"Yes, we'll pay here tonight." His voice held an edge. "Christmas lights cost, but the gardens—those beautiful flowers and shrubs, so lovingly planted and laid out—all that's free. Every day." He clamped his jaw and didn't speak again until they were inside.

He didn't propose at the garden but did get over his miff. Annalee had immediately back-pedaled, and the drive through the glorious display had warmed his heart and body. Not only did she *ooh* and *ah* appropriately, he found her even more beautiful and receptive and considered pulling out of the line of cars to make his move. But the only spaces had guards moving traffic along.

Back at rehab, they might have sat awhile, but an attendant came out to help Lawrie get her inside. Propose in her room, maybe? Rooshie, though—the ghost of Christmas Past—brought on an unforeseen attack of ambivalence, and a nurse's entrance shut down even that opportunity.

His mind worked hard on the way home. Where had she gotten her beautiful clothing? She wouldn't say and had just laughed it off. After dinner, the evening had progressed badly. Back in her room, they were both tired and short, and on leaving, he heard rude words to the nurse.

He climbed into the van and sat a moment. The proposal hadn't happened, but he could have at least kissed her somewhere along the line. Why hadn't he? He started the engine and examined the problem up and down—against Rooshie and even against Linda. But that wasn't it, he decided. If nothing else, Rooshie had taught him discipline through a deliberate, intentional act on her part. He would not throw away her lesson. As Chase had said, kissing was "cheap currency." A kiss had to mean something; he knew that—one of those important stepping stones. Keeping his body out of the relationship was serviceable discipline until he finally committed to Annalee. His D.C. guys would back him on that, even if Nathan didn't.

Linda sat in front of her cold, empty fireplace on Christmas night, thinking through the implications of what she had just read online. Was Satan showing up her weakness, or was God saying definitively, "Get over him." The line she had read said, "Has Annalee Adams landed her man? Sources close to her say yes."

Lawrie did not actually see that report, but Judge Albert alerted him to it. The senator was not happy, and Annalee seemed as mystified as he. It served, though, to put proposal plans on hold.

Chapter 44

LINDA DID NOT PARTICULARLY LIKE Florida; but having been asked to participate in an important panel discussion on invasive plants and what to do about them, she gathered a few scraps of enthusiasm and bought her airline ticket. Although Florida is far from prime in January, it would be considerably warmer than Westchester County, New York. Then, too, her birthday fell during that week, and her removal might defer whatever celebration Bonnie might pull together.

It didn't. In fact, Bonnie came up with something so splendid that Linda's eyes stayed wide for an entire day. Somehow, she had finagled a dinner date in Florida with the noted horticulturalist, Stephan Van Grooten. Linda could hardly imagine sitting down, one on one, with this man from whose publications she had drawn heavily for her own presentations. Would she have wit enough to converse intelligently with him?

A conversation with Charles and Emily of her garden club didn't help matters. "Oh, my!" said Emily. "I read something about that man. A skirt-chaser, maybe?"

"Oh, my, indeed!" Linda's eyes doubled in size.

Emily shrugged. "Could be gossip. He's one heck of a horticulturalist, I know that."

"My dear, your eager-man repellent would keep moose flies away," said Charles. "You'll be safe enough." He winked and batted Linda's arm.

Still, Linda was apprehensive when she and Stephan finally connected at a cozy, upscale eatery. She soon relaxed, though, finding him warm and engaging. Handsome, yes, but manageable. They laughed and chatted comfortably through dinner, and she felt valued and appreciated, far more than she had anticipated.

After eating their fill and sitting back, Stephan crumpled his napkin. "The next course is my garden. It lacks the magnificence of northern gardens, of course, but I think you'll find it interesting." His eyes crinkled a compelling invitation.

Emily's warning popped up. But how could Linda refuse such an opportunity, especially after such a gracious tête-à-tête?

"I'd love to see your garden, but, alas, I have significant prep work before tomorrow's event."

"Oh, but you must see it!" replied Stephan. "I value your assessment. Tell you what," he went on disarmingly, "after a quick peek at the garden, I'll whisk you to your hotel in plenty of time for your prep. No complicated questions to hold you up. Promise."

Linda drew in her breath but could not bring herself to be rude. "Thank you. I do need to work and get a good night's rest."

They drove to his waterfront home at the remote end of a guarded luxury community; Linda's eyes went wide at the wealth paving his street. Not pure gold, but close. But when he led her into his garden, breath failed her. She desperately wished she dared snap photos or surreptitiously take notes like some neophyte botany student, but she drew out her inspection as long as she could. But when he suggested going into the house for a drink, alarm bells clanged. No. She would not be caught in this sort of trap, but before she could refuse with any degree of grace, Stephan cut through.

"My wife probably has goodies. We did miss dessert, but we'll tell her we're only thirsty."

What wife? Emily had told her that Stephan was not currently married, but that he did have his women. The house was dark. *Definitely* not good. He had her firmly in his grip, however, and was steering her toward the ornate, Spanish-style villa. *Lord, help!*

Her chest grew tight as he opened the door and almost shoved her into cool darkness. Heart pounding, she braced for a fight. He put his arm around her. She stiffened and tried to twist away.

Suddenly, lights came on with blinding brilliance, and shadowed voices in the cavernous living room whooped out, "Surprise!"

Linda almost fainted, but Stephan's arm tightened and drew her toward a chair. "I think we need that drink—right now." He laughed, and the disembodied voices morphed into at least a dozen of Linda's friends who were wintering in Florida, with Bonnie at the forefront.

"Happy birthday, dear Linda!"

Linda burst into tears and clung to Bonnie.

Toward the end of January, Annalee startled Lawrie with a forceful warning about her ex-fiancé. "I dreamed about him last night, Lawrie, and he was terrible!"

"Well, dreams can be like that, but they're not real. Set it aside. Get your mind on other things."

"But he was going after you, and I couldn't stop him!"

"That's not real, either."

"Lawrie, he's evil! After he left me, things were okay, but then he said he'd get you. You've got to promise you'll never go near him or talk to him."

"Farthest thing from my mind." He frowned abruptly and looked at her. "What do you mean *after he left you?* When was that?"

Confusion seized her eyes but only momentarily. She looked away, waving dismissively.

"See? The dream is messing with my mind! I meant to say *after I left him.*" She gestured nervously toward her nightstand. "Get my Bible, Lawrie. Please read something about not being afraid."

Alarms went off in his mind, and the background check he'd never done clanged loudest. Her fear was immediate and palpable, though, so he opened the Bible to Psalm four, ending, "In peace I will lie down and sleep, for you alone, Lord, make me dwell in safety."

He returned the book to the nightstand and smiled brightly. "Now, turn off the dreams. Forget the night stalker."

"Lawrie, you're not taking me seriously. Promise me you won't talk to him!"

He paused and bit his lip, the smile unraveling. "Annalee, I don't make silly promises. I have no intention of going anywhere near him. Please be satisfied with that."

In the corridor, he greeted Annalee's aide but got only a wintery smile in return. What had turned her sour? Was it . . . Annalee? Her rude remarks to the nurse came back, and the hair on his neck rose as he unlocked his car.

Chapter 45

TWO THINGS WRECKED FEBRUARY FOR Lawrie. The first was a rare meeting with the boys at home, where Nathan asked, "Have you told Annalee about Linda?"

Lawrie huffed and turned away, kneading his hands.

"Well, I guess I got my answer on—"

"I will tell her!" Lawrie almost shouted. "I just haven't had the right opportunity."

Nathan said nothing, his raised eyebrows speaking volumes.

The other men seemed more understanding.

"Yah, we got questions," said Mike, "but we know you're smart enough to make the right choice when the time comes."

Billy, though, remained inscrutable. He said nothing until just before Lawrie left. With a hand on Lawrie's arm, he said, "My daddy taught me tracking. Started me on a slug track. Silvery trail. Easy to trace—except he made me figure out which way the thing had been going. Took me three weeks. You can't track something till you know which direction it's going. I never forgot that lesson."

Lawrie stopped breathing and couldn't think of a thing to say. Billy simply dropped his hand and backed his wheelchair away from the door. Lawrie went out into the cold.

The second month-wrecker was a minor bombshell in the form of an online accusation that Senator Crofter's campaign had accepted an illegal contribution.

> Senator Lawrence Crofter of North Dakota has put his foot in it—again. His lady friends seem to have a fondness for tracking mud into his living room.
>
> A contribution of one thousand dollars has been made to the senator's re-election war chest by an organization that reportedly received it from an unknown woman who obviously does not want the connection revealed. The donor's political motives might be solid, but her reputation may quickly tarnish.
>
> The Code of Federal Regulations, 11 CFR 110.4(b), specifically states that contributions made by one person in the name of another are prohibited. 'No person shall knowingly permit the use of his or her name to effect such a contribution.' It also prohibits 'knowingly . . . assist[ing] someone in making a contribution . . . or accept[ing] a contribution . . . in the name of another.'
>
> Perhaps Senator Crofter should pay more attention to his political bankroll than to his women.

The name attached to the article was Ewen MacClerhan.

Lawrie was furious. Normally, he would have blasted Martin, who had by now recovered from surgery, but residual guilt over his shabby treatment of his aide sent him to Connie instead. Her back went up, and like the Ghost of Christmas Future, she pointed wordlessly at Martin, disappearing into his office. Lawrie had no choice.

He walked carefully, focusing his anger on Ewen instead of Martin. "What does the man have against me? The actual contribution is peanuts. A thousand dollars. Anyone other than McClerhan, I could just say I didn't know about it, just slipped by, end of story. Is the man underemployed and down to nickel and diming? Get on it, Martin."

But before Martin had a chance to ferret out the miscreants, the matter exploded, splatting peanut butter in every direction and especially on Lawrie's political suit. "Crofter Nervous About Re-election." "Crofter Top GOP Presidential Contender? Not Any More." "The Real Crofter Comes Out." "Honest Lawrie Less than Honorable." "Does North Dakota Need to Rethink Its Prime Senator?" Journalists all but slobbered in their pursuit of yet another sex alliance. Even friendly venues played hardball.

"Martin, what have you found so far? It's been nearly a week. Any clues yet? *Why* is this happening?" Lawrie's face was haggard.

Martin shifted what remained of his dieted bulk uncomfortably. "I've checked every thousand-dollar contrib, and they all look legit. Now it's your turn." He looked over his glasses balefully. "Check your women."

Lawrie blew in exasperation. "I have checked each one—in my mind, anyway."

"C'mon, Lawrie. Gotta do better than that. Go down the list. Who've you gone out with? Name them."

Lawrie swung around angrily, huffed a few times, then sat down. "All right. Rooshie is the least likely of the bunch. Ellen and Sheila. Both are too smart to pull a stunt like that. Annalee doesn't have that kind of money. Then, some I went out with once or twice. Jennifer. Natalie. Lois. Who else . . . what was her name? Bridget. I may have forgotten one, but that's pretty much it. None of them were into contributing, let alone a thou."

Linda walked uninvited into his mind, and his heart froze. Linda had means and possible motive. And yes, Ewen was capable of finding her, digging her out, and piling dirt on them both.

Martin was watching him, squinty-eyed. Lawrie had to leave the room. Now. Before his thoughts shifted to teleprompter mode.

Spring was on the doorstep, the time of year Linda loved best. Anticipation of the coming season was better than the actuality. Once new greenery appeared, the subsequent explosion of growth and beauty would be overwhelming, leaving her soul in tatters.

Though patches of snow still lingered, this was a busy time. The greenhouse was pumping warm, humid air across trays of seedlings. She and Felipe were making final decisions in preparation for this year's grand garden tour. All the heavy work was finally complete and replanting well started. From the look of things, winter losses were minimal, with sufficient snow to protect vulnerable plants.

Eight women had signed up for her Pinchpenny Planters project, and Linda would soon be holding their hands and sniffing out bargain plants. She was under no illusions that the job would be easy. These people were not the rich, well-educated crowd she normally worked with. One woman held two jobs just to keep food on the table. Two had been abused, and others were single moms. Linda's bottom line for group membership was a passion for growing things that would get them past the grunt work. And she would demonstrate that plunging one's face in a fragrant peony blossom could float them through an entire day.

Bonnie suggested tacking a fifteen-minute Bible study onto the end of each session, and to Linda's surprise, only one woman left early. The ladies loved being prayed for and fussed over. And they raved over the high tea Bonnie laid out after a Saturday session.

"You'd think I'd given each of them a hundred dollars!" Bonnie said after the women left. "I hope you're writing an article about this."

She would. And yes, busy was good. For the first time in three years, Linda felt fully energized. Busy also kept her thoughts out of trouble.

Chapter 46

THE DONOR HAD TO HAVE been Linda. Lawrie lay awake nights trying to decide what to do. He could address the problem only so many ways, most of them intolerable. He could go see her. His breathing stopped on that one. *Oh, and by the way,* he heard himself saying, *I'm about to get married.* He grimaced and pounded his head. He could call. Almost as bad. He could email. He didn't have her address, but Martin could find it easily enough. He could send someone. Martin. No. Nathan. No. He could write a letter. Possibly, but a hard, cold way of going about it, and what would he say? He could have Connie or Dori from his home office write a formal . . . No, no, no. Not to Linda. If he chose a letter, he'd have to write it.

And right away. His work was suffering, and he hadn't seen Annalee in over a week. He had called twice and been scolded. First, though, a draft.

Dear Linda,

Could he even say "Dear"?

This is an extremely awkward letter I wish I didn't have to write. I've thought long and hard and prayed much, but here I am, being a pain.

Our "friend" Ewen MacClerhan has stirred up trouble again, and I guess our feelings are mutual about him! This time he alerted the entire world that someone contributed a sizeable amount of money to my re-election campaign, but wanting to remain anonymous, said person donated through a third party—which is illegal, according to the Code of Federal Regulations, 11 CFR 110.4(b).

Aaugh! Legalese.

My staff is searching diligently but hasn't been able to solve the mystery. All along, though, I've remembered your great kindness to me in the past.

No, strike "in the past." Too pro forma, insincere.

. . . kindness to me and thought you might somehow have heard that my coffers were low and decided to do the generous thing—not knowing about the CFR rule. <u>If not, then please accept my heartfelt apology.</u>

Maybe double underline there.

I wouldn't accuse or hurt you for the world. But with characters like MacClerhan around, I need to make things right and get him off my back.

Okay, how to end it? *What vapid thing can I say?* "I hope your garden is growing nicely." "Wish I were there." Bad. And the complimentary close. Yours truly? Sincerely? Cordially? "I'll love you forever, Kileenda"? *Lord, help me!*

"Bonnie, *what* is going on with Jay? First that horrible Ewen attack, and of course that woman. Is she really the one for him? I'm so afraid."

Bonnie had dragged Linda out of her house and to the nature preserve next door, its trails threading the great hemlocks. Bonnie was silent a moment.

"This probably sounds stupid, but will your being afraid of this woman do Jay any good or change his mind? I know you're praying, and that's good, but rubbing your arms and hyperventilating?"

Linda started to cry but bit her lip and took several big breaths. "Okay. You're right. Worry can't help him or me. An idea just popped into my head, and I know you'll laugh. It's just the opposite of what I'm feeling. Bonnie, I'm going to fast for Lent."

Bonnie looked at her oddly. "As in not eating for forty days? Or maybe just giving up chocolate?"

Linda laughed. "Well, giving up chocolate would get my attention, but I'm thinking a different kind of fast, and I'm speaking it so you can keep me accountable. I'm not—"

Bonnie broke in. "You're going to fast for Jay! What a super idea! Way better than rubbing your arms."

"No, not fast *for* Jay; fast *from* Jay. That's where it gets weird." She put a fist to her mouth for a moment, then spoke decisively. "My fast will consist of not visiting any websites or videos that feature Jay. I'll simply trust God for him and try to refocus on life as it is and not as I wish it were. Winter is over. The garden will take on new life, and I, the gardener, will try to blossom, as well."

Bonnie's eyes went wide. "That's big," she said softly. "Especially now with all this stuff going on."

"Exactly. And now I'll see how strong my addiction actually is."

"Well, it's not like pornography."

"No, but is one addiction better than another?"

Bonnie pulled her friend to the side as a service vehicle went by. "I'll pray, Linda." Then she added softly, "Lent's almost here, and Easter's coming."

Lawrie's letter to Linda still had not been finalized. After two more bad drafts, he called Nathan.

"Buddy, I need your help," he said. "Linda's my prime suspect for the illegal contribution, and I'm trying to write a letter but can't get it right."

"Wow! That's tough! Makes sense, though. Read what you've got, bro. Let me hear it."

Lawrie read and was not heartened by a long silence. "You still with me?"

"Oh, yes. Just trying to think it through. Somewhere up near the beginning you ought to say something like you're hoping she's not the culprit, so she doesn't think you're out to pin her to the mat. And I don't think you said anything about the money needing to be returned to her."

"Oh, right! That's good. And I didn't tell her how to respond. Directly to me? That would be really awkward."

"No. How about to one of your offices? Dori up here, maybe?"

"Of course! Why didn't I think of that? And I'm stuck on how to close. 'Very truly yours' won't do."

"I think you had an apology in there, but why not end with one? 'With many apologies,' blah blah."

"That's good. 'With many apologies for intruding on you—again.' Is that too crass?"

Again, Nathan was silent, but finally, he said, "That'll work. I think she'll take it right. This is tough for you, bro, and thanks for asking my help."

Lawrie returned to his computer, made his additions and a few more corrections, then wrote it out by hand, and put it in an envelope. He laid it on the floor and knelt before it. He stayed there, long beyond his actual prayer, heartsick over having to put that letter in the mail.

He couldn't, though—not right away. He'd see Annalee tomorrow, then drop it at the post office around the corner from rehab.

He stood, brushed nonexistent dirt from his slacks, and went to bed whispering, *Kileenda, Kileenda...*

That night, however, Lady Cool Water came to him in a dream. He was still on the floor, the letter now a foot thick. She glided through the closed door, cloak shimmering in a ragged sort of way as though her passage had been difficult, as though she, too, were battling right along with him. She knelt to his level and put her hands on either side of his head, eyes full of melted compassion.

"My poor, dear Lawrie." Her voice, blanket warm, sounded inside his head. "You are so loved, my dear. Your heart is hurting dreadfully. But take it out and lay it beside the envelope. God will see it and bring healing, but only after you lay it down."

Her fingers kneaded his head, and she leaned forward as though to kiss him. Before her lips touched his forehead, though, she disintegrated into glittering flecks of gold.

Lawrie rolled face down on his bed and wept into the pillow.

Late the following afternoon, Lawrie dragged himself to the rehab facility, the letter burning his chest. He didn't want to see Annalee today, but he had to before posting the letter. He didn't quite know why, but here he was.

Annalee welcomed him anxiously. "It's like forever since I saw you!" she cried. "At least, you're all right. I know you've been busy, but Lawrie, dearest, you look terribly tired."

Lawrie sighed, his spirit nestling into her welcome concern. He wheeled her toward the window and pulled a chair close. "I didn't sleep well last night, so yes, I am tired."

"What—besides . . . well, you know who—was bothering you?"

He shrugged and tried to look noncommittal. "Oh, lots of things. The usual—Senate skirmishes, long Martin sessions—always stressful." He smiled bleakly.

"Can't you get rid of Martin? Find somebody else!"

"No." He sighed. "He's indispensable. I couldn't do without him. Right now, we're working through the illegal contribution that touched off a nasty news report."

"Oh, that! You started to tell me the other night, then something else came up."

"One of those nuisance things, but it's made life difficult, for many reasons."

This would be the perfect time to tell her about Linda, but he could not. Not now. Not ever? "Someone sent a sizeable sum to my campaign fund, but—"

"Is your fund coming up any? You said it was alarmingly low. I think those were your words."

"Yes, it's doing better, thanks to staff and faithful volunteers. But I'll still need to get out there and hustle. A one-thousand-dollar donation, though, has to be returned, but we don't know who sent it. The money was given anonymously to a third party, and that's illegal. I have a good idea who might've, but it's a sticky—" He broke off and looked at Annalee. "What?"

Eyes wide, she clapped her hands over her mouth. *"Illegal!* Oh, Lawrie, I was going to surprise you on your birthday. I couldn't go buy a gift, so I got a friend who knew someone. Lawrie, I didn't realize it was illegal."

"You sent that contribution? *A thousand dollars?"*

Her face was stricken. "I had no *idea* it would get you into trouble. I just thought . . . "

Lawrie closed his eyes and brought a fist to his mouth. A storm of emotions sent him reeling. Astonishment. *Annalee*—the last person he would have guessed. Anger. Why would she do this?

Where did she get the money? She'd pled poverty ever since he'd known her. Sorrow. This changed—

A sudden thought shot a ray of light into his heart. *It wasn't Linda. He didn't have to send the letter!* He drew a big breath. "Annalee, you meant well, but the law says that illegal contributions must be returned."

"But this friend does it all the time and said it would be all right. How would anyone know where it came from?" Her voice was tight, accusatory.

Lawrie's voice became knife-sharp. "The reporter who broke the story has it in for me. His talent lies in digging dirt. Without him, probably no one would notice. But now, everyone in the world knows."

"Lawrie, I'm *sorry!*" She began to cry.

Lawrie stood, put his hands in his pockets and stared out the window. He should turn back and comfort her, assure her of his love and forgiveness, but unexpectedly, he watched his love–now a thick, black, tar ball—roll across the driveway. A long parade of witnesses marched through his mind: Nathan—stubbornly faithful Nathan. Billy and his slug warning. The rehab staff with their too-bright smiles and assurances. Grumpy aides. Annalee herself carping about the cost of gardens. *How many missionaries could be supported . . . ?* What would she say about Linda's garden? Charlotte's signed warning at Brookside Gardens. *Watch your step, buddy!* And his dream about Lady Cool Water. Was she, too, another witness for the prosecution?

He had to do something besides just walk out. He bit his lip and turned. "Annalee, I'm sorry, but I need to go, to step back and think through a lot of things. I'll take care of your contribution and do my best to keep your name out of the public. No promises because I don't know how much MacClerhan knows. I'll call in a few days."

"Lawrie, please don't leave, not right now!" Her sobs escalated.

Lawrie studied the trembling, grasping hand thrust toward him. He stepped forward, laid his hand on her shoulder, then turned and walked from the room.

"Lawrie!" Her shrieks followed him down the hall.

Chapter 41

LINDA WAS MANAGING HER THOUGHTS quite well by carefully monitoring early spring things. Snowdrops. Blackbirds back. Daffodils sending up periscopes to check conditions. The sun tracking northward. Green blades of grass in wet areas. The odd peeper singing tentatively. They had a mountain of work to do, but the garden tour was a distinct possibility, with the major rehabbing finished and just planting left to do. Which plants still needed to be decided, and where they would perform their specific duty.

Linda felt pleased with her Lenten fast. Going without news of Jay had been hard at first; but as the days went along, her mind turned to garden-tour plans, church involvement, and her ongoing "Pinchpenny Planters." Life was brightening. Easter was coming.

A mugging topped off Lawrie's five-part, day-long birthday bash, two weeks after Easter. Connie and Scheduler Ben had milked the occasion, arranging a ladies' breakfast, a university appearance, a meeting with the only union that would have him, a late-afternoon event with black school administrators, and finally, a major energy speech in the evening. How much birthday cake could he manage in one day?

While contemplating his fourth piece, he suddenly realized that one of the event servers had been at the three previous affairs. Had the man been normal-sized, Lawrie might not have noticed. But this was a specimen, a hulk. Annalee's warnings about her ex came to mind. Was this him? She'd given no description, but her fear might justify a connection. A black-gospel rendition of "Happy Birthday" shifted his focus, and he tried hard to enjoy that piece of birthday.

One event to go. Buoyed by that knowledge, he began his evening speech with energy and focus—until his eye caught the impeccably-dressed man standing at the side of the room, eyes scanning the crowd. What was going on? Had Connie arranged for muscle without telling him? Or was this somebody else's muscle? Threats, phone messages, Annalee's warnings, the slow, intestinal burn of fear . . .

What could he do in the middle of a speech? Only one option: hang tough, pray—and visit Linda's garden. *Lord . . .*

After the obligatory cake and song, the crowd thinned to a couple of die-hard talkers, and to Lawrie's relief, the big man had disappeared with the crowd.

Lawrie thanked the cleanup crew individually and made his way to the empty parking lot, where he dug out his car keys and pushed the Unlock button. As he circled the rear of the car, an oversized figure rose and punched him in the stomach and jaw, then kicked his writhing body. Lawrie rolled into a ball, eyes squeezed shut against the pain. The man fell hard on him, but to Lawrie's surprise, his assailant got dragged to a totally different fight yards away. Lawrie could see only shapeless, grunting forms. One shadow finally downed the other and ran toward the exit ramp. The other scrabbled after him, leaving Lawrie alone, in total shock, seized-up lungs once again clawing for air.

Mugged. Big man. The other—same size, a fighter. Why go after each other and not his pockets? He ordered his shaking hand to find his cell phone and his brain to stay with it so he could dial . . . what number?

He must've dialed, for flashing red and blue lights suddenly hurt his eyes. A man and woman on either side were vandalizing his head. He hissed and grimaced.

"Hey, Senator," the man said. "Startin' to feel, are you? Gotta stop the bleed."

A policeman came over and squatted. "You Senator Crofter?"

Lawrie managed a weak reply.

"Can you tell us what happened?"

The woman interrupted. "Get in line, officer. What day is it, Senator? What year?"

Lawrie sucked air as pressure on his head increased. "My birthday, but maybe not anymore. What time . . . ?"

"Some way to celebrate. Where d' you hurt—besides your head?"

"Where *don't* I hurt? You catch them?" He looked toward the policeman.

"More than one, then? We'll need info when you're ready."

Lawrie took several stiff breaths. "Two guys . . . one big . . . shadowed me all day. That's . . . all I know." He began shaking.

The woman broke in. "Sharp pain anywhere? Anything feel broken?"

Lawrie closed his eyes and shook his head numbly.

"Okay, let's get you to the hospital. They'll do X-rays. You guys follow," she flung at the policeman.

Chase and Lucas arrived at the hospital while Lawrie was being stitched and X-rayed. Nathan heard about the attack and was ready to fly down, but Lawrie called to say he was on the way home, that they'd kept him just overnight. He still hurt bad but was basically okay.

Police and FBI interviews consumed the day following the incident. No one had seen the actual attack, and only sketchy descriptions of the "big man" came from event witnesses. They questioned people at the other venues, with little success. The breakfast people called him "Mike" but knew only that he had offered to help. The university and union officials hadn't a clue, and the school administrators thought a man called Charlie fit the description.

He heard nothing for three days—until the local assistant district attorney came to his office, report in hand. "Senator, there's good news, bad news, and incomplete news. Which would you like first?"

Lawrie worked up a smile. "Well, start at the top."

The D.A. leafed through his file, then closed it and began talking. "The good news is your big guy probably saved at least your wallet. There had been a creditable warning of action against you that day, and he was put on duty by somebody—he won't say who—as an unofficial bodyguard. He stayed nearby, and finally, after the last event, waited outside till you left but didn't check behind the car. Feels bad about that. He came forward, by the way, on his own."

Lawrie's eyes went wide, and he sucked a shaky breath. "And the first guy?" he finally managed.

"He got away but wasn't hard to find. A man called Jeremy Felders. You know him?"

Lawrie frowned and shook his head. "Doesn't sound familiar."

"Well, the bad news part. He was once your girlfriend's fiancé. And the relationship apparently went on for quite a while afterward."

Lawrie sagged in his chair. "Jeremy! She tried to warn me. Said he was out to get me, but I thought she was paranoid. Doesn't make sense at all!"

"As best we can figure, he knew about you and Ms. Adams and didn't like it one bit."

"Her warning." He looked away and slapped his head. *Background check.* He swiveled back. "What's the *incomplete* part?"

The Assistant D.A. shook his head. "A lot we don't know—like who hired the operative. We can't make him talk. No crime involved. He and his boss seem like good guys, so far as we can tell. And then the Felders-Adams tie-in. Maybe you can help with that."

"Huh! I'll try. I'll talk with her as soon as I can. Has this *hero* got a name?"

"You'll laugh. His name is Tad—Tad O'Rourke."

Lawrie laughed uproariously. "Tad. As in *Tiny.* What was his mother thinking when she named him? He must've weighed twenty-five pounds straight out of the womb!"

He tried calling Annalee a couple of times but got no answer. He called again the following day, and a strange voice responded after several rings. Lawrie frowned. "Is Annalee out of her room?" he asked.

"Who?"

"Annalee Adams. Are you one of the aides—new, maybe?"

"No, my name is Hildur. I yust come this morning."

"Is this Room two-o-six? Has Annalee been moved?"

"I tink dat's da room number. I don't know no Annalee."

"I'm sorry. I'll check the desk to find out where she went."

The desk informed him that she had gone home.

"Gone home! She can't manage on her own. How could she go home?"

The desk connected him to the appropriate charge nurse, who informed him that Annalee had, indeed, gone home, well able to manage herself. She evidently had been hiding her skills until whatever dramatic moment.

This blow hit harder than his attacker's kicks, and he grabbed at the nearest chair, once again fighting for breath. *What* was going on? He instinctively looked around for the familiar hulk. He could use someone big in his life right now.

Lawrie made a phone call. "Nathan, we need to talk."

But before his flight could be arranged, Connie led in a police officer, who handed him a legal-type envelope. Lawrie opened it. Plaintiff Annalee Adams had filed a lawsuit against him for personal damages during a rescue attempt wherein unnecessary force was applied to extract her from her car that had crashed but did not burn.

Chapter 48

IN LATE APRIL, STEPHAN APPEARED unannounced at Linda's gate and pleaded entrance to view her bulbs in all their northern glory. She rolled her eyes before pushing the button to let him in.

"You are unpredictable," she said with a whimsical smile. "I still haven't decided how to categorize you; but if you don't behave, I'll sic my pit bull on you."

He laughed. "Ah! You mean Bonnie. She's formidable! With a friend like that, no bodyguard is needed."

"She told me the threats she hung over your head, and maybe if I'd known she was inside, I might have trusted you. Anyway, it was a splendid party, and I am grateful. You are welcome here. Can I make you some tea before we face the bulbs?"

"Not enough time. This time, I'm the one who has to prepare for an event. We're even." He grinned.

She led him through the kitchen to the deck, and he stopped under the wisteria, his eyes sweeping panoramically. He pointed.

"The line of your border trees drops to the ground and picks up the line of that bed there." His finger traced the arc. "And the whole of your garden moves the viewer—dramatically, emotionally—toward the gazebo. *You* designed all this?" He looked at her incredulously.

"The broad lines, yes—or, rather, my parents conceived the basic layout, and my marvelous Hispanic gardener did the . . . the dramatic *sweep* you seem to see." Her eyes seemed permanently wide. "I didn't know. As you can see, things are not totally in place, but by July's tour, they will be."

"Where did you find such a man?" His voice held a touch of awe.

"Actually, he came straight out of prison. A . . . friend sent him in my direction, and I think he would've come for pocket money. Evidently, his father had worked at some big Puerto Rican garden—San Juan, perhaps?"

"What was his father's name?"

"I don't know his first name, but Felipe's name is Hierro. He—"

"*You* have Hierro's *son* working for you?" Stephan looked incredulous.

Linda's eyes again went wide. "You knew his father?"

"Not personally, but he's an important name in horticulture. Seems I heard talk of a son getting into trouble." He looked around again and shook his head. "The boy's got the genes. This is breathtaking."

They walked from bed to bed, through the garden "rooms." Linda, still shaking, pointed here and there. "If only you could see it a few weeks from now. It would be—"

"Oh, but I *can* see it. Peonies, clematis, iris, the fine cascades of your gorgeous Beauty Bush that will touch the ground. It must be five centuries old!" He grinned. "And I can see tall delphiniums and stands of shastas and whatever annuals you'll install in the blank spots. I'm awed," was all he could say.

They came to the gazebo, and he sank onto a chair to breathe in beauty, then looked at his watch. "I'm truly sorry, but I must go. Linda, dearest—and I don't say that lightly—I have great respect for you on numerous levels, and I would not *dare* trespass on your good will. I'd be honored to take you to dinner before I head south, if only to prove myself a gentleman." He leaned toward her and kissed her cheek. "Are we truly friends now?"

But dinner didn't actually happen, as Linda had an important engagement on Stephan's only free night, and she found herself genuinely disappointed.

Nine days after Lawrie's beating, he sat in Nathan's apartment, hunched over, elbows on his knees, hands clasped. After a long silence, he looked up.

"Nathan, what does it mean?" His voice mined each word, dredging for even a fleck of comprehension. "What is God doing? Flying my 'stupid flag' for everyone to see? Yah—not the first time. Maybe He's taking me apart, piece by piece, to find that one last stubborn cell." He studied his clasped hands. "Or He's smashing the fancy vase that used to be me."

"What are you mourning most? Annalee? The attacks? The lawsuit?"

"Huh!" Lawrie waved both arms helplessly. "God's lawsuit, not Annalee's. I'm in His courtroom, waiting for the gavel to fall."

"Well," replied Nathan, "I'm in the dock with you. Neither of us acted well in this thing."

"Yah, but you were right; I was wrong. I should have listened and done the background check. I know better, and you had every right to call me out."

Silence lay between them. Then, Nathan spoke. "Do you want to talk more or just lay it down and get on with life?"

"You said 'mourning.' There are losses, yes, but Annalee isn't one of them. I should have seen the fault lines. Plenty of signals. You stood up to me first, but other signs followed: Charlotte through the deaf couple, the rehab staff, and Billy's slug story." He looked up plaintively. "Nathan, you knew without ever meeting her. How could you do that?"

Nathan laughed. "Buddy, your face is writ in large print. Easy to read. And who knows you better than I do?" He looked down a moment, then back. "What have you learned about the real Annalee, or is that off-limits?"

Lawrie shrugged. "It's common knowledge." He leaned back, eyes drooping basset-like. "As best I know, Annalee's version of her engagement breakup was only partly true. He dumped her, not the other way around. She let it slip, though I didn't catch it at the time. But apparently, they kept some sort of *working relationship* till he exploded over her imminent engagement and threatened to bring us both down. Annalee's warnings were real." He paused a moment. "But apart from Jeremy, some invisible person or network kept passing him info he couldn't possibly have known. And c'mon—a thousand bucks against the millions that fall into the hog trough? Shouldn't even have been noticed." He grimaced with exasperation. "Only Ewen . . . "

Lawrie got up and walked the room. "Nathan, I believe she really cared about me—deeply. She showed that in so many ways. I don't think it was an act. Only God knows her heart. But somewhere along the line . . . " He swung back to the window.

"Somewhere along the line, I closed my eyes to weeds in the garden. I desperately wanted a kindred spirit and a warm body, and that's my point of shame." He stopped abruptly. "Like when Nels visited me in the hospital and revealed who he really was." He ran his fingers through his hair.

Nathan looked at him compassionately. "Sit down, Lawrie. Sit and sip the Lord's forgiveness. Yes, it burns your gut, but you can't heal without it."

Lawrie studied the chair but remained standing. "Nathan, I feel like a spider dangling a hundred feet in the air, looking down on the whole, crazy episode, trying to figure it out. Like God hung me there to search through the mess till I get my bearings."

"Don't be a garbage picker, Lawrie. Come back down and stand on the rock. Eat and drink from the King's table. The mess will settle out. Welcome home, my friend!"

Chapter 49

STEPHAN CALLED LINDA FOUR TIMES, the first on a Sunday—probably knowing that Felipe wouldn't be working, but nevertheless asking to talk to him. Linda laughed. "Why didn't you just say you called to talk to me? Couldn't you be a little subtler?"

"Well, I figured if he did happen to be there, he'd have time to talk on a Sunday. He doesn't go to church five times like you do, does he?"

Linda laughed. "Actually, he does, though maybe only four to my five."

"I'll have to put up with you, then. Take your phone outside. Walk me around the garden. Tell me what's blooming, and I'll run the video in my mind."

He did call three days later and had an energetic conversation with Felipe. Linda had never heard her employee so full of words—all in Spanish, of course. He tramped from bed to bed, gesticulating enthusiastically, with a grin the length of a banana. She silently blessed Stephan for making this humble gardener of hers so ecstatically happy. She also blessed him for alerting her to the treasure Jay had sent her way.

After the third phone call, Linda knew she was being pursued. And after the fourth, she wondered what she should do about it.

Lawrie was totally wrung out when his home workweek began in June. Life had settled somewhat. His lawyer was working with Annalee's attorney on the "botched rescue" aspect of the case, hoping for a reasonable settlement. Jeremy had been indicted for assault, but how would that play out? Lawrie's hard-fought energy bill had failed by one vote, and that hurt.

Nathan met him at the airport, took one look, and heaved his bags into the car. "We'll stop for lunch, then you're going home to bed, and you'll stay there till I say you can get up."

"Till Sunday, no matter what you say."

"All right, Sunday." Nathan looked at Lawrie and shook his head. "A tough two months. You lost big, got scared out of your wits, came home in tatters, but won where it really counts. Can you rest easy with that?"

Lawrie clicked his seatbelt and took a big breath. "No . . . yah . . . I guess . . . but there's still unfinished business—the New York boys. Got to go check on Jerry. Should have gone weeks ago. I have reason to believe his dad is banging on him and his sibs. It'll be another fight, but—"

"Lawrie, no. This isn't the time. And besides, you can't *do* any more for those kids, at least legitimately."

"*Legitimately* is beside the point. I have a moral responsibility, no matter what anyone says. I took on the role of friend and advocate and have to see it through. I *care* about kids, Nathan. I lost one of my own. Ephraim would've been seven next month. Helping those boys helps make up that loss. I can't just walk away from them!"

"Give it a rest, Lawrie, at least till you've had time to rest."

"Then there's Neela Hermandez and little girls like her—sex slaves, sometimes dying horribly. I'm not on the frontlines in that rescue effort, but I can be in the trenches with my boys.

" . . . And besides," he went on, his voice lifting, "I'll have a car rental and could explore New York State a bit while I'm out that far." His mouth curved slightly. "A pleasant, green state."

Nathan glanced quickly at him, then settled into smiling in silence.

When they got to the house, Carol greeted both men. "Go upstairs," Nathan told Lawrie. "I'll get the rest of your stuff."

When he brought up the big suitcase, he found Lawrie flopped in a stuffed chair, staring at the overhead fan as it distributed coolness. "What's the matter?" he asked. "What can I get you?"

Lawrie rolled his head but said nothing.

"You need sleep. Take a shower and crawl into bed. I'll tell Carol to hold meals till you're ready."

Lawrie continued the head shaking. "It'll be three days before my eyes will even shut. I feel like I just drank five cans of N-r-G— everything tight inside, ready to explode." He slumped even further. "I need Charlotte to sing over me." He paused a minute, then smiled wryly. "Do you sing, Nathan?"

"Huh! Not as good as Charlotte. But that's not a bad idea. Just pretend she's here. Go to bed and park your mind somewhere. Sit there as long as you need to, and let Charlotte sing over you. Peace will come, my friend. It will."

Lawrie's expression shifted toward wonder. "Peace, Nathan, a tiny shred, is one I never expected to get." He worked the thought into words. "The other day, after I had moaned—again—about the enormous political cost of losing the election, Lucas handed it to me—a cloak of grace. He said if I had become vice president, I probably would never have connected with him or the group. That hit me—an epiphany. Not only would I have missed *them*, I wouldn't know *you* and the guys here. Or Billy . . . " He stopped breathing, then spoke with ragged awe. "Would I even know Jesus?"

Nathan sank onto the bed, then looked at Lawrie and spoke softly. "Is it possible that your dropping out may have saved the country from an even worse president? I'm not talking politics. I'm talking God's Sovereign power over the affairs of men."

Lawrie looked at him, thunderstruck, his mind whirling through the Nels debacle, through Billy's trauma and the Sundance episode. Through Annalee. God's Sovereign power . . .

He studied the fan again and bit his forefinger abstractedly. "Y'know," he said, "Nels could well have failed the country, and I flubbed up on just about every relationship. But none of that matters. Right now, every ounce of me is caught up in God, the troll part gone. I've seen a lot of good and bad these past years, but no matter what comes, this is where I want to be, even if the only thing left holding me together is God's love. And the cool part is He decided to show that love through you and Lucas and Billy and Chase and all the guys."

Lawrie hugged the thought for a moment, then stood and headed for the bathroom. "I'm going to bed, but tell Carol that if Charlotte happens to come, I'll see her. The same goes for Lady Cool Water."

"Lady Cool Water! Who's that?"

"I have no idea, but I'd get out of my casket to talk with her, awake or asleep—especially right now."

Chapter 50

WITH LITTLE JOY AND RESIDUAL pain in his heart, Lawrie drove from Syracuse to Welton. He looked forward to meeting with the boys but not with the parents, especially Jerry's dad, and that was the purpose of his trip. The speech he would make to an audience of one might be the most important of his political career.

He called ahead to arrange some fun with the boys before having their serious talk.

"I've got a ball and a couple of gloves. Think you could round up a few more gloves for a game of catch? I know Peter's the pro, but the rest of us will give it a go."

Caleb's response surprised him. "Well . . . we'd kinda like to meet in our friend's back meadow. Kinda small, but maybe we could . . ." His voice trailed off.

"Oh? What's your friend's name? Will he be with you?"

"Well, no. He's a she, actually. In our church." He laughed nervously. "It'll just be us. It's a good place to meet. Once you get into town, you go left after the gas station, then past the fourth house on the right. You'll see a place to park down a ways, under some trees. My truck'll be there. There's a path goes to the meadow, maybe a hundred yards. We'll watch for you."

Lawrie pursed his mouth thoughtfully but agreed to the strange arrangement. "I should be there about nine-thirty. Hope you've had breakfast. McDonald's doesn't hang out in meadows, I'd guess." He laughed.

The meadow wasn't close to anything. Lawrie did find the parking spot and worked his way along a wooded trail until he came to the starkly isolated clearing where the five boys were waiting. They looked stiff, nervous, and less than welcoming, and the hairs on Lawrie's neck began talking.

"Hey, guys! How you doin'? Thanks, Caleb, for parking your truck there. I don't think I'd 've found the spot without—"

He stopped as Jerry broke his statue-like stance and ran, throwing his arms around Lawrie with the grace and emotion of a robot. Alarm bells screamed. Lawrie grabbed Jerry's shoulders and pushed him away.

"Wait a minute," he said sternly. "Something's going on, and I want to know before we go any further." His eyes had become slits. "Sit down, right on the ground. Good. Now, if you want to tell me the setup outright, that's fine. Otherwise, I'll figure it out myself."

He stayed standing and turned a tight circle to search the surrounding woods, spotting a house some distance away. "How many high-zoom video cams are on us, would you say? At least one from the house, and who knows how many in the woods?" He looked at the boys sitting cross-legged, eyes tethered to the ground, and said angrily, "Unless you can tell me something different, I see this as intentional entrapment. Usually, it's police who set up a victim, and maybe that's not far from the truth here. Somehow, your parents convinced you that I was using and abusing you, but they needed evidence. Does anyone want to tell me otherwise?" He looked from one to the other, but the boys remained silent, hunching hard into themselves.

Lawrie spun away, grabbing hair and exhaling fumes. Then he turned back. "I don't think this is your doing. They set you up as bait. You go tell your parents that I will talk with them at noon sharp in the church. I could take legal action, and if they don't show, I will press charges. And not just your dads. I want your moms, too. Now, go. I'll talk with you after I finish with your parents."

Four of the boys scrambled to their feet and ran rabbit-like toward the house. Caleb started toward his truck, then turned back. "Lawrie—" he began, but the older man waved him on and said, kindlier, "We'll talk later, Caleb."

Nine of the ten parents appeared at the church, Jerry's mother being the absentee. Lawrie, standing in front of a plain, rough-hewn pulpit, ran steely eyes over the pew-sitters.

"We have a problem here that has escalated from five boys—six, actually—who were set up to harass an Indian tribe in the name of evangelism, to parents who are now using the five remaining boys to trap me, and I'm not sure why. Is it self-justification—you wanting to get back at me for making you look bad, or you don't like competition for your boys' affection and obedience? Perhaps your actions were based on some theological stance like 'spare the rod, spoil the child.'" Lawrie studied the wide-board flooring a moment, then looked up. "The root cause probably doesn't matter, but the end results do, and I'll cut to the bottom line."

Peter's dad stood and said, "Now, listen—"

Lawrie ignored him and continued as though he hadn't been interrupted. "First, but of secondary importance, entrapment is a crime."

Peter's father sat down.

"You were hoping I'd respond to Jerry's awkward hug in some inappropriate, incriminating way. Hugging is evidently not allowed in your community, or certainly not encouraged. I'm wondering if love in any form is allowed." He watched two women shift uncomfortably. "If I were caught on video and prosecuted, life would get back to normal—no one left to interfere. I suppose I could shrug my shoulders and say, 'I gave it my best shot, but these people don't want or need love.' I could walk away." He stopped and strode across the front.

"But that would leave the boys in a tough spot at a time when they badly need an advocate. They need *love*. Love is not a dirty word. Yes, they need discipline, a firm hand to guide them. But discipline and guidance won't work unless love is solidly underneath. If you don't speak the language of love to these kids, you might as well be talking Mandarin Chinese."

He shifted and looked each of the women in the eye. "I'm being straight with you. Your kids are at great risk, and I'll be even more specific. Of these five boys, Jerry is most vulnerable. He's on the verge of cracking, and without immediate help, he's going to go under."

Jerry's father gripped the pew in front of him and half rose, his face livid. Lawrie leaned toward him. "You can argue all you want, but do you really want to risk suicide or some other self-destructive behavior? Even if he leaves home alive, he'll be an easy target for whatever ghastly sort of love comes along. He's badly broken, and what you did to him today may have already put him over the edge. I might have been able to help him, but now, with your little entrapment game, I can't hold him and lead him into the light. This is your doing, and may God have mercy on your soul."

The men rose and walked out in silence, shoving their women along. Caleb's mother, however, broke loose and came back to Lawrie, tears spilling down her face. She said nothing and simply gripped his hand as tight as she could, her entire body trembling. Lawrie leaned close and whispered, "I have hope for your boy."

Lawrie went outside and sat on the church steps, waiting for the boys, but only Caleb came. He sat beside Lawrie, who reached over and gripped his knee. They said nothing for several minutes. Finally, Caleb spoke. "I'm thinking I need to leave here, maybe sign up for the army." He shifted his eyes sideways, then stared ahead.

Lawrie stared with him. "The leave part is probably good, but I'm not sure about the army. If I wanted to grow tomatoes in North Dakota, I don't think I'd take them from the hothouse in April and plant 'em outdoors. I'd hardened them off first, but even then, I doubt they'd survive. April can be cold—and cruel."

Caleb looked at him, then down quickly.

Lawrie went on. "The army is tough, and I'm not talking about the training part. You could do that, no sweat. Maybe someday, but not till you're hardened off."

Caleb remained silent a moment, then "Yeah" was all he said.

Lawrie examined the church driveway. "I'd like to see you working for Christians somewhere, maybe a summer job—a farm, maybe, where you can work and learn and give back. The pay wouldn't be great, maybe enough for bed and board." He grinned sideways. "Let me scratch around and call you. Do you have a cell phone? Do you text?"

The boy snorted. "You kidding? A tool of the devil!" His head sank an inch or two lower.

Lawrie laughed sadly. "You could be right on that, but it doesn't have to be bad unless you let it be. Maybe this is tied to the "leave" part, Caleb. Get yourself a plain, no-frills phone and call me at this number." He fished a card from his wallet. "Senators aren't good for a whole lot, but I do have some clout. Would you like me to see what I can find for you?"

Caleb's back straightened just a bit, nascent light in his eyes. "Well, yah—you betcha!"

Lawrie batted his shoulder. "Hey—a real North Dakotan!"

"Nathan, I've just been run over, but I can still sit up and take nourishment, as my dad used to say."

"Where are you?"

"At a Motel 6 not far from Welton."

"Tell me what happened."

"Try entrapment."

"You're kidding!"

"Nope. When I first went to D.C., I took a course on self-protection, and walking into this situation, I felt the classic signals."

"Tell me about it."

Lawrie lined out the whole interchange, mourning especially the no-show boys. "Caleb said he didn't know why they wouldn't talk, but we both think they just couldn't face me. I was really angry when I sent them to get their parents, and even though I said I wasn't mad at them, they probably didn't believe me and expected I'd lay it on. Nathan, what can I do for those boys?"

"Is their church some sort of cult?"

"I don't think so. While I was waiting for the boys to come, I looked at some of their literature, and they seem theologically straight. But they're a rigid bunch—don't ever, *ev-er* step outside the lines. It's some sort of toxic cell that wants to block even the smell of light and love. The kids in that community don't have a chance."

"Well, seems you got through to one, anyway."

"Yah, maybe. But it's possible my going there to help just made everything worse. Huh—shades of my visit to the Wolf Runner family." He laughed sardonically.

"Nathan, I'm heading to the Catskills for a couple of days. I need a good dose of mountains and trails and maybe even . . . silence. That can terrify a city guy, y'know, especially one dealing with war wounds." He paused to gather breath. "And maybe I'll head further east and, if nothing else, nail shut that particular casket, once and for all."

"Lawrie—"

"But first a big hill, maybe Mount Slide—a four-thousand footer. Listen to brooks and birds—" He laughed. "Maybe I'll practice rock climbing for the next cliff." His voice lifted, then settled back. "I'll be in touch, Nathan. Have I ever told you how much I appreciate you, by the way?"

"Yah, bro, you have, but just don't color outside my lines. I'm fussy about that."

Chapter 51

MOUNT SLIDE DID NOT GET climbed, and a bolt of lightning accepted the blame. When Lawrie left Motel 6, the weather was fine and looked promising for an afternoon attempt. But by the time he got to the campground and set up his dome tent, clouds had gathered. He didn't mind wet, but a sharp clap of thunder directly overhead sent him scuttling into his tent. *Whoo! Where did that come from?* No warning rumbles; just BLAM! Mountains do spawn storms, and they have to start somewhere. Why not here? He pushed away thoughts of God speaking through forked lightning and settled down to wait it out.

The thunder part didn't amount to much, but the rain did. No Mount Slide that afternoon. Maybe in the morning. This could be a long night with nothing but thoughts for company.

As rain pounded overhead, a toxic miasma engulfed him that almost shut down his lungs. Elijah came to mind. After the prophet's long, hard day, he had hidden his depression under a broom tree. His Jezebel was more evil than Annalee, but the similarities were striking. Nothing in Annalee's situation made sense, and attempts to dismiss it simply moved Lawrie toward the equally black cloud of the boys, their parents, and utter hopelessness.

Why had he come to the Catskills? The fragile thread that had drawn him could never sustain a return to the Garden of Eden.

After a cold, tasteless supper, he forced himself into decision-making mode. He had three choices: he could pack up and head home in the morning—by far, the easiest of the three. He could climb the mountain, but was that even possible? Like Elijah, he felt too beat—physically and emotionally—to even try. Or, he could head east and expose himself to yet another beating. Kindly given, of course, but clear and unambiguous. That would settle the matter and would in itself bring a sense of relief. How could he do it, though? How could he bring himself to knock on Linda's door? Face it—even her gate might be fast barred.

Too tired to finalize anything, he prepared for bed and slept wretchedly, even with the white noise of rain on the tent. At twenty-five past three, he gave up, his bladder driving him from the tent. The rain had become a lambent mist, the air smelling new and clean. As liquid flowed from him, he drew in great drafts of sweetness.

Suddenly, without warning, he had his decision about tomorrow—and, equally surprising, on his presidency run.

With a satisfied smile, he crawled back in the tent and slept soundly until nearly seven o'clock.

June fifteenth was a bad day for Linda. After waiting a half hour in the gazebo, air thick with ozone from a shower that wouldn't quit, she decided to make a dash for the house, despite being dressed for her talk at noon on Flowers for Peace. She hadn't wanted to do that—not today—but the Peace ladies had pressed, and she felt embarrassed to refuse. She would have much preferred locking her doors, ignoring the phone, refusing even Bonnie. She sighed.

The ladies wanted her to talk outdoors in the modest gardens of the Boniface Center, but even if it stopped raining, everything would be wet. The showers might end, but her soul would be waterlogged.

June fifteenth. Three years ago, Jay had appeared in her garden. She had served him and fallen in love. He had told her he'd never forget, but three years for a busy senator could suck his memory dry. His wife had died; he could have come, or at least contacted her, had he cared. He was seeing other women. At least Rooshie was gone. This gave her some comfort, but Annalee was a far greater threat.

The day couldn't have been much worse, a soggy Boniface Center ruling out the garden walk. She did survive the luncheon, however, and the Peace ladies left full of cheer.

Later that afternoon back at home, she slumped again into her morass. This time, though, it was Stephan adding bilge water. He was after her; she knew that. But why? Was he hoping to add a notch to his woman belt—one that represented more of a challenge than the others? Was that his game? Yes, they shared a common horticultural language and passion. They knew and respected each other's talents. He was fun and funny—even more handsome than Jay. But he'd never gotten physical—except for dragging her into his house. She had enjoyed their multifaceted conversations and discovered that he was, in fact, sensitive to her spiritual commitment.

But he was not a Christian and didn't even pretend to be one. This could not go on. Better to cut the cord before it got too thick. She didn't want to cut the cord, though. If she couldn't have Jay, this man at least gave her male companionship—if only it could stay on that level.

Her phone rang with Bonnie's ringtone. Linda sighed and let the answering machine determine the importance of her news. Nothing much, really. Bonnie had had a super day at work, sold bunches of candles, and wondered how Linda's day had gone. It had cleared nicely, she said, and sunset should be spectacular.

"Be sure to watch it." Her voice squeaked from excitement. Maybe she'd watch it, maybe not.

Television wouldn't do—not tonight. Her new CD might be safe, but it wasn't. The second song took her prisoner, and she might have sat crying until bedtime, but Bonnie's phone message got her up. The sun had long set, but maybe a lingering glow . . .

She stepped to the garden window—and froze. Light. A sinuous path of bagged candles from the patio, around the annuals, behind the arbor, past the Stella d'Oro "mountain" and across the bridge to the gazebo. Her heart exploded there at the window, and she dashed toward the kitchen door.

Chapter 52

LINDA PAUSED UNDER THE WISTERIA, then stepped onto the wondrous, magic walkway of shrouded candles. Fear grabbed her momentarily. A rapist out there? If so, she had to admire his panache. She moved barefoot across the damp grass—slowly at first, with her pace rapidly overtaking her heart rate. She began to cry, but just over the bridge she stopped, horrified. No one was in the gazebo. Looking around frantically, she cried out, "Jay!"

Then she heard it in the shrubbery. One word—a hoarse voice, hardly more than an ardent whisper: *"Kileenda!"*

She spun around, and in seconds, their bodies slammed together like powerful magnets—twirling, laughing, crying, hugging. Finally, he took her face in trembling hands and searched her eyes as though mining the depths of her soul. Seemingly satisfied, he put his lips to hers—softly, yet with an intensity that was akin to an altar experience for Linda. She drew a quick, tremulous breath.

Jay stepped back. "Yes." He spoke almost inaudibly. "That kiss was right. It was good." He leaned down and kissed her again.

Linda's eyes widened under the jagged, ragged, Olympic torch flaring within her.

Heart pounding under such passion, she reached desperately for a deflecting tactic.

"Jay," she said, voice trembling, "why were you hiding? Why weren't you in the gazebo?"

His answer jarred her.

"I was afraid."

"Afraid!"

"Yes." He stepped back, his voice in panic mode. "I didn't know if . . . I went to the Catskills, searching for courage to come here instead of heading home. Why would you still care? Would you even remember my name? 'Let's see—some single letter, wasn't it?' you'd ask, then sigh. 'I'm *so* sorry. Help me out here. Refresh my—'"

Linda laughed. "You're too funny! Me—forget you? How could I?"

"Oh, you could." He chortled sardonically. "If you only knew. So much has happened. Life has knocked me around a bit, so why not face the worst of all beatings—'Get lost, buddy; no longer interested'—and get it behind me once and for all?"

"Oh, Jay, I would never . . . "

"I didn't know that; but early this morning, I had a God moment, there in the Catskills, and it gave me courage. I had to go, so I crawled out of the tent. Standing there in the drizzle, everything became clear—what I was to do and how I could pull it off."

He put a hand on her arm. "And tonight, when you crashed into me, I knew, I *knew* I'd done it right. If you'd been even slightly tentative, I would have slunk away. But you *showed* you loved me, and I couldn't give that up." He grinned and cocked his head whimsically. "Maybe this is another of your *unpresentable glories*?"

Delight lit Linda's eyes. "Oh!" She put her hands to her cheeks. "You did see the TV thing! It was so awful. It seemed right at the time—or at least before I said it out loud—but afterward, my lawyer was sure I'd gotten you into *big* trouble. Did I?"

He laughed ruefully. "Made things . . . um . . . *interesting* for a bit. But watching you speak shook me so much I couldn't process what you were saying. And Martin was beside me, parsing every word, which rattled me even more. He cleaned up the mess pretty quickly, but I needed time to absorb what you were getting at. A long time, actually. I think I understand now, but . . . lining out God's glory on national TV. That took *courage*!" He shook his head in wonder.

"Ohhh," Linda moaned. "I beat myself up for months over what I said, but I felt then—and still do—that, bad as they sounded in the public glare, my words were right. All but the 'bad behavior' part." She grimaced ruefully. "That was awful and stupid!

"But Jay," she went on, cocking her head pertly, "do you realize that's *twice* you've been *unpresentable*? Three years ago, and again today. How do you manage such timing?"

He laughed and slapped at a mosquito. "Ha! Senators *learn* timing."

"Jay, let's go in the gazebo." She pulled him toward the screen door and felt him shaking. As he settled in a chair, she inspected the table with its large hurricane chimney sheltering multiple taupe candles. "This is beautiful, Jay! How did you come up with all this and the pathway candles?"

"I bought them this afternoon in the center of town."

Linda's eyes widened. "Bonnie!" she gasped.

Lawrie frowned. "Bonnie?"

"She knew! That's why she squeaked. You met her three years ago. Remember that day in Philly? Of course, you do," she added, seeing his eyes light.

"Yes! I thought she looked familiar. But she never let on! Bent over backwards to find enough candles. We decided shapes and colors wouldn't matter, and she grasped right away what I wanted to do. Tore the store apart for me."

"Not for you." Linda shook her head sadly. "For me. She was the 'close friend' who tipped off Ewen, and she's never forgiven herself. But she recognized you and grasped what you were doing. I wish I could've seen her—totally out of control! She called but gave no hint, other than telling me to watch the sunset. I missed the sunset, but—"

"Good thing. I wasn't ready. I had candles in the bags but not lit. I didn't want you to see it that early. And the garden is changed—everything's different. You've been busy!"

"Oh! One of the bags is burning!"

"Huh! The candle must've tipped. I was hurrying and not too careful."

"Is there sand in the bags? How did you bring enough to fill—"

"Not sand." He dug in his pocket. "Bonnie had these gadgets that poke through the bottom of the bag. See?" He held up a pointed holder.

"How clever! I've never seen them."

Linda sank into her chair. "Jay, tell me about the Catskills. Why did you go there?"

He sat silent against the night music of frogs and peepers, then looked into the darkness and spoke as though unmindful of her question. "This is incredibly wonderful, Linda. I can't tell you. My heart has been here countless times, but this place, right here . . . " His voice trailed off.

Linda reached out, but Lawrie folded his hands tightly and went on. "Linda, not even this place is safe. Any connection with me is dangerous. My political enemies are legion. Others, too, are out to get me and could destroy us both. And there's Ewen."

"Ewen! He's been busy on my end, too, y'know."

"Well, I know he got us both into big—"

"Oh, there's more! Why would he want to unravel the sins of my former gardener?"

Lawrie frowned incredulously. "Your gardener! He'd stoop that low?" He shook his head. "Anyway, with all this in my mind, I knew coming here—"

Her hand reached his. "Dear one, you were safe here once, and now you're back home. And I love you madly. Can you rest in that?"

She examined his face closely. He was thinner and older, with unfamiliar lines etching his face. "I see now who you really are, deep inside that powerful persona. Three years ago and now—everything false stripped away, terribly vulnerable, desperately afraid. You carry wounds, Jay, even more than when you first came."

He closed his eyes. "I've come back here so many times." He laughed. "Only a few weeks ago, I was giving a talk I didn't think I could get through. Your garden worked its magic, but right after, a big lunk knocked me flat and—"

"I heard about that! Are you all right? You had stitches." She leaned to feel the side of his head.

He laughed. "Linda, what *don't* you know about me? If Charlotte were here, she'd flip a fast hand sign: 'Watch your step, buddy! This woman has smarts you know nothing about!'" His laughter dropped away. "Do you know Charlotte? Can you tell me where she is?"

Linda reached out compassionately. "I'm sorry, I don't know Charlotte. She must be—"

"No, you wouldn't know her. She was Glynneth's angel, and after my wife died . . . "

He straightened and shifted the subject.

"It bothers me that Ewen came after you. I'm sorry, Linda. I truly am. If I hadn't collapsed here, none of that would have happened."

"Jay, it's not your fault. God laid out a murky path for us both. One bright spin-off is the splendid, new gardener you sent to replace Jorge. Please tell me about Felipe."

She smiled brightly, but he stared across the dark water and spoke haltingly toward it. "Ewen . . . Annalee . . . " The whispered names scarcely registered, but Linda's heart recoiled.

Annalee! In her excitement she'd forgotten Annalee—a haunting shadow that had sucked up all her oxygen. *Annalee...*

She had to respond, but as she opened her mouth, Lawrie spoke in a rush of words.

"Linda, you're probably thinking you're second in line, but you were never, *ever* second choice. You've always been first, but so far out of reach . . . " He stopped, gripping the chair arms as though bracing against some dangerous onslaught. "While I was lighting candles around the flower beds, it struck me that gardens don't just happen. They must be created and . . . *disciplined*. Weeds have to go." He stopped again, struggling for words. "Linda, you created this garden. And as God prunes His garden, cuts off bad branches, burns them—"

"Jay, don't go there. I'm not God, and—"

"I know that, but you don't know my weed capacity. I don't belong in this garden, Linda, and Annalee is clear evidence of that."

Linda uncurled his fingers from the chair. "Lay it down, Jay. We'll talk about Annalee, but first, do the words *love* and *grace* mean anything to you?"

Lawrie slumped with a shamefaced smile. "You been talking to my guys? They're all over me on that."

"Then you know that God loves you. And now you know that I love you."

"But you don't know *me*, Linda. One week's exposure isn't enough to dig through all my weeds."

"Oh, I know more than you realize. I was so addicted to following you on the internet that I decided to fast from you this past Lent. That's my weed patch." She laughed ruefully.

"First, though—" She settled back with a grin. "Some other important stuff. Before we start on Annalee, I want to know how you latched onto Rooshie. What*ever* possessed you to pick *her* out of the crowd?"

Lawrie gasped as though she'd doused him with ice water.

"You *have* been poking through my rubble! Actually, it was a matter of her picking me, not me picking her. I *survived* Rooshie . . . well, mostly." He looked down. "Blame my personal angel, Lady Cool Water. It was her idea for me to get out there, find some women, and start looking juicy."

"And Rooshie was the one."

"Like I said, she picked me. A hotwire, you betcha. Taught me a lot." He winked mischievously.

Linda's eyes narrowed. "Well, I know Rooshie, and I was horrified. I couldn't conceive of your ever marrying her!"

"You *know* Rooshie?"

"From way back. Some remote family connection. I never liked her when we were children." Linda looked at him sideways as though finding him hard to believe. "And Lady—what did you call her? Who is she?"

"Lady Cool Water. I have no idea. An old woman who came to see me twice—plus a dream when I badly needed her." His face slumped momentarily but then brightened. "Before the election, she showed up and said, 'We share a love for Linda Jensen's island gazebo.' My heart stopped cold. I didn't know what to think or what her game was, so I just asked, 'What do you want?'"

Linda frowned. "Who in the world could it be? Huh! With all the old ladies who parade through my garden, I couldn't begin to guess."

"Well, she was something else. A wisp of a woman—elegant, intelligent. Her eyes digested the whole of me in seconds. 'Lady Cool Water' was the only name she'd give. 'I admire your virtue,' she said, 'appreciate your choices, your commitment. But I want you to know that this creaky old lioness will be watching closely to make sure you don't tarnish.'

"'Don't worry!' I told her. 'My inner lions are as formidable as yours.' They were hollow words, it turned out, but once my pack of lions got on me—"

"*Pride* of lions, not pack."

"Pride, I've learned, *is* a lion." He grinned. "Two prides—guys on both ends—every bit as formidable as my elegant angel. They work to keep me on track.

"Getting back to the dangerous part of our associating . . ." he went on. "That, as much as anything, is what kept me away. I brought grief on your head three years ago and couldn't bear to add more. But Lady Cool Water was trying to turn attention away from you by linking me with other women. This morning, outside the tent, I made another decision that took a huge weight off of me. The danger will likely diminish when I say—out loud— that I will not run for president. I would not subject you to that, and my decision removes at least that barricade." He looked at her with a grin. "Any problem there?"

Linda's eyes went wide. "Whoo! I think that requires a little conversation! I hadn't given it a thought, and—"

He laughed. "I couldn't believe how much better it made me feel, even in the rain. My other decision suddenly got much easier."

He reached into his pocket. "I brought my ticket along, hoping it would get me inside your door." He pulled out the paper, now worn and tattered, that Linda had given him in the hospital.

Her eyes lit. "You still have it!"

"It goes with me everywhere. It's my second link to God."

She touched the paper gently, then looked up with delight. "It didn't upset you, then! I was so afraid. And I have my ticket." She grinned mischievously.

"*Your* ticket? Not this one?" He waved the paper.

"No. Your guy, Felipe. He came through like a tornado and—"

"Felipe? My guy?"

"You sent him to me—with the paper."

"I'm lost. Give me a context."

Linda frowned. "You know. He'd been in prison. You must've met him there, though he didn't recognize your name."

"Ah! The gardener! Yes, Felipe sounds right." Then Lawrie looked at her sharply. "He came *here*?"

"You sent him with that paper."

"What paper?"

"C'mon! You're playing with me."

"I'm not. What paper are you talking about?"

Linda eyed him quizzically. "A totally blank piece, with only a teeny *J* in the middle—practically invisible."

Lawrie leaned forward, frowning. "Linda, this is scary. Felipe was a funny guy—shy, an emotional mess—but once I got him talking, his love for gardening came pouring out, and I wished I could hook him up with you. I told the employment lady about his potential, but I swear I didn't give him a paper, blank or otherwise, and I certainly didn't mention your name."

"He said a woman gave it to him and told him to use it only if I decided not to hire him—which, in fact, is what happened. Jorge had given me tons of grief and had to go, but when Felipe first came, he was awful! A beat-up dog who could hardly talk. I couldn't deal with it. But when he pulled that paper out, everything changed. I took him to the garden, and just like that—a totally different person."

"You still have the paper? I'd like to see it."

"I do. I'll show you when we go inside. Are you warm enough? We could go in now."

"Not just yet. This is where I need to be, where I've longed to be. So much to talk about, so many things to lay on the table."

He looked at her and took a big breath. "That week I was here, God showed me something I'd never known. You *were* love—the face of God, if you will. You planted my garden, so to speak, and my guys cultivated it. But had it not been for you, the rest probably wouldn't have happened."

Linda shifted with a smile. "I couldn't figure you out. You obviously knew the Bible. Anyone who can find Hosea knows his way around."

Lawrie grunted. "Hosea eleven—"

"I'm so sorry about that! When I heard about your little boy, I realized I'd stepped in it."

"Well, after Glynneth died, my guys messed up even more with that same passage."

"Tell me about them. Wait! That shooting outside of Bismarck. When you gave your statement, a guy with light hair put his hand on your shoulder. Was that one of them?"

"Yes, Nathan."

"Tell me about him. I realized—no, I *saw* that night that God had you tight."

Lawrie hunched forward, hands clasped, and said, "Nathan . . . salvaged my life. He dragged me from the jaws of hell and shoved me into a Bible study with a small band of men who started rehabbing me. Kevin, Mike, Len, Bruce, Laddie, Jake . . . and Billy." He leaned back, eyes searching the roof rafters. "Christmas day. Nathan. Billy." Again, he stopped, throat tight and words taut. "I'm sorry. I didn't realize it would be this hard."

Linda slid from her chair onto her knees in front of Lawrie, tears running down her face. He wrapped his arms around her and clung tightly, kissing her head and hair, her neck, her shoulder, more and more ardently. Linda drew a shuddering breath and let out a low cry. Immediately and with an anguished growl, Lawrie pushed her aside and jerked out of his chair to lean panting against a post in a posture of shame.

"I'm sorry, Linda. I'm *sorry!*" His voice was husky and came in gasps. "One minute, I'm caught up over my friends, the next it's totally *wrong*. I'm sorry!"

Linda sat staring, trying to calm her own physical response, not knowing what to do or say. Slowly, she rose. "Did I do—"

He turned and helped her up. "No, I'm the weed." He groaned. "If my guys were here, I'd get it, both barrels."

"Maybe we should go indoors, have a cool drink. Would that help?"

He took a big breath. "Yes. I'm okay. I just need to learn how to color inside the lines."

Chapter 53

THEY STEPPED FROM THE GAZEBO, and Lawrie bent to the first of the candles, inadvertently setting the bag on fire. Linda laughed as he stomped it out.

"Just leave them. We'll blow out the candles, and I'll get them in the morning." Linda took his arm and pulled him along. "A cool drink. What would you like? Juice? Some sun tea? And, by the way, what would you like me to call you?" She smiled self-consciously. "I've tried both names and would be happy with either, but which would you like?"

He blew out another candle, then straightened with a smile. "Call me whatever fits the moment, and I'll be happy." He led her up the deck stairs and under the trellis. "Wisteria!" He stopped to pull in the scent, then looked toward the sound of water. "The troll! Is he still there?"

"Oh, yes. I could turn on a light, but tomorrow might be better."

He nodded. "Yes. Tomorrow. It's enough that he's on duty. I know that fellow well."

As he slid open the screen door to go indoors, Lawrie drew a deep breath, eyes taking in every wall of the kitchen. "That's a new painting." He pointed. "I like it."

"It's a Galda oil—*Roses in a Silver Vase with Bowl*."

He studied it. "Yah—it evokes. And the bar chairs pick up the rose color. They're new." He grinned.

"Just new covers. They were pretty shabby."

He went slowly out of the kitchen and down the hall to *his* bedroom and stepped in almost reverently. He said nothing and just stood in place, eyes carefully handling every item in the room as though each was terrifyingly precious.

Linda, waiting behind him, put her hand softly on his back. He turned reluctantly and moved into the vast area that incorporated living and dining space and the less-formal sitting area that overlooked the garden. Lawrie planted himself in front of the massive stone fireplace, relaxing visibly.

"This is home, right here, my place of peace. I couldn't decide whether it was this or the gazebo, but now I know. The gazebo is my place of rest and beauty, but this is peace. I'll never forget the small fire you built for me. It was cool but not cold, and I think you did it just for my pleasure." He halted and put mirrored hands to his mouth. "It pleased me—very much."

"Sit down," she said softly. "I'll get your tea. No, wait." She turned to the mantel and handed him a small object. "Do you recognize this?" She bit her lip, eyes twinkling.

He examined it carefully, and his eyes lit. "You kept it! You dried the rose and kept it with the vase!"

"Of course, I kept it. Not even Bonnie knows what it meant or who it was from. I was a wreck when it came. I *had* to put it in the gazebo, and my helpers thought I was crazy. People loved it, though, the way I set it up." Her hands went around his as he held the vase. "This was a precious gift, and I now understand the risk you took in sending it. Is this what they call a paper trail?" She took the vase and replaced it on the mantel.

He looked away. "I had to. It was my only way to say thank you. No matter the cost, I had to. We paid, you and I, but not because of the rose."

"Sit down," she said gently, "while I get tea."

She put ice in the glasses and poured a small measure of dark brew from a pint-sized jar. Lawrie exclaimed from the other room, "Oh! Your paper with the small J. You said—"

"Yes. Let me finish the tea, and I'll get it." She pushed the cold-water lever to fill the glasses, then carried them to the living room. "Here you go. I'll find the paper." She returned with it, and he held his glass high.

"This is fine. What's in it?"

"I hadn't invented it when you were here. Mostly Darjeeling with lemon and a sprig of mint." She grinned. "Put it down and look at this." She opened the paper and held it out.

His eyes searched the seemingly empty page. "Um . . . "

"I told you it was small. Look close—center of the page."

He peered closely, then pointed. "You have no idea how Felipe got this?"

"He says a woman gave it to him in case I turned him away. He'll be here in the morning. We can ask him more."

They sat and talked through many things—his wretched trip home three years earlier and the traumatic aftermath, her visit in the hospital and how it impacted him. "I thought I was dreaming that night. I heard you speak, but the mute button was on, and your voice wouldn't come through. And then you were gone. You spoke the word, then left."

"Pain meds make your brain fuzzy. By the way, I wrote you a letter one day but, of course, didn't send it."

"You wrote to me? Tell me!"

"I needed to write what I was feeling, but when I got home, I burned it—reverently. That's all."

"You *wrote* to me . . . " A ray of awe broke through. "I wrote a letter to *you*, Linda, but thank *God* I didn't have to send it!" The awe lingered, but he waved off questions. "Never mind. I'll tell you sometime.

"That hospital visit," he went on. "I can't tell you how important it was. You had the word of the Lord for *me*." Lawrie rubbed a finger down the moisture on his glass.

"Thank you. I needed to hear that. I saw it as yet another *unpresentable glory* the Lord asked me to do. With all my heart, I wanted to serve you and through that, serve God."

He sat back, as though studying his thoughts. "*Unpresentable.* Yes. I felt it, too, after you left."

She checked the level of tea in his glass, then assessed his face. "Is this the time to talk about Annalee?"

Lawrie set his glass carefully on the coffee table and clasped his hands.

"Maybe later, perhaps?" Linda looked toward him anxiously.

"Annalee." He leaned back and stared at the ceiling beams. "It's so obvious now, but not at first, and that's my only excuse." He shifted his focus and laughed awkwardly. "If I'd known you were watching that closely, it might have kept me out of trouble. I wish I could erase it all, but maybe this is one more *unpresentable.* After wading out of the muck and mire of that relationship, the shimmering glory of God's forgiveness came to rest on me. And with that, I could at least consider coming here. But no matter how much I thought I was in love with Annalee, I never mistook her as being a better person than you. You were the impossible dream. Annalee was the warm, attractive, in-the-flesh person who, of course, would be flattered and fortunate to have me—and my money." He blew through his teeth, got up, and stood in front of the fireplace, running self-deprecating fingers through his hair. "Brazen, arrogant, presumptuous!"

He swung around sharply. "This is *me*, Linda. My only plea is that I come to you, having been flat on my face before God, laying everything before Him and now before you. I have received His forgiveness and now ask yours. You may—you should—think long and hard about that. What I have done is an indicator of what I'm capable of doing."

Linda's voice trembled. "Jay, you've been my dream these three years. You were an idol, and as I said, you became my Lenten fast." She laughed ruefully. "But you coming tonight blew away the dream person and revealed a real person—with foibles and strengths—the man I love, a man *this* real person can live with—forever. And now that you've shown it's *me* you love, Annalee no longer matters. And," she added, almost to herself, "neither does my friendship with Stephan."

She stood and opened her arms.

Lawrie stiffened. "You *trust* me?"

Linda laughed. "You wouldn't *dare* lose it this time. You know perfectly well I'd deck you! You're safe," and her fingers beckoned him.

Their hearts met, and they clung as though never to let go.

Finally, Lawrie backed away. "Linda, my D.C. guys harp on a kiss being inflated currency. I don't want that for us. I want to save full-value kisses for our marriage bed—if or when that happens."

Linda's eyes opened wide, but she responded softly. "I will try not to make it hard for you. And Senator Crofter, I admire you!" She smiled, but then looked at her watch. "Oh!" she lamented. "I should call Bonnie. She's probably skittering through her apartment, waiting for news. This is a horrible time, but I don't think she'll go to bed until I call. Do you mind?"

"Not at all. Tell her I owe her."

Linda pushed Bonnie's number, and Lawrie reached out for the phone. Linda looked at him quizzically but handed it over.

"Well—hi back to you, Bonnie. Lawrie Crofter here . . . Yes, really." Laughingly, he held the phone away from his ear, and Linda hooted. "Just wanted to report on our candle caper. Huge success. She didn't follow through on the sunset thing, but I wasn't ready then, so the timing was perfect . . . Yes, the fasteners worked well. A couple bags burned, but that was user error . . . You were super, Bonnie, and I want to apologize for not recognizing you. We were all a bit distracted that day in Philadelphia . . . Yah, I want your perspective on that sometime. You've put up with a lot from us both. Thank you again, and I owe you a big hug. Maybe tomorrow . . . Thanks. And Bonnie, I'm asking another favor. Would you make a phone call for me, to my friend Nathan? Here's the number . . . Tell him, 'The jay has landed.' Would you do that? I think he'll get it, but if not, you can connect the dots for him . . . Bless you, Bonnie, and we'll talk to you later." He handed the phone back to Linda with a big grin. "I badly want to call Nathan myself, but I'm guessing this might be payback for Bonnie."

"You couldn't have given her anything more valuable."

"I'll call him from the motel. He'll be awake."

They sat quietly for a few moments, neither knowing how to go on. Finally, Lawrie stood. "This has been a day, and we both have a lot to process. I'll head out, but what are you having for breakfast and at what time?" He grinned. "Maybe you can tell me about . . . um . . . "

Linda's eyes crinkled mischievously. "Stephan. Not much to tell, but how about eight o'clock? Is that too early?"

"Eight it is. Is it all right to come to the gate this time instead of tromping through the woods?" He grinned.

"Yes, please! Let me drive you to your car. I don't want you going through the woods this time of night."

"I'll stay out of the woods. The preserve is just down the road, and I have a small flashlight in my pocket. I'll be all right. The walk'll do me good." He looked away, then back to her. "Will you be all right?"

"I am forever all right. Thank you, dear heart, for being brave enough to come to me."

"Nathan, buddy, did you get a phone call?"

"I did. So, the jaybird hit the ground running."

"I almost chickened out but then got an idea, and there *happened* to be a candle shop in the center of town. Did Bonnie tell you what we cooked up?"

"She did. She only knew that it worked and pumped me with questions. I told her what I thought you wouldn't mind her knowing, but she wants the whole story."

"She'll get it, probably tomorrow. Nathan, I almost blew it right at the start. Linda followed the candles to the gazebo, and first thing you know, hormones took over. Why wasn't I prepared for that? Good grief! I'm a grown man, not some teenager who can't keep his jeans on."

"Well, I'm hardly the one to talk to about that, but tell you what—you keep your pants zipped, and I'll pray."

Chapter 54

LAWRIE ARRIVED FIVE MINUTES BEFORE eight o'clock. Linda buzzed him through the gate. "Park your car and come on in. Door's open."

Breakfast was joyous, and after tending to the dishes, they stepped onto the deck to find Felipe. "I'm anxious to see if he remembers you. There he is. Felipe!" she shouted, motioning to him. "Come say hello to a friend of yours."

As the gardener headed their way, Lawrie bent to the troll garden and knelt for closer inspection. "Incredible!" he whispered. "How did you get it to look so . . . ancient?" He touched the rickety cabin, the gloomy shrubbery, rotting mushrooms. "I've been here often, y' know, under that bridge." He dipped his finger reverently in the tiny flow of water. "Maybe I've finally been washed of troll-ishness." Hearing voices, he stood to greet Felipe.

The gardener stopped uncertainly on the stone patio, then his face, habitually morose and wintery, brightened like sun after rain. *"Señor!"* he cried.

Lawrie, hand extended, immediately shifted to hug stance. "Felipe, *amigo! Cómo estás? Cómo va?"*

"Buena, buena," and he began to weep for joy. "You talk to me. You listen, ask me about gardens. And here you are, in this most *maravilloso* garden! How are you here?"

"Your garden, Felipe. You have made it *maravilloso*. And I am here because I loved this garden three years ago and longed to see it again. And here you are!" He gave the gardener another hug.

"Come sit down, Felipe," said Linda, "and tell me again about the paper with the little *J* on it. This is the man I thought had sent it, but he says he didn't. Can you tell us more about the person who gave it to you?"

Felipe sat stiff and apprehensive. Lawrie reached over with a reassuring pat. "This isn't a test, *amigo*. No right or wrong. You say a woman gave it to you?"

"*Sí.*" His hands gripped the armrests.

"Do you remember what she looked like? Tall? Short?"

He considered a moment. "Sort of in between?"

"Did she wear a uniform?"

He shook his head woefully. "I don't know . . . "

Lawrie asked more questions, but Felipe looked sadder and sadder.

"Well," said Lawrie, "whoever it was did get you here, and that's all that really matters. Now, how about a tour of your *gran obra de arte*. I want to drink in all the improvements you've made."

The phone rang indoors. "Let me get that," said Linda. The men settled back as she went into the house. After a moment, she stuck her head out the door. "My mom's just down the street and wants to come in for a few minutes. I tried to push her off till later, but she'd like to drop something off. Do you mind? She's a dear and won't stay long. Then we'll do the tour."

"If you don't think she'll mind my being here, I'd love to meet her."

"Okay, I'll tell her. Come inside. She doesn't like the sun. Felipe, go back to work, and we'll find you." Lawrie joined her in the living room. "You'll like her." She smiled as they sat down. "She's been awfully good to me since my dad died."

"It will be an honor." He took a breath. "And I need to get on her good side, right from the start!" He smiled wryly.

"She won't give you trouble." Linda laughed and got up as the doorbell rang. Lawrie listened to the mother-daughter greetings in the hall and checked his shirt and trousers to make sure all was in order.

As Linda ushered her mother into the living room, Lawrie rose with his well-crafted political smile to meet her. They both stopped for a moment, and Lawrie's smile turned to pure shock. Linda froze in dismay, which intensified as the two rushed toward each other.

"My dear Lawrie, it *is* you! The circular pathway did lead you to the right door. I am *so* relieved!"

He enveloped her slender frame, tears running down his cheeks.

"Dear, dear Lawrie! When Linda told me she had company, I had to come see if this *company* might be worth my while to meet." She backed off and put her hands on his face. "Are you all right, my dear?"

He nodded. "I'm more all right now than ever in my entire life." His voice trembled. "You have given me an inestimable gift."

Linda stared, helpless and speechless. Finally, she stepped forward uncertainly. "It seems—Am I on the same planet as you two? Somewhere, somehow, you've met?"

Lawrie turned with a radiant smile. "Linda, dearest, I want you to meet Lady Cool Water. This wonderful woman—this mother of yours—is my angel! I never knew. She never told me, not even a hint—well, except that word about the gazebo." He looked at her, smiling.

"Oh, we did have a romp, didn't we, dear one?" The old lady's eyes twinkled. "I didn't want to prejudice you. Potential mothers-in-law can be formidably intimidating."

"Well, we need to change that, right now." Lawrie got down on one knee and took the two wrinkled hands, eyes crinkling. "Lady Cool Water," he said, "will you be my mother-in-law?"

She tipped her head in riotous laughter, then studied his face. "Oh, my dear, you are prodigiously handsome and look so much better than last I saw you. I think I love you fully as much as my daughter does, but really, aren't we getting things the wrong way around? Are we truly on marriage terms?" She looked expectantly at them both.

Lawrie stood and put his arm around her. "We're working on it, but with scarcely a half day into the conversation, we have a way to go."

She looked at him pertly. "How long can you be here, my dear?"

Lawrie grimaced. "Not long enough. I need to head back to D.C. Monday morning. Work does pile up."

"Oh! Well, then, we must get busy! No time to waste, and I know just the thing. I will arrange entrance for you both at to-night's gala in Greenburgh. They're renaming some old relic of a building—if only I could remember who died needing an appropriate structure to embellish his name. I'll look him up so we won't be embarrassed—Carson somebody? I'm thinking Lawrie will need to rent a suit, but that can be arranged, and—"

"*Moth-er*, stop!" Linda's face had become a thundercloud. "You may be Lawrie's angel, but you're pushing your wealthy entitlement envelope here. You're engineering events and using people."

"My dear—" She turned with equal ferocity. "I have worked long and hard getting the two of you together again, and this is *necessary,* an essential part of the overall plan. Important people will be there, and you must let them see you together. Lawrie understands the messy world of gossip; but with our careful groundwork, I don't think your being together will cause a stir." She turned to Lawrie. "After our talk, you got the hang of things nicely, once Rooshie broke you in." On his quick intake of breath, she waved her hand. "Oh, I know, but you needed shaking up. She made a bold statement right up front, something people would notice. And you caught on well and created your own relational embroidery from there on."

Lightning bolted from Linda's eyes. "*You* put Rooshie onto Lawrie?"

"Oh, yes! Rooshie needed a bit of bullying at first, but she agreed to mind her manners."

"Why didn't you *tell* me?"

"Linda, dear, do calm yourself. This was a classified, highly sensitive operation, and I believe Lawrie and I managed quite adequately."

She turned back to Lawrie, who looked with alarm from one to the other. Mischief played around her mouth. "Rooshie alone would not do, but you picked up nicely after she disappeared. I must say, though," she went on, mouth pursed primly, "your attentions to that unfortunate accident woman frightened me. I considered another visit, but decided prayer would be the better weapon. God had brought you through so much. Surely, He would bring you all the way home. This whole, convoluted relationship was, after all, His doing. That much was clear from the beginning."

Linda rubbed her face and stalked the room perimeter. Her mother's eyes followed her compassionately. "Yes, my dear. It's quite a story, isn't it? But this meaningless frippery tonight will legitimize you both in the public eye." She cocked her head and smiled impishly. "Though, perhaps another stitch or two in Washington before an announcement is made would be good. And that's what we're after, isn't it? In due time, of course."

Linda huffed and rolled her eyes. Lawrie moved to her side and put his arm around her, but she turned on him. "Jay, my mother may look fragile and weak, but—"

He laughed. "Oh, no question there! I believe she could run the entire universe if God were to shift that chore to her shoulders.

And—" He turned to the woman. "You did visit me a third time—by way of a dream! You came at a moment of great desperation, and your hands on my head . . . " His hands tented over his mouth. "Please don't be upset with her, Linda. She's a woman of incredible love who brought balm and healing into my life. She risked much on our behalf, and I doubt we'll ever know the full cost. She is my angel, and I will be highly honored to be her son-in-law."

After an awkward silence, Lady Cool Water straightened spritely and went on. "Now, we might give Tailor Time a call, don't you think, and see what our friend Josef can do for us."

Linda sighed resignedly, but her nose went up. "That's fine, Mother, but *I* need to shop, too! After all—" Mock sarcasm pursed her lips. "Without the right purse and shoes for such an affair, I'm *nothing*."

This time Lawrie showed alarm, and Linda saw her wrong turn. She had to respond quickly and carefully, without referencing Glynneth's spending habits. "I'm sorry!" She reached for his arm. "That was supposed to be a joke. A bunch of snooty women at one of my garden tours were measuring women by the quality of their shoes and purses. If that's all I had to lean on . . . !"

Lawrie breathed again and relaxed visibly.

Lady Cool Water's eyes caught the interaction and swiveled from face to face. Then with a captivating smile, she took Lawrie's other arm. "Can you give us your sizes, dear?"

Chapter 55

ON SATURDAY NIGHT, THEY WENT to the Carson A. Rumboldt Memorial Gala in Greensburgh, both of them clothed appropriately, according to Lady Cool Water's dictates: noticeable but not flashy. Lawrie, comfortable in the schmooze saddle, moved Linda around the elegant entrance hall, introducing her as a local friend, making their relationship seem casual and natural. As planned, they were observed and talked about, but few noted their prior connection.

Lady Cool Water, on the far side of the hall, nodded approvingly.

"You're good at this," said Linda. "I saw you operating way off, but up close, you're awesome!" She smiled.

"With you at my side, how could I not be?" He squeezed her arm but carefully kept to nonchalant.

The doors to the banquet hall opened, and Lawrie and Linda sat with three of the dignitaries. Conversation was light, with only a smattering of defanged and even humorous politics.

When dessert forks were at last put down and napkins crumpled beside them, Lawrie leaned back, then jolted upright when gentle hands rested on his shoulders and a soft voice behind him said, "Mistuh."

He leaped to his feet. "Charlotte!" His eyes took in the slender, gold-sheathed figure before him, and with face crumbling, he lifted and whirled her around, both of them laughing and crying.

Charlotte whispered in his ear. "Senators are expected to act dignified. Start thinking how to explain this—maybe to Missy first?" Smiling, she gave his cheek a final kiss and slid from his arms.

He began explaining to his table of dignitaries, then saw nearly every eye in the room watching them. Arm firmly around Charlotte, he morphed into political mode and raised his voice. "I want you all to meet my long-lost Charlotte who, in the wake of our tragedy some years ago, came upon my wife and me like a benign tsunami. Her wave of love and grace swept over us at a time of great need; but after my wife died, she went into the sunset, only to pop up here tonight." He squeezed her tightly. "Now, dear Charlotte, it's your turn to explain."

The banquet hall erupted in happy applause. She waited till it stopped, then held up her left hand. "I've been busy, you know, tidying up the world and getting married. Even senators sometimes have to wait in line." More riotous applause, and the crowd turned back to chit-chat and a final cup of coffee.

Lawrie, astonished, took her hand with its glittering rings and then looked unbelievingly into her face. "Married! Charlotte, who *ever* would attach himself to you? I need to meet this man, to find out if he knows he's taken a tiger to his bosom."

"Oh, you'll meet him, and yes, he knows, but he being a professional tiger tamer balances us pretty well. And you are Kileenda," she said, turning to Linda with a dazzling smile.

Linda's eyes went wide, and Lawrie's mouth once more became cod-like.

Charlotte's eyes danced, but she spoke softly. "I know a fair amount about you but had to see up close what this man's been fixated on all this time. And from what I've seen, I believe you'll make a well-matched team of mules able to draw a straight furrow."

"Charlotte," said Lawrie, "why didn't you write? In the hospital, you promised you'd be back. Why didn't you at least let me know you were all right?"

She leaned back and bit her lip. "Short answer, I couldn't stop crying. For you, for Glynneth, for not having recognized her intention. Looking back, it should have been easy enough to figure, but not then. I failed her; I failed you."

Sadness bent her forward, but then her iron backbone straightened, and she faced him. "Honey, you never saw Angry Charlotte. The whole time I lived in your house, she never showed up, except to nip you into line now and again. You wouldn't want to see that woman. Uh-uh. You were hurting so bad, I didn't want to lay that on you. I needed to carry it off to where it might do some good. But here I am!" She smiled and raised her arms. "I did write, but I'm not sure that letter got forwarded to you."

He shook his head. "I didn't get any letters."

"*One* letter? As in a very small *J*?"

Lawrie and Linda looked at each other with an astonished, "Oh!"

"*You* gave that to Felipe?" asked Linda, her eyes wide and eager.

"Thought it might get your attention." She smiled and waved it off, but her face turned serious. "Before we get into that, you need to brace up to meeting my husband. Another sip of wine, perhaps, to steady your nerves? Come." And she led them out of the banquet hall and down the corridor to a small, well-appointed sitting room with a *Private* sign posted outside the door.

A man, thin and sallow, rose slowly from a leather chair as they entered the room, and at the sight of him, Linda let out a cry. "Steady on, love!" Charlotte reached for her arm. "Honey, you need some courage here."

Lawrie stared at the man, his face abruptly cold, angry, and devoid of color. "*You!*" he cried.

"Aye," the man replied. "Some call me that, and some a lot wairse, but generally, I go by Ewen." He didn't put out his hand.

Charlotte held Linda's arm and rubbed her back gently. "Come, sweetie—sit down. A ghost might be easier to cope with right now. Sit on this loveseat till Lawrie starts breathing again." Linda sank down but continued to stare in disbelief at Ewen.

"So," said Lawrie, voice and eyes diamond hard, "the professional tiger tamer."

Charlotte's eyes took on an edge. "I think you've forgotten how hard I can bite. Like I said out there, you don't want to get on my bad side. Mmm-mmm." A smile softened her words, but no one in the room misread the power of her presence.

"Charlotte, you're telling me you *married* this man?" He spoke, eyes not leaving Ewen's face.

She moved directly in front of him, head tipped slightly down with eyes looking up as though at a naughty child. "Look at me," she said softly, hands drawing his head around. "Mistuh, have I ever given you reason to mistrust me?"

Linda caught her breath and looked at her sharply. Charlotte saw but didn't move her eyes. "Yes'm, I said *Mistuh.* That's one of those things you'll need to catch up on that's gone on between him and me." She flipped her head, eyes dancing again. "And Mistuh, I take the look on your face to mean that I don't generally do stupid things. I'm asking you to trust me now. I want you to sit down next to Linda and do some listening. Hear?"

Lawrie sat, pale and shaken.

"I said I needed to take my anger where it might do some good. I hunted down this man but found right away that God had gotten there first. I want you to hear him."

Ewen leaned forward, elbows on his knees, hands clasped between them, head bowed momentarily. Then he looked up, face oozing pain and emotion. "The fairst words I must say is I'm sorry.

I did you grrait damage and have no excuse. Seemed fine and good for my career at the time, until I realized that my popping the lid on the relationship between you and Linda indirectly caused Glynneth's death. Weighed heavy."

He looked down again as though to collect new strength. "Then when Charlotte came aftair me wi' her God-fire eyes and began her *tidying,* I knew I had *railly* staipped over a serious line. Once we got that straightened out, she began to poosh me—no, *draw* is the better word—she drew me toward God, got me convairted, and redirrected my talents toward seeing what we might be able t' fix in the awful mess. I began to resairch the matter of Glynneth's death and back-pedaled my hint of you pooshing her off the cliff."

He stopped, eyes on Charlotte as she settled beside Lawrie and adroitly took over the conversation. "Coming back to the *J* letter," she said, "Ewen's dirt-digging turned up Jorge's pilfering, and we were able put him down with minimal wash. But all that came after we found Felipe and learned that Lawrie had talked with him."

"How do you find out this kind of stuff," Lawrie asked, face teetering on good weather, bad weather.

"If you know whair t' look," replied Ewen, "it's aisy to find. A phone call here, conversation there. Y' have to be borrn wi' a devious gene." He smiled impishly. "I considered bringing Tad along in case your taimper got out of—"

"*Tad!* You know *Tad?* No." His face reflected sudden understanding. "*You're* Tad's handler."

"Ay." Ewen smiled wryly. "Your head okay? Tad felt bad aboot that but couldna' take time to explain."

Lawrie sank back, stared at Ewen, and shook his head.

Charlotte, forefinger gyrating, said, "Back to Felipe." She smiled disarmingly. "I stepped in as a temp social worker, talked with him, then handed him the *J* paper and sent him on. He's worked out well, hasn't he?" Her eyes reflected satisfaction.

Linda put hands to her mouth. "A Godsend!"

Ewen's face brightened. "Did you na' figure," he went on, "Lawrie's little scheme of dating other women to throw the public off scent? Annalee, though . . . " He shook his head.

"Huh!" said Lawrie, his face turning hard. "If even you couldn't figure out Annalee—"

"Oh, but I did. Knew about the boyfriend and their funky relationship. Offered the donation thought, and she grabbed for it. No—" He put up his hand. "Made sure she knew exactly what she was doing. The illegal part—"

"I thought Jeremy did that."

Ewen's eyes twinkled. "Whair d'y think he got the idea? He's not that smart. Her leaving the rehab did surprise me. But wi' Jeremy safely off her map, she no longer had t' fake impairment and could retairn home. But I do na think she'll show up in church." He grinned.

Lawrie grunted sardonically. "The lawsuit—did you see that coming, too?"

Ewen laughed. "Didna see it but nae surprised. I wouldna' worry too much. *Botched Rescue* laws are on your side."

He looked down. "Other things way back I should ha' sniffed out, but I didna' have Charlotte on my back then—or at least she hadna' got seriously into my sins."

"Ewen," said Lawrie, "if you don't already know, I'm telling you now: this lady is smarter than both of us put together."

Ewen cocked his head wryly. "I took her on as a challenge but didna' ken her cunning. In the end, the ony way I could make peace was to marry her." He flicked his eyebrows facetiously, but his humor quickly morphed into a look of intense love laced with pain. Neither Lawrie nor Linda could misinterpret the depth of what had gone on between them.

Linda suddenly stiffened as though plugged into a wall outlet. "Yes!" she cried. "That's it! The *unpresentable glory!*" She scrunched her eyes, unable to go on.

"What is it, Linda?" Lawrie leaned to search her face.

With deep-sucked breath, she looked up, eyes radiant. "Do you see it? Do you *feel* God's glory here right now? All of this . . . " Her finger circled the room. "One hidden thing after another. Events we considered terrible—dastardly, even." She turned a rueful smile on Ewen. "But now, in the end, *dastardly* is blossoming into *splendid.* The two of you—Charlotte, Ewen, my *mother,* even—went about righting terrible wrongs, all out of love. God . . . did . . . this! Made the unpresentable *glorious!*"

She leaned forward with vibrant intensity. "Think of it! My words on TV that spawned ugly jokes, made big trouble for Lawrie and a horrible mess for me—they've been validated, vindicated! Yes!" She pumped both arms, tears streaming down her face. "There in the studio, I felt I was saying it right. Now I *know* for *sure!*"

No one else spoke. The silence pulsed with a palpable energy that caught them up, drew them inside an ethereal tabernacle that smelled faintly of smoke and crackled with the glory of God.

Sudden laughter and applause from the hall broke the spell, allowing them to breathe again in a less daunting, sacred space.

Charlotte was first to speak. She grasped Lawrie's arm. "I have another unpresentable for you—a letter I'm almost afraid to give. I have not read it, but I think I know what it says. If you needed great courage to face Ewen, you may need even more for this." She squeezed his arm, compassion lining a safe path for him to step onto.

Fear-filled eyes clung to hers. "Glynneth?" he whispered.

She nodded. "If I'd come across it right away, it would've put me on high alert, but she hid it too well—in a silk bag containing a lace chemise I'd shown her and laughed over when it first arrived—from my straitlaced, maiden aunt, of all things." Charlotte's tortured smile lasted only a millisecond. "I didn't find it till I moved yet again and felt something in the bag that didn't belong."

She bit her lip and turned to Ewen, who pulled a small envelope from an inner pocket. She held it tight to her breast for a moment, head bowed, allowing tears to roll. Then without further word, she handed it to Lawrie.

He turned the envelope over and over, as though to decipher its contents without actually having to read it. It bore his name and Linda's. Finally, with shaking hands, he worked it open and read silently.

> My dearest Lawrie,
>
> If you are reading this, then all is well. You are with Linda now, and I am glad and happy for you. Yes, you held me and said again and again you loved only me, but I know in my heart. After all, what's left of me to love? You did love me, even when it was hard, so hard. Both of us were broken, yet you stayed and gave me your whole self—even let me pretend I was helping your campaign by visiting those dear children.
>
> And you gave me Charlotte. She was God to me, Lawrie. I know she wouldn't want me to say that, but if God is like Charlotte, then I want Him to take me. I asked Charlotte once if God could sing, and she said of course. He sang the world into existence, and He sings over us every day. I want to give myself to God, along with the baby within me.

Lawrie put the letter down and wept. Both Linda and Charlotte put their arms around him. "I guessed right, didn't I?" said Charlotte. "She was pregnant?"

"I can't finish. You read," and he handed it to her.

Charlotte scanned the first part of the letter, biting her lip against tears, then picked up where Lawrie had left off.

> I know how much you want another baby, but Lawrie, dear, I cannot do it. I would be so afraid. I cannot face the pain again—the pain of bearing, the pain of caring. I cannot do it! Just the idea of getting fat all over again! You know how much I love babies and children, but I just can't. I can't. Not after [and here she had scribbled out the rest of her sentence].

> But now you have Linda. She'll know how to have babies and how to take care of them. Please have at least three—one for each of my two and one just for her. Maybe more—a bouquet of babies! She'll be a good mother. Raising babies can't be harder than raising flowers. I want to get out of the way to make the two of you as happy as we should have been. Love her, Lawrie. PLEASE. Even when it's hard. You're good at that.

> And Charlotte, dear Charlotte. Please tell her—no, thank her for loving me. I will miss her, but maybe I'll see Charlotte in God's face.

Charlotte dropped her face into the letter, shoulders heaving.

They sat long, clinging to each other but saying nothing. The party outside broke up, and one person opened the door to look in but shut it quickly.

When nothing else could be said and it was time to go, Ewen stood with some difficulty. Charlotte reached under his chair for a cane and gave it to him with a squeeze of tender affection.

Lawrie looked at him with puzzled surprise. "As often as I've pic-tured you, a cane's the last thing I'd expect. Doesn't fit your style."

Ewen laughed somberly. "Noo, perhaps not, and I havna' used it all that long." He looked down at Charlotte, who was rubbing cheer onto his chest. "And perhaps I willna' need it much longer." He paused a moment, then said simply, "Bone cancer run amok."

"Like I said—" Charlotte smiled up at her husband. "God got to him first. His heart was ready for me and for Jesus."

Lawrie's entire body vibrated with shock. He stepped toward Ewen and held him tight, not letting go for nearly a minute.

Ewen, face wet with tears, said only, "Thank you."

Charlotte put her arm around him, her head on his shoulder. "My bonnie braw laddie!"

Other than cleanup people, the only person waiting at the fa-cility was Lady Cool Water. She took in the brokenness. "Oh, my dears! Such deep, deep pain. But if I'm not mistaken, some holy flame is transforming all that anguish into breath-taking glory. My heart wants to give comfort, but I must not interfere with God." She turned to her daughter. "Take Lawrie home, dear one. Sit with him in the garden until the eyes of his heart adjust to the unbearable light of this new *unpresentable glory.*"

Epilogue

Loving Lord, with all devotion I desire you now. You are fully aware of my weakness, my troubled life, my depression. I come to you for healing, tranquility, and confidence. You know all there is to know about me, even my secret thoughts, and you alone can help me. You know what I need and how great is my emptiness. I stand naked before you.[8]

The wedding of Lawrie Crofter and Linda Jensen—the real one, that is—had no equal. The church in which it was held was chosen more for its architectural aspects than for geographical location. The building itself had to be large for the number of people who would attend, but even more importantly, they needed a downstairs chapel, with a couple of small rooms and a lavatory nearby—requirements not easy to accommodate. They had considered the National Cathedral and its crypt-level chapels, but another D.C. church came to light.

Ewen came up with the germ idea for this arrangement, and Charlotte's fertile mind plumped it somewhat. When they presented it to Lawrie, he made it his own. He talked at length with Nathan before lining out the basic premise, if not the details, to Linda. Other participants were enlisted and enthusiastically agreed to lift their end of the complex scheme.

---

8   Thomas à Kempis. *The Imitation of Christ.* In *Christian Classics in Modern English.* Chicago: Harold Shaw Publishers, 1983. 149.

At first, Ewen and Charlotte declined to attend this preliminary event. "This is prrivate, your moment. Only those who—"

"Nonsense," said Lawrie. "I want you both there, and I want Charlotte to sing. I don't care how she does it or what, but—" He struggled to keep his voice even. "She must be part of this. She told me once that she often sang over me. I need her now."

The day of the wedding, December fifteenth, was relatively warm but misty, cloaking the D.C. landscape in a diaphanous glow. At ten a.m., a small party made its way into the church and headed downstairs. They did glance at the lavish arrangements in the upstairs sanctuary and saw Pastor Drew from Linda's church talking with the organist. They hurried below, where two people greeted them, seated the guests, and led the principals to separate rooms to dress appropriately.

The audience was little more than a dozen strong, but most sat eager, expectant—except for Caleb, who was clearly uncomfortable about what might happen here. He had come at Lawrie's insistence and provision, yet seemed fearful of this exposure to raw love.

"I'm not ready for this," he had moaned. "Something weird is gonna happen here. I know it is. I'm not ready."

Lawrie had laughed. "Hey, I'm the one doing *weird*. You'll just be sitting there, watching. Hang with us, buddy. *Weird* might fit better than you think."

Up front, the low, plain platform held a table with candles, flowers, and communion elements. On the left was a chair, and with it a basin, pitcher, and artfully draped towel.

At the appointed time, Pastor Dan from Bismarck took his place at the front edge of the platform. Charlotte was first to appear. Dressed in cream, gold, and an ever-changing expression of tenderness, she regally paced the perimeter of the chapel, first humming, then singing what sounded like "Amazing Grace," ornamented almost beyond recognition. Her voice stroked each word and drew from it an exact color and texture of tone. It started softly, then built to vibrant intensity, twisting and whirling against the ceiling until everyone had to draw breath so tight that it could not be released until, mercifully, she hauled in her passion to a more breathable level.

The principals were supposed to have entered during this prelude, but none of them could move. Finally, Nathan led Lawrie, dressed in a loose, white gown, directly to the platform.

By a more circuitous route, Bonnie brought Linda, also barefoot and similarly gowned, to a filthy strip of carpeting. When Linda halted in revulsion, her friend pressed her forward. "Come. You must walk on this," she said.

Surprised, Linda looked at Lawrie, then caught her breath and stepped onto the mess. At the far end, Lawrie took her hand and settled her on the chair, then bent to the task of pouring water, washing her feet and wiping them dry. He kissed her feet and looked full into her face. She touched his cheek. "Please, may I wash your feet, too?"

"Well, it's not scripted, but I would be honored."

She flashed a smile as he sat, then lifted his foot and washed it lovingly. "This act," she said, hands and voice shaking, "*especially* with dirty water, is symbolic of the forgiveness I will need to ask again and again. I know myself too well—quick with anger, quick to speak. I'm sorry, my dearest, for the times I will hurt you by speaking harshly. I'm *sorry*." She bent her forehead to his foot.

Charlotte continued to slide along, singing softly. "Hallelujah! For our Lord God Almighty reigns . . . Worthy is the Lamb."

After his feet were dried, Lawrie stood and took both of Linda's hands. Voice unsteady, he said, "I, Lawrence Joseph Crofter, stand with you, Kileenda Clarissa Jensen, declaring my love and intention of becoming your husband. But before that can happen, I ask you to humble yourself with me before our Lord, giving ourselves in covenantal agreement for Him to use in whatever service He chooses. Will you do that?"

Linda, shaking visibly, gripped his right hand and allowed him to lead her onto the platform, where they laid themselves facedown, foreheads resting on folded hands. Lawrie spoke softly. "Lord God Almighty, You brought us together in a garden, and we lie here before You, naked and unashamed."

Under his words, Linda spoke a running polyphony of "Thank You, Lord, thank You. Your mercy, Your grace . . . cover our sins . . . forgive our hurtful words against those we love."

Charlotte sang, *"Before the throne of God above/ I have a strong and perfect plea. A great High Priest whose Name is Love/ Who ever lives and pleads for me."*

"Yes, Lord," said Lawrie. "You led us through deep valleys of pain, but here and now, we hold out that pain, those wounds, for You to transform into glory—for You, Lord, for You."

"We give our lives," said Linda. "Dead to ourselves, alive to You."

"How deep the Father's love for us, how vast beyond all measure . . ."

Lawrie cleared his throat. "We have been in crisis places, but You gave us good people to . . . hold our ropes." He could not go on. As though on signal, the integral company of men rose from their chairs, trying without success to pull Caleb along, then knelt to lay hands on the couple. With Pastor Dan at the head, they worked down the parallel bodies, praying for whatever progeny God would give them.

Charlotte circled with a dark, soulful litany: "You know us, Lord. You know our coming in, our going out. You know our weakness, our troubled souls. You know our secret thoughts. You know our need, our great emptiness. You alone can help us, and so we lie before You. We come for healing, for tranquility, for confidence. How deep Your love, how vast beyond all measure."

While this was happening, two figures slid silently into the chapel and moved slowly to the platform. As they did, Charlotte shifted seamlessly to the haunting "Dakota Hymn"—*"Many and great, O God, are Your works, Maker of earth and sky."* Without looking at her, the man lifted his hand in response, then leaned sideways from his wheelchair, in obvious pain, to grasp Lawrie's heel. Voice husky, he began to pray. "Maker of earth and sky, lift up Lawrie and—"

Lawrie stiffened as though plugged into an electric socket. "Billy!" he cried, scrambling to his feet. "And Joey!" He grabbed the boy, then knelt beside Billy.

At that point, Caleb slid to the floor, sobbing aloud.

But the service was not over. Nathan shifted the foot-washing chair and settled Joey onto it as the pastor prepared the communion elements. As Dan spoke the ritual words, Charlotte chanted, "Blessed are Thou, O Lord our God, King of the universe, who bringest forth bread from the earth."[9] The pastor broke off two pieces of bread and gave them to the couple. Linda gave hers to Lawrie and said with a trembling voice, "This, too, is *my* body that I give now to you as your wife till death us do part."

Lawrie had trouble swallowing.

When the wine was offered, they drank, and Charlotte sang, *"Blessed are Thou, O Lord our God, King of the universe, Creator of the fruit of the vine."*[10]

Lawrie said, "As Jesus poured out his life for me, so I, as your husband, pour out my life for you."

Pastor Dan's eyes widened at this unplanned dialogue, but he took their cups, set them on the table, then turned back. "You have come together before the Lord and before this company. You

---

9   *The Standard Prayer Book (Siddur, a Jewish Prayer Book)*. Mariana de Lacerda Oliveira, 2013.

10   Ibid.

have sanctified yourselves. Though Pastor Drew will be the one to say the official, legal words upstairs, I do declare that before God, you may now retire to the bridal chamber prepared for you and there celebrate your oneness—in the name of our Lord and Savior Jesus Christ." He turned and took Linda's hand. "Three-and-a-half years ago, you gave Lawrie a touch of care and compassion that brought scandal onto both your heads. It seemed then an impossibly fragile thread of love, but we are witnesses to what proved to be an unbreakable bond."

His focus broadened to the room. "Each of us here has been either a primary player in this captivating drama or has been profoundly impacted by it. But—" His voice took on special emphasis, "—when we go upstairs, we will not speak of this ceremony. Many folks would find it far too unpresentable. Who here, though, can deny that God's glory has been on display? Covering what is done in private gives greater honor to our Lord. As the Scripture says, 'If one part is honored, every part rejoices with it.'"[11]

Silently, Charlotte crossed the platform behind the pastor, her hands signing, *Deep love honors God.*

He addressed the couple. "Lawrie and Linda," he said, "this is your time to come together—one flesh—under God's blessing and stamp of approval. Go—" His eyes twinkled, "—and please save your kiss for your immediate, private ceremony."

Lawrie's smile was radiant. "Come, my bride, to the place where I can serve you, where I can touch you and bring healing to both our hearts."

Nathan and Bonnie moved to the couple's side and led them from the chapel and down the hallway to the bridal chamber they had lovingly appointed. They returned to the chapel doorway

---

11   1 Corinthians 12:26b

and stood guard against intrusion, hands held, eyes fixed on each other with unmistakable affection.

Almost like a shadow crossing the floor, Charlotte moved to the platform and knelt, lowering her head to the floor. Pastor Dan had already stepped down to talk with the others, and no one noticed until Ewen picked up his crutches and painfully pulled himself to his feet. Billy's tracker eyes caught the move, and he swiveled his wheelchair to accompany the man's slow passage to the front. Everyone stopped talking when they saw what was happening. Billy motioned for Joey to fetch the foot-washing chair. Ewen nodded gratefully.

The men again moved to lay hands on the couple up front, this time with Caleb in the vanguard. Billy began and prayed long and hard, first for Charlotte, then for Ewen. He allowed others to pray but cut them off if their prayers shifted toward him. Once Caleb got the pattern, he, too, prayed for the MacClerhans, but after Billy's final "Amen," the young man took over. He shifted both hands to Billy and forced words through his tight throat.

"Lord, You said, 'Greater love hath no man than this, that a man lay down his life for his friends.'[12] God, this man right here," and he squeezed Billy's shoulders, "showed me what real love looks like—the lay-down-your-life kind. Not just here, not just now. Others showed me, too, but Billy came a long way today, maybe just for me, but maybe he didn't know that. You sent him, God, and I'm asking you to show him love he can really see, like You showed me. You brought my stony heart alive. Maybe You could bring his legs alive the same way."

12 John 15:13 KJV

Billy reached up and put his iron-tough hand over Caleb's and squeezed hard.

The End

For more information about
Eleanor K. Gustafson
&

An Unpresentable Glory
please visit:

www.eleanorgustafson.com
www.facebook.com/eleanorgustafsonauthor
@EgusEllie
www.goodreads.com/author/show/1969775.Eleanor_Gustafson
www.linkedin.com/in/ellie-gustafson-a7752446

....

For more information about
AMBASSADOR INTERNATIONAL
please visit:

www.ambassador-international.com
www.facebook.com/AmbassadorIntl
Twitter: @AmbassadorIntl

*If you enjoyed this book, please consider leaving us a review on
Amazon, Goodreads, or our website.*

Continued Praise for *An Unpresentable Glory*

"When a stranger collapses near Master Gardener Kileenda Jensen's delphiniums, her ensuing act of kindness for the ill man she knows only as Jay initiates a "love event." Will it survive the crushing weight of an election, a press bent on destruction, grief for a lost son, a suicide, a traumatic accident, and attempted entrapment? *An Unpresentable Glory* spans the breadth of the country and condenses the hope we all find in relationship to a garden, a very special place of beauty and healing. With a delightful, narrative style, Eleanor Gustafson offers insight into the world's inability to discern Christian virtue and the glory of service that is, in the minds of many, unpresentable."

—SAM PAKAN
Author of *Jesse's Seed* and upcoming *A Bed in Sheol*

"*An Unpresentable Glory* is an unusual and compelling story. I quickly became engrossed in the storylines following the lives of the two main characters. Not only did I wonder—and sometimes fret—about what would happen to them next, I couldn't keep from guessing how—or whether—things would ever work out right. To my delight, not only was the ending extremely satisfying, it was filled with surprises galore.

"Ellie Gustafson handles the Christian elements lovingly, biblically, and realistically. And the strong presence of Native American and Latino characters and the extremely knowledgeable references to flowers and gardening help to make *An Unpresentable Glory* a potentially award-winning novel."

—ROGER E. BRUNER
Author of *Rosa No-Name*, three quirky romantic novels, and the young adult *Altered Hearts* series